The Reminiscences Of Sir Henry Hawkins

Baron Brampton

Edited By

Richard Harris, K.C.

The Echo Library 2006

Published by

The Echo Library

Echo Library
131 High St.
Teddington
Middlesex TW11 8HH

www.echo-library.com

Please report serious faults in the text to complaints@echo-library.com

ISBN 1-84702-910-8

PREFACE.

As a preface I wish to say only a very few words--namely, that but for the great pressure put upon me I should not have ventured to write, or allowed to be published, any reminiscences of mine, being very conscious that I could not offer to the public any words of my own that would be worth the time it would occupy to read them; but the whole merit of this volume is due to my very old friend Richard Harris, K.C., who has already shown, by his skill and marvellously attractive composition in reproducing my efforts in the Tichborne case, what interest may be imparted to an otherwise very dry subject.

In that work[A] he has done me much more than justice, and for this I thank him, with many good wishes for the success of this his new work, and with many thanks to those of the public who may take and feel an interest in such of my imperfect reminiscences as are here recorded.

BRAMPTON.

HARROGATE, *August 17, 1904*

[Footnote A: "Illustrations in Advocacy" (fourth edition, Stevens and Haynes).]

EDITOR'S PREFACE.

This volume is the outcome of many conversations with Lord Brampton and of innumerable manuscript notes from his pen. I have endeavoured, as far as possible, to present them to the public in such a manner that, although chronological order has not been strictly adhered to, it has been, nevertheless, considering the innumerable events of Lord Brampton's career, carefully observed.

Apocryphal stories are always told of celebrated men, and of no one more than of Sir Henry Hawkins during his career on the Bench and at the Bar; but I venture to say that there is no doubtful story in this volume, and, further, that there is not one which has ever been told exactly in the same form before. Good stories, like good coin, lose by circulation. If there should be one or two in these reminiscences which have lost their image and superscription by much handling, I hope that the recasting which they have undergone will give them, not only the brightness of the original mint, but a wider circulation than they have ever known.

The distinguishing characteristics by which Lord Brampton's stories may be known I have long been familiar with, and have no hesitation in saying that one or other, some or all, may be found in every anecdote that bears the genuine stamp. They are

WIT, HUMOUR, PATHOS, AND TRAGEDY.

My claims in the production of this volume are confined to its *defects*, although Lord Brampton has been generous enough toattribute to me a share in its merits.

RICHARD HARRIS.
27 FITZJOHN'S AVENUE,
HAMPSTEAD,
October 6, 1904.

CONTENTS

CHAPTER

I.	AT BEDFORD SCHOOL
II.	IN MY UNCLE'S OFFICE
III.	SECOND YEAR--THESIGER AND PLATT--MY FIRST BRIEF
IV.	AT THE OLD BAILEY IN THE OLD TIMES
V.	MR. JUSTICE MAULE
VI.	AN INCIDENT ON THE ROAD TO NEWMARKET
VII.	AN EPISODE AT HERTFORD QUARTER SESSIONS
VIII.	A DANGEROUS SITUATION--A CASE OF FORGETFULNESS
IX.	THE ONLY "RACER" I EVER OWNED--SAM LINTON, THE DOG-FINDER
X.	WHY I GAVE OVER CARD-PLAYING
XI.	"CODD'S PUZZLE"
XII.	GRAHAM, THE POLITE JUDGE
XIII.	GLORIOUS OLD DAYS--THE HON. BOB GRIMSTON, AND MANY OTHERS--CHICKEN-HAZARD
XIV.	PETER RYLAND--THE REV. MR. FAKER AND THE WELSH WILL
XV.	TATTERSALL'S--BARON MARTIN, HARRY HILL, AND THE OLD FOX IN THE YARD
XVI.	ARISING OUT OF THE "ORSINI AFFAIR"
XVII.	APPOINTED QUEEN'S COUNSEL--A SERIOUS ILLNESS--SAM LEWIS
XVIII.	THE PRIZE--FIGHT ON FRIMLEY COMMON
XIX.	SAM WARREN, THE AUTHOR OF "TEN THOUSAND A YEAR"
XX.	THE BRIGHTON CARD-SHARPING CASE
XXI.	THE KNEBWORTH THEATRICAL ENTERTAINMENTS--SIR EDWARD BULWER LYTTON--CHARLES DICKENS, CHARLES MATHEWS, MACREADY, DOUGLAS JERROLD
XXII.	CROCKFORD'S--"HOOKS AND EYES"--DOUGLAS JERROLD
XXIII.	ALDERSON, TOMKINS, AND A FREE COUNTRY--A PROBLEM IN HUMAN NATURE
XXIV.	CHARLES MATHEWS--A HARVEST FESTIVAL AT THE VILLAGE CHURCH
XXV.	COMPENSATION--NICE CALCULATIONS IN OLD DAYS--EXPERTS--LLOYD AND I
XXVI.	ELECTION PETITIONS
XXVII.	MY CANDIDATURE FOR BARNSTAPLE
XXVIII.	THE TICHBORNE CASE
XXIX.	A VISIT TO SHEFFIELD--MRS. HAILSTONE'S DANISH BOARHOUND

XXX.	AN EXPERT IN HANDWRITING--"DO YOU KNOW JOE BROWN?"
XXXI.	APPOINTED A JUDGE--MY FIRST TRIAL FOR MURDER
XXXII.	ON THE MIDLAND CIRCUIT
XXXIII.	JACK
XXXIV.	TWO TRAGEDIES
XXXV.	THE ST. NEOTS CASE
XXXVI.	A NIGHT AT NOTTINGHAM
XXXVII.	HOW I MET AN INCORRIGIBLE PUNSTER
XXXVIII.	THE TILNEY STREET OUTRAGE--"ARE YOU NOT GOING TO PUT ON THE BLACK CAP, MY LORD?"
XXXIX.	SEVERAL SCENES
XL.	DR. LAMSON--A CASE OF MISTAKEN IDENTITY--A WILL CASE
XLI.	MR. J.L. TOOLE ON THE BENCH
XLII.	A FULL MEMBER OF THE JOCKEY CLUB
XLIII.	THE LITTLE MOUSE AND THE PRISONER--THE BRUTALITY OF OUR OLD LAWS
XLIV.	THE LAST OF LORD CAMPBELL--WINE AND WATER--SIR THOMAS WILDE
XLV.	HOW I CROSS-EXAMINED PRINCE LOUIS NAPOLEON
XLVI.	THE NEW LAW ALLOWING THE ACCUSED TO GIVE EVIDENCE--THE CASE OF DR. WALLACE, THE LAST I TRIED ON CIRCUIT
XLVII.	A FAREWELL MEMORY OF JACK
XLVIII.	OLD TURF FRIENDS
XLIX.	LEAVING THE BENCH--LORD BRAMPTON
L.	SENTENCES
LI.	CARDINAL MANNING--"OUR CHAPEL"
APPENDIX	

THE REMINISCENCES OF SIR HENRY HAWKINS.
(NOW LORD BRAMPTON.)

CHAPTER I.

AT BEDFORD SCHOOL.

My father was a solicitor at Hitchin, and much esteemed in the county of Hertford. He was also agent for many of the county families, with whom he was in friendly intercourse. My mother was the daughter of the respected Clerk of the Peace for Bedfordshire, a position of good influence, which might be, and is occasionally, of great assistance to a young man commencing his career at the Bar. To me it was of no importance whatever.

My father had a large family, sons and daughters, of whom only two are living. I mention this as an explanation of my early position when straitened circumstances compelled a most rigid economy. During no part of my educational career, either at school or in the Inn of Court to which I belonged, had I anything but a small allowance from my father. My life at home is as little worth telling as that of any other in the same social position, and I pass it by, merely stating that, after proper preparation, I was packed off to Bedford School for a few years.

My life there would have been an uninteresting blank but for a little circumstance which will presently be related. It was the custom then at this very excellent foundation to give mainly a classical education, and doubtless I attained a very fair proficiency in my studies. Had I cultivated them, however, with the same assiduity as I did many of my pursuits in after-life, I might have attained some eminence as a professor of the dead languages, and arrived at the dignity of one of the masters of Bedford.

However, if I had any ambition at that time, it was not to become a professor of dead languages, but to see what I could make of my own. It is of no interest to any one that I had great numbers of peg-tops and marbles, or learnt to be a pretty good swimmer in the Ouse. There was a greater swim prepared for me in after-life, and that is the only reason for my referring to it.

In the year 1830 Bedford Schoolhouse occupied the whole of one side of St. Paul's Square, which faced the High Street. From that part of the building you commanded a view of the square and the beautiful country around. The sleepy old bridge spanned the still more sleepy river, over which lay the quiet road leading to the little village of Willshampstead, and it came along through the old square where the schoolhouse was.

It was market day in Bedford, and there was the usual concourse of buyers and sellers, tramps and country people in their Sunday gear; farmers and their wives, with itinerant venders of every saleable and unsaleable article from far and near.

I was in the upper schoolroom with another boy, and, looking out of the window, had an opportunity of watching all that took place for a considerable space. There was a good deal of merriment to divert our attention, for there were clowns and merry-andrews passing along the highroad, with singlestick players, Punch and Judy shows, and other public amusers. Every one knows that the smallest event in the country will cause a good deal of excitement, even if it be so small an occurrence as a runaway horse.

There was, however, no runaway horse to-day; but suddenly a great silence came over the people, and a sullen gloom that made a great despondency in my mind without my knowing why. Public solemnity affects even the youngest of us. At all events, it affected me.

Presently--and deeply is the event impressed on my mind after seventy years of a busy life, full of almost every conceivable event--I saw, emerging from a bystreet that led from Bedford Jail, and coming along through the square and near the window where I was standing, a common farm cart, drawn by a horse which was led by a labouring man. As I was above the crowd on the first floor I could see there was a layer of straw in the cart at the bottom, and above it, tumbled into a rough heap, as though carelessly thrown in, a quantity of the same; and I could see also from all the surrounding circumstances, especially the pallid faces of the crowd, that there was something sad about it all. The horse moved slowly along, at almost a snail's pace, while behind walked a poor, sad couple with their heads bowed down, and each with a hand on the tail-board of the cart. They were evidently overwhelmed with grief.

Happily we have no such processions now; even Justice itself has been humanized to some extent, and the law's cruel severity mitigated. The cart contained the rude shell into which had been laid the body of this poor man and woman's only son, *a youth of seventeen, hanged that morning at Bedford Jail for setting fire to a stack of corn!*

He was now being conveyed to the village of Willshampstead, six miles from Bedford, there to be laid in the little churchyard where in his childhood he had played. He was the son of very respectable labouring people of Willshampstead; had been misled into committing what was more a boyish freak than a crime, and was hanged. That was all the authorities could do for him, and they did it. This is the remotest and the saddest reminiscence of my life, and the only sad one I mean to relate, if I can avoid it.

But years afterwards, when I became a judge, this picture, photographed on my mind as it was, gave me many a lesson which I believe was turned to good account on the judicial bench. It was mainly useful in impressing on my mind the great consideration of the surrounding circumstances of every crime, the *degree* of guilt in the criminal, and the difference in the degrees of the same kind of offence. About this I shall say something hereafter.

I remained at this school until I had acquired all the learning my father thought necessary for my future position, as he intended it to be, and much more than I thought necessary, unless I was to get my living by teaching Latin and Greek.

In due course I was articled to my worthy uncle, the Clerk of the Peace, and, had I possessed my present experience, should have known that it was a diplomatic move of the most profound policy to enable me, if anything happened to him, to succeed to that important dignity.

Had I been ambitious of wealth, there were other offices which my uncle held, to the great satisfaction of the county as well as his own. These would naturally descend to me, and I should have been in a position of great prominence in the county, with a very respectable income.

But I hated the drudgery of an attorney's office. In six months I saw enough of its documentary evidence to convince me that I hated it from my heart, and that nothing on earth would induce me to become a solicitor. I took good care, meek as I was, to show this determination to my friends. It was my only chance of escape. But while remaining there it was my duty to work, however hateful the task, and I did so.

Even this, to me, most odious business had its advantages in after-life. I attended one morning with my uncle the Petty Sessions of Hertford, where, no doubt, I was supposed to enlarge my knowledge of sessions practice; it certainly did so, for I knew nothing, and received a lesson, which is not only my earliest recollection, but my first experience in *Advocacy*.

At this Hertford Petty Sessional Division the chairman was a somewhat pompous clergyman, but very devoted to his duties. He was strict in his application of the law when he knew it, but it was fortunate for some delinquents, although unfortunate for others, that he did not always possess sufficient knowledge to act independently of his clerk's opinion, while the clerk's opinion did not always depend upon his knowledge of law.

An impudent vagabond was brought up before this clergyman charged with a violent and unprovoked assault on a man in a public-house. He was said to have gone into the room where the prosecutor was, and to have taken up his jug of ale and appropriated the contents to his own use without the owner's consent. The prosecutor, annoyed at the outrage, rose, and was immediately knocked down by the interloper, and in falling cut his head.

There was to my untutored mind no defence, but the accused was a man of remarkable cunning and not a little ingenuity. He knew the magistrate well, and his special weakness, which was vanity. By his knowledge the man completely outwitted his adversary, and shifted the charge from himself on to the prosecutor's shoulders. The curious thing was he cross-examined the reverend chairman instead of the witness, which I thought a master-stroke of policy, if not advocacy.

"You know this public-house, sir?" he asked.

The reverend gentleman nodded.

"I put it to yourself, sir, as a gentleman: how would you have liked it if another man had come to your house and drunk your beer?"

There was no necessity to give an answer to this question. It answered itself. The reverend gentleman would not have liked it, and, seeing this, the accused continued,--

"Well, your honour, this here man comes and takes my beer.

"'Halloa, Jack!' I ses, 'no more o' that.'

"'No,' he says, 'there's no more; it's all gone.'

"'Stop a bit," says I; 'that wun't do, nuther.'

"'That wun't do?' he says. 'Wool that do?' and he ups with the jug and hits me a smack in the mouth, and down I goes clean on the floor; he then falls atop of me and right on the pot he held in his hand, which broke with his fall, bein' a earthenware jug, and cuts his head, and 'Sarve him right,' I hopes your honour'll say; and the proof of which statement is, sir, that there's the cut o' that jug on his forehead plainly visible for anybody to see at this present moment. Now, sir, what next? for there's summat else.

"'Jack,' says I, 'I'll summon you for this assault.'

"'Yes,' he says, 'and so'll I; I'll have ee afore his Worship Mr. Knox.'

"'Afore his Worship Mr. Knox?' says I. 'And why not afore his Worship the Rev. Mr. Hull? He's the gentleman for my money--a real gentleman as'll hear reason, and do justice atween man and man.'

"'What!' says Jack, with an oath that I ain't going to repeat afore a clergyman--'what!' he says, 'a d--d old dromedary like that!'

"'Dromedary, sir,' meaning your worship! Did anybody ever hear such wile words against a clergyman, let alone a magistrate, sir? And he then has the cheek to come here and ask you to believe him. 'Old dromedary!' says he--' a d--d old dromedary.'"

Mr. Hull, the reverend chairman, was naturally very indignant, not that he minded on his own account, as he said--that was of no consequence--but a man who could use such foul language was not to be believed on his oath. He therefore dismissed the summons, and ordered the prosecutor to pay the costs.

I think both my father and uncle still nursed the idea that I was to become the good old-fashioned county attorney, for they perpetually rang in my ears the praises of "our Bench" and "our chairman," our Bench being by far the biggest thing in Hertfordshire, except when a couple of notables came down to contest the heavy-weight championship or some other noble prize.

For myself, I can truly say I had no ambition at this time beyond earning my bread, for I pretty well knew I had to trust entirely to my own exertions. The fortunate have many friends, and it is just the fortunate who are best without them. I had none, and desired none, if they were to advise me against my inclinations. My term being now expired, for I loyally pursued my studies to the bitter end, my mind was made up, ambition or no ambition, for the Bar or the Stage.

Like most young men, I loved acting, and quite believed I would succeed. My passion for the stage was encouraged by an old schoolfellow of my father's when he was at Rugby, for whom I had, as a boy, a great admiration. I forget whether in after-life I retained it, for we drifted apart, and our divergent ways continued their course without our meeting again.

Any worse decision, so far as my friends were concerned, could not be conceived. They both remonstrated solemnly, and were deeply touched with what they saw was my impending ruin, especially the ruin of their hopes. In vain, however, did they attempt to persuade me; my mind was as fixed as the mind of two-and-twenty can be. Having warned me in terms of severity, they now addressed me in the language of affection, and asked how I could be so headstrong and foolish as to attempt the Bar, at which it was clear that I could only succeed after working about twenty years as a special pleader.

They next set before me, as a terrible warning, my uncle, another brother of my father's, who had gone to the Bar, and I will not say never had any practice, for I believe he practised a good deal on the Norfolk Broads, and once had a brief at sessions concerning the irremovability of a pauper, which he conducted much to the satisfaction of the pauper, although I believe the solicitor never gave him another brief.

However, our family trio could not go on for ever quarrelling, and at last they made a compromise with me, much to my satisfaction. My father undertook to allow me a hundred a year for five years, and after that time it was to cease automatically, whether I sank or swam, with this solemn proviso, however, for the soothing of his conscience: that if I sank *my fate was to be upon my own head*! I agreed also to that part of the business, and accepting the terms, started for London.

CHAPTER II.

IN MY UNCLE'S OFFICE.

I ought to mention, in speaking of my ancestors, that I had a very worthy godfather who was half-brother to my father. He was connected with a family of great respectability at Royston, in Cambridgeshire, and inherited from them a moderate-sized landed estate. A portion of this property was a little farm situate at *Brampton*, in Huntingdonshire, from which village I took the title I now enjoy.

The farm was left, however, to my aunt for life, who lived to a good old age, as most life-tenants do whom you expect to succeed, and I got nothing until it was of no use to me. When I came into possession I was making a very fair income at the Bar, and the probability is my aunt did me, unconsciously, the greatest kindness she could in keeping me out of it so long.

So much for my ancestors. About the rest of them I know nothing, except an anecdote or two.

There was one more event in my boyhood which I will mention, because it is historic. I assisted my father, on my little pony, in proclaiming William IV. on his accession to the throne, and I mention it with the more pride because, having been created a Peer of the Realm by her late gracious Majesty Queen Victoria, I was qualified to assist as a member of the Privy Council at the accession of his present most gracious Majesty, and had the honour to hear him announce himself as *King Edward of England* by the title of *Edward the Seventh*!

Arrived in London, full of good advice and abundance of warnings as to the fate that awaited me, I entered as a pupil the chambers of a famous special pleader of that time, whose name was Frederick Thompson. This was in the year 1841.

I have the right to say I worked very hard there for several months, and studied with all my might; nor was the study distasteful. I was learning something which would be useful to me in after-life. Moreover, being endowed with pluck and energy, I wanted to show that my uncles--for the godfather warned me as well--and my father were false prophets. So I gave myself up entirely to the acquisition of knowledge, this being absolutely necessary if I was to make anything of my future career. "Sink or swim," my father said, was the alternative, so I was resolved to keep my head above water if possible.

After being at Thompson's my allotted period, I next went to Mr. George Butt, a very able and learned man, who afterwards became a Queen's Counsel, but never an advocate. I acquired while with him a good deal of knowledge that was invaluable, became his favourite pupil, and was in due course entrusted with papers of great responsibility, so that in time it came to pass that Mr. Butt would send off my opinions without any correction.

These are small things to talk of now, but they were great then, and the foundation of what, to me, were great things to come, although I little suspected any of them at that time; and as I look back over that long stretch of years, I have the satisfaction of feeling that I did not enter upon my precarious career without doing my utmost to fit myself for it.

In those early days of the century prize-fights were very common in England. The noble art of self-defence was patronized by the greatest in the land. Society loved a prize-fight, and always went to see it, as Society went to any other fashionable function. Magistrates went, and even clerical members of that august body. As magistrates it may have been their duty to discountenance, but as county gentlemen it was their privilege to support, the noble champions of the art, especially when they had their money on the event.

The magistrates, if their presence was ever discovered, said they went to prevent a breach of the peace, but if they were unable to effect this laudable object, they looked on quietly so as to prevent any one committing a breach of the peace on themselves. Their individual heads were worth something.

It was to one of these exhibitions of valour, between *Owen Swift* and *Brighton Bill*, that a reverend and sporting magistrate took my brother John, a nice good schoolboy, in a tall hat. He thought it was the right thing that the boy should *see the world.* I thought also that what was good for John, as prescribed by his clerical adviser, would not be bad for me, so I went as well.

There was a great crowd, of course, but I kept my eye on John's tall chimney-pot hat, knowing that while I saw that I should not lose John.

Presently there was a stir, for Brighton Bill had landed a tremendous blow on the cheek of Owen Swift, and while we were applauding, as is the custom at prize-fights and public dinners, a cunning pickpocket standing immediately behind John pushed the tall chimney-pot hat tightly down over the boy's eyes.

His little hands, which had been in his pockets, went up in a moment to raise his hat, so that he might see the world, the big object he had come to see; and immediately in went two other hands, and out came the savings of John's life--two precious half-crowns, which he had shown to me with great pride that very morning! When he saw the world again the rogue had disappeared.

The famous place for these pugilistic encounters, or one of the famous places, was a spot called Noon's Folly, which was within a very few miles of Royston, where the counties of Cambridge, Suffolk, Essex, and Hertfordshire meet, or most of them. That was the scene of many a stiff encounter; and although, of course, there were both magisterial and police interference when the knowledge reached them that a fight was about to take place within their particular jurisdiction, by some singular misadventure the knowledge never reached them until their worships were returning from the battle. All was over before any *official* communication was made.

I was entered of the Middle Temple on April 16, 1839, and remained with Mr. Butt until I had kept sufficient terms to qualify me to take out a licence to plead on my own account, which I did at the earliest possible date. This was a great step in my career, although, of course, the licence did not enable me to plead in court, as I was not called to the Bar.

If work came I should now be in a fair way to attain independence. But the prospect was by no means flattering; it was, in fact, all but hopeless while the position of a special pleader was not my ambition. The lookout, in fact, was anything but encouraging from the fifth floor of *No. 3 Elm Court*--I mean prospectively. It was a region not inaccessible, of course, but it looked on to a landscape of chimney-pots, not one of which was likely to attract attorneys; it was cheap and lonely, dull and miserable--a melancholy altitude beyond the world and its companionship. Had I been of a melancholy disposition I might have gone mad, for hope surely never came to a fifth floor. But there I sat day by day, week by week, and month by month, waiting for the knock that never came, hoping for the business that might never come.

Hundreds of times did I listen with vain expectations to the footsteps on the stairs below--footsteps of attorneys and clerks, messengers and office-boys. I knew them all, and that was all I knew of them. Down below at the bottom flight they tramped, and there they mostly stopped. The ground floor was evidently the best for business; but some came higher, to the first floor. That was a good position; there were plenty of footsteps, and I could tell they were the footsteps of clients. A few came a little higher still, and then my hopes rose with the footsteps. Now some one had come up to the third floor: he stopped! Alas! there was the knock, one single hard knock: it was a junior clerk. The sound came all too soon for me, and I turned from my own door to my little den and looked out of my window up into the sky, from whence it seemed I might just as well expect a brief as from the regions below.

This was not quite true. On another occasion some bold adventurer ascended with asthmatical energy to the *fourth floor*, and I thought as I heard him wheeze he would never have breath enough to get down again, and wondered if the good-natured attorneys kept these wheezy old gentlemen out of charity. But it was rare indeed that the climber, unless it was the rent collector, reached that floor.

The fifth landing was too remote for the postman, for I never got a letter--at least so it seemed; and no squirrel watching from the topmost bough of the tallest pine could be more lonely than I.

At last I thought a step had passed even the fourth landing, and was approaching mine; but I would not think too fast, and damped my hopes a little on purpose lest they should burn too brightly and too fast. I was not mistaken: there *was* a footstep on my landing, and I listened for the one heavy knock. It seemed to me I waited about an hour and a half, judging by the palpitations of my heart, and wished the man had knocked as vigorously. But I was rewarded: the knocker fell, and as my boy was away with the toothache, I opened the door myself. He was the same wheezy man I had heard below some time before; and I really seem to have liked asthmatical people ever since--except when I became a judge and they disturbed me in court.

"Papers!"

That is enough to say to any one who understands the situation. You may be sure I gave them my best attention, that they were finished promptly, and, as I hoped, in the best style. If I had required any additional incentive to keep me to my daily task of watching, this would have been sufficient; but I wanted none. I knew that my whole future depended upon it, and there I was from ten in the morning till ten at night.

My first fee was small, but it was the biggest fee I ever had. It was 10s. 6d. I was only a special pleader, and with some papers our fees were even less; we only had to *draw* pleadings, not to open them in court--that comes after you are called to the Bar. Drawing them means really drawing the points of the case for counsel, and opening them means a gabbling epitome of them to the jury, which no jury in this world ever yet understood or ever will.

This little matter was the forerunner of others, and by little and little I steadily went on, earning a few shillings now and a few shillings then, but, best of all, becoming known little by little here and there.

I was aware that some knowledge of the world would be necessary for me when I once got into it by way of business as an advocate, so I came to the conclusion that it would be well to commence that branch of study as soon as I closed the other for the day--or rather for the night.

I had not far to go to school, only to the Haymarket and its delightful purlieus; and there were the best teachers to be found in the world, and the most recondite studies. For all these I kept, as the great politicians say, an open mind, and learned a great deal which stood me in good stead in after-life.

It is not necessary, I suppose, in writing these reminiscences, to describe all I saw--at least I hope not. Manners have so changed since that time that people who have no imagination would not believe me, and those who have would imagine I was exaggerating. So I must skip this portion of my youthful studies, merely saying that I saw nearly, if not *quite*, all the life which was to be seen in London; and I am sure I am not exaggerating when I say that that would nearly fill an octavo volume of itself. There is so much to be seen in London, as a dear old lady I used to drink tea with once told me.

But she did not know more than I, for she had never seen the night-houses, gambling hells, and other places of amusement that at that time were open all night long, nor had she seen the ghastly faces of the morning. I attribute my escaping the consequences of all these allurements to the beautiful influence which my mother in early life exercised over me, as I attribute my knowledge of them to the removal of the restraint with which my earlier years had been curbed.

My mother died before I came to London, but undoubtedly her influence was with me, although I broke loose, as a matter of course, from all paternal control.

But I was never a "man about town." To be that you must have plenty of money or none at all, and in either case you are an object to avoid. I had, nevertheless, a great many pleasures that a young man from the country can enjoy. I loved horse-racing, cricket, and the prize-ring. It was not because pugilism was a fashionable amusement in those days that I attended a "set-to" occasionally; I went on my own account, not to ape people in the fashionable world, and enjoyed it on my own account, not because they liked it, but because I did.

My rent at this time of my entrance into the fashionable world was £12 a year; my laundress, perhaps, a little less. She earned it by coming up the stairs; but she was a good old soul. I remembered her long years after, and always with gratitude for her many kindnesses in those gloomy days. Her name was Hannem.

Of course, I had to buy the necessary books for my professional use, coals, and other things, and after paying all these I had to live on the narrow margin of my £100 a year.

This recollection is very pleasing. I never got into debt, and never wanted; but I had to be frugal and avoid every unnecessary expense.

But the time at last came when I was no longer to rest on my lonely perch at the top of Elm Court. I had kept my terms, and was duly called to the Bar of the Middle Temple on May 3, 1843.

Just fifty years after, when I was a judge, and almost the Senior Bencher of my Inn, our illustrious Sovereign, then Prince of Wales, who is also a Bencher of the Middle Temple, favoured us with his presence at dinner, and did me the honour to propose my health in a gracious speech. On returning thanks for this kindness, I told the crowded audience of my *jubilee*, and pointed out the spot where fifty years before I had held my call party.

CHAPTER III.

SECOND YEAR--THESIGER AND PLATT--MY FIRST BRIEF.

In my second year I made fifty pounds, the sweetest fifty pounds I ever made. I had no longer any weary waiting, for there was no weariness in it, and I confess at this time my sole idea, and I may add my only ambition, was to relieve myself of all obligations to my father. If I could accomplish this, I should have vindicated the step I had taken, and my father would have no further right, whatever reason he might think he had, to complain.

My third year came, and then, to my great joy, finding that I was earning more than the hundred pounds he allowed me, I wrote and informed him, with all proper expressions of gratitude, that I should no longer need his assistance, and from that time I never had a single farthing that I did not earn.

I am sure I was prouder of that than of my peerage, for I experienced for the first time the joyous pride of independence. There is no fruit of labour so sweet as that.

But I no sooner began to obtain a little success than my rivals and others tried to deprive me of the merit of it, if merit there was--"Oh, of course his father and uncle are both solicitors in the county;" while one of the local newspapers years after was good enough to publish a paragraph which stated that I owed all my success to my father's office.

This, of course, does not need contradiction. An occasional small brief from Hitchin was the beginning and the end of my father's influence, while sessions practice was not the practice I hoped to finish my career with, although I had little hopes of eminence. Certainly if I had I should have known that eminence could not come from Hitchin.

I chose the Home Circuit, and did not leave it till I was made a judge. It is impossible to forget the kindness I received from its members throughout my whole career. There was a brotherly feeling amongst us, which made life very pleasant.

There were several celebrated men on the Home Circuit when I joined. Amongst them were Thesiger and Platt.

This was long before the former became Attorney-General, which took place in 1858. He afterwards was Lord Chancellor, and took his title from the little county town where probably he obtained his start in the career which ended so brilliantly.

Platt became a Baron of the Exchequer.

Thesiger was a first-rate advocate, and, I need not say, was at all times scrupulously fair. He had a high sense of honour, and was replete with a quiet, subtle humour, which seemed to come upon you unawares, and, like all true humour, derived no little of its pleasure from its surprise. In addition to his abilities, Thesiger was ever kind-hearted and gentle, especially in his manner towards juniors. I know that he sympathized with them, and helped them whenever he had an opportunity. It did not fall to my lot to hold many briefs with him, but I am glad to say that I had some, because I shall not forget the kindness and instruction I received from him.

Platt was an advocate of a different stamp. He also was kind, and in every way worthy of grateful remembrance. He loved to amuse especially the junior Bar, and more particularly in court. He was a good natural punster, and endowed with a lively wit. The circuit was never dull when Platt was present; but there was one trait in his character as an advocate that judges always profess to disapprove of--he loved popular applause, and his singularly bold and curious mode of cross-examination sometimes brought him both rebuke and hearty laughter from the most austere of judges.

He dealt with a witness as though the witness was putty, moulding him into any grotesque form that suited his humour. No evidence could preserve its original shape after Platt had done with it. He had a coaxing manner, so much so that a witness would often be led to say what he never intended, and what afterwards he could not believe he had uttered.

Thesiger, who was his constant opponent, was sometimes irritated with Platt's manner, and on the occasion I am about to mention fairly lost his temper.

It was in an action for nuisance before Tindal, Chief Justice of the Common Pleas, at Croydon Assizes.

Thesiger was for the plaintiff, who complained of a nuisance caused by the bad smells that emanated from a certain tank on the defendant's premises, and called a very respectable but ignorant labouring man to prove his case.

The witness gave a description of the tank, not picturesque, but doubtless true, and into this tank all kinds of refuse seem to have been thrown, so that the vilest of foul stenches were emitted.

Platt began his cross-examination of poor Hodge by asking him in his most coaxing manner to describe the character and nature of the various stenches. Had Hodge been scientific, or if he had had a little common sense, he would have simply answered "*bad* character and *ill*-nature;" but he improved on this simplicity, and said,--

"Some on 'em smells summat *like paint*."

This was quite sufficient for Platt.

"Come now," said he, "that's a very sensible answer. You are aware, as a man of undoubted intelligence, that there are various colours of paint. Had this smell any *particular colour*, think you?"

"Wall, I dunnow, sir."

"Don't answer hurriedly; take your time. We only want to get at the truth. Now, what colour do you say this smell belonged to?"

"Wall, I don't raightly know, sir."

"I see. But what do you say to *yellow*? Had it a yellow smell, think you?"

"Wall, sir, I doan't think ur wus yaller, nuther. No, sir, not quite yaller; I think it was moore of a blue like."

"A blue smell. We all know a blue smell when we see it."

Of course, I need not say the laughter was going on in peals, much to Platt's delight. Tindal was simply in an ecstasy, but did all he could to suppress his enjoyment of the scene.

Then Platt resumed,--

"You think it was more of a blue smell like? Now, let me ask you, there are many kinds of blue smells, from the smell of a Blue Peter, which is salt, to that of the sky, which depends upon the weather. Was it dark, or--"

"A kind of sky-blue, sir."

"More like your scarf?"

Up went Hodge's hand to see if he could feel the colour.

"Yes," said he, "that's more like--"

"Zummut like your scarf?"

"Yes, sir."

Then he was asked as to a variety of solids and liquids; and the man shook his head, intimating that he could go a deuce of a way, but that there were bounds even to human knowledge.

Then Platt questioned him on less abstruse topics, and to all of his questions he kept answering,--

"Yes, my lord."

"Were fish remnants," asked Platt, "sometimes thrown into this reservoir of filth, such as old cods' heads with goggle eyes?"

"Yes, my lord."

"*Rari nantes in gurgite vasto?*"

"Yes, my lord."

Thesiger could stand it no longer. He had been writhing while the court had been roaring with laughter, which all the ushers in the universe could not suppress.

"My lord, my lord, there must be some limit even to cross-examination by my friend. Does your lordship think it is fair to suggest a classical quotation to a respectable but illiterate labourer?"

Tindal, who could not keep his countenance--and no man who witnessed the scene could--said,--

"It all depends, Mr. Thesiger, whether this man understands Latin." Whereupon Platt immediately turned to the witness and said,--

"Now, my man, attend: *Rari nantes in gurgite vasto*. You understand that, do you not?"

"Yes, my lord," answered the witness, stroking his chin.

Tindal, trying all he could to suppress his laughter, said:

"Mr. Thesiger, the witness says he understands the quotation, and as you have no evidence to the contrary, I do not see how I can help you." Of course, there was a renewal of the general laughter, but Thesiger, in his reply, turned it on Platt.

This was my first appearance on circuit, and my first lesson from a great advocate in the art of caricature.

No man at the Bar can forget the joy of his first brief--that wonderful oblong packet of white papers, tied with the mysterious pink tape, which his fourth share of the diminutive clerk brings him, marked with the important "I gua."

I speak not to stall-fed juniors who have not to wait till their merits are discovered, and who know that whosoever may watch and wait and hope or despair, they shall have enough. All blessings go with them; I never envied them their heritage. They are born to briefs as the sparks fly upwards. I tell my experience to those who will understand and appreciate every word I say--to men who have to make their way in the world by their own exertions, and live on their own labour or die of disappointment. There is one consolation even for the wretched waiters on solicitors' favours, and that is, that the men who have never had to work their way seldom rise to eminence or to any position but respectable mediocrity. They never knew hope, and will never know what it is to despair, or to nibble the short herbage of the common where poorer creatures browse.

A father never looked on his firstborn with more pleasure than a barrister on his first brief. If the Tower guns were announcing the birth of an heir to the Throne, he would not look up to ask, "What is that?"

It was the turning-point of my life, for had there been no first brief pretty soon, I should have thought my kind relations' predictions were about to be verified. But I should never have returned home; there was still the Stage left, on which I hoped to act my part.

Strange to say, my first brief, like almost everything in my life, had a little touch of humour in it.

I was instructed to defend a man at Hertford Sessions for stealing a wheelbarrow, and unfortunately the wheelbarrow was found on him; more unfortunate still--for I might have made a good speech on the subject of the *animus furandi*--the man not only told the policeman he stole it, but pleaded "Guilty" before the magistrates. I was therefore in the miserable condition of one doomed to failure, take what line I pleased. There was nothing to be said by way of defence, but I learnt a lesson never to be forgotten.

Being a little too conscientious, I told my client, the attorney, that in the circumstances I must return the brief, inasmuch as there was no defence for the unhappy prisoner.

The attorney seemed to admire my principle, and instead of taking offence, smiled in a good-natured manner, and said it was no doubt a difficult task he had imposed on me, and he would exchange the brief for another. He kept his word, and by-and-by returned with a much easier case--a prosecution where the man pleaded "Guilty." It was a grand triumph, and I was much pleased.

Those were early days to begin picking and choosing briefs, for no man can do that unless he is much more wanted by clients than in want of them; but I learned the secret in after life of a great deal of its success.

I was, however, a little chagrined when I saw the mistake I had made. Rodwell was leader of the sessions, and ought to have been far above a guinea brief; judge then of my surprise when I saw that same brief a few minutes after accepted by that great man--the brief I had refused because there was nothing to be said on the prisoner's behalf. My curiosity was excited to see what Rodwell would do with it, and what defence he would set up. It was soon gratified. He simply admitted the prisoner's guilt, and hoped the chairman, who was Lord Salisbury, would deal leniently with him.

I could have done that quite as well myself, and pocketed the guinea. From that moment I resolved never to turn a case away because it was hopeless.

I subjoin a copy of my first brief for the prosecution.

It must be remembered that in those days the gallows was a very popular institution. They punished severely even trivial offences, and this case would have been considered a very serious one; while a sentence of seven years' transportation was almost as good as an acquittal.

>*Herts. No. 10.*
>Michaelmas Sessions, 1844.
>Regina *v.*
>Elizabeth Norman.
>Brief for the Prosecution.
>Mr. Hawkins.
>I Gua.
>*H. Hawkins.*
>Plea--Guilty.
>H.H.
>Oct. 14, 1844.
>Transported for 7 years.
>H.H.
>*Cobliam.*
>Ware.

These are my notes:--

>*Sep.* 20.
>Mr. Page.
>Silk shawl.
>Apprehension.
>Various accounts.
>Exam. before J---- J----.
>Propy found.
>Mrs. Stevens,}
>Mr. Johnson, } Witnesses.

I made a rule throughout my professional life to note my cases with the greatest care.

CHAPTER IV.

AT THE OLD BAILEY IN THE OLD TIMES.

It is a vast space to look back over sixty years of labour, and yet there seems hardly a scene or an event of any consequence, that is not reproduced in my mind with a vividness that astonishes me.

In my earlier visits to her Majesty's Courts of Justice my principal business was to study the Queen's Counsel and Serjeants, and they were worthy the attention I bestowed on them. They all belonged to different schools of advocacy, and some knew very little about it.

I went to the Old Bailey, a den of infamy in those times not conceivable now, and I verily believe that no future time will produce its like--at least I hope not. Its associations were enough to strike a chill of horror into you. It was the very cesspool for the offscourings of humanity. I had no taste for criminal practice in those days, except as a means of learning the art of advocacy. In these cases, presided over by a judge who knows his work, the rules of evidence are strictly observed, and you will learn more in six months of practical advocacy than in ten years elsewhere. The Criminal Court was the best school in which to learn your work of cross-examination and examination-in-chief, while the Courts of Equity were probably the worst. But I shall not dwell on my struggles in connection with the Old Bailey at that early period of my life. What will be more interesting, perhaps, are some curious arrangements which they had for the conduct of business and the entertainment of the Judges.

These are a too much neglected part of our history, and when referred to in reminiscences are generally referred to as matters for jocularity. They exercised, however, a serious influence on the minds and feelings of the people, as well as their manners; more so than a hundred subjects with which the historian or the novelist sometimes deals.

In all cases of unusual gravity three Judges sat together. Offences that would now be treated as not even deserving of a day's imprisonment in many cases were then invariably punished with death. It was not, therefore, so much the nature of the offence as the importance of it in the eyes of the Judges that caused three of them to sit together and try the criminals.

They sat till five o'clock right through, and then went to a sumptuous dinner provided by the Lord Mayor and Aldermen. They drank everybody's health but their own, thoroughly relieved their minds from the horrors of the court, and, having indulged in much festive wit, sometimes at an alderman's expense, and often at their own, returned into court in solemn procession, their gravity undisturbed by anything that had previously taken place, and looking the picture of contentment and virtue.

Another dinner was provided by the Sheriffs; this was for the Recorder, Common Serjeant, and others, who took their seats when their lordships had arisen.

I ought to mention one important dignitary--namely, the chaplain of Newgate--whose fortunate position gave him the advantage over most persons: for he *dined at both these dinners*, and assisted in the circulation of the wit from one party to another; so that what my Lord Chief Justice had made the table roar with at five o'clock, the Recorder and the Common Serjeant roared with at six, and were able to retail at their family tables at a later period of the evening. It was in that way so many good things have come down to the present day.

The reverend gentleman alluded to of course attended the court in robes, and his only, but solemn, function was to say "Amen" when the sentence of death was pronounced by the Judge.

There were curious old stories, too, about my lords and old port at that time which are not of my own reminiscences, and therefore I shall do no more than mention them in order to pass on to what I heard and saw myself.

The first thing that struck me in the after-dinner trials was the extreme rapidity with which the proceedings were conducted. As judges and counsel were exhilarated, the business was proportionately accelerated. But of all the men I had the pleasure of meeting on these occasions, the one who gave me the best idea of rapidity in an after-dinner case was Mirehouse.

Let me illustrate it by a trial which I heard. Jones was the name of the prisoner. His offence was that of picking pockets, entailing, of course, a punishment corresponding in severity with the barbarity of the times. It was not a plea of "Guilty," when perhaps a little more inquiry might have been necessary; it was a case in which the prisoner solemnly declared he was "Not Guilty," and therefore had a right to be tried.

The accused having "held up his hand," and the jury having solemnly sworn to hearken to the evidence, and "to well and truly try, and true deliverance make," etc., the witness for the prosecution climbs into the box, which was like a pulpit, and before he has time to look round and see where the voice comes from, he is examined as follows by the prosecuting counsel:--

"I think you were walking up Ludgate Hill on Thursday, 25th, about half-past two in the afternoon, and suddenly felt a tug at your pocket and missed your handkerchief, which the constable now produces. Is that it?"

"Yes, sir."

"I suppose you have nothing to ask him?" says the judge. "Next witness."

Constable stands up.

"Were you following the prosecutor on the occasion when he was robbed on Ludgate Hill? and did you see the prisoner put his hand into the prosecutor's pocket and take this handkerchief out of it?"

"Yes, sir."

Judge to prisoner: "Nothing to say, I suppose?" Then to the jury: "Gentlemen, I suppose you have no doubt? I have none."

Jury: "Guilty, my lord," as though to oblige his lordship.

Judge to prisoner: "Jones, we have met before--we shall not meet again for some time--seven years' transportation. Next case."

Time: two minutes fifty-three seconds.

Perhaps this case was a high example of expedition, because it was not always that a learned counsel could put his questions so neatly; but it may be taken that these after-dinner trials did not occupy on the average more than *four minutes* each.

CHAPTER V.

MR. JUSTICE MAULE.

Of course, in those days there were judges of the utmost strictness as there are now, who insisted that the rules of evidence should be rigidly adhered to. I may mention, one, whose abilities were of a remarkable order, and whose memory is still fresh in the minds of many of my contemporaries--I mean Mr. Justice Maule. His asthmatic cough was the most interesting and amusing cough I ever heard, especially when he was saying anything more than usually humorous, which was not infrequently. He was a man of great wit, sound sense, and a curious humour such as I never heard in any other man. He possessed, too, a particularly keen apprehension. To those who had any real ability he was the most pleasant of Judges, but he had little love for mediocrities. No man ever was endowed with a greater abhorrence of hypocrisy. I learnt a great deal in watching him and noting his observations. One day a very sad case was being tried. It was that of a man for killing an infant, and it was proposed by the prosecution to call as a witness a little brother of the murdered child.

The boy's capacity to give evidence, however, was somewhat doubted by the counsel for the Crown, John Clark, and it did honour to his sense of fairness. Having asked the little boy a question or two as to the meaning of an oath, he said he had some doubt as to whether the witness should be admitted to give evidence, as he did not seem to understand the nature of an oath, and the boy was otherwise deficient in religious knowledge.

He was asked the usual sensible questions which St. Thomas Aquinas himself would have been puzzled to answer; and being a mere child of seven--or at most eight--years of age, without any kind of education, was unable to state what the exact nature of an oath was.

Having failed in this, he was next asked what, when they died, became of people who told lies.

"If he knows that, it's a good deal more than I do," said Maule.

"Attend to me," said the Crown counsel. "Do you know that it's wicked to tell lies?"

"Yes, sir," the boy answered.

"I don't think," said the counsel for the prosecution, "it would be safe to swear him, my lord; he does not seem to know anything about religion at all.--You can stand down."

"Stop a minute, my boy," says Maule; "let me ask you a question or two. You have been asked about a future state--at least I presume that was at the bottom of the gentleman's question. I should like to know what you have been taught to believe. What will become of *you*, my little boy, when you die, if you are so wicked as to tell a lie?"

"*Hell fire*," answered the boy with great promptitude and boldness.

"Right," said Maule. "Now let us go a little further. Do you mean to say, boy, that you would go to hell fire for telling *any* lie?"

"*Hell fire*, sir," said the boy emphatically, as though it were something to look forward to rather than shun.

"Take time, my boy," said Maule; "don't answer hurriedly; think it over. Suppose, now, you were accused of stealing an apple; how would that be in the next world, think you?"

"*Hell fire*, my lord!"

"Very good indeed. Now let us suppose that you were disobedient to your parents, or to one of them; what would happen in that case?"

"*Hell fire*, my lord!"

"Exactly; very good indeed. Now let me take another instance, and suppose that you were sent for the milk in the morning, and took *just a little sip* while you were carrying it home; how would that be as regards your future state?"

"*Hell fire!*" repeated the boy.

Upon this Clark suggested that the lad's absolute ignorance of the nature of an oath and Divine things rendered it imprudent to call him.

"I don't know about that," said Maule; "he seems to me to be very sound, and most divines will tell you he is right."

"He does not seem to be competent," said the counsel.

"I beg your pardon," returned the judge, "I think he is a very good little boy. He thinks that for every wilful fault he will go to hell fire; and he is very likely while he believes that doctrine to be most strict in his observance of truth. If you and I believed that such would be the penalty for every act of misconduct we committed, we should be better men than we are. Let the boy be sworn."

On one occasion, before Maule, I had to defend a man for murder. It was a terribly difficult case, because there was no defence except the usual one of insanity.

The court adjourned for lunch, and Woollet (who was my junior) and I went to consultation. I was oppressed with the difficulty of my task, and asked Woollet what he thought I could do.

"Oh," said he in his sanguine way, "make a hell of a speech. You'll pull him through all right. Let 'em have it."

"I'll give them as much burning eloquence as I can manage," said I, in my youthful ardour; "but what's the use of words against facts? We must really stand by the defence of insanity; it is all that's left."

"Call the clergyman," said Woollet; "he'll help us all he can."

With that resolution we returned to court. I made my speech for the defence, following Woollet's advice as nearly as practicable, and really blazed away. I think the jury believed there was a good deal in what I said, for they seemed a very discerning body and a good deal inclined to logic, especially as there was a mixture of passion in it.

We then called the clergyman of the village where the prisoner lived. He said he had been Vicar for thirty-four years, and that up to very recently, a few days before the murder, the prisoner had been a regular attendant at his church. He was a married man with a wife and two little children, one seven and the other nine.

"Did the wife attend your ministrations, too?" asked Maule.

"Not so regularly. Suddenly," continued the Vicar, after suppressing his emotion, "without any apparent cause, the man became *a Sabbath-breaker*, and absented himself from church."

This evidence rather puzzled me, for I could not understand its purport. Maule in the meantime was watching it with the keenest interest and no little curiosity. He was not a great believer in the defence of insanity--except, occasionally, that of the solicitor who set it up--and consequently watched the Vicar with scrutinizing intensity.

"Have you finished with your witness, Mr. Woollet?" his lordship inquired.

"Yes, my lord."

Maule then took him in hand, and after looking at him steadfastly for about a minute, said,--

"You say, sir, that you have been Vicar of this parish for *four-and-thirty years?*"

"Yes, my lord."

"And during that time I dare say you have regularly performed the services of the Church?"

"Yes, my lord."

"Did you have week-day services as well?"

"Every Tuesday, my lord."

"And did you preach your own sermons?"

"With an occasional homily of the Church."

"Your own sermon or discourse, with an occasional homily? And was this poor man a regular attendant at all your services during the whole time you have been Vicar?"

"Until he killed his wife, my lord."

"That follows--I mean up to the time of this Sabbath-breaking you spoke of he regularly attended your ministrations, and then killed his wife?"

"Exactly, my lord."

"Never missed the sermon, discourse, or homily of the Church, Sunday or week-day?"

"That is so, my lord."

"Did you write your own sermons, may I ask?"

"Oh yes, my lord."

Maule carefully wrote down all that our witness said, and I began to think the defence of insanity stood on very fair grounds, especially when I perceived that Maule was making some arithmetical calculations. But you never could tell by his manner which way he was going, and therefore we had to wait for his next observation, which was to this effect:--

"You have given yourself, sir, a very excellent character, and doubtless, by your long service in the village, have richly deserved it. You have, no doubt, also won the affection of all your parishioners, probably that of the Bishop of your diocese, by your incomparable devotion to your parochial duties. The result, however, of your indefatigable exertions, so far as this unhappy man is concerned, comes to this--"

His lordship then turned and addressed his observations on the result to me.

"This gentleman, Mr. Hawkins, has written with his own pen and preached or read with his own voice to this unhappy prisoner about one hundred and four Sunday sermons or discourses, with an occasional homily, every year."

There was an irresistible sense of the ludicrous as Maule uttered, or rather growled, these words in a slow enunciation and an asthmatical tone. He paused as if wondering at the magnitude of his calculations, and then commenced again more slowly and solemnly than before.

"These," said he, "added to the week-day services--make--exactly *one hundred and fifty-six sermons, discourses, and homilies for the year*." (Then he stared at me, asking with his eyes what I thought of it.) "These, again, being continued over a space of time, comprising, as the reverend gentleman tells us, no less than *thirty-four years*, give us a grand total of *five thousand three hundred and four sermons, discourses, or homilies* during this unhappy man's life."

Maule's eyes were now riveted on the clergyman as though he were an accessory to the murder.

"Five thousand three hundred and four," he repeated, "by the same person, however respectable and beloved as a pastor he might be, was what few of us could have gone through unless we were endowed with as much strength of mind as power of endurance. I was going to ask you, sir, did the idea ever strike you when you talked of this unhappy being suddenly leaving your ministrations and turning Sabbath-breaker, that after thirty-four years he might want a little change? Would it not be reasonable to suppose that the man might think he had had enough of it?"

"It might, my lord."

"And would not that in your judgment, instead of showing that he was insane, prove that he was *a very sensible man*?"

The Vicar did not quite assent to this, and as he would not dissent from the learned Judge, said nothing.

"And," continued Maule, "that he was perfectly sane, although he murdered his wife?"

All this was very clever, not to say facetious, on the part of the learned Judge; but as I had yet to address the jury, I was resolved to take the other view of the effect of the Vicar's sermons, and I did so. I worked Maule's quarry, I think, with some little effect: for after all his most strenuous exertions to secure a conviction, the jury believed, probably, that no man's mind could stand the ordeal; and, further, that any doubt they might have, after seeing the two children of the prisoner in court dressed in little black frocks, and sobbing bitterly while I was addressing them, would be given in the prisoner's favour, which it was.

This incident in my life is not finished. On the same evening I was dining at the country house of a Mr. Hardcastle, and near me sat an old inhabitant of the village where the tragedy had been committed.

"You made a touching speech, Mr. Hawkins," said the old inhabitant.

"Well," I answered, "it was the best thing I could do in the circumstances."

"Yes," he said; "but I don't think you would have painted the little home in such glowing colours if you had seen what I saw last week when I was driving past the cottage. No, no; I think you'd have toned down a bit."

"What was it?" I asked.

"Why," said the old inhabitant, "the little children who sobbed so violently in court this morning, and to whom you made such pathetic reference, were playing on an ash-heap near their cottage; and they had a poor cat with a string round its neck, swinging backwards and forwards, and as they did so they sang,--

This is the way poor daddy will go!
This is the way poor daddy will go!'

Such, Mr. Hawkins, was their excessive grief!"

Yes, but it got the verdict.

CHAPTER VI.

AN INCIDENT ON THE ROAD TO NEWMARKET.

My first visit to Newmarket Heath had one or two little incidents which may be interesting, although of no great importance. The Newmarket of to-day is not quite the same Newmarket that it was then: many things connected with it have changed, and, above all, its frequenters have changed; and if "things are not what they seem," they do not seem to me, at all events, to be what they were "in my day."

Sixty years is a long space of time to traverse, but I do so with a very vivid recollection of my old friend Charley Wright.

It was on a bright October morning when we set out, and glad enough was I to leave the courts at Westminster and the courts of the Temple--glad enough to break loose from the thraldom of nothing to do and get away into the beautiful country.

Charley and I were always great friends; we had seen so much together, especially of what is called "the world," which I use in a different sense from that in which we were now to seek adventures. We had seen so much of its good and evil, its lights and shades, and had so many memories in common, that they formed the groundwork of a lasting friendship.

He was the only son of an almost too indulgent father, who was the very best example of an old English gentleman of his day you could ever meet. He also had seen a good deal of life, and was not unfamiliar with any of its varied aspects. He was intellectual and genial, and dispensed his hospitality with the most winning courtesy. To me he was all kindness, and I have a grateful feeling of delight in being able in these few words to record my affectionate reverence for his memory. It was at his house in Pall Mall that I met John Leech and Percival Leigh.

But I digress as my mind goes back to these early dates, and unless I break away, Charley and I will not reach Newmarket in time for the first race. It happened that when we made this memorable visit I had an uncle living at The Priory at Royston, which was some five-and-twenty miles from Newmarket, where the big handicap, I think the Cesarewitch, was to be run the following day, or the next--I forget which.

But an interesting episode interrupted our journey to the Heath. To our surprise, and no little to our delight, there was to be an important meeting of the "Fancy" to witness a great prize-fight between Jack Brassy and Ben Caunt.

Ben Caunt was the greatest prize-fighter, both in stature and bulk, as well as in strength, I ever saw. He looked what he was--then or soon after--the champion of the world.

Brassy, too, was well made, and seemed every whit the man to meet Caunt. The two, indeed, were equally well made in form and shape, and as smooth cut as marble statues when they stripped for action.

The advertisements had announced that the contest was to come off at, "or as near thereto as circumstances permitted" (circumstances here meaning the police), the village of Little Bury, near Saffron Walden.

At the little inn of the village some of the magnates of the Ring were to assemble on the morning of the fight for an early breakfast, to which Charley and I had the good fortune to be invited by Jack Brassy's second, Peter Crawley, another noted pugilist of his day.

It was different weather from that we enjoyed in the early morning, for the rain was now pouring down in torrents, and we had a drive of no less than fifteen miles before us to the scene of action. Vehicles were few, and horses fewer. Nothing was to be had for love or money, as it seemed. But there was at last found one man who, if he had little love for the prize-ring, had much reverence for the golden coin that supported it. He was a Quaker. He had an old gig, and, I think, a still older horse, both of which I hired for the journey--the Quaker, of course, pretending that he had no idea of any meeting of the "Fancy" whatever. Nor do I suppose he would know what that term implied.

If ever any man in the world did what young men are always told by good people to do--namely, to persevere--I am sure we did, Charley and I, with the Quaker's horse. Whether he suspected the mission on which we were bent, or was considering the danger of such a scene to his morals, I could not ascertain, but never did any animal show a greater reluctance to go anywhere except to his quiet home.

Your happiness at these great gatherings depended entirely upon the distance or proximity of the police. If they were pretty near, the landlord of the inn would hesitate about serving you, and if he did, would charge a far higher price in consequence of the supposed increased risk. He would never encourage a breach of the peace in defiance of the county magistrates, who were the authority to renew his licence at Brewster Sessions. So much, then, if the officers of justice were *near*.

If they happened to be absent--which, as I have said, occasionally occurred when a big thing was to come off--there was then a dominant feeling of social equality which you could never see manifested so strongly in any other place. A gentleman would think nothing of putting his fingers into your pockets and abstracting your money, and if you had the hardihood to resent the intrusion, would think less of putting his fist into your eyes.

We were by no means certain, as I learned, that our fight would come off after all, for it appeared the magistrates had given strict and specific instructions to the police that no combat was to take place in the county of Essex. Consequently the parties whose duty it was to make preparations had fled from that respectable county and gone away towards Six Mile Bottom, just in one of the corners of Cambridgeshire, as if the intention was that the dons of the University should have a look in. Constables slept more soundly in Cambridgeshire than in Essex. Moreover, the Essex magistrates would themselves have a moral right to witness the fight if it did not take place in their county.

Thus we set out for the rendezvous. Charley soon discovered that our steed was not accustomed to the whip, for instead of urging him forward it produced the contrary effect. However, we got along by slow degrees, and when we came up with the crowd--oh!

Such a scene I had never witnessed in my life, nor could have conceived it possible anywhere on this earth or anywhere out of that abyss the full description of which you will find in "Paradise Lost."

It was a procession of the blackguardism of all ages and of all countries under heaven. The sexes were apparently in equal numbers and in equal degrees of ugliness and ferocity. There were faces flat for want of noses, and mouths ghastly for want of teeth; faces scarred, bruised, battered into every shape but what might be called human. There were fighting-men of every species and variety--men whose profession it was to fight, and others whose brutal nature it was; there were women fighters, too, more deadly and dangerous than the men, because they added cruelty to their ferocity. Innumerable women there were who had lost the very nature of womanhood, and whose mouths were the mere outlet of oaths and filthy language. Their shrill clamours deafened our ears and subdued the deep voices of the men, whom they chaffed, reviled, shrieked at, yelled at, and swore at by way of *fun*.

Amidst this turbulent rabble rode several members of the peerage, and even Ministerial supporters of the "noble art," exchanging with the low wretches I have mentioned a word or two of chaff or an occasional laugh at the grotesque wit and humour which are never absent from an English crowd.

As we approached the famous scene, to which every one was looking with the most intense anticipation, the crowd grew almost frenzied with expectancy, and yet the utmost good-humour prevailed. In this spirit we arrived at Bourne Bridge, and thence to the place of encounter was no great distance. It was a little field behind a public-house.

Every face was now white with excitement, except the faces of the combatants. They were firm set as iron itself. Trained to physical endurance, they were equally so in nerve and coolness of temperament, and could not have seemed more excited than if they were going to dinner instead of to one of the most terrible encounters I ever witnessed.

To those who have never seen an exhibition of this kind it was quite amazing to observe with what rapidity the ropes were fixed and the ring formed; nor were the men less prompt. Into the ring they stepped with their supporters, or seconds, and in almost an instant the principals had shaken hands, and were facing each other in what well might be deadly conflict. There were illustrious members of all classes assembled there, members probably of all professions, men who afterwards, as I know, became great in history, politics, law, literature, and religion; for it was a very great fight, and attracted all sorts and conditions from all places and positions. Nothing since that fight, except Tom Sayers and the "Benicia Boy," has attracted so goodly and so fashionable an audience and so fierce an assembly of blackguards.

But in the time of the latter battle the decadence of the Ring was manifest, and was the outcome of what is doubtless an increasing civilization. At the time of which I am now speaking the Prize Ring was one of our fashionable sports, supported by the wealthy of all classes, and was supposed to contribute to the manliness of our race; consequently our distinguished warriors, as well as the members of our most gentle professions, loved a good old-fashioned English "set-to," and nobody, as a rule, was the worse for it, although my poor brother Jack never recovered his half-crowns.

We had been advised to take our cushions from the gig to sit upon, because the straw round the ring was soddened with the heavy rains, and I need not say we found it was a very wise precaution. The straw had been placed round the ring for the benefit of the *élite*, who occupied front seats.

The fight now began, and, I must repeat, I never saw anything like it. Both pugilists were of the heaviest fighting weights. Caunt was a real giant, ugly as could be by the frequent batterings he had received in the face. His head was like a bull-dog's, and so was his courage, whilst his strength must have been that of a very Samson; but if it was, it did not reside in his hair, for that was short and close as a mouse's back.

At first I thought Brassy had the best of it; he was more active, being less ponderous, and landed some very ugly ones, cutting right into the flesh, although Caunt did not appear to mind it in the least. Brassy, however, did not follow up his advantage as I thought he ought to have done, and in my opinion dreaded the enormous power and force of his opponent in the event of his "getting home."

With the usual fluctuations of a great battle, the contest went on until nearly a *hundred rounds* were fought, lasting as many minutes, but no decisive effect was as yet observable. After this, however, Brassy could not come up to time. The event, therefore, was declared in Caunt's favour, and his opponent was carried off the field on a hurdle into the public-house, where I afterwards saw him in bed.

Thus terminated the great fight of the day, but not thus my day's adventures.

The sport was all that the most enthusiastic supporters of the Ring could desire. It no doubt had its barbarous aspects, regarded from a humanitarian point of view, but it was not so demoralizing as the spectacle of some poor creature risking his neck in a performance for which the spectator pays his sixpence, and the whole excitement consists in the knowledge that the actor may be dashed to pieces before his eyes.

It was time now to leave the scene, so Charley and I went to look for our gig (evidence of gentility from the time of Thurtell and Hunt's trial for the murder of Mr. Weare).

Alas! our respectability was gone--I mean the gig.

In vindication of the wisdom and foresight of Charley and myself, I should like to mention that we had entrusted that valuable evidence of our status to the keeping of a worthy stranger dressed in an old red jacket and a pair of corduroy trousers fastened with a wisp of hay below the knees.

When we arrived at the spot where he promised to wait our coming, he was gone, the horse and gig too; nor could any inquiries ascertain their whereabouts.

Whether this incident was a judgment on the Quaker, as Wright suggested, or one of the inevitable incidents attendant on a prize-fight, I am not in a position to say; but we thought it served the Quaker right for letting us a horse that would not go until the gentleman in the red jacket relieved us of any further trouble on that account.

Mistakes are so common amongst thieves that one can never tell how the horse got away; but if I were put on my oath, knowing the proclivities of the animal, I should say that he was backed out of the field.

We were now, as it seemed, the most deplorable objects in creation: without friends and without a gig, wet through, shelterless, amidst a crowd of drunken, loathsome outcasts of society, with only one solitary comfort between us--a pipe, which Charley enjoyed and I loathed. Drink is always quarrelsome or affectionate, generally the one first and the other after. When the tears dry, oaths begin, and we soon found that the quarrelsome stage of the company had been reached.

Amidst all this excitement we had not forgotten that this little matter of the prize-fight was but an incident on our journey to Newmarket. We knew full well that our present appearance would have found no recognition in the Mall. But we cared nothing for the Mall, as we were not known by the fashion in the racing world; and as for the others, we should like to avoid them in any world.

You will wonder in these circumstances what we did. We waited where we were through the whole of that wet afternoon, and then, on a couple of hacks--how we obtained them I don't know; I never asked Charley, and nothing of any importance turns upon them--we arrived at our comfortable Royston quarters about eight o'clock, tired to death.

We were received with a hearty welcome by my uncle, who was much entertained with our day's adventures. He liked my description of the fight, especially when I told him how Brassy "drew Caunt's claret," and showed such other knowledge of the scientific practice that no one could possibly have learnt had he not read up carefully *Bell's Life* for the current week.

I am sure my uncle thought I was one of the best of nephews, and I considered him in reality "my only uncle." Long, thought I, may he prove to be; and yet I never borrowed a penny from him in my life.

On the next day, fully equipped, and with all that was necessary for our distinguished position, we set out for Newmarket Heath, even now the glory of the racing world, not forgetting Goodwood, which is more or less a private business and fashionable picnic.

I shall not attempt to describe Newmarket. No one can describe, the indescribable. I will only say it was not the Newmarket which our later generation knows. It was then in its crude state of original simplicity. There were no stands save "the Duke's," at the top of the town, and one other, somewhat smaller and nearer to the present grand stand. Those who could afford to do so rode on horseback about the Heath; those who could not walked if they felt disposed, or sat down on the turf--the best enjoyment of all if you are tired. We did all three: we rode, walked, and sat down. At last, after a thoroughly enjoyable outing, such as the Bar knows nothing of in these respectable times, we returned to our business quarters in the Temple.

CHAPTER VII.

AN EPISODE AT HERTFORD QUARTER SESSIONS.

Hearsay is not, as a rule, evidence in a court of justice. There are one or two exceptions which I need not mention. If you want, therefore, to say what Smith said, you cannot say it, but must call Smith himself, and probably he will swear he never said anything of the sort.

The Marquis of Salisbury, in the early days that I speak of, was a kind-hearted chairman, and would never allow the quibble of the lawyer to stand in the way of justice to the prisoner. In those days at sessions they were not so nice in the observances of mere forms as they are now, and you could sometimes get in something that was not exactly evidence, strictly speaking, in favour of a prisoner by a side-wind, as it were, although it was not the correct thing to do.

It happened that I was instructed to defend a man who had been committed to Hertford Quarter Sessions on a charge of felony. The committing magistrates having refused to let the man out on bail, an application was made at Judges' Chambers before Mr. Baron Martin to reverse that decision, which he did.

"Not a rag of evidence," said the attorney's clerk when he delivered the little brief--"not a shadder of evidence, Mr. 'Awkins. It's a walk-over, sir."

I knew that meant a nominal fee, but wondered how many more similes he was going to deliver instead of the money. But to the honour of the solicitor, I am bound to say that point was soon cleared up, and the practice of magistrates, supposed to be in their right minds, committing people for trial with no "shadder" of evidence against them, it now became my duty to inquire into. I asked how he knew there was no evidence, and whether the man bore a respectable character.

"Oh, I was up before the Baron," he answered. ("Yes," I thought, "but you must wake very early if you are up too soon for Baron Martin.") "And the Baron said, as to grantin' bail, 'Certainly he should; the magistrates had no business to commit him for trial, for there was not a rag of a case against the man.' So you see, sir, it's a easy case, Mr. 'Awkins; and as the man's a poor man, we can't mark much of a fee."

The usual complaint with quarter sessions solicitors.

Such were my instructions. I was young in practice at that time, and took a great deal more in--I mean in the way of credulity--than I did in after life. Nor was I very learned in the ways of solicitors' clerks. I knew that hearsay evidence, even in the case of a Judge's observation, was inadmissible, and therefore what the Baron said could not strictly be given; but I did not know how far you might go in the country, nor what the Marquis's opinion might be of the Baron. I therefore mentioned it to Rodwell, who, of course, was instructed for the prosecution; he was in everything on one side or the other--never, I believe, on both.

This stickler for etiquette was absolutely shocked; he held up his hands, began a declamation on the rules of evidence, and uttered so many Pharisaical platitudes that I only escaped annihilation by a hair's-breadth. He was always furious on etiquette.

Much annoyed at his bumptious manner, I was resolved now, come what would, to pay him off. I wanted to show him he was not everybody, even at Hertford Sessions. So when the case came on and the policeman was in the box, I rose to cross-examine him, which I did very quietly.

"Now, policeman, I am going to ask you a question; but pray don't answer it till you are told to do so, because my learned friend may object to it."

Rodwell sprang to his feet and objected at once.

"What is the question?" asked the Marquis. "We must hear what the question is before I can rule as to your objection, Mr. Rodwell."

This was a good one for Mr. Rodwell, and made him colour up to his eyebrows, especially as I looked at him and smiled.

"The question, my lord," said I, "is a very simple one: Did not Mr. Baron Martin say, when applied to for bail, that there was not a rag of a case against the prisoner?"

"This is monstrous!" said the learned stickler for forms and ceremonies--"monstrous! Never heard of such a thing!"

It might have been monstrous, but it gave me an excellent grievance with the jury, even if the Marquis did not see his way to allow the question; and a grievance is worth something, if you have no defence.

The Marquis paid great attention to the case, especially after that observation of the Baron's. Although he regretted that it could not be got in as evidence, he was good enough to say I should get the benefit of it with the jury.

All this time there was a continuous growl from my learned friend of "Monstrous! monstrous!"--so much so that for days after that word kept ringing in my ears, as monotonously as a muffin bell on a Sunday afternoon.

But I believe he was more irritated by my subsequent conduct, for I played round the question like one longing for forbidden fruit, and emphasized the objection of my learned friend now and again: all very wrong, I know now, but in the heyday of youthful ardour how many faults we commit!"

"Just tell me," I said to the policeman, "did the learned Judge--I mean Mr. Baron Martin--seem to know what he was about when he let this man out on bail?"

"O yes, sir," said the witness, "he knowed what he was about, right enough," stroking his chin.

"You may rely on that," said the Marquis. "You may take that for granted, Mr. Hawkins."

"I thought so, my lord; there is not a judge on the Bench who can see through a case quicker than the Baron."

The grumbling still continued.

"Now, then, don't answer this."

"You have already ruled, my lord," said Rodwell.

"This is another one," said I; "but if it's regular to keep objecting before the prisoner's counsel has a chance of putting his question, I sit down, my lord. I shall be allowed, probably, to address the jury--that is. if Mr. Rodwell does not object."

The noble Marquis, on seeing my distress, said,--

"Mr. Hawkins, the question needs no answer from the policeman; you will get the benefit of it for what it is worth. The jury will draw their own conclusions from Mr. Rodwell's objections."

As they did upon the whole case, for they acquitted, much to Mr. Rodwell's annoyance.

"Now," said the Marquis, "let the officer stand back. I want to ask what the Baron really did say when he let this man out on bail."

"My lord," answered the witness, "his lordship said as how he looked upon the whole lot as a *gang of thieves*."

"You've got it now," said Rodwell.

"And so have you," said I. "You should not have objected, and then you would have got the answer he has just given."

CHAPTER VIII.

A DANGEROUS SITUATION--A FORGOTTEN PRISONER.

I had been to Paris in the summer of 18-- for a little holiday, and was returning in the evening after some races had taken place near that city. I had not attended them, and was, in fact, not aware that they were being held; but I soon discovered the fact from finding myself in the midst of the motley Crowds which always throng railway stations on such occasions, only on this particular day they were a little worse than usual. The race meeting had brought together the roughs of all nations, and especially from England. As it seemed to me, my fellow-countrymen always took the lead in this kind of competition.

I was endeavouring to get to the booking-office amongst the rest of the crowd, and there was far more pushing and struggling than was at all necessary for that purpose. Presently a burly ruffian, with a low East End face of the slum pattern and complexion, rolled out a volley of oaths at me. He asked where the ---- I was pushing and what game I was up to, as though I were a professional pickpocket like himself. He had the advantage of me in being surrounded by a gang of the most loathsome blackguards you could imagine, while I was without a friend. I spoke, therefore, very civilly, and said the crowd was pushing behind and forcing me forward. The brute was annoyed at my coolness, and irritated all the more.

Hitherto his language had not been strong enough to frighten me, so he improved its strength by some tremendous epithets, considerably above proof. I think he must have enjoyed the exclusive copyright, for I never knew his superlatives imitated. He finished the harangue by saying that he would knock my head off if I said another word.

To this I replied, with a look stronger than all his language, "No, you won't."

My look must have been strong, because the countenances of the bystanders were subdued.

"Why won't I, muster?" he asked.

"For two reasons," I said: "first, because you won't try; and secondly, because you could not if you did."

He was somewhat tamed, and then I lifted my hat, so that he could see my close-cropped hair, which was as short as his own, only not for the same reason. "You don't seem to know who I am," I added, hoping he would now take me for a member of the prize-ring. But my appearance did not frighten him. I had nothing but my short-cropped hair to rely on; so in self-defence I had to devise another stratagem. To frighten him one must look the ruffian in the face, or look the ruffian that he was. He continued to abuse me as we passed on our way to the booking-office window, and I have no doubt he and his gang were determined to rob me. One thing was common between us--we had no regard for one another. I now assumed as bold a manner as I could and a rough East End accent. "Look-ee 'ere," said I: "I know you don't keer for me no more 'an I keers for you. I ain't afraid o' no man, and I'll tell you what it is: it's your ignorance of who I am that makes you bold. I know you ain't a bad un with the maulers. Let's have no more nonsense about it here. I'll fight you on Monday week, say, for a hundred a side in the Butts, and we'll post the money at Peter Crawley's next Saturday. What d'ye say to that?"

Peter Crawley, whom I have already mentioned as inviting me to breakfast, was like a thunderclap to him. I must be somebody if I knew Peter Crawley, and now he doubtless bethought him of my short hair.

I must confess if the fellow had taken me at my word I should have been in as great a funk as he was, but he did not. My challenge was declined.

A curious incident happened once in the rural district of Saffron Walden. It is a borough no doubt, but it always seemed to me to be too small for any grown-up thing, and its name sounded more like a little flower-bed than anything else. On the occasion of which I speak there was great excitement in the place because they had got a prisoner—an event which baffled the experience of the oldest inhabitant.

The Recorder was an elderly barrister, full of pomp and dignity; and, like many of his brother Recorders, had very seldom a prisoner to try. You may therefore imagine with what stupendous importance he was invested when he found that the rural magistrates had committed a little boy for trial for stealing a *ball of twine*. Think of the grand jury filing in to be "charged" by this judicial dignitary. Imagine his charge, his well-chosen sentences in anticipation of the one to come at the end of the sitting. Think of his eloquent disquisition on the law of larceny! It was all there!

After the usual proclamation against vice and immorality had been read, and after the grand jury had duly found a true bill, the next thing was to find the prisoner and bring him up for trial.

We may not be sentimental, or I might have cried, "God save the child!" as the usher said, "God save the Queen!" But "Suffer little children to come unto Me" would not have applied to our jails in those miserable and inhuman times. Mercy and sympathy were out of the question when you had law and order to maintain, as well as all the functionaries who had to contribute to their preservation.

"Put up the prisoner!" said the Recorder in solemn and commanding tones.

Down into the jaws of the cavern below the dock descended the jailer of six feet two--the only big thing about the place. He was a resolute-looking man in full uniform, and I can almost feel the breathless silence that pervaded the court during his absence.

Time passed and no one appeared. When a sufficient interval had elapsed for the stalwart jailer to have eaten his prisoner, had he been so minded, the Recorder, looking up from behind the *Times*, which he appeared to be reading, asked in a very stern voice why the prisoner was not "put up."

They did not put up the boy, but the jailer, with a blood-forsaken face, put himself up through the hole, like a policeman coming through a trap-door in a pantomime.

"I beg your honour's pardon, my lord, but they have forgot to bring him."

"Forgot to bring him! What do you mean? Where is he?"

"They've left him at Chelmsford, your honour."

It seemed there was no jail at Saffron Walden, because, to the honour of the borough be it said, they had no one to put into it; and this small child had been committed for safe custody to Chelmsford to wait his trial at sessions, and had been there so long that he was actually forgotten when the day of trial came. I never heard anything more of him; but hope his small offence was forgotten as well as himself.

CHAPTER IX.

THE ONLY "RACER" I EVER OWNED--SAM LINTON, THE DOG-FINDER.

I have been often asked whether I ever owned a racer. In point of fact, I never did, although I went as near to that honour as any man who never arrived at it--a racer, too, who afterwards carried its owner's colours triumphantly past the winning-post.

The reader may have been shocked at the story I told of those poor ill-brought-up children whose mother was murdered, from the natural feeling that if pure innocence is not to be found in childhood, where are we to seek it?

I will indicate the spot in three words--*on the Turf.*

True, you will find fraud, cunning, knavery, and robbery, but you will find also the most unsophisticated innocence.

I went as a spectator, a lover of sport, and a lover of horses; and took more delight in it than I ever could in any haunt of fashionable idleness.

I amused myself by watching the proceedings of the betting-ring, where there is a good deal more honesty than in many places dignified by the name of "marts."

But if there was no innocence on the turf, rogues could not live; they are not cannibals--not, at all events, while they can obtain tenderer food. And are there not commercial circles also which could not exist without their equally innocent supporters?

Experience may be a dear school, but its lessons are never forgotten. A very little should go a long way, and the wisest make it go farthest. If any one wants a picture of innocence on the turf, let me give one of my own drawing, taken from nature.

All my life I have loved animals, especially horses and dogs; and all field sports, especially hunting and racing. But I went on the turf with as much simplicity as a girl possesses at her first ball, knowing nothing about public form or the way to calculate odds, to hedge, or do anything but wonder at the number of fools there were in the world. I did not know "a thing or two," like the knowing ones who lose all they possess. Who could believe that men go about philanthropically to inform the innocent how to "put their money on," while they carefully avoid putting on their own? Tipsters, in short, were no part of my racing creed. I was not so ignorant as that. I believed in a good horse quite as much as Lord Rosebery does, and much more than I believed in a good rider. But there were even then honest jockeys, as well as unimpeachable owners. All you can say is, honesty is honesty everywhere, and you will find a good deal of it on the turf, if you know where to look for it; and its value is in proportion to its quantity. The moment you depart a hair's-breadth from its immaculate principle there is no medium state between that and roguery.

However, be that as it may, I was once the owner of a pedigree thoroughbred called Dreadnought, which was presented to me when a colt. Dreadnought's dam Collingwood was by Muley Moloch out of Barbelle. Dreadnought was good for nothing as a racer, and had broken down in training. As a castaway he was offered to me, and I gladly accepted the present.

As he was too young to work, I sent him down to ---- Park, to be kept till he was fit for use. He was there for a considerable time, and was then sent back in a neglected and miserable condition.

I rode him for some time, until one day he took me to Richmond Park, and on going up the hill fell and cut both his knees to pieces and mine as well. This was a sad mishap, and, of course, I could have no further confidence in poor Dreadnought, fond of him as I was; so he was placed under the care of a skilful veterinary surgeon, who gave him every attention. His bill was by no means heavy, and he brought him quite round again.

In the course of time he acquired a respectable appearance, although his broken knees, to say nothing of his "past," prevented his becoming valuable so far as I was concerned. Certainly I had no expectation of his ever going on to the turf. How could one believe that any owner would think of entering him for a race?

One morning my groom came to me and said, "I think, sir, I can find a purchaser for Dreadnought, if you have no objection to selling him; he's a gentleman, sir, who would take great care of him and give him a good home."

"Sell him!" said I. "Well, I should not object if he found a good master. I cannot ride him, and he is practically useless. What price does he seem inclined to offer?"

"Well, he ain't made any offer, sir; but he seems a good deal took with him and to like the look of him. Perhaps, sir, he might come and see you. I told him that I thought a matter o' *fifteen pun* might buy un. I dunnow whether I did right, sir, but I told un you would never take a farden less. I stuck to that."

"No," said I, "certainly not, when the vet.'s bill was twelve pounds ten--not a farthing less, James."

When the proposed purchaser came, he said, "It's a poor horse--a very poor horse; he wants a lot of looking after, and I shouldn't think of buying him except for the sake of seeing what I could do with him, for I am not fond of lumber, Mr. Hawkins--I don't care for lumber."

It was straightforward, but I did not at the time see his depth of feeling. He was evidently intending to buy him out of compassion, as he had some knowledge of his ancestors. But I stuck to my fifteen pounds hard and fast, and at last he said, "Well, Mr. Hawkins, I'll give you all you ask, if so be you'll throw in the saddle and bridle!"

I was tired of the negotiations, and yielded; so away went poor Dreadnought with his saddle and bridle, never for me to look on again. I was sorry to part with him, and the more so because his life had been unfortunate. But I was deceived in him as well as in his new master. From me he had concealed his merits, only to reveal them, as is often the case with latent genius, when some accidental opportunity offered.

At that time Bromley in Kent was a central attraction for a great many second-class patrons of the sporting world. I know little about the events that were negotiated at Bromley and other small places of the kind, but there was, as I have been informed, a good deal of blackguardism and pickpocketing on its course and in its little primitive streets--lucky if you came out of them with only one black eye. They would steal the teeth out of your mouth if you did not keep it shut and your eyes open.

However, Bromley races came on some time after the sale of my Dreadnought.... The next morning my groom came with a look of astonishment that seemed to have kept him awake all night, and said,--

"You'll be surprised to hear, sir, that our 'oss has won a fifty-pound prize at Bromley, and a pot of money besides in bets for his owner."

"Won a prize!" said I. "Was it by standing on his head?"

"Won a *race*, sir."

"Then it must have been a walk-over."

"Oh no, sir; he beat the cracks, beat the favourites, and took in all the knowing ones. I always said there was something about that there 'oss, sir, that I didn't understand and nobody couldn't understand, sir."

I was absolutely dumbfounded, knowing very little about "favourites" or "cracks." My groom I knew I could rely upon, for he always seemed to be the very soul of honour. I thought at first he might have been misled in some Bromley taproom, but afterwards found that it was all true--he had heard it from the owner himself, in whom the public seemed to place confidence, for they laid very long odds against Dreadnought.

The animal was famous, but not in that name; he had, like most honest persons, an alias. How he achieved his victory is uncertain; one thing, however, is certain--it must have been a startling surprise to Dreadnought to find himself in a race at all, and still more astonishing to find himself in front.

"How many ran?" I asked.

"Three, sir; two of 'em crack horses."

At this time I took little interest in pedigrees, and knew nothing of the "cracks," so the names of those celebrated animals which Dreadnought had beaten are forgotten. One of them, it appeared, had been heavily backed at 9 to 4, but Dreadnought did not seem to care for that; he ran, not on his public form, but on his merits. My eyes were opened at last, and the whole mystery was solved when James told me that *all three horses belonged to the same owner*!

From that time to this I never heard what became of Dreadnought, and never saw the man who bought him, even in the dock. It is strange, however, that animals so true and faithful as dogs and horses should be instruments so perverted as to make men liars and rogues; while for intelligence many of them could give most of us pounds and pass us easily at the winning-post.

Speaking of dogs reminds me of dog-stealers and *their* ways, of which some years ago I had a curious experience. I have told the story before, but it has become altered, and the true one has never been heard since. Indeed, no story is told correctly when its copyright is infringed.

There was a man at the time referred to known as old Sam Linton, the most extraordinary dog-fancier who ever lived, and the most curious thing about him was that he always fancied other people's dogs to his own. He was a remarkable dog-*finder*, too. In these days of dogs' homes the services of such a man as Linton are not so much in request; but he was a home in himself, and did a great deal of good in his way by restoring lost dogs to their owners; so that it became almost a common question in those days, when a lady lost her pet, to ask if she had made any inquiry of old Sam Linton. He was better than the wise woman who indicated in some mysterious jargon where the stolen watch might or might not be found in the future, for old Sam *brought* you the very dog on a *specified day*! The wise woman never knew where the lost property was; old Sam did.

I dare say he was a great blackguard, but as he has long joined the majority, it is of no consequence. There was one thing I admired about Sam: there was a thorough absence in him of all hypocrisy and cant. He professed no religion whatever, but acted upon the principle that a bargain was a bargain, and should be carried out as between man and man. That was his idea, and as I found him true to it, I respected him accordingly, and mention his name as one of the few genuinely honest men I have met.

The way I made his acquaintance was singular. I was dining with my brother benchers at the Middle Temple Hall, when a message was brought that a gentleman would like to see me "partickler" after dinner, if I could give him a few minutes.

When I came out of the hall, there was a man looking very like a burglar. His dress, or what you should call his "get-up," is worth a momentary glance. He had a cat-skin cap in his hand about as large as a frying-pan, and nearly of the same colour--this he kept turning round and round first with one hand, then with both--a pea-jacket with large pearl buttons, corduroy breeches, a kind of moleskin waistcoat, and blucher shoes. He impressed one in a moment as being fond of drink. On one or two occasions I found this quality of great service to me in matters relating to the discovery of lost dogs. Drink, no doubt, has its advantages to those who do not drink.

"Muster Orkins, sir," said he, "beggin' your pardon, sir, but might I have a word with you, Muster Orkins, if it ain't a great intrusion, sir?"

I saw my man at once, and showed him that I understood business.

"You are Sam Linton?"

It took his breath away. He hadn't much, but poor old Sam did not like to part with it. In a very husky voice, that never seemed to get outside his mouth, he said,--

"*Yus, sur*, that's it, Mr. Orkins." Then he breathed, "Yer 'onner, wot I means to say is this--"

"What do you want, Linton? Never mind what you mean to say; I know you'll never say it."

"Well, Mr. Orkins, sir, ye see it is as this: you've lost a little dorg. Well, you'll say, 'How do you know that 'ere, Sam?' 'Well, sir,' I says, "ow don't I know it? Ain't you bin an' offered *fourteen pun* for that there leetle dorg? Why, it's knowed dreckly all round Mile End--the werry 'ome of lorst dorgs--and that there dorg, find him when you wool, why, he ain't worth more'n *fourteen bob*, sir.' Now, 'ow d'ye 'count for that, sir?"

"You've seen him, then?"

"Not I," says Sam, unmoved even by a twitch; "but I knows a party as 'as, and it ain't likely, Mr. Orkins, as you'll get 'im by orferin' a price like that, for why? Why, it stands to reason--don't it, Mr. Orkins?--it ain't the *dorg you're* payin' for, but *your feelins* as these 'ere wagabonds is *tradin' on, Mr. Orkins*; that's where it is. O sir, it's abominable, as I tells 'em, keepin' a gennelman's dorg."

I was perfectly thunderstruck with the man's philosophy and good feeling.

"Go on, Mr. Linton."

"Well, Mr. Orkins, they knows--damn 'em!--as your feelins ull make you orfer more and more, for who knows that there dorg might belong *to a lidy*, and then *her* feelins has to be took into consideration. I'll tell 'ee now, Mr. Orkins, how this class of wagabond works, for wagabonds I must allow they be. Well, they meets, let's say, at a public, and one says to another, 'I say, Bill,' he says, 'that there dawg as you found 'longs to Lawyer Orkins; he's bloomin' fond o' dawgs, is Lawyer Orkins, so they say, and he can pay for it.' 'Right you are,' says Bill, 'and a d---- lawyer *shall* pay for it. He makes us pay when we wants him, and now we got him we'll make him pay.' So you see, Mr. Orkins, where it is, and whereas the way to do it is to say to these fellers--I'll just suppose, sir, I'm you and you're me, sir; no offence, I hope--'Well, I wants the dawg back.' Well, they says; leastways, I ses, ses I,--

"'Lawyer Orkins, you lost a dawg, 'ave yer?'

"'Yes,' ses you, 'I have,' like a gennelman--excuse my imitation, sir--' and I don't *keer a damn for the whelp*!' That's wot you ortersay. 'He's only a bloomin' mongrel.'"

"Very good; what am I to say next, Mr. Linton?"

"'Don't yer?' says the tother feller; 'then what the h---- are yer looken arter him for?'

"'Well,' you ses, Mr. Orkins, 'you can go to h----. I don't keer for the dawg; he ain't my fancy.'"

"A proper place for the whole lot of you, Sam."

"But, excuse me, Mr. Orkins, sir, that's for futue occasions. This 'ere present one, in orferin' fourteen pun, you've let the cat out o' the bag, and what I could ha' done had you consulted me sooner I can't do now; I could ha' got him for a *fi'-pun note* at one time, but they've worked on your feelins, and, mark my words, they'll want *twenty pun* as the price o' that there dawg, as sure as my name's Sam Linton. That's all I got to say, Mr. Orkins, and I thought I'd come and warn yer like a man--he's got into bad hands, that there dawg."

"I am much obliged, Mr. Linton; you seem to be a straightforward-dealing man."

"Well, sir, I tries to act upright and downstraight; and, as I ses, if a man only does that he ain't got nothin' to fear, 'as he, Muster Orkins?"

"When can I have him, Sam?"

"Well, sir, you can have him--let me see--Monday was a week, when you lost him; next Monday'll be another week, when I found him; that'll be a fortnit. Suppose we ses next Tooesday week?"

"Suppose we say to-morrow."

"Oh!" said Sam, "then I thinks you'll be sucked in! The chances are, Mr. Orkins, you won't see him at all. Why, sir, you don't know how them chaps carries on their business. Would you believe it, Mr. Orkins, a gennelman comes to me, and he ses, 'Sam,' he ses, 'I want to find a little pet dawg as belonged to a lidy'--which was his wife, in course--and he ses the lidy was nearly out of her mind. 'Well,' I ses, 'sir, to be 'onest with you, don't you mention that there fact to anybody but me'--because when a lidy goes out of her mind over a lorst dawg up goes the price, and you can't calculate bank-rate, as they ses. The price'll go up fablous, Mr. Orkins; there's nothin' rules the market like that there. Well, at last I agrees to do my best for the gent, and he says, just as you might say, Mr. Orkins, just now, 'When can she have him?' Well, I told him the time; but what a innercent question, Mr. Orkins! 'Why not before?' says he, with a kind of a angry voice, like yours just now, sir. 'Why, sir,' I ses, 'these people as finds dawgs 'ave their feelins as well as losers 'as theirs, and sometimes when they can't find the owner, they sells the animal.' Well, they sold this gennelman's animal to a major, and the reason why he couldn't be had for a little while was that the major, being fond on him, and 'avin' paid a good price for the dawg, it would ha' been cruel if he did not let him have the pleasure of him like for a few days--or a week."

Sam and I parted the best of friends, and, I need not say, on the best of terms I could get. I knew him for many years after this incident, and say to his credit that, although he was sometimes hard with customers, he acted, from all one ever heard, strictly in accordance with the bargain he made, whatever it might be; and what is more singular than all, I never heard of old Sam Linton getting into trouble.

CHAPTER X.

WHY I GAVE OVER CARD-PLAYING.

Like most men who are not saints, I had the natural instinct for gambling, without any passion for it; but soon found the necessity for suppressing my inclination for cards, lest it should interfere with my legitimate profession. It was necessary to abandon the indulgence, or abandon myself to its temptations.

I owe my determination never to play again at cards to the bad luck which befell me on a particular occasion at Ascot on the Cup Day of the year 18--. I was at that time struggling to make my way in my profession, and carefully storing up my little savings for the proverbial rainy day.

Having been previously to the Epsom summer races, and had such extraordinary good luck, nothing but a severe reverse would have induced me to take the step I did. Good luck is fascinating, and invariably leads us on, with bad luck sometimes close behind.

I went to Epsom with my dear old friend Charley Wright, and we soon set to work in one of the booths to make something towards our fortunes at *rouge et noir*. The booth was kept by a man who seemed--to me, at all events--to be the soul of honour. I had no reason to speak otherwise than well of him, for I staked a half-crown on the black, and won two half-crowns every time, or nearly every time.

I thought it a most excellent game, and with less of the element of chance or skill in it than any game I ever played. My pockets were getting stuffed with half-crowns, so that they bulged, and caused me to wonder if I should be allowed to leave the racecourse alive, for there were many thieves who visited the Downs in those days.

But my friend Charley was with me, and I knew he would be a pretty trustworthy fellow in a row. This, however, was but a momentary thought, for I was too much engrossed in the game and in my good luck to dwell on possibilities. Nor did I interest myself in Charley's proceedings, but took it for granted that a game so propitious to me was no less so to him. He was playing with several others; who or what they were was of no moment to me. I pursued my game quietly, and picked up my half-crowns with great gladness and with no concern for those who had lost them.

Presently, however, my attention was momentarily diverted by hearing Charley let off a most uncontrollable "D--n!"

"What's the matter, Charley?" I asked, without lifting my head.

"Matter!" says Charley; "rooked--that's all!"

"Rooked! That's very extraordinary. I'm winning like anything. Look here!" and I pointed to my pockets, which were almost bursting.

"Yes," said he, "I see how it is: you've been winning on twos to one, and I've been losing on threes."

"Black's the winning colour to-day, Charley--*noir; you should have backed noir.* Besides, long odds are much too risky. I am quite content with two to one."

Here there was a general break-up of the party, because Charley being out of it as well as several others, it left only one, and, of course, the keeper of the booth was not so foolish, however honourable, to pay me two half-crowns and win only one. So there it ended.

That night I made this game a study, and the sensible conclusion came to me that if you would take advantage of the table you should play for the lower stakes, because you have a better chance of winning than those who play high. At least, that was the result of my policy; for while those who played high were ruined, my pockets were filled, and, by that cautious mode of playing, I was so lucky that, had there been enough at threes to one, I could have kept on making money as long as they had any to lose.

I changed my half-crowns with the booth-keeper for gold, and reached my chambers safely with the spoil. And how pleasant it was to count it!

It has occurred to me since that the keeper of the booth had carefully noted my proceedings (such was my innocence), and that he made his calculations for a future occasion. One thing he was quite sure of--namely, that he would see me again on the first opportunity there was of winning more half-crowns.

It is possible that a succession of runs of luck might have put an end to my professional career; it is certain that the opposite result put an end to my card-playing aspirations.

In about a fortnight, all eager for a renewal of my Epsom experience, I went down to the Ascot meeting, taking with me not only all my previous winnings, but my store of savings for the rainy day, and was determined to pursue the same moderate system of cautious play.

There was the same booth, the same little flag fluttering on the top, and the same obliging proprietor. He recognized me at once, and looked as if he was quite sure I would be there--as if, in fact, he had been waiting for me. After a pleasant greeting and a few friendly words, I thought it a little odd that a man should be so glad to meet one who had come to fill his pockets at the booth-keeper's expense--at least, I thought this afterwards, not at the time. He looked genuinely pleased, and down I sat once more, quite sure that two to one would beat three.

The proprietor kept his eye on my play in a very thoughtful manner, nor was it surprising that he knew his game as well as I; in fact, it turned out that he knew it better. To this day I am unable to explain how he manoeuvred it, how he adjusted his tactics to counteract mine; but that something happened more than mere luck would account for was certain, for, as often as the half-crown went on black, red was the lucky colour. But I persevered on black because it had been my friend at Epsom, and down went the half-crowns, to be swept up by the keeper of the booth. I cannot even now explain how it was done.

Intending to make a good day's work and gather a rich harvest, I took with me every shilling I had in the world--not only my previous winnings, but my hard-earned savings at the Bar. I began to lose, but went on playing, in the vain hope--the worst hope of the gambler--of retrieving what I had lost and recovering my former luck. But it was not to be; the table was against me. I forsook my loyalty to black and laid on red. Alas! red was no better friend. I lost again, and knew now that all my Epsom winnings had found their way once more into the keeper's pocket. A fortnight's loan was all I had of them. It was a pity they had not been given to some charity. But I kept on bravely enough, and did not despair or leave off while I had a half-crown left. That half-crown, however, was soon raked up with the rest into the keeper's bag.

I was bankrupt, with nothing in my pocket but twopence and a return ticket from Paddington.

Hopeless and helpless, I had learnt a lesson--a lesson you can only learn in the school of experience.

I little thought then that the only certain winner at the gaming-table is *the table itself*, and made up my mind as I walked alone and disappointed through Windsor Park, on my way to the station, that I would never touch a card again-- and I never did.

For the first time since setting out in the morning I felt hungry, and bought a pennyworth of apples at a little stall kept by an old woman, and a bottle of ginger-beer. Such was my frugal meal; and thus sustained I tramped on, my return ticket being my only possession in the world. I reached Paddington with a sorry heart, and walked to the Temple, my good resolution my only comfort; but it was all-sufficient for the occasion and for all time to come.

CHAPTER XI.

"CODD'S PUZZLE."

Having somewhat succeeded in my practice at Quarter Sessions, I enlarged my field of adventure by attending the Old Bailey, hoping, of course, to obtain some briefs at that court; and although I abandoned the practice as a rule, I was, in after-life, on many occasions retained to appear in cases which are still fresh in my memory. I was with Edwin James, who was counsel for Mr. Bates, one of the partners of Strahan and Sir John Dean Paul, bankers of the Strand, and who were sentenced to fourteen years' transportation for fraudulently misappropriating securities of their customers. I was counsel for a young clerk to Leopold Redpath, the notorious man who was transported for extensive forgeries upon the Great Northern Railway. The clerk was justly acquitted by the jury.

My recollection of this period brings back many curious defences, which illustrate the school of advocacy in which I studied. Whether they contributed to my future success, I do not know, but that they afforded amusement is proved by my remembering them at all.

Hertford and St. Albans were my chief places, my earliest attachments, and are amongst my pleasantest memories. It seems childish to think of them as scenes of my struggles, for when I come to look back I had no struggles at all. I was merely practising like a cricketer at the nets; there was nothing to struggle for except a verdict when it would not come without some effort.

But dear old Codd was the man to struggle. He struggled and wriggled; tie him up as tightly as you could, you saw him fighting to get free, as he did in the following great duck case. He was a very amiable old barrister, a fast talker--so fast that he never stayed to pronounce his words--and of an ingenuity that ought to have been applied to some better purpose, such as the making of steam-engines or writing novels, rather than defending thieves. He reminded me on this occasion of the man in the circus who rode several horses at a time. In the case I allude to, he set up no less than *seven defences* to account for the unhappy duck's finding its way into his client's pocket, and the charm of them all was their variety. Inconsistency was not the word to apply reproachfully. Inconsistency was Codd's merit. He was like a conjurer who asks you to name a card, and as surely as you do so you draw it from the pack.

This particular duck case was known long after as "Codd's Puzzle."

"First," says Codd, "my client bought the duck and paid for it."

He was not the man to be afraid of being asked where.

"Second," says Codd, "my client found it; thirdly, it had been given to him; fourthly, it flew into his garden; fifthly, he was asleep, and some one put it into his pocket." And so the untiring and ingenious Codd proceeded making his case unnaturally good.

But the strange thing was that, instead of sweeping him away with a touch of ridicule, the young advocate argued the several defences one after the other with great dialectical skill, so that the jury became puzzled; and if the defence had not been so extraordinarily good, there would have been an acquittal forthwith.

There had been such a bewildering torrent of arguments that presently Codd's head began to swim, and he shrugged his shoulders, meaning thereby that it was the most puzzling case *he* had ever had anything to do with.

At last it became a question whether, amidst these conflicting accounts, there ever was any duck at all. Codd had not thought of that till some junior suggested it, and then he was asked by the Marquis of Salisbury, our chairman, whether there was any particular line of defence he wished to suggest.

"No," says Codd, "not in particular; my client wished to make a clean breast of it, and put them all before the jury; and I should be much obliged if those gentlemen will adopt any one of them."[A]

The jury acquitted the prisoner, not because they chose any particular defence, but because they did not know which to choose, and so gave the prisoner the benefit of the doubt.

The client was happy, and Codd famous.

[Footnote A: Sixty years after this event, in the reply in the great Tichborne case, Mr. Hawkins, Q.C., quoted this very defence as an illustration of the absurdity of the suggestion that one of several *Ospreys* picked up Sir Roger Tichborne--as will hereafter appear.]

CHAPTER XII.

GRAHAM, THE POLITE JUDGE.

Just before my time the punishment of death was inflicted for almost every offence of stealing which would now be thought sufficiently dealt with by a sentence of a week's imprisonment. The struggle to turn King's evidence was great, and it was almost a competitive examination to ascertain who knew most about the crime; and he, being generally the worst of the gang, was accepted accordingly.

I remember when I was a child three men, named respectively Marshall, Cartwright, and Ingram, were charged with having committed a burglary in the house of a gentleman named Pym, who lived in a village in Hertfordshire, Marshall being at that time, and Cartwright having previously been, butler in the gentleman's service. Ingram had been a footman in London.

The burglary was not in itself of an aggravated character. Plate only was stolen, and that had been concealed under the gravel bed of a little rivulet which ran through the grounds.

No violence or threat of violence had been offered to any inmate of the house, yet the case was looked upon as serious because of the position of trust which had been held by the two butlers.

Ingram was admitted as King's evidence. The butlers were convicted, sentenced to death, and hanged, whilst Ingram was, according to universal practice, set at liberty. Before the expiration of a year, however, he was convicted of having stolen a horse, and as horse-stealing was a capital offence at that time, he suffered the penalty of death at Hereford.

It was a curious coincidence that only a year or two afterwards a man named Probert, who had given King's evidence upon which the notorious Thurtell and Hunt were convicted of the brutal murder of Weare and executed, was also released, and within a year convicted of horse-stealing and hanged.

An old calendar for the Assize at Lincoln, which I give as an Appendix, reminds me of the condition of the law and of its victims at that time. At every assize it was like a tiger let loose upon the district. If a man escaped the gallows, he was lucky, while the criminals were by no means the hardened ruffians who had been trained in the school of crime; they were mostly composed of the most ignorant rural labourers--if, indeed, in those days there were any degrees of ignorance, when to be able to read a few words by spelling them was considered a prodigious feat.

Jurors often endeavoured to mitigate the terrors of the law by finding that the stolen property, however valuable it might be, was of less value than five shillings. May the recording angel "drop a tear over this record of perjury and blot it out for ever."

It was in those days that Mr. Justice Graham was called upon to administer the law, and on one occasion particularly he vindicated his character for courtesy to all who appeared before him. He was a man unconscious of humour and yet humorous, and was not aware of the extreme civility which he exhibited to everybody and upon all occasions, especially to the prisoner.

People went away with a sense of gratitude for his kindness, and when he sentenced a batch of prisoners to death he did it in a manner that might make any one suppose, if he did not know the facts, that they had been awarded prizes for good conduct.

He was firm, nevertheless--a great thing in judges, if not accompanied with weakness of mind. I may add that there was a singular precision in his mode of expression as well as in his ideas.

At a country assize, where he was presiding in the Crown Court, a man was indicted for murder. He pleaded "Not guilty." The evidence contained in the depositions was terribly clear, and, of course, the judge, who had perused them, was aware of it.

The case having been called on for trial, counsel for the prosecution applied for a postponement on the ground of the absence of a most material witness for the Crown.

I should mention that in those days counsel were not allowed to speak for the prisoner, but the judge was always in theory supposed to watch the case on his behalf. In the absence of a *material* witness the prisoner would be acquitted.

The learned Mr. Justice Graham asked the accused if he had any objection to the case being postponed until the next assizes, on the ground, as the prosecution had alleged, that their most material witness could not be produced. His lordship put the case as somewhat of a misfortune for the prisoner, and made it appear that it would be postponed, if he desired it, as a favour to *him*.

Notwithstanding the judge's courteous manner of putting it, the prisoner most strenuously objected to any postponement. It was not for him to oblige the Crown at the expense of a broken neck, and he desired above all things to be tried in accordance with law. He stood there on his "jail delivery."

Graham was firm, but polite, and determined to grant the postponement asked for. In this he was doubtless right, for the interests of justice demanded it. But to soften down the prisoner's disappointment and excuse the necessity of his further imprisonment, his lordship addressed him in the following terms, and in quite a sympathetic manner:--

"Prisoner, I am extremely sorry to have to detain you in prison, but *common humanity* requires that I should not let you be tried in the absence of an important witness for the prosecution, although at the same time I can quite appreciate your desire to have your case speedily disposed of; one does not like a thing of this sort hanging over one's head. But now, for the sake of argument, prisoner, suppose I were to try you to-day in the absence of that material witness, and yet, contrary to your expectations, they were to find you guilty. What then? Why, in the absence of that material witness, I should have to sentence you to be hanged on Monday next. That would be a painful ordeal for both of us.

"But now let us take the other alternative, and let us suppose that if your trial had been put off, and the material witness, when called, could prove something in your favour--this sometimes happens--and that that something induced the jury to acquit you, what a sad thing that would be! It would not signify to you, because you would have been hanged, and would be dead!"

Here his lordship paused for a considerable time, unable to suppress his emotion, but, having recovered himself, continued,--

"But you must consider what my feelings would be when I thought I had hanged an innocent man!"

At the next assizes the man was brought up, the material witness appeared; the prisoner was found guilty, and hanged.

The humane judge's feelings were therefore spared.

At the Old Bailey he was presiding during a sessions which was rather light for the times, there being less than a score left for execution under sentence of death. There were, in fact, only sixteen, most of them for petty thefts.

His lordship, instead of reading the whole of the sixteen names, omitted one, and read out only fifteen. He then politely, and with exquisite precision and solemnity, exhorted them severally to prepare for the awful doom that awaited them the following Monday, and pronounced on each the sentence of death.

They left the dock.

After they were gone the jailer explained to his lordship that there had been *sixteen* prisoners capitally convicted, but that his lordship had omitted the name of one of them, and he would like to know what was to be done with him.

"What is the prisoner's name?" asked Graham.

"John Robins, my lord."

"Oh, bring John Robins back--by all means let John Robins step forward. I am obliged to you."

The culprit was once more placed at the Bar, and Graham, addressing him in his singularly courteous manner, said apologetically,--

"John Robins, I find I have accidentally omitted your name in my list of prisoners doomed to execution. It was quite accidental, I assure you, and I ask your pardon for my mistake. I am very sorry, and can only add that you will be hanged with the rest."

CHAPTER XIII.

GLORIOUS OLD DAYS--THE HON. BOB GRIMSTON, AND MANY OTHERS--CHICKEN-HAZARD.

The old glories of the circuit days vanished with stage-coaches and post-chaises. If you climbed on to the former for the sake of economy because you could not afford to travel in the latter, you would be fined at the circuit mess, whose notions of propriety and economy were always at variance.

Those who obtained no business found it particularly hateful to keep up the foolish appearance of having it by means of a post-chaise. You might not ride in a public vehicle, or dine at a public table, or put up at an inn for fear of falling in with attorneys and obtaining briefs from them surreptitiously. The Home Circuit was very strict in these respects, but it was the cheapest circuit to travel in the kingdom, so that its members were numerous and, I need not say, various in mind, manner, and position.

But it was a circuit of brilliant men in my young days. Many of them rose to eminence both in law and in Parliament. It was a time, indeed, when, if judges made law, law made judges.

I should like to say a word or two about those times and the necessary studies to be undergone by those who aspired to eminence.

In the days of my earliest acquaintance with the law, an ancient order of men, now almost, if not quite, extinct, called Special Pleaders, existed, who, after having kept the usual number of terms--that is to say, eaten the prescribed number of dinners in the Inn of Court to which they belonged--became qualified, on payment of a fee of £12, to take out a Crown licence to plead under the Bar. This enabled them to do all things which a barrister could do that did not require to be transacted in court. They drew pleadings, advised and took pupils.

Some of them practised in this way all their lives and were never called. Others grew tired of the drudgery, and were called to the Bar, where they remained *junior* barristers as long as they lived, old age having no effect upon their status. Some were promoted to the ancient order of Serjeants-at-Law, or were appointed her Majesty's Counsel, while some of the Serjeants received from the Crown patents of precedence with priority over all Queen's Counsel appointed after them, and with the privilege of wearing a silk gown and a Queen's Counsel wig.

There was, however, this difference between a Queen's Counsel and the holder of a Patent of Precedence: that the former, having been appointed one of her Majesty's Counsel, could not thenceforth appear without special licence under the sign-manual of the Queen to defend a prisoner upon a criminal charge. The Serjeant-at-Law is as rare now as a bustard.

I mention these old-fashioned times and studies, not because of their interest at the present day, but because they produced such men as Littledale,

Bayley, Parke (afterwards Lord Wensleydale), Alderson, Tindal, Patteson, Wightman, Crompton, Vaughan Williams, James, Willes, and, later, Blackburn.

The contemplation of these legal giants, amongst whom my career commenced, somewhat checked the buoyant impulse which had urged me onward at Quarter Sessions, but at the same time imparted a little modest desire to imitate such incomparable models. Those of them who were selected from the junior Bar were good examples of men whose vast knowledge of law was acquired in the way I have indicated, and who were chosen on their merits alone.

But even these successful examples, however encouraging to the student, were, nevertheless, not ill-calculated to make a young barrister whose income was small, and sometimes, as in my case, by no means *assured* to him, sicken at the thought that, study as he liked, years might pass, and probably would, before a remunerative practice came to cheer him. Perhaps it would never come at all, and he would become, like so many hundreds of others of his day and ours, a hopeless failure. All were competitors for the briefs and even the smiles of solicitors; for without their favour none could succeed, although he might unite in himself all the qualities of lawyer and advocate.

The prospect was not exhilarating for any one who had to perform the drudgery of the first few years of a junior's life; nevertheless, I was not cast down by the mere apprehension, or rather the mere possibility of failure, for when I looked round on my competitors I was encouraged by the thought that dear old Woollet knew more about a rate appeal than Littledale himself, while old Peter Ryland, with his inimitable Saxon, was quite as good at the irremovability of a pauper as Codd was in accounting for the illegal removal of a duck, and both in their several branches of knowledge more learned than Alderson or Bayley. But here I was, launched on that wide sea in which I was "to sink or swim," and, as I preferred the latter, I struck out with a resolute breast-stroke, and, as I have said, never failed to keep my head above water. It was some satisfaction to know that, if the judges were so learned, there was yet more learning to come; much yet to come down from, the old table-land of the Common Law, and much more from the inexhaustible fountain of Parliament.

The Quarter Sessions Court was the arena of my first eight years of professional life. I watched and waited with unwearied attention, never without hope, but often on the very verge of despair, of ever making any progress which would justify my choosing it as a profession. My greatest delight, perhaps, was the obtaining an acquittal of some one whose guilt nobody could doubt. All the struggle of those times was the fight for the "one three six," and the hardest effort of my life was the most valuable, because it gave me the key which opened the door to many depositories of unexplored wealth.

There were many men who outlived their life, and others who never lived their lives at all; many men who did nothing, and many more who would almost have given their lives to do something.

There was, however, one man of those days whom I cannot here pass over, as he remained my companion and friend to his life's end, and will be remembered by me with affection and reverence to the end of my own. It was old Bob Grimston, whom I first met at the benefit of "the Spider," one of the famous prize-fighters of the time. The Hon. Bob Grimston was known in the sporting world as one of its most enthusiastic supporters, and acknowledged as one of the best men in saddle or at the wicket. But Bob was not only a sportsman--he was a gentleman of the finest feeling you could meet, and the keenest sense of honour.

Having thus spoken of some of the eminent men of my early days, I would like to mention a little incident that occurred before I had fairly settled down to practise, or formed any serious intention as to the course I should pursue--that is to say, whether I should remain a sessions man like Woollet, or become a master of Saxon like old Peter Ryland, a sportsman like Bob Grimston, or a cosmopolitan like Rodwell, so as to comprehend all that came in my way. I chose the latter, for the simple reason that in principle I loved what in these days would be called "the open door," and received all comers, even sometimes entertaining solicitors unawares.

Accordingly I laid myself open to the attention of kind friends and people whose manner of life was founded on the Christian principle of being "given to hospitality."

But before I come to the particular incident I wish to describe, I must briefly mention a remarkable case that was tried in the Queen's Bench, and which necessarily throws me back a year or two in my narrative.

It was a case known as "Boyle and Lawson," and the incident it reveals will give an idea of the state of society of that day. I am not sure whether it differs in many respects from that of the present, except in so far as its *honour* is concerned, for what was looked upon then as a flagrant outrage on public morality is now regarded as an error of judgment, or a mistake occasioned by some fortuitous combination of unconsidered circumstances. Such is the value in literature and argument of long words without meaning.

However, the action was brought against the proprietors of the *Times* newspaper for libel. The libel consisted in the statement that the respectable plaintiff--a lady--had conspired with persons unknown to obtain false letters of credit for large sums of money.

The hospitable friends I refer to lived in excellent style in Norwich. How they had attained their social distinction I am unable to say, but they were, in fact, in the "very best set," which in Norwich was by no means the fastest.

I was travelling at this time with Charles Willshire and his brother Thomas, who was a mere youth. There was also an undergraduate of Cambridge of the name of Crook with us, and another who had joined our party for a few days' ramble.

We were enjoying ourselves in the old city of Norwich as only youth can, when we received an invitation to pass an evening in a very fashionable circle. How the invitation came I could not tell, but we made no inquiry and accepted it. Arrived at the house, which was situated in the most aristocratic neighbourhood that Norwich could boast, we found ourselves in the most agreeable society we could wish to meet. This was a group of exalted and fashionable personages arrayed in costumes of the superb Prince Regent style. Nothing could exceed this party in elegance of costume or manners. You could tell at once they were, as it was then expressed, "of the quality." Their cordiality was equalled only by their courtesy, and had we been princes of the blood we could not have received a more polite welcome. There was an elegance, too, about the house, and a refinement which coincided with the culture of the hosts and guests. Altogether it was one of the most agreeable parties I had ever seen. There were several gentlemen, all Prince Regents, and one sweet lady, charming in every way, from the well-arranged blonde tresses to the neatest little shoe that ever adorned a Cinderella foot. She was beautiful in person as she was charming in manner. You saw at once that she moved in the best Norwich society, and was the idol of it. Crook was perfectly amazed at so much grace and splendour, but then he was much younger than any of us.

I don't think any one was so much smitten as Crook. We had seen more of the world than he had--that is to say, more of the witness-box--and if you don't see the world there, on its oath, you can see it nowhere in the same unveiled deformity.

We enjoyed ourselves very much. There was good music and a little sweet singing, the lady being in that art, as in every other, well trained and accomplished. If I was not altogether ravished with the performance, Crook was. You could see that by the tender look of his eyes.

After the music, cards were introduced, and they commenced playing *vingt-et-un*, Crook being the special favourite with everybody, especially with the ladies. I believe much was due to the expression of his eyes.

As I had given up cards, I did not join in the game, but became more and more interested in it as an onlooker. I was a little surprised, however, to find that in a very short while, comparatively, our friend Crook had lost £30 or £40; and as this was the greater part of his allowance for travelling expenses, it placed him in a rather awkward position.

Some men travel faster when they have no money; this was not the case with poor Crook, who travelled only by means of it. Alas, I thought, *twenty-one* and *vingt-et-un*! It was a serious matter, and the worse because Crook was not a good loser: he lost his head and his temper as well as his money; and I have ever observed through life that the man who loses his temper loses himself and his friends.

He was disgusted with his bad luck, but nurtured a desperate hope--the forlorn hope that deceives all gamblers--that he should retrieve his losses on some future occasion, which he eagerly looked for and, one might say, demanded.

The occasion was not far off; it was, in fact, nearer than Crook anticipated. His pleasant manner and agreeable society at *vingt-et-un* procured us another invitation for the following night but one, and of course we accepted it. It was a great change to me from the scenery of the Elm Court chimney-pots.

Whatever might be Crook's happily sanguine disposition and hope of retrieving his luck, there was one thing which the calculator of chances does not take into consideration in games of this kind. We, visiting such cultured and fashionable people, would never for a moment think so meanly of our friends; I mean the possibility of their cheating, a word never mentioned in well-bred society. A suspicion of such conduct, even, would be tantamount to treason, and a violation of the rules that regulate the conduct of ladies and gentlemen. It was far from all our thoughts, and the devil alone could entertain so malevolent an idea. Be that as it may, as a matter of philosophy, the onlooker sees most of the game, and as I was an onlooker this is what I saw:--

The elegant lady *exchanged glances with one of the players while she was looking over Crook's hand*. Crook was losing as fast as he could, and no wonder. I was now in an awkward position. To have denounced our hosts because I interpreted a lady's glances in a manner that made her worse than a common thief might have produced unknown trouble. But I kept my eye on the beautiful blonde, nevertheless, and became more and more confirmed in my suspicions without any better opportunity of declaring them.

The charming well-bred lady thus communicating her knowledge of Crook's cards, I need not say he was soon reduced to a state of insolvency; and as the party was too exclusive and fashionable to extend their hospitality to those who had not the means of paying, it soon broke up, and we returned to our rooms, I somewhat wiser and Crook a great deal poorer.

Such was the adventure which came to my mind when I saw in the Queen's Bench at Westminster the trial of "Boyle and Lawson" against the *Times* for calumnious insinuations against the character of a lady and others, suggesting that they obtained false letters of credit to enable them to cheat and defraud.

This was the select party which Norwich society had lionized--the great unknown to whom we had been introduced, and where Crook had been cheated out of his travelling-money!

The lady was the fair plaintiff in this action, seeking for the rehabilitation of her character; and she succeeded in effecting that object so far as the outlay of one farthing would enable her to do so, for that was all the jury gave her, and it was exactly that amount too much. Her character was worth more to her in Crook's time.

Speaking of a man running society on his fees--that is, endeavouring to cope with the rich on the mere earnings of a barrister, however large they may be--I have met with several instances which would have preserved me from the same fate had I ever been cursed with such an inclination. The number of successful men at the Bar who have been ruined by worshipping the idol which is called "Society," and which is perhaps a more disastrous deity to worship than any other, is legion. This is one unhappy example, the only one I intend to give.

While I was living in Bond Street, and working very hard, I had little time and no inclination to lounge about amongst the socially great; I had, indeed, no money to spend on great people. The entrance-fee into the portals of the smart society temple is heavy, especially for a working-man; and so found the bright particular star who had long held his place amidst the splendid social galaxy, and then disappeared into a deeper obscurity than that from which he had emerged, to be seen no more for ever.

He was a Queen's Counsel, a brilliant advocate in a certain line of business, and a popular, agreeable, intellectual, and amusing companion. He obtained a seat in Parliament, and a footing in Society which made him one of its selected and principal lions. In every Society paper, amongst its most fashionable intelligence, there was he; and Society hardly seemed to be able to get along without him.

One Sunday afternoon I was reading in my little room when this agreeable member of the *élite* called upon me. My astonishment was great, because at that time of my career not only did I not receive visitors, but *such* a visitor was beyond all expectation, and I wondered, when his name was announced, what could have brought him, he so great and I comparatively nothing. It is true I had known him for some time, but I knew him so little that I thought of him as a most estimable great man whose career was leading him to the highest distinction in his profession.

Another extraordinary thing that struck me long after, but did not at the time, was that the business he came upon made no particular impression on my mind, any more than if it had been the most ordinary thing in the world. That to me is still inexplicable.

My visitor did not let troubles sit upon him, if troubles he ever had, for he seemed to be in the highest spirits. Society kept him ever in a state of effervescent hilarity, so that he never let anything trouble him. At this time he was making at the Bar seven or eight thousand a year, and consequently, I thought, must be the happiest of men.

His manner was agreeable, and his face wore a smile of complacency at variance with the nature of his errand, which he quickly took care to make known by informing me that he was in a devil of a mess, and did not know what he should do to get out of it.

"Oh," I said quite carelessly, "you'll manage." And little did I think I should be the means of fulfilling my own prophecy.

"The fact is, my dear Hawkins," said the wily intriguer, for such he was, "I'll tell you seriously how I stand. To-morrow morning I have bills becoming due amounting to £1,250, and I want you to be good enough to lend me that sum to enable me to meet them."

I was perfectly astounded! This greatness to have come down to £1,250 on the wrong side of the ledger.

"I have no such amount," said I, "and never had anything like it at my bank." I must say I pitied him, and began to wonder in what way I *could* help him. He was so really and good-naturedly in earnest, and seemed so extremely anxious, that at last I said, "Well, I'll see what I can do," and asked him to meet me in court the following morning, when I would tell him whether I could help him or not.

His gratitude was boundless; my kindness should never be forgotten--no, as long as he lived! and if he had been addressing a common jury he could not have used more flowers of speech or shed more abundant tears to water them with. I was the best friend he had ever had. And, as it seemed afterwards, very foolishly so, because he told me he had not one farthing of security to offer for the loan. A man who ought to have been worth from fifty to a hundred thousand pounds!

However, I went to my bankers' and made arrangements to be provided with the amount. I met him at the place of appointment, and was quite surprised to see the change in his demeanour since the day before. He was now apparently in a state of deeper distress than ever, and thinking to soothe him, I said, "It's all right; you can have the money!"

Once more he overwhelmed me with the eloquence of a grateful heart, but said it was of no use--no use whatever; that instead of £1,250 he had other bills coming in, and unless they could all be met he might just as well let the others go.

"How much do you *really* want to quite clear you?" I asked, with a simplicity which astonishes me to this day.

"Well," he said, "nothing is of the least use under £2,500."

I was a little staggered, but, pitying his distress of mind, went once more to my bankers' and made the further necessary arrangements. I borrowed the whole amount at five per cent., and placed it to the credit of this brilliant Queen's Counsel.

The only terms I made with him on this new condition of things was that he should, out of his incoming fees, pay my clerk £500 a quarter until the whole sum was liquidated. This he might easily have done, and this he arranged to do; but the next day he pledged the whole of his prospective income to a Jew, incurred fresh liabilities, and left me without a shadow of a chance of ever seeing a penny of my money again. I need not say every farthing was lost, principal and interest. I say interest, because it cost me five per cent, till the amount was paid.

His end was as romantic as his life, but it is best told in the words of my old friend Charley Colman, who never spares colour when it is necessary, and in that respect is an artist who resembles Nature. Thus he writes:--

"What a coward at heart was ----! He allowed himself to be sat upon and crushed without raising a hand or voice in his defence of himself. When he returned from America he accepted a seat in ---- office--in the office of the man who urged Lord ---- to prosecute him.

"After your gift to him--a noble gift of £3,000--he called at my chambers, spoke in high terms of your generosity, and wished all the world to know it, so elated was he. I was to publish it far and wide. He went away. In half an hour he returned, and begged me to keep the affair secret. 'Too late,' said I. 'Several gentlemen have been here, and to them I mentioned the matter, and begged them to spread it far and wide.' His heart failed him when he thought he would be talked about.

"He was a kind-hearted fellow at times--generous to a fault, always most abstemious; but he had a tongue, and one he did not try to control. He used to say stinging things of people, knowing them to be untrue.

"What a life! What a terrible fate was his! Turned out of Parliament; made to resign his Benchership; his gown taken from him by the Benchers; driven to America by his creditors to get his living; not allowed to practise in the Supreme Court in America. At forty-five years of age his life had foundered. He returns to England--for what! Simply to find his recklessness had blasted his life, and then--?

"Sometimes, in spite of *all*, I feel a moisture in my eye when I think of him. Had he been true to himself what a brilliant life was open to him! What a practice he had! Up to the last he told me that he turned £14,000 a year. He worked hard, very hard, and his gains went to ---- or to chicken-hazard! Poor fellow!"

CHAPTER XIV.

PETER RYLAND--THE REV. MR. FAKER AND THE WELSH WILL.

I was retained at Hertford Assizes, with Peter Ryland as my leader, to prosecute a man for perjury, which was alleged to have been committed in an action in which a cantankerous man, who had once filled the office of High Sheriff for the county, was the prosecutor. Wealthy and disagreeable, he was nevertheless a henpecked tyrant.

Mrs. Brown, his wife, was a witness for the prosecution in the alleged perjury--which was unfortunate for her husband, because she had the greatest knowledge of the circumstances surrounding the case; while Mr. Brown had the best knowledge of the probable quality of his wife's evidence.

When we were in consultation and considering the nature of this evidence, and arranging the best mode of presenting our case to the jury, Brown interposed, and begged that Mr. Ryland should call Mrs. Brown as the *last* witness, instead of first, which was the proper course. "Because," said he, "*if anything goes wrong during the trial or anything is wanting, Mrs. Brown will be quite ready to mop it all up.*"

This in a prosecution for perjury was one of the boldest propositions I had ever heard.

I need not say that good Mrs. Brown was called, as she ought to have been, first. The lady's mop was not in requisition at that stage of the trial, and the jury decided against her.

I was sometimes in the Divorce Court, and old Jack Holker was generally my opponent. He was called "Long Odds." In one particular case I won some *éclat*. It is not related on that account, however, but simply in consequence of its remarkable incidents. No case is interesting unless it is outside the ordinary stock-in-trade of the Law Courts, and I think this was.

The details are not worth telling, and I therefore pass them by. Cresswell was the President, and the future President, Hannen, my junior.

We won a great victory through the remarkable over-confidence and indiscretion of Edwin James, Q.C., who opposed us. James's client was the husband of the deceased. By her will the lady had left him the whole of her property, amounting to nearly £100,000. The case we set up was that the wife had been improperly influenced by her husband in making it, and that her mind was coerced into doing what she did not intend to do, and so we sought to set aside the will on that ground.

Edwin James had proved a very strong case on behalf of the validity of the will. He had called the attesting witnesses, and they, respectable gentlemen as they undoubtedly were, had proved all that was necessary--namely, that the testator, notwithstanding that she was in a feeble condition and almost at the last stage, was perfectly calm and capable in mind and understanding--exactly, in fact, as a testator ought to be who wills her property to her husband if he retains her affection.

The witnesses had been cross-examined by me, and nothing had been elicited that cast the least doubt upon their character or credibility. Had the matter been left where it was, the £100,000 would have been secured. But James, whatever may have been his brilliance, was wanting in tact. He would not leave well alone, but resolved to call the Rev. Mr. Faker, a distinguished Dissenting minister.

In fiction this gentleman would have appeared in the melodramatic guise of a spangled tunic, sugar-loaf hat, with party-coloured ribbons, purple or green breeches, and motley hose; but in the witness-box he was in clerical uniform, a long coat and white cravat with corresponding long face and hair, especially at the back of his head. A soberer style of a stage bandit was never seen. He was just the man for cross-examination, I saw at a glance--a fancy witness, and, I believe, a Welshman. As he was a Christian warrior, I had to find out the weak places in his armour. But little he knew of courts of law and the penetrating art of cross-examination, which could make a hole in the triple-plated coat of fraud, hypocrisy, and cunning. I was in no such panoply. I fought only with my little pebblestone and sling, but took good aim, and then the missile flew with well-directed speed.

I had to throw at a venture at first, because, happily, there were no instructions how to cross-examine. Not that I should have followed them if there had been; but I might have got a *fact* or two from them.

It is well known that artifice is the resource of cunning, whether it acts on the principle of concealing truth or boldly asserting falsehood. Here the reverend strategist did both: he knew how a little truth could deceive. You must remember that at this point of the case, when the Rev. Faker was called, there was nothing to cross-examine about. I knew nothing of the parties, the witnesses, the solicitors, or any one except my learned friends. It would not have been discreditable to my advocacy if I had submitted to a verdict. I will, therefore, give the points of the questions which elicited the truth from the Christian warrior; and probably the non-legal reader of these memoirs may be interested in seeing what may sometimes be done by a few judicious questions.

"Mr. Faker," I said.

"Sir," says Faker.

"You have told us you acted as the adviser of the testatrix."

"Yes, sir."

"Spiritual adviser, of course?"

A spiritual bow.

"You advised the deceased lady, probably, as to her duties as a dying woman?"

"Certainly."

"Duty to her husband--was that one?"

A slight hesitation in Mr. Faker revealed the vast amount of fraud of which he was capable. It was the smallest peephole, but I saw a good way. Till then there was nothing to cross-examine about, but after that hesitation there was £100,000 worth! He had betrayed himself. At last Faker said,--

"Yes, Mr. Hawkins; yes, sir--her duty to her husband."

"In the way of *providing* for him?" was my next question.

"Oh yes; quite so."

"You were careful, of course, as you told your learned counsel, to avoid any undue influence?"

"Certainly."

"The will was not completed, I think, when you first saw the dying woman-- on the day, I mean, of her death?"

"No, not at that time."

"Was it kept in a little bag by the pillow of the testatrix? Did she retain the keys of the bag herself?"

"That is quite right."

"Had it been executed at this time? I think you said not?"

"Not at this time; it had to be revised."

"How did you obtain possession of the keys?"

"I obtained them."

"Yes, I know; but without her knowledge?"

It was awkward for Faker, but he had to confess that he was not sure. Then he frankly admitted that the will was taken out of the bag--in the lady's presence, of course, but whether she was quite dead or almost alive was uncertain; and then he and the husband spiritually conferred as to what the real intention of the dying woman in the circumstances was *likely to be*, and having ascertained that, they made *another will*, which they called "settling the former one" by carrying out the lady's intentions, the lady being now dead to all intentions whatsoever.

This was the will which was offered for probate!

Cresswell thought it was a curious state of affairs, and listened with much interest to the further cross-examination.

"Had you ever seen any other will?" I inquired. It was quite an accidental question, as one would put in a desultory sort of conversation with a friend.

"Er--yes--I have," said Faker.

"What was that?"

"Well, it was a will, to tell you the truth, Mr. Hawkins, executed in my favour for £5,000."

"Where is it?"

"I have not the original," said the minister, "but I have a copy of it."

"Copy! But where is the original?"

"Original?" repeats Faker.

"Yes, the original; there must have been an original if you have a copy."

"Oh," said the Rev. Faker, "I remember, the original was destroyed after the testatrix's death."

"How?"

"Burnt!"

Even the very grave Hannen, my ever-respected friend and junior, smiled; Cresswell, never prone to smile at villainy, smiled also.

"The original burnt, and only a copy produced! What do you mean, sir?"

The situation was dramatic.

"Is it not strange," I asked, "even in *your* view of things, that the original will should be burnt and the copy preserved?"

"Yes," answered the reverend gentleman; "perhaps it would have been better--"

"To have burnt the copy and given us the original, and more especially after the lady was dead. But, let me ask you, *why* did you destroy the original will?"

I pressed him again and again, but he could not answer. The reason was plain. His ingenuity was exhausted, and so I gave him the finishing stroke with this question,--

"Will you swear, sir, that an original will ever existed?"

The answer was, "No."

I knew it *must* be the answer, because there could be no other that would not betray him.

"What is your explanation?" asked Cresswell.

"My explanation, my lord, is that the testatrix had often expressed to me her intention to leave me £5,000, and I wrote the codicil which was destroyed to carry out her wishes."

Cresswell had warned James early in the case as to the futility of calling witnesses after the two who alone were necessary, but to no purpose; he hurried his client to destruction, and I have never been able to understand his conduct. The most that can be said for him is that he did not suspect any danger, and took no trouble to avoid incurring it.

It is curious enough that on the morning of the trial we had tried to compromise the matter by offering £10,000.

The refusal of the offer shows how little they thought that any cross-examination could injure their cause.

Hannen said he could not have believed a cross-examination could be conducted in that manner without any knowledge of the facts, and paid me the compliment of saying it was worth at the least £80,000.

CHAPTER XV.

TATTERSALL'S--BARON MARTIN, HARRY HILL, AND THE OLD FOX IN THE YARD.

Tattersall's in my time was one of the pleasantest Sunday afternoon lounges in London. There was a spirit of freedom and social equality pervading the place which only belongs to assemblies where sport is the principal object and pleasure of all. There was also the absence of irksome workaday drudgery; I think that was, after all, the main cause of its being so delightful a meeting-place to me.

There was, however, another attraction, and that was dear old Baron Martin, one of the most pleasant companions you could meet, no matter whether in the Court of Exchequer or the "old Ring." A keen sportsman he was, and a shrewd, common-sense lawyer--so great a lover of the Turf that it is told of him, and I know it to be true, that once in court a man was pointed out to him bowing with great reverence, and repeating it over and over again until he caught the Baron's attention. The Judge, with one pair of spectacles on his forehead and another on his eyes, immediately cried aloud to his marshal, "Custance, the jockey, as I'm alive!" and then the Baron bowed most politely to the man in the crowd, the most famous jockey of his day.

Speaking of Tattersall's reminds me of many things, amongst them of the way in which, happily, I came to the resolution never to bet on a horse-race. It was here I learnt the lesson, at a place where generally people learn the opposite, and never forgot it. No sermon would ever have taught me so much as I learnt there.

Like my oldest and one of my dearest friends on the turf, Lord Falmouth, I never made a bet after the time I speak of. No one who lives in the world needs any description of the Tattersall's of to-day. But the Tattersall's of my earlier days was not exactly the same thing, although the differences would not be recognizable to persons who have not over-keen recollections.

The institution has perhaps known more great men than Parliament itself-- not so many bishops, perhaps, as the Church, but more statesmen than could get into the House of Lords; and all the biographies that have ever been written could not furnish more illustrations of the ups and downs of life, especially the downs, nor of more illustrious men. The names of all the great and mediocre people who visited the famous rendezvous would fill a respectable Court guide, and the money transactions that have taken place would pay off the National Debt. All this is a pleasant outcome of the national character.

Do not suppose that Judges, other than Baron Martin, never looked in, for they did, and so did learned and illustrious Queen's Counsel and Serjeants-at-Law, authors, editors, actors, statesmen, and, to sum it up in brief, all the real men of the day of all professions and degrees of social position.

At first my visits were infrequent; afterwards I went more often, and then became a regular attendant. I loved the "old Ring," and yet could never explain why. I think it was the variety of human character that charmed me. I was doing very little at the Bar, and was, no doubt, desirous to make as many acquaintances as possible, and to see as much of the world as I could. It is a long way back in my career, but I go over the course with no regrets and with every feeling of delight. Everything seems to have been enjoyable in those far-off days, although I was in a constant state of uncertainty with regard to my career. There were three principal places of pleasure at that time: one was Tattersall's, one Newmarket, and the Courts of Law a third.

There used to be, in the centre of the yard or court at Tattersall's, a significant representation of an old fox, and I often wondered whether it was set up as a warning, or merely by way of ornamentation, or as the symbol of sport. It might have been to tell you to be wary and on the alert. But whatever the original design of this statue to Reynard, the old fox read me a solemn lesson, and seemed to be always saying, "Take care, Harry; be on your guard. There are many prowlers everywhere."

But there was another monitor in constant attendance, who was deservedly respected by all who had the pleasure of his acquaintance--that is to say, by all who visited Tattersall's more than once. He was not in the least emblematic like the old fox, but a man of sound sense, with no poetry, of an extremely good nature, and full of anecdote. You might follow his advice, and it would be well with you; or you might follow your opinion in opposition to his and take your chance. His name was Hill--Harry Hill they familiarly called him--and although you might have many a grander acquaintance, you could never meet a truer friend.

He was an old and much-respected friend of the Baron, and that says a great deal for him; for if anybody in the world could understand a *man*, it was Baron Martin. Whether it was the Prime Minister or the unhappy thief in the dock, he knew all classes and all degrees of criminality. He was not poetical with regard to landscapes, for if one were pointed out to him by some proprietor of a lordly estate, he would say, "Yes, a vera fine place indeed; and I would have the winning-post *there*!"

The old fox and Harry Hill! The two characters at Tattersall's in those days can never be forgotten, by those who knew them.

It may seem strange in these more enlightened days that at that time I was under the impression that no one could make a bet unless he had the means of paying if he lost. This statement will provoke a smile, but it is true. The consequence was that I was debarred from speculating where I thought I had a most excellent chance of winning, having been brought up to believe that the world was almost destitute of fraud--a strange and almost unaccountable idea which only time and experience proved to be erroneous. Judge of the vast unexplored field of discovery that lay before me! Harry Hill was better informed. He had lived longer, and had been brought in contact with the cleverest men of the age. He knew at a glance the adventurous fool who staked his last chance when the odds were a hundred to one, and also the man of honour who staked his life on his honesty--and sometimes *lost*!

There were "blacklegs" in those days who looked out for such honest gentlemen, and *won*--scoundrels who degrade sport, and trade successfully on the reputations of men of honour. You cannot cope with these; honesty cannot compete with fraud either in sport or trade.

It was a very brief Sunday sermon which Harry preached to me this afternoon, but it was an effective one, and out of the abundance of his good nature he gave me these well-remembered words of friendly warning,--

"Mr. Hawkins, I see you come here pretty regularly on Sunday afternoons; but I advise you not to speculate amongst us, for if you do we shall beat you. We know our business better than you do, and you'll get nothing out of us any more than we should get out of you if we were to dabble in your law, for you know *that* business better than we do."

This disinterested advice I took to heart, and treated it as a warning. I thanked Mr. Hill, promised to take advantage of his kindness, and kept my word during the whole time that Tattersall's remained in the old locality, which it did for a considerable period.

The establishment at this time was at Hyde Park Corner, and had been rented from Lord Grosvenor since 1766. It was used for the purpose of selling thoroughbreds and other horses of a first-rate order, until the expiration of the lease, which was, I think, in 1865. It was then removed to Knightsbridge, where I still continued my visits.

The new premises, or, as it might be called, the new institution, was inaugurated with a grand dinner, chiefly attended by members of the sporting world, including Admiral Rous, George Payne, and many other well-known and popular patrons of our national sport. There were also a great many who were known as "swells," people who took a lively interest in racing affairs, and others who belonged to the literary and artistic world, and enjoyed the national sports as well. It was a large assembly, and if any persons can enjoy a good dinner and lively conversation, it is those who take an interest in sport. Mixed as the company might be, it was uniform in its object, which was to be happy as well as jolly.

That I should have been asked to be present on this historic occasion was extremely gratifying, but I could find no reason for the honour conferred upon me, except that it 'might be because I had always endeavoured to make myself agreeable--a faculty, if it be a faculty, most invaluable in all the relations and circumstances of life. I was flattered by the compliment, because in reality I was the guest of all the really great men of the day.

But a still more striking honour was in store. I was called upon to respond for somebody or something; I don't remember what it was to this day, nor had I the faintest notion what I ought to say. I was perfectly bewildered, and the first utterance caused a roar of laughter. I did not at that time know the reason. It is of no consequence whether you know what you are talking about in an after-dinner speech or not, for say what you may, hardly anybody listens, and if they do few will understand the drift of your observations. You get a great deal of applause when you stand up, and a great deal more when you sit down. I seemed to catch my audience quite accidentally by using a word tabooed at that time in sporting circles, because it represented the blacklegs of the racecourse, and was used as a nickname for rascaldom. "Gentlemen," I said, "I have been unexpectedly called upon my *legs*--" Then I stammered an apology for using the word in that company, and the laughter was unbounded. Next morning all the sporting papers reported it as an excellent joke, although the last person who saw the joke was myself.

After dinner we adjourned to the new premises, which included a betting-room, since christened "place," by interpretation of a particular statute by myself and others. Oh the castigation I received from the Jockey Club on that account! Whether the monitory fox was anywhere within the precincts I do not know, but I missed him at that time, and attributed to his absence the lapse from virtue which undermined my previous resolution, and in a moment undid the merits of exemplary years. However, it brought me to myself, and was, after all, a "blessing in disguise"--and pleasant to think of.

We were in the betting-room, and there was Harry Hill, my genial old friend, who had advised me to take care, and never to bet, "because we know our business better than you do." Alas! amidst the hubbub and excitement, to say nothing of the joviality of everybody and the excellence of the champagne, I said in a brave tone,--

"Come now, Mr. Hill, I *must* have a bet, on the opening of the new Tattersalls. I will give you evens for a fiver on ---- for the Derby!"

Alas! my friend, who *ought* to have known better, forgot the good advice he had given me only a few years before, and I, heedless of consequences in my hilarity, repeated the offer of evens on the *favourite*.

"Done!" said two or three, and amongst them Hill. I might have repeated the offer and accepted the bet over and over again, so popular was it. "Done, done, done!" everywhere.

But Hill was the man for my money, and he had it. Before morning the *favourite was scratched*!

It was the race which Hermit won! Poor Hastings lost heavily and died soon after. I had backed the wrong horse, and have never ceased to wonder how I could have been so foolish. "Let me advise you not to speculate amongst us," were Hill's words, "for if you do we shall beat you;" and it cost me five pounds to learn that. A lawyer's opinion may be worth what is paid for it in a case stated; but of the soundness of of a horse's wind, or the thousand and one ailments to which that animal's flesh and blood are heir, I knew nothing--not so much as the little boy who runs and fetches in the stable, and who could give the ablest lawyer in Great Britain or Ireland odds on any particular favourite's "public form" and beat him.

Put not your trust in tipsters; they no more knew that Hermit had a chance for the Derby than they could foretell the snowstorm that was coming to enable him to win it.

This was the last bet I ever made; and I owe my abandonment of the practice to Harry Hill, who gave me excellent advice and enforced it by example.

CHAPTER XVI.

ARISING OUT OF THE "ORSINI AFFAIR."

The "Orsini Affair" was one of high treason and murder. It was the attempt on the part of a band of conspirators to murder Napoleon III. In order to accomplish this *political* object, they exploded a bomb as nearly under his Majesty's carriage as they could manage, but instead of murdering the Emperor they killed a policeman.

Orsini was captured, tried, and executed in the good old French fashion. His political career ended with the guillotine--a sharp remedy, but effective, so far as he was concerned.

One Dr. Simon Bernard was more fortunate than his principal, for he was in England, the refuge of discontented foreign murderers, who try to do good by stealth, and sometimes feel very uncomfortable when they find that it turns out to be assassination.

Bernard was a brother conspirator in this famous Orsini business, and being apprehended in England, was taken to be tried before Lord Chief Justice Campbell, Edwin James and myself being retained for the defence.

There was no defence on the facts, and no case on the law. He was indicted for conspiracy with Orsini to murder the Emperor in Paris.

I had prepared a very elaborate and exhaustive argument in favour of the prisoner, on the law, and had little doubt I could secure his acquittal; but the facts were terribly strong, and we knew well enough if the jury convicted, Campbell would hang the prisoner, for he never tolerated murder. With this view of the case, we summoned Dr. Bernard to a consultation, which was held in one of the most ghastly rooms of Newgate.

No more miserable place could be found outside the jail, and it could only be surpassed in horror by one within. It might have been, and probably was, an anteroom to hell, but of that I say nothing. I leave my description, for I can do no more justice to it. The only cheerful thing about it was Dr. Bernard himself. He was totally unconcerned with the danger of his situation, and regarded himself as a hero of the first order. Murder, hanging, guillotine--all seemed to be the everyday chances of life, and to him there was nothing sweeter or more desirable, if you might judge by his demeanour.

I thought it well to mention the fact that, if the jury found him guilty, Lord Campbell would certainly sentence him to death. He exhibited no emotion whatever, but shrugging his shoulders after the manner of a Frenchman who differed from you in opinion, said,--

"Well, if I am hanged, I must be hanged, that is all."

With a man like him it was impossible to argue or ask for explanations. He seemed to be possessed with the one idea that to remedy all the grievances of the State it was merely necessary to blow up the Emperor with his horses and carriage, and coolly informed us, without the least reserve, that the bombs manufactured with this political object had been sent over to Paris from England concealed in firkins of butter. I can find no words in which to express my feelings.

So ended our first consultation. The "merits" of the case were gone; there was no defence. But whatever might be our opinion on Dr. Bernard's state of mind, we could not abandon him to his fate. We were retained to defend him, and defend him we must, even in spite of himself, if we could do so consistently with our professional honour and duty.

Accordingly we had another consultation, and as I have said there was one other room in England more ghastly than that where we held our first interview, so now I reluctantly introduce you to it.

If a man about to be tried for his life could look on this apartment and its horrors unmoved, he would certainly be a fit subject for the attentions of the hangman, and deserving of no human sympathy. It was enough to shake the nerves of the hangman himself.

We were in an apartment on the north-east side of the quadrangular building, where the sunshine never entered. Even daylight never came, but only a feeble, sickening twilight, precursor of the grave itself. It was not merely the gloom that intensified the horrors of the situation, or the ghastly traditions of the place, or the impending fate of our callous client; but there was a tier of shelves occupying the side of the apartment, on which were placed in dismal prominence the plaster-of-Paris busts of all the malefactors who had been hanged in Newgate for some hundred years.

No man can look attractive after having been hanged, and the indentation of the hangman's rope on every one of their necks, with the mark of the knot under the ear, gave such an impression of all that can be conceived of devilish horror as would baffle the conceptions of the most morbid genius.

Whether these things were preserved for phrenological purposes or for the gratification of the most sanguinary taste, I never knew, but they impressed me with a disgust of the brutal tendency of the age.

Dr. Bernard, however, seemed to take a different view. Probably he was scientific. He went up to them, and examined, as it seemed, every one of these ghastly memorials with an interest which could only be scientific. It did not seem to have occurred to his brain that *his* head would probably be the next to adorn that repository of criminal effigies.

He was in charge of a warder, and looked round with the utmost composure, as though examining the Caesars in the British Museum, and was as interested as any fanatical fool of a phrenologist. He shrugged his shoulders, raised his eyebrows, and repeated his old formula, "Well, if I am to be hanged, I must be hanged."

He was acquitted. My elaborate arguments on the law were not necessary, for the jury actually refused to believe the evidence as to the facts!

Such are the chances of trial by jury!

As a relief to this gloomy chapter I must tell you of a distinguished Judge who had to sentence a dishonest butler for robbing his master of some silver spoons. He considered it his duty to say a few words to the prisoner in passing sentence, in order to show the enormity of the crime of a servant in his position robbing his master, and by way of warning to others who might be tempted to follow his example.

"You, prisoner," said his lordship, "have been found guilty, by a jury of your country, of stealing these articles from your employer--mark that--*your employer*! Now, it aggravates your offence that he is your employer, because he employs you to look after his property. You *did* look after it, but not in the way that a butler should--mark that!" The judge here hemmed and coughed, as if somewhat exhausted with his exemplary speech; and then resumed his address, which was ethical and judicial: "You, prisoner, have *no* excuse for your conduct. You had a most excellent situation, and a kind master to whom you owed a debt of the deepest gratitude and your allegiance as a faithful servant, instead of which you paid him by *feathering your nest with his silver spoons*; therefore you must be transported for the term of seven years!"

The metaphor was equal to that employed by an Attorney-General, who at a certain time in the history of the Home Rule agitation, addressing his constituents, told them that *Mr. Gladstone had sent up a balloon to see which way the cat jumped with regard to Ireland!* He was soon appointed a Judge of the High Court.

Judges, however, are not always masters of their feelings, any more than they are of their language; they are sometimes carried away by prejudice, or even controlled by sentiment. I knew one, a very worthy and amiable man, who, having to sentence a prisoner to death, was so overcome by the terrible nature of the crime that he informed the unhappy convict that he could expect *no mercy either in this world or the next!*

Littledale, again, was an uncommonly kind and virtuous man, a good husband and a learned Judge; but he was afflicted with a wife whom he could not control. She, on the contrary, controlled him, and left him no peace unless she had her will. At times, however, she overdid her business. Littledale had a butler who had been in the family many years, and with whom he would not have parted on any account. He would sooner have parted with her ladyship. One morning, however, this excellent butler came to Sir Joseph and said, with tears in his eyes,--

"I beg your pardon, my lord--"

"What's the matter, James?"

"I'm very sorry, my lord," said the butler, "but I wish to leave."

"Wish to leave, James? Why, what do you wish to leave for? Haven't you got a good situation?"

"Capital sitiwation, Sir Joseph, and you have always been a good kind master to me, Sir Joseph; but, O Sir Joseph, Sir Joseph!"

"What then, James, what then? Why do you wish to leave? Not going to get married, eh--not surely going to get married? O James, don't do it!"

"Heaven forbid, Sir Joseph!"

"Eh, eh? Well, then, what is it? Speak out, James, and tell me all about it. Tell me--tell me as a friend! If there is any trouble--"

"Well, Sir Joseph, I could put up with anything from *you, Sir Joseph*, but I *can't get on with my lady*!"

"My lady be--. O James, what a sinner you make of me! Is that all, James? Then go down on your knees at once and *thank God my lady is not your wife*!"

It was a happy thought, and James stayed.

I don't think I have mentioned a curious reason that a jury once gave for *not* finding a prisoner guilty, although he had been tried on a charge of a most terrible murder. The evidence was irresistible to anybody but a jury, and the case was one of inexcusable brutality. The man had been tried for the murder of his father and mother, and, as I said, the evidence was too clear to leave a doubt as to his guilt.

The jury retired to consider their verdict, and were away so long that the Judge sent for them and asked if there was any point upon which he could enlighten them. They answered no, and thought they understood the case perfectly well.

After a great deal of further consideration they brought in a verdict of "*Not Guilty.*"

The Judge was angry at so outrageous a violation of their plain duty, and did what he ought not to have done--namely, asked the reason they brought in such a verdict, when they knew the culprit was guilty and ought to have been hanged.

"That's just it, my lord," said the foreman of this distinguished body. "I assure you we had no doubt about the prisoner's guilt, but we *thought there had been deaths enough in the family lately, and so gave him the benefit of the doubt*!"

There was a young solicitor who had been entrusted with a defence in a case of murder. It was his first case of importance, and he was, of course, enthusiastic in his devotion to his client's interests. Indeed, his enthusiasm rather overstepped his prudence.

By dint of perseverance and persuasion he obtained a promise from a juror-in-waiting that if he should be on the jury he would consent to no other verdict than manslaughter, which would be a tremendous triumph for the young solicitor.

The case was a very strong one for wilful murder. The friendly juror-in-waiting took his seat in the box. Everything went well except the evidence, and the solicitor's heart almost failed for fear his man should give way. The jury for a long time were unable to agree.

Now the young solicitor felt it was his faithful juror who was standing out.

"All agreed but one, my lord."

"Go back to your room," said the Judge; which they did, and after another long absence returned with a verdict of "Manslaughter."

Jubilant with his success, the young solicitor met his juryman, congratulated him on his firmness, and thanked him for his exertions.

"How did you manage it, my good friend--how did you manage? It was a wonderful verdict--wonderful!"

"Oh," said he, "I was determined not to budge. I never budge. Conscience is ever my guide."

"I suppose there were eleven to one against you?"

"Eleven to one! A tough job, sir--a tough job."

"Eleven for wilful murder, eh?" said the jubilant young man. "Dear me, what a narrow squeak!"

"Eleven for *murder*! No, sir!" exclaimed the juror.

"What, then?"

"*Eleven for an acquittal*! You may depend upon it, sir, the other jurors had been 'got at.'"

Lord Watson, dining with me one Grand Day at Gray's Inn, said he recollected a very stupid and a very rude Scottish Judge (which seems very remarkable) who scarcely ever listened to an advocate, and pooh-poohed everything that was said.

One day a celebrated advocate was arguing before him, when, to express his contempt of what he was saying, the cantankerous old curmudgeon of a Judge pointed with one forefinger to one of his ears, and with the other to the opposite one.

"You see this, Mr. ----?"

"I do, my lord," said the advocate.

"Well, it just goes in here and comes out there!" and his lordship smiled with the hilarity of a Judge who thinks he has actually said a good thing.

The advocate looked and smiled not *likewise*, but a good deal more wise. Then the expression of his face changed to one of contempt.

"I do not doubt it, my lord," said he. "What is there to prevent it?"

The learned judge sat immovable, and looked--like a judicial--*wit*.

I was now getting on so well in my profession that in the minds of many of the unsuccessful there was a natural feeling of disappointment. Why one man should succeed and a dozen fail has ever been an unsolved problem at the Bar, and ever will be. But the curious part of this natural law is that it manifests itself in the most unexpected manner.

Coming one day from a County Court, where I had had a successful day, and humming a little tune, whom should I meet but my friend Morgan ----. He was a very pleasant man, what is called a *nice man*, of a quiet, religious turn of mind, and nobody was ever more painstaking to push himself along. He was a great stickler for a man's doing his duty, and was possessed with the idea that, getting on as I was, it was my duty to refuse to take a brief in the County Court.

Coming up to me on the occasion I refer to, Morgan said, "What, *you* here, Hawkins! I believe you'd take a brief before the devil in h----."

I was quite taken aback for the moment by the use of such language. If he had not been so religious a man, perhaps I should not have felt it so much; as it was, I could hardly fetch my breath.

When I recovered my equanimity I answered, "Yes, Morgan, I would, and should get one of my devils to hold it."

He seemed appeased by my frank avowal, for he loved honesty almost as much as fees.

CHAPTER XVII.

APPOINTED QUEEN'S COUNSEL--A SERIOUS ILLNESS--SAM LEWIS.

On January 10, 1859, the Lord Chancellor did me the honour of recommending my name to Her Most Gracious Majesty, and I was raised to the rank and dignity of a Queen's Counsel.

This is a step of doubtful wisdom to most men in the legal profession, for it is generally looked upon as the end of a man's career or the beginning. I had no doubt about the propriety of the step; it had been the object of my ambition, and I believe I should unhesitatingly have acted as I did even if it had been the termination of my professional life. My idea was to go forward in the career I had chosen. The junior work, if it had not lost its emoluments, no longer possessed the pleasurable excitement of the old days. It was never my ambition merely to "mark time;" that is unsatisfactory exertion, and leads no whither.

But enough; I took silk, and a new life opened before me. I was a leader.

My business rolled on in ever-increasing volume, so that I had to fairly pick my way through the constant downpour of briefs, but was always pressed forward by that useful institution known as the "barrister's clerk."

Whatever business overwhelms the counsel, no amount of it would disconcert the clerk, and it is wonderful how many briefs he can arrange in upstanding attitude along mantelpieces, tables, tops of dwarf cupboards, windows--anywhere, in fact, where there is anything to stand a brief on--without that gentleman feeling the least exhausted. It would take as long to wear him out as to wear to a level the rocks of Niagara. The loss of a brief to him is almost like the loss of an eye. It would take a week after such a disaster to get the right focus of things.

My clerk came rushing into my room one day so pale and excited that I wondered if the man had lost his wife or child. He did not leave me long in suspense as soon as he could articulate his words.

"Sir," said he, "you know those Emmets that you have done so much for?"

I remembered.

"Well, sir, they've taken a brief to another counsel."

It was a serious misfortune, no doubt, and I had to soothe him in the best manner I could; so to lessen the calamity I made the best joke I could think of in the circumstances, and said the Emmets were small people, almost beneath notice.

I don't wonder that he did not see it with tears in his eyes; his distress was painful to witness. The poor fellow was dumbfounded, but at last shook his head, saying,--

"We've had a good deal from those Emmets, sir."

"But you need not make mountains out of ant-hills."

He did not see that either.

I was now living in Bond Street, and for the first time in my life was taken seriously ill. My clerk's worry then came home to me; not about a single brief, but about a great many. Illness would be a very serious matter, as I had arrived at an important stage in my career. A barrister in full practice cannot afford to be ill. In my distress I sent to Baron Martin, as I was in every case in his list for the following day, and begged him to oblige me by adjourning his court. It was a large request, but I knew his kindness, and felt I might ask the favour. Baron Martin, I should think, never in his life did an unkind act or refused to do a kind one. He instantly complied with my request, and did not listen for a moment to the "public interest," as the foolish fetish is called which sometimes does duty for its neglect. The "public interest" on this occasion was the interests of all those who had entrusted their business to my keeping. The public interests are the interests of the suitors.

My illness threatened to be fatal. I had been overworked; and nothing but the greatest care and skill brought me round. One never knows what friendship is and what friends are till one is ill.

At length there was a consultation, Drs. Addison, Charles Johnson, Duplex, and F. Hawkins, my cousin, being present.

It was a kind of medical jury which sat upon me. I will pass over details, and come to the conclusion of the investigation. After considering the case, Dr. Addison, who acted as foreman of the jury, said,--

"We find a verdict of 'Guilty,' under mitigating circumstances. The prisoner has not injured himself with intent to do any grievous bodily or mental harm, but he has been guilty of negligence, not having taken due care of himself, and we hope the sentence we are about to pass will act as a warning to him, and deter others from following a like practice. The prisoner is released on bail, to come up for judgment when called upon; and the meaning of that is," said Dr. Addison, "that if you behave yourself you will hear no more of this; but if you return to your former practice without any regard to the warning you have had, you will be promptly called up for judgment, and I need not say the sentence will be proportioned to the requirements of the case. You may now go."

To carry on Dr. Addison's joke, I heartily thanked him for taking my good character into consideration, and practically acquitting me of all evil tendencies. Acting upon his good advice, from that time to this I have never been in trouble again.

Watson, Q.C., afterwards Baron Watson, advised me to take a long rest; but as he was not a doctor of medicine, I did not act upon his advice. A long rest would have killed me much faster than any amount of work, so I worked with judgment; and although my business went on increasing to an extent that would not have pleased Dr. Addison, I suffered no evil effects, but seemed to get through it with more ease than ever, and was soon in a fair way to achieve the greatest goal of human endeavour--a comfortable independence. The reason of getting through so much work was that I had to reject a great deal, and, of course, had my choice of the best, not only as to work, but as to clients. To use a sporting phrase, I got the best "mounts," and therefore was at the top of the record in wins.

Good cases are easy--they do not need winning; they will do their own work if you only leave them alone. Bad cases require all your attention; they want much propping, and your only chance is that, if you cannot win, your opponent may *lose*.

But nothing in the chatter about the Bar is more erroneous than the talk of the tremendous incomes of counsel. A man is never estimated at his true worth in this world, certainly not a barrister, actor, physician, or writer; and as for incomes, no one can estimate his neighbour's except the Income-tax Commissioners. They get pretty near sometimes, however, without knowing it.

One morning I was riding in the Park when old Sam Lewis, the great money-lender, a man for whom I had much esteem, and about whom I will relate a little story presently, came alongside. We were on friendly and even familiar terms, although I never borrowed any money of him in my life.

"Why, Mr. Hawkins," said he, "you seem to be in almost everything. What a fortune you must be piling up!"

"Not so big as you might think," I replied.

"Why, how many," he rejoined, "are making as much as you? A good many are doing twenty thousand a year, I dare say, but--"

Here I checked his curiosity by asking if he had ever considered what twenty thousand a year meant.

He never had.

"Then I will tell you, Lewis. *You* may make it in a day, but to us it means five hundred golden sovereigns every week in the working year!"

It somewhat startled him, I could see, and it effected my object without giving offence. What did it matter to Sam Lewis what my income was?

"There are men who make it," he answered.

"Some men have made it," I said; "and I know some who make more, but will never own to it, ask who may."

I may say I liked Sam Lewis, and having told the story of the Queen's Counsel who *borrowed* my money in so dishonest a manner, I will tell one of Sam, the professional money-lender.

He never was known to take advantage of a man in difficulties, and he never did, nor to charge any one exorbitant interest. I have known him lend to men and allow them to fix their own time of payment, their own rate of interest, and their own security. He often lent without any at all. He knew his men, and was not fool enough to trust a rogue at any amount of interest. He was known and respected by all ranks, and never more esteemed than by those who had had pecuniary transactions with him. He was the soul of honour, and his transactions were world-wide; business passed through his hands that would have been entrusted nowhere else; so that he was rich, and no one was more deservedly so.

Here is an incident in Lewis's business life that will show one phase of his character.

He held a number of bills, many of which were suspected by him to be forged--that is to say, that the figures had been altered after the signature of the acceptor had been written.

They were all in the name of Lord ----.

One day Lewis met his lordship in the Park, and mentioned his suspicion, at the same time inviting him to call and examine the bills. The noble lord was a little amazed, and proceeded at once to Lewis's office. Seating himself on one side of the table with his lordship on the other, Lewis handed to him the bills one by one and requested him to set aside those that were forged.

The separation having been made, it appeared that over *twenty thousand-pounds' worth of the bills were forged*! The noble lord was a little startled at the discovery, but his mind was soon eased by Lewis putting the whole of the forged bills into the fire.

"There's an end of them, my lord," said he. "We want no prosecution, and I do not wish to receive payment from you. I ought to have examined them with more care, and you ought not to have left space enough before the first figure to supplement it by another. The rogue could not resist the temptation."

So ended this monetary transaction, creditable alike to the honour and generosity of the money-lender.

The most steady of minds will sometimes go on the tramp. This was never better illustrated than when the young curate was being married, and the officiating clergyman asked him the formal question, "Wilt thou have this woman to thy wedded wife?"

The poor bridegroom, losing self-control, and not having yet a better half to keep him straight, answered, "That is my desire," anticipating by a considerable period a totally different religious ceremony of the Church--namely, the Baptism of Infants. In his anticipation the young man had overreached the necessities of the situation.

This momentary digression leads me to the following story. I was staying at the house of an old friend, a wealthy Hebrew, while another of the guests was Arthur A'Becket. As will sometimes happen when you are in good spirits, the conversation took a religious turn. We drifted into it unconsciously, and our worthy host was telling us that he was in the habit of praying night and morning. Being in a communicative mood, I said, "Well, since you name it, I sometimes say a little prayer myself." The Hebrew was attentive, and seemed not a little surprised. "This is especially the case in the morning," I added. "But once upon a time my mind wavered a little between business and prayer, and I found myself in the midst of my devotional exercise saying, 'Gentlemen of the jury.'"

"Thank God!" cried A'Becket, "our friend Hawkins is not a Unitarian."

I often wonder how I was able to get through the amount of business that pressed upon me and retain my health, but happily I did so. One great factor in my fortunate condition of health was, perhaps, that I had no ridiculous ambition. What was to come would come as the result of hard work, for I was born to no miraculous interpositions or official friendships.

Having dropped gambling, I set to work, and after a long spell of *nisi prius*, in all its phases, had engaged my attention, a new sphere of action presented itself in the shape of Compensation Cases--an easy and lucrative branch, which seemed to be added to, rather than have grown out of, our profession; but whatever was its connection, it was a prolific branch, hanging down with such good fruit that it required no tempter to make you taste it.

Railway, Government, and Municipal authorities were everywhere taking land for public improvements, and where they were, as a rule, my friend Horace Lloyd and myself were engaged in friendly rivalry as to the amount to be paid.

CHAPTER XVIII.

THE PRIZE-FIGHT ON FRIMLEY COMMON.

I must now describe a remarkable event that occurred a great many years ago, and which caused no little amusement at the time; indeed, for years after Baron Parke used to tell the story with the greatest pleasure.

In those old days there was a prize-fight on Frimley Common, and it was known long after as the "Frimley Common Prize-Fight," although many a battle had taken place on Frimley Ridges before that time, and many a one since. This particular fight was the more celebrated because one of the combatants was killed, and I remember the events connected with it as clearly as if they had taken place only yesterday. At the following Kingston Assizes the victorious pugilist was indicted for manslaughter. It was an awful charge, especially before the Judge who was then presiding. The man, however, escaped for the moment, and a warrant was issued for his apprehension.

At a later period I was at Guildford, where the Assizes were being held. Even at that time the man "wanted" for the manslaughter could be easily identified, for he still bore visible signs of the punishment he had undergone in the encounter.

I was sitting in court one afternoon when a country sporting attorney of the name of Morris quietly sidled up to me. I ought to mention that at these Assizes Lord Chief Justice Erle was sitting, and it was well known that he also detested the Prize Ring, and had therefore, no sympathy with any of its members. He was consequently a dangerous Judge to have anything to do with in a case of this kind. His punishment would be sure to be one of severity, and a conviction a dead certainty. There was a sparkle in the sporting solicitor's eye, as he glanced at me over his shoulder, which plainly intimated that he had something good to communicate.

As he came in front of the seat where I was, he said, in a subdued whisper, that he had been instructed by Lord ---- to defend the accused prize-fighter; that the man was at that moment in the town, and would like to have my opinion as to whether it would be prudent to surrender at these Assizes--surrender, that is to say, to the constables who were on the lookout for him; or whether it would be better, as they were ignorant of his whereabouts, to delay his trial until the next Assizes, when he would be better prepared to face the tribunal, as by that time he would have recovered from the punishment he had received.

It is certain the jury would have taken his battered appearance as evidence of the damage he had inflicted on his adversary, whom he had unfortunately killed; and even more likely that Erle should have regarded his injuries in the same light, and punished him more severely for having received them. I had a perfect right to answer the question put to me, and felt that it was my duty to the accused to answer frankly. So I said there was little doubt, as the man was dead, and the accused still bore unmistakable signs of the contest, there would be pretty clear evidence of identity; that as Erle was not a fool, he would most certainly convict him; while, being opposed to everything connected with the "noble art of self-defence," he might send him to penal servitude for a number of years.

I had no need to say more. The solicitor, who was a ready-witted and voluble man, was anxious to amalgamate his opinion with mine. He was shrewd, and caught an idea before you could be sure you had one yourself.

"The most prudent thing, sir," he said, "would be to surrender at the next Assizes, and not at these. That is just what I thought, sir, and so I told him, advising in the meantime that he should carefully avoid putting himself in the way of the police."

I have no doubt he acted on this opinion, for I heard that he left the town immediately, and was neither seen nor heard of again till the eve of the Spring Assizes, which were to be held at Kingston, and at which Baron Parke was to preside. The Baron was one of the shrewdest of men, as any one would discover who attempted to deceive him.

On the Commission day the attorney for the accused presented himself to me again, and once more sought my opinion with regard to the trial and the surrender of the accused.

"Would it be proper," he asked, "for my client to show his respect for the court and dress in a becoming manner; or should he appear in his everyday clothes as a working bricklayer, dirty and unwashed?"

Again I advised, as was my duty, that he should scrupulously regard the dignity of the Bench, and show the greatest respect to the learned Judge who presided; that he ought not to come in a disgraceful costume if he could help it, but appear as becomingly attired as possible. That was all I said. Let me also observe, what perhaps there is no occasion to say, that I impressed upon the attorney that his client should abstain from any appearance of attempting to deceive the Judge, and informed him, as the fact was, that his lordship was scrupulously particular in all points of etiquette and decorum. Moreover, I added as a last word, "The Judge is too shrewd to be taken in."

After thus duly impressing upon him the importance of a quiet behaviour, I suggested that any costume other than that of the man when actually engaged in the fight *might* throw some difficulty in the way of a young and inexperienced country constable identifying him. It was never too late for even a bricklayer to mend his garments or his manners and adjust them to the occasion. The policeman who alone could identify the Frimley champion had not seen him for many months--not since the fight, in fact; and the prisoner ought not to appear in the dock in fighting costume, as the young Surrey constable saw him on that one occasion. Moreover, Baron Parke would not like him to appear in that dress.

This was, as nearly as I can remember, all that took place between us. Judge, now, of my surprise, if you can, when the case was called on, to see the prisoner appear in the dock looking like a *young clergyman*, dressed in a complete suit of black, a long frock coat, fitting him up to the neck and very nearly down to the heels. He had the appearance of a very tame curate. His hair, instead of being short and stumpy, as when the young policeman saw him, was now long, shiny, and carefully brushed over both sides of his forehead, which gave him the appearance so fashionable amongst the saints of the Old Masters.

I was utterly astounded at the change from the rude, rough bricklayer, scarred all over the face, to the clergyman-like appearance of this gentlemanly prisoner. I dared not laugh, but it was difficult to maintain my countenance. Deceive Baron Parke! I thought; he would deceive the devil himself, who knew a great deal more about parsons than Parke did.

The learned Judge looked at him for a considerable time, as though he had never seen a prize-fighter before, and was determined to make the most of him. If the ghost of Hamlet had stood in the dock instead of the prisoner, he would not have surprised dear old Parke more than the prisoner did.

It was a masterpiece of deception, notwithstanding my serious warning.

On the jury, it so happened, was an elderly Quaker, in his full array of drab coat, vest, and breeches, with the regulation blue stockings. He had long whitish hair, and a Quaker hat in front of him on the ledge of the jury-box. He was what might be called a "factor" in the situation, which it was no easy matter to know in a moment how to deal with. He would be against prize-fighting to a certainty, but how far he might be inclined to convict a prize-fighter was another matter. At last I made up my mind in what way to deal with him, and it was this--not on the merits of the noble art itself, but on those of the case. If I could convince this conscientious juror that there *might be* (that would be good enough) a doubt as to identity, it would be sufficient for my purpose; so I mainly addressed myself to *him*, after disposing of the young policeman pretty satisfactorily, leaving only his bare belief to be dealt with in argument. The young policeman's belief that *that there* was the man showed what a strong young policeman he was.

I asked the Quaker to allow me to suggest, for the sake of argument only, that *he*, the Quaker, should imagine himself putting off his Quaker dress, and assuming the costume of a prize-fighter, his hair cut so short that it would present the appearance of an aged rat; "then," said I, "divest yourself of your shirt and flannel--strip yourself, in fact, quite to the skin above your belt--and with only a pair of cotton drawers of a sky blue, or any other colour you might prefer, and, say, a bird's-eye *fogle* round your waist, your lower limbs terminating in cotton socks and high-lows--with the additional ornamentation to all this elegant drapery of a couple of your front teeth knocked out--and I will venture to ask you, sir, and any one of the gentlemen whom I am addressing, whether you think your own good and respectable wife herself would recognize the partner of her joys?"

The burst of laughter which this little transformation of the respectable, stout old Quaker occasioned I was in no way responsible for; but even Old Parke fell back in his seat, and said,--

"Mr. Hawkins! Mr. Hawkins!"

I knew what that meant, and when the usher, by dint of much clamour, secured me another hearing, I continued,--

"Nay, sir, and if you looked at yourself in a looking-glass you would not be able to recognize a single feature you possessed, had you been battered about the face as the unfortunate man was. Why, the young policeman says in his evidence his nose was flattened, his eyes were swollen black, blue, and red, his cheeks gashed and bloody! But it is enough: if that is a correct description, although a mild one, of the man as he appeared after the scene of the conflict, how can you expect the young constable to recognize such an individual months afterwards, or any of the witnesses, although to their dying day they would not forget the terrible disfigurement of the poor fellow whom you are supposed to be trying?"

All this time there was everywhere painfully suppressed laughter, and even the jury, all of them Epsom men, and many of whom I knew well enough, were hardly able to contain themselves.

His lordship, after summing up the case to the jury, looked down quietly to me, as I was sitting below him, and murmured,--

"Hawkins, you've got all Epsom with you!"

"Yes," I answered, "but you have got the Quaker; he was the only one I was afraid of."

"You have transformed him," said the Judge.

In a few minutes the verdict showed the accuracy of his lordship's observation, for the jury returned a verdict of "Not guilty."

I must say, however, that Parke did his utmost to obtain a conviction, but reason and good sense were too much for him.

CHAPTER XIX.

SAM WARREN, THE AUTHOR OF "TEN THOUSAND A YEAR."

Amongst the illustrious men whom I have met, the name of Sam Warren deserves remembrance, for he was a genial, good-natured man, full of humour, and generally entertained a good opinion of everybody, including himself. He not only achieved distinction in his profession and became a Queen's Counsel, but wrote a book which attained a well-deserved popularity, and was entitled "Ten Thousand a Year."

He was a member of the Northern Circuit, and I believe was as popular as his book. That he did not become a Judge, like several of his friends, was not Sam's fault, for no man went more into society, cultivated acquaintances of the best style, or had better qualifications for the honour than he.

But although he did not achieve this distinction, he was made a little lower than that order, and became in due time a *Master in Lunacy*, a post, as it seemed from Sam's description, of the highest importance and no little fun.

A part of his duties was to visit lunatic asylums and other places where these patients were confined, with a view to report to the authorities his opinion of the patients' mental condition. No doubt to a man of Sam's observant mind this work presented many studies of interest, as well as situations of excitement, and at times of no little humour. He found, for instance, that many of these poor creatures were possessed of a much larger income than ten thousand a year. Some of them were Dukes and some supernatural beings, who were just on a visit to this little clod of a world to see how things were going.

Soon after his appointment, and before he had become used to the work, he told me of a singular experience he once had with a particular gentleman whom he was intending to report as having perfectly recovered from any mental aberration with which he might have been afflicted. Sam wondered how it was possible that a gentleman of such culture and understanding should be considered a fit subject for confinement, for he had several pleasant and intellectual conversations with him, and found him quite agreeable and refined, and of a perfectly balanced mind.

"I had been told," said the Master, "that the peculiar form of derangement with this gentleman was that he had aspired to distinction in the English Church; and on one memorable occasion when I called he received me, not with the usual familiarity, but with a certain stiffness and solemnity of bearing which was hardly in keeping with his courteous demeanour on other occasions. One had to be on one's guard at all times, or he might get a knife plunged into him without notice. I chatted for some time in a kind and easy manner, hoping to find that the mild restraint and discipline had done the poor fellow good. Alas! how deceived I was, when, in a sudden rage, he turned upon me, and asked *who the devil I thought I was talking to?*"

"I told him a gentleman of a kind nature, I was sure, and of an amiable disposition.

"'Yes,' said he, 'but that is no reason why you should not treat me with proper deference and with due respect for my exalted position.'

"I bowed politely, and expressed a hope that I should never forget what was due from one gentleman to another.

"'No, no,' said he, 'that kind of excuse will not do. One gentleman to another, indeed! Whom are you talking to? I insist on your treating me with reverence and respect. Perhaps you do not know that I am *St. Paul?*'

"'Indeed!' said I, 'I was not aware that I was speaking to that holy Apostle, to one whom I hold in extreme reverence, and whose writings I have made my study.'"

After that, it seems, they got on very well together for the rest of the interview. Warren was able to delight him with his knowledge of Cappadocia, Phrygia, and Pamphylia, and the little incident of leaving his cloak at Troas, his shipwreck, and a vast number of things which the Apostle seemed very pleased to hear, while he conducted himself with that pious dignity which well deserved the obsequious reverence of the official visitor. On parting, St. Paul said,--

"You are rather *mixed in your Scriptures*; the only thing you are accurate about is *leaving my cloak at Troas*."

On Warren's next visit he resolved to conduct himself with more reverence. St. Paul was looking much the same as on the previous occasion. Sam genuflected, and held down his head, putting his hands devoutly together, and making such other manifestations of reverence as he thought the case required.

St. Paul looked at Warren with wonderment, and was evidently by no means satisfied with his salutations.

"Who the devil," said the madman, "do you think you are making those idiotic signs to? Whom do you take me for?"

"St. Paul, your holiness."

"'St. Paul, your holiness,' he repeated. 'My ----, you ought to be put into a lunatic asylum and looked after. You must be stark mad to think I am the holy Apostle St. Paul. What put that into your silly brains? Down on your knees, villain, at once, and prostrate yourself before *the Shah of Persia*--the dawn of creation and the light of the universe!'

"I thought this was coming it pretty strong," continued Sam, "but as it was all in my day's work, I conformed as well as I could to my instructions. The difficulty was in knowing how to address His Majesty, so I stammered, 'Dread potentate!' and seeing it pleased him, 'Light of the universe,' I cried, 'it is morning! May I rise?'

"'I perceive,' said the Shah, 'you are a genius,'"

"What did you think of his state of mind after that?" I asked.

Sam laughed and answered: "I thought he was getting better, more rational, and thanked him for his good opinion. 'Mighty potentate,' said I, 'monarch of the universe, I apologize for my mistake, but I was at *St. Luke's* yesterday,'

"'My faithful Luke!' said he, and clapped his hands. I knew once more where he was.

"'The last time,' said I (thinking I would rather have him the amiable Paul than the savage Shah), 'your Majesty informed me that you were the holy Apostle St. Paul!'

"'So I am,' answered the Shah.

"'I am at a loss, your Majesty, I humbly confess, to understand how your immortal Highness can be at one and the same time the blessed Apostle St. Paul and the Shah of Persia,'

"'Because you are such a damned fool!' replied His Highness.

"Here was the fierceness of the Shah, but immediately the gentleness of the Apostle restored him to a more amiable mood, and coming towards me with a smile, he said,--

"'The explanation, my dear sir, is simple;' and then, in a quiet, confidential tone, he added: '*It was the same mother, but two fathers!*'"

"I had another experience not long after in the same asylum," continued Warren. "One of my patients told me he had married the devil's daughter when I was asking him about his relations. 'She was a nice girl enough,' he said, 'and although my people thought I had married beneath me, I was satisfied with her rank, seeing she was a Prince's daughter. We went off on our honeymoon in a chariot of fire which her father lent us for the occasion, and had a comfortable time of it at Monte Carlo, where all the hotels are under her father's special patronage.'

"'I hope,' said I, 'your marriage was a happy one.'

"'Yes,' said he with a sigh, '*but we don't get on well with the old folks!*'"

No writer was ever more solicitous of fame than Sam Warren. It was a proud moment whenever there was the remotest allusion to his authorship, and I always loved to compliment him on his books.

In the famous case of Lord St. Leonards's will, which had been lost, I supported the lost will, and proved its contents from the evidence of Miss Sugden and others.

Sam Warren had been in the habit of visiting Lord St. Leonards at Boyle Farm, Ditton. He gave evidence as to what Lord St. Leonards had told him respecting his intentions as to the disposal of his property.

After examining him, I said with a polite bow: "Mr. Warren, I owe you an apology for bringing you into the Probate Court. I am sure no one will ever dream of disputing *your* will, because you have left everybody '*Ten Thousand a Year*!'"

Whereupon Warren bowed most politely to me in acknowledgment of the compliment; then bowed to the *Judge*, and received his lordship's bow in return; then bowed to the *jury*, then to the *Bar*, and, lastly, to the *gallery*.

Writing of the Probate and Divorce Court reminds me of a curious application for the postponement of a trial made by George Brown, who was as good a humorist as he was a lawyer.

I have said that Judges in those days were more strict in refusing these applications than in ours, and Cresswell was no exception to the rule. He disliked them, and rarely yielded. But Brown was a man of a very persuasive manner, and it was always difficult to refuse him anything. I was sitting in Cresswell's court when George rose as soon as the Judge had taken his seat, and asked if a case might be postponed which would be in the next day's list.

"Have you an affidavit, Mr. Brown, as to the reason?"

"Yes, my lord; but I can hardly put the real ground of my application into the affidavit. I have communicated with the other side, and they are perfectly agreeable under the circumstances."

"I cannot agree to postpone without some adequate cause being stated," said Cresswell.

"I am very sorry, my lord, but it will be very inconvenient to me to be here to-morrow."

There was a laugh round the Bar, which Cresswell observing, asked what the real reason was.

Brown smiled and blushed; nothing would bring him to state plainly what the reason of his application was. At last, however, he stammered,--

"My lord, the fact is I am going to take the first step towards a divorce."

The appeal touched the Judge; the reason was sufficient. Every step in a divorce was to be encouraged, especially the first. The application was granted, and Brown was married the next day.

CHAPTER XX.

THE BRIGHTON CARD-SHARPING CASE.

From the courts of justice to the prize-ring is an easy and sometimes pleasant transition, especially in books. I visited from time to time such well-known persons as "Deaf Burke," Nat Langham, "Dutch Sam," and Owen Swift, all remarkable men, with constitutions of iron, and made like perfect models of humanity. Their names are unknown in these days, although in those of the long past gentlemen of the first position were proud of their acquaintance; and these men, although their profession was battering one another, were as little inclined to brutality as any. And when it is remembered that they played their game in accordance with strict rules and on the most scientific principles, it will be seen that cruelty formed no part of their character.

The true sportsmen of the period, amongst whom were the highest in the social and political world, took the same interest in contests in the ring as they did on the turf or in the cricket-field, and for the same reason. Whether Jem Mace would beat Tom Sayers had as much interest at fashionable dinner-tables as whether Lord Derby would dispose of Aberdeen or Palmerston. Lords and dukes backed their opinion in thousands, and the bargee and the ostler gave or took the odds according to the tips, in shillings. The gentleman of the long robe, therefore, was not to be supposed as altogether out of his element in sporting circles any more than the gentleman who had not a rag to cover him.

Nor was it uncommon to meet what was called the cream of society at the celebrated rendezvous of Ben Caunt, which was the Coach and Horses, St. Martin's Lane, or at the less pretentious resort of the Tipton Slasher; and what will our modern ladies think of their fair predecessors, who in those days witnessed the drawing of a badger or a dog-fight on a Sunday afternoon?

All mankind will attend exhibitions of skill and prowess, and although prize-fights are illegal, you never can suppress the spirit which engendered that form of competition.

I spent sometimes, with many eminent spectators, a quiet hour or two at Tom Spring's in Holborn, and met many of the best men there in all ranks and professions, always excepting the Church. After one of these entertainments I was travelling with John Gully, once a formidable champion of the ring, and at that time a great bookmaker, as well as owner of racehorses--afterwards presented at Court to her most gracious Majesty the late Queen--and Member of Parliament. We were travelling on our way to Bath, and as we approached a tunnel not far from our destination, Gully pointed out a particular spot "where," said he, "I won my first fight;" and so proud was he of the recollection that he might have been in a picture like that of Wellington pointing out the Field of Waterloo to a young lady.

This knowledge of the world, seen as I saw it, was of the greatest use in my profession. If you would know the world, you must not confine yourself to its virtues. There *is* another side, and it is well to look at it. I thought on one particular occasion how useful a little of this knowledge would have been during a certain cross-examination of Arthur Orton in Chancery by a member of the Chancery Bar. He put this question and many others of a similar kind,--

"Do you swear, sir, that you were on board the *Bella*?" in a very severe tone.

"Yes, sir," says the Claimant, "I do."

"Stop," says the advocate; "I'll take that down;" and he did, with a great deal besides, his cross-examination materially assisting the man in prolonging his fraudulent claim.

I was engaged in the Brighton card-sharping case, upon which so much stress was laid by the Claimant as proving his identity with Roger Tichborne, Roger not having been in the matter at all. I was counsel for one of the persons, the notorious Johnny Broom, who was indicted for fraud, and whose trial ought to have come on before Lord Chief Justice Jervis. He was not a good Judge, so far as the *defendant* was concerned, to try such a case, and that being Johnny's opinion, he absconded from his bail. The Lord Chief Justice had a great knowledge of card-sharping and of all other rogueries, so that he was an apt man to deal with delinquents who practised them. Conviction before him would have been certain in this case. He was, in fact, waiting for Johnny, as it was a case of great roguery, and intended to deal severely with him.

You may imagine, then, how angry he was when he heard that his man had flown. But there was one consolation: the Broom gang consisted of a number of men who acted on all occasions as confederates when the frauds were practised. Two of these rogues were also indicted, and placed on their trial at this assize.

A Mr. Johnson appeared for the prosecution, and in opening the case for the Crown, in order to show his uncommon fairness, was so impartial as to state that he could find no ground of complaint in respect of the *cards*, which, he said, had been most carefully examined by the Brighton magistrates.

Who these Brighton magistrates were I never heard, but probably they were gentlemen who knew nothing of sharpers and their ways, and whose only experience of cards was a quiet rubber with the ladies of their household. However, such was their unanimous opinion, and upon it the counsel for the Crown informed the Lord Chief Justice that he had no case so far as the fairness of the cards was concerned.

The Lord Chief Justice saw in a moment the importance of that admission on the part of the prosecution. If that were accepted the case was gone, since the fraud for which these men were indicted could not have been perpetrated by honest cards.

"The Brighton magistrates!" said the Chief Justice, with becoming emphasis. "Give me the cards; I should like to have a look at them."

They were handed up, and then a little scene took place which was picturesque and instructive. The Judge took up the cards one by one after carefully wiping and adjusting his glasses to his nose, while his confidential clerk leant over his shoulder with clerk-like familiarity. Having scrutinized them with the minutest observation, Jervis packed them up, and, turning to Mr. Johnson, said,--

"Mr. Johnson, I will show you how the trick was done. If you will take that card"--handing him one from the pack "--you will see that to the ordinary eye there is nothing to attract your attention. That is precisely as it should be in all games of cheating, for if every fool could see the private marks the rogues could not carry on their calling."

Johnson took the card, and, instructed by the Lord Chief Justice, carefully looked it over, but saw nothing. His face was a perfect blank, and his mind could not have been much more picturesque.

"Turn it over," said his lordship. Johnson obeyed. Still the cryptic hierograph did not appear. The Judge stared at his pupil. "Do you see," asked his lordship, "a tiny mark on the corner of the card at the back?"

"Oh, I see it!" says Johnson, with a face beaming with delight and simplicity.

"That means *the ace of diamonds*" said the Chief--"ace of diamonds, Mr. Johnson!" And thus, after a while, the cards and their secret signs were explained to the counsel for the Crown, who, on the intelligence of the Brighton magistrates, declared that, so far as the *cards* were concerned, he must acquit these card-sharping rogues of all intention to deceive.

In all cases the back of the card showed what was on the face; that was the simple secret of the whole contrivance, although the Brighton magistrates could not discover it, as the whole of them combined had not a hundredth part of the intelligent cuteness of Lord Chief Justice Jervis.

Two of this gang were standing near me, and I heard one of them say to the other,--

"Joey, how would you like to play blind hookey with that ---- old devil?"

"O my G----!" exclaimed Joey.

The prisoners were convicted principally upon the evidence of the Lord Chief Justice, and sentenced to long terms of imprisonment. My client Johnny got away. He read about Jervis and this trial in the papers, and declared he would sooner abandon his profession than be tried by such an old thief. "Why," said he, "that old bloke knows every trick on the board."

His escape was rather interesting. He came into Lewes fully intending to take his trial, and went out of Lewes with the determination not to be tried at those assizes, for the simple reason, as he said, that Jervis was too heavy weight for his counsel.

He took a room and showed himself publicly; but at night the police--those stalwart county men--paid a tiptoe visit to his bedroom. They had no right to this privilege, but perhaps Harry thought it would be better for his brother if they did so. Why they went on tiptoe was that Harry told them his brother was in so weak a state that he woke up with the least noise. The police very kindly believed him, and paid their first and second visit on tiptoe.

When they went the third time, however, their bird had flown. Johnny had let himself down by the window, and, evading the vigilance of those who may have been on the lookout, escaped.

But he did not go without providing a substitute. Harry was to answer all inquiries, and waited the arrival of his watchers, lying in Johnny's bedroom. When the officers came he opened the door in his night apparel, and said, "Hush! don't disturb him; poor Johnny ain't slept hardly for a week over this 'ere job. But you can have a peep at him, only don't make a noise. There he is!" and he pointed to a fancy nightcap of his brother's, which only wanted Johnny's head to make the story true.

The good constables, having seen it as they saw it the night before, left the house as quietly as mice, still on tiptoe.

Harry described this performance to me himself.

Jervis had the whole country scoured for him, but unless he had scoured it himself, there was little chance of any one else finding the culprit.

CHAPTER XXI.

THE KNEBWORTH THEATRICAL ENTERTAINMENTS--SIR EDWARD

BULWER--LYTTON--CHARLES DICKENS, CHARLES MATHEWS, MACREADY, DOUGLAS

JERROLD, AND MANY OTHERS.

Among my pleasantest reminiscences were the partly amateur and partly professional entertainments that took place at the celebrated seat of the distinguished author, Sir Edward Bulwer-Lytton, about the year 185-.

At that time a gentleman of position usually sought to enhance the family dignity by a seat in Parliament. The most brilliant mediocrity even could not succeed without the patronage of the great families, while the great families were dependent upon those who had the franchise for the seats they coveted.

Forty-shilling freeholders were of some importance in those days; hence these theatrical performances at Knebworth Park, for Sir Edward wanted their suffrages without bribery or corruption.

Those who were the happy possessors of what they called the "frankise" were also distinguished enough, to be invited to the great performances at the candidate's beautiful estate.

It was a happy thought to give a succession of dramatic entertainments, amongst which "Every Man in his Humour" was one. Sir Edward knew his constituents and their tastes; it would be better than oratory at some village inn to ask them to the stately hall of Knebworth, and give them one of our fine old English plays.

I have already said that I had made up my mind in my earliest days to go to the Bar or on the Stage, and that love for the histrionic art (sometimes called the footlights) never left me.

For some reason or other I was invited to join the illustrious company which assembled on those eventful evenings, although I was cast for a very humble part in the performance. Nor is there much to wonder at when I tell you who my colleagues were.

First comes that most distinguished comedian of his day, Charles Mathews. I had known him for many a year, and liked him the better, if that was possible, the longer I knew him.

Mathews was the leader of the company; next was another illustrious man whose name will live for ever, and who was not only one of the greatest authors of his time, but also the most distinguished of the non-professional actors. Had he been on the stage, Mathews himself could not have surpassed him. This was Charles Dickens.

After him comes a great friend of Sir Edward, John Foster, a barrister of Lincoln's Inn, and author of the "Life of Goldsmith," as well as editor of the *Examiner* newspaper.

I am not quite sure whether Macready was present on this particular occasion, but I think he was; there were really so many illustrious names that it is impossible at this distance of time to be sure of every one. Macready was a great friend of Bulwer, and with Dickens and others was engaged in giving stage representations for charitable purposes in London and the provinces, so that it is at least possible I may be confounding Knebworth with some other place where I was one of the company.

Amongst us also was another whose name will always command the admiration of his countrymen, Douglas Jerrold. There were also Mark Lemon, Frank Stone, and another Royal Academician, John Leech, Frederick Dickens, Radcliffe, Eliot Yorke, Henry Hale, and others whose names escape my memory at the present moment.

No greater honour could be shown to a young barrister than to invite him to meet so distinguished a company, and what was even more gratifying to my vanity, asking me to act with them in the performance. There were many ladies, some of them of the greatest distinction, but without the leave of those who are their immediate relatives, which I have no time now to obtain, I forbear to mention their names in this work.

The business--for business it was, as well as the greatest pleasure--was no little strain on my energies, for I was now obtaining a large amount of work, and appearing in court every day. I had the orthodox number of devils--at least seven--to assist me, and every morning they came and received the briefs they were to hold.

Alas! of the illustrious people I have mentioned all are dead, all save one lady and myself.

When will such a company meet again?

I was no sooner in the midst of Knebworth's delightful associations than I was anxious to return to the toilsome duties of the Law Courts, with their prosaic pleadings and windbag eloquence. I was wanted in several consultations long before the courts met, so that it was idle to suppose I could stay the night at Knebworth. But what would I have given to be able to do so?

Not my briefs! They were the business of my life, without which the Knebworth pleasures would not have been possible. I never looked with any other feeling than that of pleasure on my work, and whenever the question arose I decided without hesitation in favour of the more profitable but less delightful occupation.

But I managed a compromise now and then. For instance, after I had done my duty in the consultations, and seen my work fairly started in court, I contrived to take the train pretty early to Knebworth, in order to attend rehearsals as well as perform in the evening.

Sir Edward's good-nature caused him much distress at my having to journey to and fro. What *could* he do? He offered me the sole use of his library during the time I was there if I could make it in any way helpful, and said it should be fitted up as a bedroom and study. But it was impossible to do other than I did. The rehearsals were nearly always going on--we had audiences as though they were *matinées*--and they afforded much amusement to us as well as the spectators when we made our corrections or abused one another for some egregious blunder. This, of course, did not include Mathews, who coached us from an improvised royalty box, where he graciously acted as George IV., got up in a wonderful Georgian costume for the occasion. George was so good that he diverted the attention of the audience from us, and made a wonderful hit in his new character.

I will not say that at our regular performances we always won the admiration, but I will affirm that we certainly received the forbearance, of our audience, which says a great deal for them. This observation, however, does not, of course, apply to the professional artists, but only to myself, who, luckily, through all the business still kept my head.

And it will be easily understood that this was the more difficult, especially if I may include my temper with it, when the good-natured Baronet actually invited several of his Hertford friends and neighbours to take part in the performances, some of them being friends of my own and members of my profession.

So that at this electioneering time the whole of that division was alive with theatricals and "Every Man in his Humour," which was exactly what Sir Edward wanted.

It was an ordeal for some of us to rehearse with the celebrities of the stage, but I need not say their good-humour and delight in showing how this and that should be done, and how this and that should be spoken, was, I am sure, reciprocated by all the amateurs in studying the corrections. Never were lessons more kindly given, or received with more pleasurable surprise. Some could scarcely conceive how they could so blunder in accent and emphasis. However, most things require learning, even advocacy and acting.

Eliot Yorke was stage-manager, and wrote a very excellent prologue. It must have been good, it was so heartily applauded, and the same may be said of all of us. I think Radcliffe studied the part of Old Knowell, while I played Young Knowell. Speaking after this interval of many years, I believe we were all word-perfect and pretty well conscious of our respective duties. Charles Dickens arranged our costumes, while Nathan supplied them. He arranged me well. I was quite satisfied with my Elizabethan ruff wound round my throat, but must confess that it was a little uncomfortable for the first three or four hours. My hose also gave me great satisfaction and some little annoyance.

I thought if I could walk into court without changing my costume, what a sensation I should create! What would Campbell or Jervis say to *Young Knowell?*

My father, as I have mentioned, lived at Hitchin, about six miles from Knebworth, and my professional duties calling me so early to town, I arranged to sleep at Hitchin, and go to London by an early train in the morning. Sir Edward was much concerned at all this, and again wondered whether his library could not be appropriated. But the other was the only practicable plan, and was adopted. Every day I was in court by nine o'clock, sometimes worked till five, then went by rail to Stevenage and drove to Knebworth, three miles. That was the routine. It was then time to put on my Elizabethan ruff and hose. After the play I once more donned my private costume, and supped luxuriously at a round table, where all our splendid company were assembled.

After supper some of us used to retire to Douglas Jerrold's room in one of the towers, and there we spent a jovial evening, prolonging the entertainment until the small hours of the morning.

Then my fly, which had been waiting a long time, enabled me to reach Hitchin and get three hours' sleep.

All this was hard work, but I was really strong, and in the best of health, so that I enjoyed the labour as well as the pleasure. One cannot now conceive how it was possible to go through so much without breaking down. I attribute it, however, to the attendant excitement, which braced me up, and have always found that excitement will enable you to exceed your normal strength.

I had very many theatrical friends, all of them delightful in every way. Amongst them Wright and Paul Bedford. Such companions as these are not to be met with twice, each with his individuality, while the two in combination were incomparable. They kept one in a perpetual state of laughter. Paul was irresistible in his drollery, and whether it was mimicry or original humour, you could not but revel in its quaint conceits.

Such men are benefactors; they brighten the darkest hours of existence, turn sorrow into laughter, and enable men to forget their troubles and live a little while in the sunshine of humour. Banish philosophy if you please, banish ambition if you must banish something, but leave us *humour*, the light of the social world. All who have experienced its beautiful influence can appreciate its value, and understand it as one of the choicest blessings conferred on our existence.

The dullest company was enlivened when Wright entered upon the scene. I remember Paul being told one day at the Garrick Club that a certain poor barrister, who had been an actor, was going to marry the daughter of an old friend. "Ah!" said he, "yes, he's *a lover without spangles.*"

Who but Paul would have thought of so grotesque a simile? And yet its applicability was simply due to the language of the stage.

I remember Robson, too, and his wonderful acting; he had no rival. Nature had given him the talent which Art had cultivated to the highest perfection. Next come the Keelys' impersonations of every phase of dramatic life—originals in acting, and actors of originals.

But I must not linger over this portion of my story. It would occupy many pages, and time and space are limited; I therefore take my leave of one of the pleasantest chapters in my reminiscences.

All, alas! have passed away—all I knew and loved, all who made that time so happy; and reluctantly as I say it, it must be said: "Farewell, dear, grand old. Knebworth, with all thy glories and all the glad faces and merry hearts I met within your walls—a long, long, farewell!"

CHAPTER XXII.

CROCKFORD'S--"THE HOOKS AND EYES"--DOUGLAS JERROLD.

"Crockford's" has become a mere reminiscence, but worthy, in many respects, of being preserved as part of the history of London. It was historic in many of its associations as well as its incidents, and men who made history as well as those who wrote it met at Crockford's. It was celebrated alike for high play and high company.

As I never had a real passion for gambling, it was to me a place of great enjoyment, for there were some of the celebrated men of the day amongst its invited guests--wits, poets, novelists, playwrights, painters--in fact, all who had distinguished themselves in art or literature, law, science, or learning of any kind were always welcomed.

It was as pleasant a lounge as any in London, not excepting Tattersall's, which has equal claims on my memory. At Crockford's I met Captain H----, a wonderful gamester; he died early, but not too early for his welfare, seeing that all the chances of life are against the gambler. Padwick, too, I knew; he entertained with refined and lavish hospitality. He was one of the winners in the game of life who did not die early. He told good stories and put much interest into them. He knew Palmer, the Rugeley poisoner--a sporting man of the first water, who poisoned John Parsons Cook for the sake of his winnings, and his wife and mother, it was said, for the sake of the insurance on their lives. Padwick knew everybody's deeds and misdeeds who sought to increase his wealth on the turf or at the gaming-table. He was a just and honourable man, but without any sympathy for fools.

Others I could recall by the score, men of character and of no character. Some I knew afterwards professionally, and especially one, who, although convicted of crime, escaped by collusion the sentence justly passed upon him. Another was a man of position without character, whose evil habits destroyed the talent that would have made him famous.

But I need not dwell on the manifold characters and scenes of Crockford's. There has been nothing like it either in its origin or its subsequent history. There will never be anything like it in an age of refinement and laws, which have been wisely passed for the protection of fools.

The founder of this fashionable gambling place was at one time a small fishmonger in either the Strand or Fleet Street, I forget which, and lived there till he removed to St. James's Street, where he became a fisher of men, but never in any other than an honourable way.

"His Palace of Fortune" was of the grandest style of architectural beauty. It was one in which the worshippers of Fortune planked down the last acre of their patrimonial estates to propitiate the fickle goddess in the allurements of the gaming-table. But how *can* Fortune herself give two to one on all comers? Some *must* lose to pay the winners.

At this palatial abode the most sumptuous repasts were prepared by the most celebrated *chefs* the world could produce, and were eaten by the most fastidious and expensive gourmands Nature ever created; gamblers of the most distinguished and the most disreputable characters; gentlemen of the latest pattern and the oldest school, the worst of men and the best, sporting politicians and political sportsmen, place-hunters, Ministers, ex-Ministers, scions of old families and ancient pedigrees, as well as men of new families and no pedigrees, who purchased, as we do now, a coat of arms at the Heralds' tailoring shop, and selected their ancestors in Wardour Street.

Only the wealthy could be members of this club, for only the wealthy could lose money and pay it. Landscape painters might be guests, but it was only the man who belonged to the landscape who could belong to the body that gambled for it. Young barristers might visit the place, possibly with an eye to business, but only members of large practice or Judges could be members of this society.

Lord Palmerston defended it manfully before the committee appointed really for its destruction. He said it did a great deal of good--much more good than all the gambling hells of London did harm. Whether his lordship contended that there was no betting carried on at Crockford's I am not prepared to say, but when evidence is given before Parliamentary Committees it is sometimes difficult to understand its exact meaning. Palmerston, however, positively said, without any doubt as to his meaning, that candidates were not elected in order that they might be plucked of every feather they possessed, and that any one who maintained the contrary was slandering one of the most respectable clubs in London. Some men would rather have pulled down St. Paul's than Crockford's.

It was the very perfection of a club, said the statesman, and its principal game was chicken hazard. What could be stronger evidence than that of its usefulness and respectability? At this game they usually lost all they had, of little consequence to those who could not do better with their property, and perhaps the best thing for the country, because when it got into better hands it stood some chance of being applied to more legitimate purposes.

After a while Crockford quarrelled with his partner, and they separated.

Whatever men may say in these days against an institution which flourished in those, ex-Prime Ministers, Dukes, Earls, and ex-Lord Chancellors, as well as future Ministers of State and future Judges, belonged to it, or sought eagerly for admission to its membership. To be under the shadow of the fishmonger was greatness itself.

At the mention of the name of Crockford's a procession of the greatest men of the day passes before my eyes; their name would be legion as to numbers, but an army of devoted patriots I should call them in every other sense, for they were English to the backbone, whether gamblers or saints.

Of course there were some amongst them, as in every large body of men, who were not so desirable to know as you could wish; but they were easy to avoid and at all times an interesting study.

There were wise men and self-deluded fools, manly, well-bred men, and effeminate, conceited coxcombs, who wore stays and did up their back hair, used paint, and daubed their cheeks with violet powder. These men, while they had it, planked down their money with the longest possible odds against them. There was one who was the very opposite to these in the person of old Squire Osbaldistone. True, he had squandered more money than any one had ever seen outside the Bank of England, but he had done it like a gentleman and not like a fool. A real grand man was the old squire, and I enjoyed many a walk with him over Newmarket Heath, listening to his amusing anecdotes, his delightful humour and brilliant wit. His manner was so buoyant that no one could have believed he had spent hundreds of thousands of pounds, but he had, without compunction or regret.

The novelist and the painter could artistically describe Squire Osbaldistone. I can only say he was a "fine old English gentleman, one of the olden time." It was in a billiard-room at Leamington where I first met him, and as he was as indifferent a player as you could meet, he thought himself one of the best that ever handled a cue.

I neither played chicken hazard nor any other game, but enjoyed myself in seeing others play, and in picking up crumbs of knowledge which I made good use of in my profession.

The institution was not established for the benefit of science or literature, except that kind of literature which goes by the name of bookmaking. Its founder was a veritable dunce, but he was the cleverest of bookmakers, and made more by it in one night than all the authors of that day in their lives. One hundred thousand pounds in one night was not bad evidence of his calculation of chances and his general knowledge of mankind.

To be a member of this club, wealth was not the only qualification, because in time you would lose it; you had to be well born or distinguished in some other way. The fishmonger knew a good salmon by its appearance; he had also a keen respect for the man who had ancestors and ancestral estates.

I ought not to omit to mention another celebrated bookie of that day; he was second only to Crockford himself, and was called "The Librarian." He was also known as "Billy Sims."

Billy lived in St. James's Street, in a house which has long since been demolished, and thither people resorted to enjoy the idle, witty, and often scandalous gossip of the time. It was as easy to lose your reputation there as your money at Crockford's, and far more difficult to keep it. The only really innocent conversation was when a man talked about himself.

From that popular gossiping establishment I heard a little story told by the son of Sydney Smith. His father had been sent for to see an old lady who was one of his most troublesome parishioners. She was dying. Sad to say, she had always been querulous and quarrelsome. It may have been constitutional, but whatever the cause, her husband had had an uncomfortable time with her. When Sydney Smith reached the house the old lady was dead, and the bereaved widower, a religious man in his way, and acquainted with Scripture, said,--

"Ah, sir, you are too late: my poor dear wife has gone to *Abraham's bosom*."

"Poor Abraham!" exclaimed Sydney; "she'll tear his inside out."

As all these things pass through my memory, I recall another little incident with much satisfaction, because I was retained in the case. It was a scandalous fraud in connection with the gaming-table. An action was brought by a cheat against a gentleman who was said to have lost £20,000 on the cast of the dice. I was the counsel opposed to plaintiff, who was said to have cheated by means of *loaded dice*. I won the case, and it was generally believed that the action was the cause of the appointment of the "Gaming Committee," at which tribunal all the rascality of the gaming-tables was called to give evidence, and the witnesses did so in such a manner as to shock the conscience of the civilized world, which is never conscious of anything until exposure takes place in a court of law or in some other legal inquiry.

Diabolical revelations were brought to light. However, as I have said, Lord Palmerston effectually cleared Crockford's, and it almost seemed, from the evidence of those who knew Crockford's best, that they never played anything there but old-fashioned whist for threepenny points, patience, and beggar-my-neighbour.

His Royal Highness the then Prince of Wales came into court during the trial I refer to, and seemed interested in the proceedings. I wonder if his Majesty now remembers it!

In those days Baron Martin and I met once a year, he on the Bench and I in court, with a hansom cab waiting outside ready to start for the Derby. It is necessary for Judges to sit on Derby Day, to show that they do not go; but if by some accident the work of the court is finished in time to get down to Epsom, those who love an afternoon in the country sometimes go in the direction of the Downs. There is usually a run on the list on that day.

There was another club to which I belonged in those old days, called "The Hooks and Eyes," where I met for the last time poor Douglas Jerrold. He was one of the Eyes, and always on the lookout for a good thing, or the opportunity of saying one. He was certainly, in my opinion, the wittiest man of his day. But at times his wit was more hurtful than amusing. Wit should never leave a sting.

He was sometimes hard on those who were the objects of his personal dislike. Of these Sir Charles Taylor was one. He was not a welcome member of the Hooks and Eyes, and Jerrold knew it. There was really no reason why Sir Charles should not have been liked, except perhaps that he was dull and prosaic; rather simple than dull, perhaps, for he was always ready to laugh with the rest of us, whether he understood the joke or not. And what could the most brilliant do beyond that?

Sir Charles was fond of music. He mentioned in Jerrold's company on one occasion "that 'The Last Rose of Summer' so affected him that it quite carried him away."

"Can any one hum it?" asked Jerrold.

CHAPTER XXIII.

ALDERSON, TOMKINS, AND A FREE COUNTRY--A PROBLEM IN HUMAN NATURE.

Alderson was a very excellent man and a good Judge. I liked him, and could always deal with him on a level footing. He was quaint and original, and never led away by a false philanthropy or a sickly sentimentalism.

Appealed to on behalf of a man who had a wife and large family, and had been convicted of robbing his neighbours, "True," said Alderson--"very true, it is a free country. Nothing can be more proper than that a man should have a wife and a large family; it is his due--as many children as circumstances will permit. But, Tomkins, you have no right, even in a free country, to steal your neighbour's property to support them!"

I liked him where there was a weak case on the other side; he was particularly good on those occasions.

In the Assize Court at Chelmsford a barrister who had a great criminal practice was retained to defend a man for stealing sheep, a very serious offence in those days--one where anything less than transportation would be considered excessive leniency.

The principal evidence against the man was that the bones of the deceased animal were found in his garden, which was urged by the prosecuting counsel as somewhat strong proof of guilt, but not conclusive.

It must have struck everybody who has watched criminal proceedings that the person a prisoner has most to fear when he is tried is too often his own counsel, who may not be qualified by nature's certificate of capacity to defend. However, be that as it may, in this case there was no evidence against the prisoner, unless his counsel made it so.

"Counsel for the defence" in those days was a wrong description--he was called the *friend* of the prisoner; and I should conclude, from what I have seen of this relationship, that the adage "Save me from my friends" originated in this connection.

The friend of this prisoner, instead of insisting that there was no evidence, since no one could swear to the sheep bones when no man had ever seen them, endeavoured to explain away the cause of death, and thus, by a foolish concession, admitted their actual identity. It was not Alderson's duty to defend the prisoner against his own admission, although, but for that, he would have pointed out to the Crown how absolutely illogical their proposition was in law. But the "friend" of the prisoner suggested that sheep often put their heads through gaps or breakages in the hurdles, and rubbed their necks against the projecting points of the broken bars; and that being so, why should the jury not come to a verdict in favour of the prisoner on that ground? It was quite possible that the constant rubbing would ultimately cut the sheep's throat. If it did not, the prisoner submitted to the same operation at the hand of his "friend."

"Yes," said Baron Alderson, "that is a very plausible suggestion to start with; but having commenced your line of defence on that ground, you must continue it, and carry it to the finish; and to do this you must show that not only did this sheep in a moment of temporary insanity--as I suppose you would allege in order to screen it--commit suicide, but that it skinned itself and then buried its body, or what, was left of it after giving a portion to the prisoner to eat, in the prisoner's garden, and covered itself up in its own grave. You must go as far as that to make a complete defence of it. I don't say the jury may not believe you; we shall see. Gentlemen, what do you say--is the sheep or the prisoner guilty?" The sheep was instantly acquitted.

There was another display of forensic ingenuity by the same counsel in the next case, where he was once again the "friend" of the prisoner.

A man was charged with stealing a number of gold and silver coins which had been buried a few hours previously under the foundation-stone of a new public edifice.

The prisoner was one of the workmen, and had seen them deposited for the historical curiosity of future ages. Antiquity, of course, would be the essence of the value of the coins, except to the thief. The royal hand had covered them with the stone, duly tapped by the silver trowel amidst the hurrahs of the loyal populace, in which the prisoner heartily joined. But in the night he stole forth, and then stole the coins.

They were found at his cottage secreted in a very private locality, as though his conscience smote him or his fear sought to prevent discovery. His legal friend, however, driven from the mere outwork of facts, had taken refuge in the citadel of law; he was equal to the occasion. Alas! Alderson knew the way into this impregnable retreat.

Counsel suggested that it was never intended by those who placed the coins where they were found that they should remain there till the end of time; they were intended, said he, to be taken away by somebody, but by whom was not indicated by the depositors, and as no time or person was mentioned, they must belong to the first finder. It was all a mere chance as to the time of their resurrection. Further, it was certain they were not intended to be taken by their owners who had placed them there--they never expected to see them again--but by any one who happened to come upon them. Those who deposited them where they were found parted not only with the possession, but with all claims of ownership. Nor could any one representing him make any claim.

All this was excellent reasoning as far as it went, and the only thing the prosecution alleged by way of answer was that they were intended to be brought to light as antiquities.

"Very well," said the prisoner's counsel; "then there is no felonious intent in that case--it is merely a mistake. Antiquity came too soon."

And so did the conviction.

I was instructed, with the Hon. George Denman, son of my old friend, whom I have so often mentioned, to defend three persons at the Maidstone

Assizes for a cruel murder. Mr. Justice Wightman was the Judge, and there was not a better Judge of evidence than he, or of law either.

The prisoners were father, mother, and son, and the deceased was a poor servant girl who had been engaged to be married to another son of the male prisoner and his wife.

The unfortunate girl had left her service at Gravesend, and gone to this family on a visit. The prisoners, there could be no doubt, were open to the gravest suspicion, but how far each was concerned with the actual murder was uncertain, and possibly could never be proved.

The night before the trial the attorney who acted for the accused persons called on me, and asked this extraordinary question,--

"Could you secure the acquittal of the father and the son if the woman will plead guilty?"

It is impossible to conceive the amount of resolution and self-sacrifice involved in this attempt to save the life of her husband and son. It was too startling a proposal to listen to. I could advise no client to plead guilty to wilful murder. It was so extraordinary a proposition, look at it from whatever point I might, that it was perfectly impossible to advise such a course. I asked him if the woman knew what she was doing, and that if she pleaded guilty certain death would follow.

"Oh yes," said he; "she is quite prepared."

"The murder," I said, "is one of the worst that can be conceived--cruel and fiendish."

He agreed, but persisted that she was perfectly willing to sacrifice her own life if her husband and son could be saved.

This woman, so full of feeling for her own family, had thought so little of that of others that she had held down the poor servant girl in bed while her son strangled her.

"If," said I, "she were to plead guilty, the great probability is that the jury would believe they were all guilty--very probably they are; and most certainly in that case they would all be hanged." I therefore strongly advised that the woman should stand her trial "with the others," which she did. In the end they all *got off*! the evidence not being sufficiently clear against any.

It was a strange mingling of evil and good in one breast--of diabolical cruelty and noble self-sacrifice.

I leave others to work out this problem of human nature.

CHAPTER XXIV.

CHARLES MATHEWS--A HARVEST FESTIVAL AT THE VILLAGE CHURCH.

The sporting world has no greater claim on my memory than the theatrical or the artistic. I recall them with a vividness that brings back all the enjoyments of long and sincere friendships. For instance, one evening I was in Charles Mathews's dressing-room at the theatre and enjoying a little chat when he was "called."

"Come along," said he; "come along."

Why he should "call" me to come along I never knew. I had no part in the piece at that moment. But he soon gave me one. I followed, with lingering steps and slow, having no knowledge of the construction of the premises; but in a moment Mathews had disappeared, and I found myself in the middle of the stage, with a crowded house in front of me. The whole audience burst into an uproar of laughter. I suppose it was the incompatibility of my appearance at that juncture which made me "take" so well; but it brought down the house, and if the curtain had fallen at that moment, I should have been a great success, and Mathews would have been out of it. In the midst of my discomfiture, however, he came on to the stage by another entrance as "cool as a cucumber." He told me afterwards that he had turned the incident to good account by referring to me as "Every man in his humour," or, "A bailiff in distressing circumstances!"

I was visiting the country house of a respectable old solicitor, who was instructing me in a "compensation case" which was to be heard at Wakefield.

"I don't know, Mr. Hawkins," said he on Sunday morning, "whether you would like to see our little church?"

"No, thank you," I answered; "we can have a look at it to-morrow when we have a 'view of the premises.'"

"I thought, perhaps," said Mr. Goodman, "you might like to attend the service."

"No," said I, "not particularly; a walk under the 'broad canopy' is preferable on a beautiful morning like this to a poky little pew; and I like the singing of the birds better than the humming of a clergyman's nose.

"Very well," he said; "we will, if you like, take a little walk."

With surprising innocence he inflicted upon me a pious fraud, leading me over fields and meadows, stiles and rustic bridges, until at last the cunning old fox brought me out along a by-path and over a plank bridge right into the village. Then turning a corner near a picturesque farmhouse, he smilingly observed, "This is our church."

"It's a very old one, and looks much more picturesque in the distance. Shall we have a view a little farther off?"

"St. Mary's," said he; "1694 is the date--"

"St. Mary's?" said I. "Fancy! And what is the date--1694?"

"It has some fine tablets, Mr. Hawkins, if you'd like to look in--"

"I don't care for tablets," I answered; "if I go to church it is not to stare at tablets."

At last my host summed up courage to say,--

"Mr. Hawkins, this is our little harvest festival of thanksgiving, and I should not like to be absent."

"Why on earth, Mr. Goodman," I answered, "did you not say that before? Let us go in by all means. I like a good harvest as well as any Christian on earth."

The pew was the family pew--the *whole family pew*, and nothing but the family pew; bought with the estate, with the family estate; and was in an excellent situation for the congregation to have a fine view of Mr. Goodman. Indeed, his cheery face could be seen by everybody in church.

I must say the little edifice looked very nice, and had been adorned with the most artistic taste by the young ladies of the Vicarage and the Hall. Mr. Goodman was "the Hall." There were bunches of neatly-arranged turnips and carrots, with potatoes, barley, oats, and mangel-wurzel, and almost every variety of fruit from the little village; and every girl had barley and wheat-ears in her straw hat. It was an affecting sight, calculated to make any one adore the young ladies and long for dinner.

The sermon was an excellent one so far as I could pronounce an opinion, but would have been considerably improved had it been three-quarters of an hour shorter. It contained, however, the usual allusions to harvest-homes, gathering into barns, and laying up treasures; which last observation reminded Mr. Goodman that he had *left his purse at home*, and had come away without any money.

I saw him fumbling in his pocket. Now, thought I, the time has come for showing my devotion to Mr. Goodman. As soon, therefore, as he had whispered to me, I handed him all I had, which consisted of a five-pound note. He gratefully took it, and although about five times as much as *he* intended to give, when the bag was handed to him in went the five-pound note.

I knew my friend was chuckling as soon as we got into his family pew at the way in which he had lured me step by step, till we walked the last plank over the ditch, so I was not sorry to return good for evil and lend him my note.

He stared somewhat sideways at me when the bag passed, but I bore it with fortitude. I took particular notice that the crimson bag passed along the front of our family pew at a very dilatory pace, and tarried a good deal, as if reluctant to leave it. To and fro it passed in front of my nose as if it contained something I should like to smell, and at last moved away altogether. I was glad of that, because it prevented my following the words of the hymn in my book, and, unfortunately, it was one of those harvest hymns I did not know by heart.

On our way home over the meadows, where the grasshoppers were practising for the next day's sports, and were in high glee over this harvest festival, Mr. Goodman seemed fidgety; whether conscience-stricken for the Sabbath fraud he had practised upon me or not, I could not say, but at last he asked how I liked their little service.

I said it was quite large enough.

"You"--he paused--"you did not, I think"--another pause--"contribute to our little gathering?"

"No," I said, "but it was not my fault; I lent you all I had. The fund, however, will not suffer in the least, and you have the satisfaction of having contributed the whole of our joint pocket-money. It does not matter who the giver is so long as the fund obtains it." I then diverted his mind with a story or two.

Cockburn, I said, was sitting next to Thesiger during a trial before Campbell, Chief Justice, in which the Judge read some French documents, and, being a Scotsman, it attracted a good deal of attention. Cockburn, who was a good French scholar, was much annoyed at the Chief Justice's pronunciation of the French language.

"He is murdering it," said he--"*murdering* it!"

"No, my dear Cockburn," answered Thesiger, "he is not killing it, only Scotching it."

Sir Alexander was at a little shooting-party with Bethell and his son, one of whom shot the gamekeeper. The father accused the son of the misadventure, while the son returned the compliment. Cockburn, after some little time, asked the gamekeeper what was the real truth of the unfortunate incident--who was the gentleman who had inflicted the injury?

The gamekeeper, still smarting from his wounds, and forgetting the respect due to the questioner, answered,--

"O Sir Alexander--d--n 'em, it was *both*!"

A remark made by Lord Young, the Scotch Judge, one of the wittiest men who ever adorned the Bar, and who is a Bencher of the Middle Temple, struck me as particularly happy. There was a conversation about the admission of solicitors to the roll, and the long time it took before they were eligible to pass from their stage of pupilage to that of solicitor, amounting, I think, to seven years; upon which Lord Young said, "*Nemo repente fuit turpissimus.*"

CHAPTER XXV.

COMPENSATION--NICE CALCULATIONS IN OLD DAYS--EXPERTS--LLOYD AND I.

As my business continued to increase, it took me more and more from the ordinary *nisi prius*, and kept me perpetually employed in special matters. I had a great many compensation cases, where houses, lands, and businesses had been taken for public or company purposes. They were interesting and by no means difficult, the great difficulty being to get the true value when you had, as I have known, a hundred thousand pounds asked on one side and ten thousand offered on the other.

Railway companies were especially plundered in the exorbitant valuation of lands, and therefore an advocate who could check the valuers by cross-examination was sought after. Juries were always liable to be imposed upon, and generally gave liberal compensation, altogether apart from the market value. Experts, such as land agents and surveyors, were always in request, and indeed these experts in value caused the most extravagant amounts to be awarded. Even the mean sum between highest and lowest was a monstrously unfair guide, for one old expert used to instruct his pupils that the only true principle in estimating value was to ask at least twice as much as the business or other property was worth, because, he said, the other side will be sure to try and cut you down one-half, and then probably offer to split the difference. If you accept that, you will of course get one-quarter more than you could by stating what you really wanted. No one could deal with the real value, because there was no such thing known in the Compensation Court.

On one occasion I was travelling north in connection with one of these cases, retained, as usual, on behalf of a railway company. In my judgment the claim would have been handsomely met by an award of £10,000, and that sum we were prepared to give.

On my way I observed in my carriage a gentleman who was very busy in making calculations on slips of paper, and every now and again mentioning the figures at which he had arrived--repeating them to himself. When we got to a station he threw away his paper, after tearing it up, and when we started commenced again, but at every stoppage on our journey he increased his amount. After we had travelled 250 miles, the property he was valuing had attained the handsome figure of £100,000.

He evidently had not observed me. I was very quiet, and well wrapped up. The next day, when he stepped into the witness-box he had not the least idea that I had been his fellow-traveller of the previous night. He was not very sharp except in the matter of figures; but his opinion, like that of all experts, was invincible. His name was Bunce.

"When did you view this property, Mr. Bunce? I understand you come from London."

"I saw it this morning, sir."

"Did you make any calculation as to its value *before* you saw it?"

This puzzled him, and he stared at me. It was a hard stare, but I held out.

He said, "No."

"Not when you were travelling? Did it not pass through your mind when you were in the train, for instance--'I wonder, now, what that property is worth?'"

"I dare say it did, sir."

"But don't *dare say* anything unless it's true."

"I did, then, run it over in my mind."

"And I dare say you made notes and can produce them. Did you make notes?" After a while I said, "I see you did. You may as well let me have them."

"I tore them up."

"Why? What became of the pieces?"

"I threw them away."

"Do you remember what price you had arrived at when you reached Peterborough, for instance?"

The expert thought I was some one whom we never mention except when in a bad temper, and he was more and more puzzled when he found that at every stoppage I knew how much his price had increased.

As the case was tried by an arbitrator and not a jury, my task was easy, arbitrators not being so likely to be befooled as the other form of tribunal. This arbitrator, especially, knew the elasticity of an expert's opinion, and therefore I was not alarmed for my client. The amount was soon arrived at by reducing the sum claimed by no less than £90,000. Thus vanished the visionary claim and the expert. He evidently had not been trained by the cunning old surveyor whose experience taught him to be moderate, and ask only twice as much as you ought to get.

In another claim, which was no less than £10,000, the jury gave £300. This was a state of things that had to be stopped, and it could only be accomplished at that time by counsel who appeared on behalf of the companies.

Sir Henry Hunt was one of the best of arbitrators, and it was difficult to deceive him. It took a clever expert to convince him that a piece of land whose actual value would be £100 was worth £20,000.

Sir Henry once paid me a compliment--of course, I was not present.

"Hawkins," said he, "is the very best advocate of the day, and, strange to say, his initials are the same as mine. You may turn them upside down and they will still stand on their legs" (H.H.).

Sir Henry was sometimes a witness, and as such always dangerous to the side against whom he was called, because he was a judge of value and a man of honour.

One instance in which I took a somewhat novel course in demolishing a fictitious claim is, perhaps, worth while to relate, although so many years have passed since it occurred.

It was so far back as the time of the old Hungerford Market, which the railway company was taking for their present Charing Cross terminus. The question was as to the value of a business for the sale of medical appliances.

Mr. Lloyd, as usual, was for the business, while I appeared for the company. My excellent friend proceeded on the good old lines of compensation advocacy with the same comfortable routine that one plays the old family rubber of threepenny points. I occasionally finessed, however, and put my opponent off his play. He held good hands, but if I had an occasionally bad one, I sometimes managed to save the odd trick.

Lloyd had expatiated on the value of the situation, the highroad between Waterloo Station and the Strand, immense traffic and grand frontage. To prove all this he called a multitude of witnesses, who kissed the same book and swore the same thing almost in the same words. But to his great surprise I did not cross-examine. Lloyd was bewildered, and said I had admitted the value by not cross-examining, and he should not call any more witnesses.

I then addressed the jury, and said, "A multitude of witnesses may prove anything they like, but my friend has started with an entirely erroneous view of the situation. The compensation for disturbance of a business must depend a great deal on the nature of the business. If you can carry it on elsewhere with the same facility and profit, the compensation you are entitled to is very little. I will illustrate my meaning. Let us suppose that in this thoroughfare there is a good public-house--for such a business it would indeed be an excellent situation; you may easily imagine a couple of burly farmers coming up from Farnham or Windlesham to the Cattle Show, and walking over the bridge, hot and thirsty. 'Hallo!' says one; 'I say, Jim, here's a nice public; what d'ye say to goin' in and havin' a glass o' bitter? It's a goodish pull over this 'ere bridge."

"'With all my heart,' says Jim; and in they go.

"There you see the advantage of being on the highroad. But now, let us see these two stalwart farmers coming along, and--instead of the handsome public and the bitter ale there is this shop, where they sell medical arrangements--can you imagine one of them saying to the other, 'I say, Jim, here's a very nice medical shop; what d'ye say to going in and having a truss?'"

The argument considerably reduced the compensation, but what it lacked in money the claimant got in laughter.

Sometimes I led a witness who was an expert valuer for a claimant to such a gross exaggeration of the value of a business as to stamp the claim with fraud, and so destroy his evidence altogether.

Sir Henry Hunt used to nod with apparent approval at every piece of evidence which showed any kind of exaggeration, but every nod was worth, as a rule, a handsome reduction to the other side.

I shall never forget an attorney's face who, having been offered £10,000 for a property, stood out for £13,000.

It was a claim by a poulterers' company for eight houses that were taken by a railway company. I relied entirely on my speech, as I often did, because the threadbare cross-examinations were almost, by this time, things of course, as were the figures themselves mere results of true calculations on false bases.

This attorney, who had, perhaps, never had a compensation case before, was quite a great man, and took the arbitrator's assenting nods as so much cash down.

So encouraged, indeed, was he that he became almost impudent to me, and gave me no little annoyance by his impertinent asides. At last I looked at him good-humouredly, and politely requested him, as though he were the court itself, to suspend his judgment while I had the honour of addressing the arbitrator for twenty minutes, "at the end of which time I promise to make you, sir," said I, "the most miserable man in existence."

I was supported in this appeal by the arbitrator, who hoped he would not interrupt Mr. Hawkins.

As I proceeded the attorney fidgeted, puffed out his cheeks, blew out his breath, twirled his thumbs as I twirled my figures, and grated his teeth as he looked at me sideways, while I concluded a little peroration I had got up for him, which was merely to this effect, that if railway companies yielded to such extortionate demands as were made by this attorney on behalf of the poulterers' company, they would not leave their shareholders a feather to fly with.

The attorney looked very much like moulting himself, and the end of it was that he got *two thousand pounds* less than we had offered him in the morning, and consequently had to pay all the costs.

As I have stated, John Horatio Lloyd was my principal opponent in these great public works cases, and I remember him with every feeling of respect. He was an advocate whom no opponent could treat lightly, and was uniformly kind and agreeable.

Of course I had a very large experience in those times--I suppose, without vanity, I may say the very largest. I was retained to assess compensation for the immense blocks of buildings acquired for the space now occupied by the Law Courts. In the very early cases the law. officers of the Crown were concerned, but after that the whole of the business was entrusted to my care, although for reasons best known to themselves the Commissioners declined to send me a general retainer, which would have been one small sum for the whole, but gave instead a special retainer on every case. If my memory serves me, on one occasion I had ninety-four of these special retainers delivered at my chambers. This was in consequence of their refusing to retain me generally for the whole, which would have been a nominal fee of five guineas.

CHAPTER XXVI.

ELECTION PETITIONS.

Another class of work which gave me much pleasure and interest was that of election petitions. These came in such abundance that I had to put on, as I thought, a prohibitory fee, which in reality increased the volume of my labour.

One day Baron Martin asked me if I was coming to such and such an election petition.

"No," I answered, "no; I have put a prohibitory fee on my services; I can't be bothered with election petitions."

"How much have you put on?"

"Five hundred guineas, and two hundred a day."

The Baron laughed heartily. "A prohibitory fee! They must have you, Hawkins--they must have you. Put on what you like; make it high enough, and they'll have you all the more."

And I did. It turned out a very lucrative branch of my business, and my electioneering expenses were a good investment. My experience at Barnstaple, to be told hereafter, repaid the outlay, and no feature of an election ever came before me but I recognized a family likeness.

Amongst the earliest was that of W.H. Smith, who had been returned for Westminster. The petitioner endeavoured to unseat him on the ground of bribery, alleged to have been committed in paying large sums of money for exhibiting placards on behalf of the candidate. It was tried before Baron Martin.

About the payments there was no element of extravagance, but there were undoubtedly many cases of payment, and these were alleged to be illegal.

Ballantine was my junior. One of the curious matters in the case was that these payments had been principally made by, or under, the advice of my old friend, whom I cannot mention too often, the Hon. Robert Grimston.

Ballantine, as I thought, most injudiciously advised me not to call "that old fool;" but believing in Grimston, and having charge of the case, I resolved to call him. Baron Martin knew Grimston as well as I did, and believed in him as much.

"Who is this?" asked the Judge.

"Another bill-sticker, my lord."

Grimston gave his evidence, and was severely cross-examined by my friend, J. Fitzjames Stephen. He fully and satisfactorily explained every one of the questioned items, evidently to the satisfaction of Martin, who dismissed the petition, and thus Mr. Smith retained his seat.

The learned Judge said, in giving judgment, that without Grimston's evidence the seat would have been in great danger, but that he had put an innocent colour on the whole case, and that, knowing him to be an honourable man and incapable of saying anything but the truth, he had implicitly trusted to every word he spoke.

Mr. Smith, whom I met some days after, said he was perfectly assured that if I had not had the conduct of the case, and Grimston had not been called, his seat would have been lost.

In the petition against Sir George Elliot for Durham there was nothing of any importance in the case, except that Sir George gave a very interesting history of his life.

He had been a poor boy who had worked in the cutting of the pit, lying on his back and picking out from the roof overhead the coal which was shovelled into the truck. From this humble position literally and socially he had proceeded, first to his feet, and then step by step, until, from one grade to another, he had amassed a large fortune, and sufficient income to enable him to incur, not only the expenses of an election and a seat in Parliament, but also those of a bitterly hostile election petition, enormously extravagant in every way. I succeeded in winning his case, and never was more proud of a victory. It had lasted many days.

There is one matter almost of a historical character, which I mention in order to do all the justice in my power to a man who, although deserving of reprobation, is also entitled to admiration for the chivalry of his true nature. I speak of it with some hesitation, and therefore without the name. Those who are interested in his memory will know to whom I allude, and possibly be grateful for the tribute to his character, however much it may have been sullied by his temporary absence of manly discretion.

He was charged with assaulting a young lady in a railway train between Aldershot and Waterloo. There was much of the melodramatic in the incidents, and much of the righteous indignation of the public before trial. There was judgment and condemnation in every virtuous mind. The assault alleged was doubtless of a most serious character, if proved. I say nothing of what might have been proved or not proved; but, speaking as an advocate, I will not hesitate to affirm that cross-examination may sometimes save one person's character without in the least affecting that of another.

But this was not to be. Whatever line of defence my experience might have suggested, I was debarred by his express command from putting a single question.

I say to his honour that, as a gentleman and a British officer, he preferred to take to himself the ruin of his own character, the forfeiture of his commission in the army, the loss of social status, and *all* that could make life worth having, to casting even a doubt on the lady's veracity in the witness-box.

My instructions crippled me, but I obeyed my client, of course, implicitly in the letter and the spirit, even though to some extent he may have entailed upon himself more ignominy and greater severity of punishment than I felt he deserved.

He died in Egypt, never having been reinstated in the British army. I knew but little of him until this catastrophe occurred; but the manliness of his defence showed him to be naturally a man of honour, who, having been guilty of serious misconduct, did all he could to amend the wrong he had done; and so he won my sympathy in his sad misfortune and misery.

In the days when burglary was punished with death, there was very seldom any remission, I was in court one day at Guildford, when a respectably-dressed man in a velveteen suit of a yellowy green colour and pearl buttons came up to me. He looked like one of Lord Onslow's gamekeepers. I knew nothing of him, but seemed to recognize his features as those of one I had seen before. When he came in front of my seat he grinned with immense satisfaction, and said,--

"Can I get you anything, Mr. Orkins?"

I could not understand the man's meaning.

"No, thank you," I said. "What do you mean?"

"Don't you recollect, sir, you defended me at Kingston for a burglary charge, and got me off., Mr. Orkins, in flyin' colours?"

I recollected. He seemed to have the flying colours on his lips. "Very well," I said; "I hope you will never want defending again."

"No, sir; never."

"That's right."

"Would a *teapot* be of any use to you, Mr. Orkins?"

"A teapot!"

"Yes, sir, or a few silver spoons--anything you like to name, Mr. Orkins."

I begged him to leave the court.

"Mr. Orkins, I will; but I am grateful for your gettin' me off that job, and if a piece o' plate will be any good, I'll guarantee it's good old family stuff as'll fetch you a lot o' money some day."

I again told him to go, and, disappointed at my not accepting things of greater value, he said,--

"Sir, will a sack o' taters be of any service to you?"

This sort of gratitude was not uncommon in those days. I told the story to Mr. Justice Wightman, and he said,--

"Oh, that's nothing to what happened to the Common Serjeant of London. He had sent to him once a Christmas hamper containing a hare, a brace and a half of pheasants, three ducks, and a couple of fowls, which *he accepted*."

I sometimes won a jury over by a little good-natured banter, and often annoyed Chief Justice Campbell when I woke him up with laughter. And yet he liked me, for although often annoyed, he was never really angry. He used to crouch his head down over his two forearms and go to sleep, or pretend to, by way of showing it did not matter what I said to the jury. I dare say it was disrespectful, but I could not help on these occasions quietly pointing across my shoulder at him with my thumb, and that was enough. The jury roared, and Campbell looked up,--

"What's the joke, Mr. Hawkins?"

"Nothing, my lord; I was only saying I was quite sure your lordship would tell the jury exactly what I was saying."

"Go on, Mr. Hawkins--"

Then he turned to his clerk and said,--

"I shall catch him one of these days. Confine yourself to the issue, Mr. Hawkins."

"If your lordship pleases," said I, and went on.

The eccentricities of Judges would form a laughable chapter. Some of them were overwhelmed with the importance of their position; none were ever modest enough to perceive their own small individuality amidst their judicial environments; and this thought reminds me of an occurrence at Liverpool Assizes, when Huddlestone and Manisty, the two Judges on circuit, dined as usual with the Lord Mayor. The Queen's health was proposed, of course, and Manisty, with his innate good breeding, stood up to drink it, whereupon his august brother Judge pulled him violently by his sleeve, saying, "Sit down, Manisty, you damned fool! *we* are the Queen!"

I was addressing a jury for the plaintiff in a breach of promise case, and as the defendant had not appeared in the witness-box, I inadvertently called attention to an elderly well-dressed gentleman in blue frock-coat and brass buttons--a man, apparently, of good position. The jury looked at him and then at one another as I said how shameful it was for a gentleman to brazen it out in the way the defendant did--ashamed to go into the witness-box, but not ashamed to sit in court.

Here the gentleman rose in a great rage amidst the laughter of the audience, in which even the ushers and javelin-men joined, to say nothing of the Judge himself, and shouted with angry vociferation,--

"Mr. Hawkins, I am *not* the defendant in this case, Sir ----"

"I am very sorry for you," I replied; "but no one said you were."

There was another outburst, and the poor gentleman gesticulated, if possible, more vehemently than before.

"I am not the def--"

"Nobody would have supposed you were, sir, if you had not taken so much trouble to deny it. The jury, however, will now judge of it."

"I am a married man, sir."

"So much the worse," said I.

CHAPTER XXVII.

MY CANDIDATURE FOR BARNSTAPLE.

Although the House of Commons dislikes lawyers, constituencies love them. The enterprising patriots of the long robe are everywhere sought after, provided they possess, with all their other qualifications, the one thing needful, and possessing which, all others may be dispensed with.

Barnstaple was no exception to the rule. It had a character for conspicuous discernment, and, like the unseen eagle in the sky, could pick out at any distance the object of its desire.

Eminent, respectable, and rich must be the qualification of any candidate who sought its suffrages--the last, at all events, being indispensable.

Up to this time I had not felt those patriotic yearnings which are manifested so early in the legal heart. I was never a political adventurer; I had no eye on Parliament merely as a stepping-stone to a judgeship; and probably, but for the events I am about to describe, I should never have been heard of as a politician at all. There were so many candidates in the profession to whom time was no object that I left this political hunting-ground entirely to them.

In 1865 I was waited upon at Westminster by a very influential deputation from the Barnstaple electors--honest-looking electors as any candidate could wish to see--bringing with them a requisition signed by almost innumerable independent electors, and stating that there were a great many more of the same respectable class who would have signed had time been permitted. Further signatures were, however, to be forwarded. It was urged by the deputation that I should make my appearance at Barnstaple at the earliest possible date, as no time was to be lost, and they were most anxious to hear my views, especially upon topics that they knew more about than I, which is generally the case, I am told, in most constituencies. I asked when they thought I ought to put in an appearance.

"Within a week at latest," said the leading spirit of the deputation. "Within a week at latest," repeated all the deputation in chorus." Because," said the leading personage, "there is already a gentleman of the name of Cave" (it should have been pronounced as two syllables, so as to afford me some sort of warning of the danger I was confronting) "busily canvassing in all directions for the Liberal party, and Mr. Howell Gwynne and Sir George Stukely will be the Conservative candidates. However, it would be a certain seat if I would do them the honour of coming forward. There would be little trouble, and it would almost be a walk-over."

A walk-over was very nice, and the tantalizing hopes this deputation inspired me with overcame my great reluctance to enter the field of politics; and in that ill-advised moment I promised to allow myself to be nominated.

It was arranged that I should make my appearance by a specified afternoon train on a particular day in the week (apparently to be set apart as a public holiday), so that I had little time for preparation. By the next day's post I received a kind of official communication from "our committee," stating that a very substantial deputation from the general body would have the honour to meet me at the station, and accompany me to the committee-rooms for the purpose of introduction.

Down, therefore, I went by the Great Western line, and in due time arrived at my destination, as I thought.

I found, instead of the "influential body of gentlemen" who were to have the honour of conducting me to the headquarters of the Liberal party, there was only a small portion of it, almost too insignificant to admit of counting. But he was an important personage in uniform, and dressed somewhat like a commissionaire.

After much salutation and deferential hemming and stammering, he said I had better proceed to *a little station only a few miles farther on and dine*, "and if so be I'd do that, they would meet me in the evening."

Not being a professional politician, nor greatly ambitious of its honours, I was somewhat disconcerted at such extraordinary conduct on the part of my committee, and would have returned to town, but that the train was going the wrong way, and by the time I reached the little station I had argued the matter out, as I thought. It *might* be a measure of precaution, in a constituency so respectable as Barnstaple, to prevent the least suspicion of *treating* or corrupt influence. Had I dined at Barnstaple it might have been suggested that some one dined with me or drank my health. Whatever it was, the revelation was not yet.

I was to return "as soon as I had dined." Everything was to be ready for my reception.

All these instructions I obeyed with the greatest loyalty, and returned at an early hour in the evening. But if I was disappointed at my first reception, how was I elated by the second! All was made up for by good feeling and enthusiasm. We were evidently all brothers fighting for the sacred cause, but what the cause was I had not been informed up to this time.

At the station was a local band of music waiting to receive me, and to strike up the inspiring air, "See the conquering hero comes;" but, unfortunately, the band consisted only of a drum, of such dimensions that I thought it must have been built for the occasion, and a clarionet.

Before the band struck up, however, I was greeted with such enthusiastic outbursts that they might have brought tears into the eyes of any one less firm than myself. "Orkins for ever!" roared the multitude. It almost stunned me. Never could I have dreamt my popularity would be so great. "Orkins for ever!" again and again they repeated, each volley, if possible, louder than before. "Bravo, Orkins! Let 'em 'ave it, Orkins! don't spare 'em." I wish I had known what this meant.

I must say they did all that mortals could do with their mouths to honour their future member.

Hogarth's "March to Finchley" was outdone by that march to the Barnstaple town hall. An enormous body of electors, "free and independent" stamped on their faces as well as their hands, was gathered there, and it was a long time before we could get anywhere near the door.

Again and again the air was rent with the cries for "Orkins," and it was perfectly useless for the police to attempt to clear the way. They had me as if on show, and it was only by the most wonderful perseverance and good luck that I found myself going head first along the corridor leading to the hall itself.

When I appeared on the platform, it seemed as if Barnstaple had never seen such a man; they were mad with joy, and all wanted to shake hands with me at once. I dodged a good many, and by dint of waving his arms like a semaphore the chairman succeeded, not in restoring peace, but in moderating the noise.

I now had an opportunity of using my eyes, and there before me in one of the front seats was the redoubtable Cave--the great canvassing Cave--who instantly rose and gave me the most cordial welcome, trusted I was to be his future colleague in the House, and was most generous in his expressions of admiration for the people of Barnstaple, especially the voting portion of them, and hoped I should have a very pleasant time and never forget dear old Barnstaple. I said I was not likely to--nor am I.

Of course I had to address the assembled electors first after the introduction by the chairman, who, taking a long time to inform us what the electors *wanted*, I made up my mind what to say in order to convince them that they should have it. I gave them hopes of a great deal of legal reform and reduction of punishments, for I thought that would suit most of them best, and then gladly assented to a satisfactory adjustment of all local requirements and improvements, as well as a determined redress of grievances which should on no account be longer delayed. ("Orkins for ever!")

Then Cave stood up--an imposing man, with a good deal of presence and shirt-collar--who invited any man--indeed, *challenged* anybody--in that hall to question him on any subject whatever.

The challenge was accepted, and up stood one of the rank and file of the electors--no doubt sent by the Howell Gwynne party--and with a voice that showed at least he meant to be heard, said,--

"Mr. Cave, first and foremost of all, I should like to know *how your missus is to-day*?"

It was scarcely a political or public question, but nobody objected, and everybody roared with laughter, because it seemed at all political meetings Cave had started the fashion, which has been adopted by many candidates since that time, of referring *to his wife*! Cave always began by saying he could never go through this ordeal without the help and sympathy of his dear wife--his support and joy--at whose bidding and in pursuit of whose dreams he had come forward to win a seat in their uncorruptible borough, and to represent them--the most coveted honour of his life--in the House of Commons.

Of course this oratory, having a religious flavour, took with a very large body of the Barnstaple electors, and was always received with cheers as an encouragement to domestic felicity and faithfulness to connubial ties.

When this gentleman put the question, Cave answered as though it was asked in real earnest, and was cheered to the echo, not merely for his domestic felicity, but his cool contempt for any man who could so far forget connubial bliss as to sneer at it.

For a few days all went tolerably well, and then I was told that a very different kind of influence prevailed in the borough than that of religion or political morality, and that it would be perfectly hopeless to expect to win the seat unless I was prepared to purchase the large majority of electors; indeed, that I must buy almost every voter. (That's what they meant by "Give it 'em, Orkins! Let 'em 'ave it!")

This I refused to believe; but it was said they were such free and independent electors that they would vote for *either* party, and you could not be sure of them until the last moment; in fact, *if I would win I must bribe*! to say nothing of all sorts of subscriptions to cricket clubs and blanket clubs, as well as friendly societies of all kinds.

I declined to accept these warnings, and looked upon it as some kind of political dodge got up by the other side.

I resolved to win by playing the game, and made up my mind to go to the poll on the political questions which were agitating the public mind, as I was informed, by a simple honest candidature, thinking that in political as in every other warfare honesty is the best policy. On that noble maxim I entered into the contest, believing in Barnstaple, and feeling confident I should represent it in Parliament.

To indulge in bribery of any sort would, I knew, be fatal to my own interests even if I had not been actuated by any higher motive. I placed myself, therefore, in the hands of my friend and principal agent, Mr. Kingston, as well as the other agents of the party.

We did not long, however, remain true to ourselves. There was a hitch somewhere which soon developed into a split; and it was certain some of us must go to the wall. I could not, however, understand the reason of it; we professed the same politics, the same "cause," the same battle-cry, the same enemies. But, whatever it was, we were so much divided that my chances of heading the poll were diminishing.

I had been cheered to the echo night after night and all day long, so that there was enough shouting to make a Prime Minister; my horses had time after time been taken from my carriage, and cheering voters drew me along. These unmistakable signs of popular devotion to my interests had been most encouraging; and as they shouted themselves hoarse for me, I talked myself hoarse for them. We had a mutual hoarseness for each other. Everything looked like success; everything *sounded* like success; and night after night out came drum and clarionet to do their duty manfully in drumming me to my hotel.

It had been a remarkable success; everybody said so. Most of them declared solemnly they had never seen anything like it. They pronounced it a record popularity. I thought it was because the good people had selected me as their candidate on independent and purity of election principles. This explanation gave them great joy, and they cheered with extra enthusiasm for their own virtue. Judge, then, my surprise a short while after, when, notwithstanding the firm principles upon which we had proceeded, and by which my popularity was secured, I began to perceive that *money was the only thing they wanted*! Their uncorruptible nature yielded, alas! to the lowering influence of that deity.

It was at first a little mysterious why they should have postponed their demands--secret and silent--until almost the last moment; but the fact is, a large section of my party were dissatisfied with the voluntary nature of their services; they declined to work for nothing, and having shown me that the prize--that is, the seat--was mine, they determined to let me know it must be paid for. A large number of my voters would do nothing; they kept their hands in their pockets because they could not get them into mine.

This was no longer a secret, but on the eve of the election was boldly put forward as a demand, and I was plainly told that £500 distributed in small sums would make my election sure.

As, however, in no circumstances would I stoop to their offer, this demand did not in the least influence me--I never wavered in my resolution, and refused to give a farthing. Furthermore, showing the web in which they sought to entangle me, the same voice that suggested the £500 also informed me that I was closely watched by a couple of detectives set on by the other side.

I was well aware that the "other side" had given five-pound notes for votes, but I could neither follow the example nor use the information, as it was told me "in the strictest confidence."

I was therefore powerless, and felt we were drifting asunder more and more. At last came the polling day, and a happy relief from an unpleasant situation it certainly was.

A fine bright morning ushered in an exciting day. There was a great inrush of voters at the polling-booth, friendly votes, if I may call them so--votes, I mean to say, of honest supporters; these were my acquaintances made during my sojourn at Barnstaple; others came, a few for Cave as well as myself. Cave did not seem to enjoy the popularity that I had achieved. Still, he got a few votes.

Now came an exciting scene. About midday, the working man's dinner hour, the tide began to turn, for the whole body of *bribed* voters were released from work. My majority quickly dwindled, and at length disappeared, until I was in a very hopeless minority. Everywhere it was "Stukely for ever!" Some cried, "Stukely and free beer!" Stukely, who till now had hardly been anybody, and had not talked himself hoarse in their interests as I had, was the great object of their admiration and their hopes.

The consequence of this sudden development of Stukely's popularity was that Cave united his destiny with the new favourite, and such an involution of parties took place that "Stukely and Cave" joined hand in hand and heart to heart, while poor Howell Gwynne and myself were abandoned as useless candidates. At one o'clock it was clear that I must be defeated by a large majority.

The Cave party then approached me with the modest request that, as it was quite clear that I could not be returned, would I mind attending the polling places and give my support to Cave?

This piece of unparalleled impudence I declined to accede to, and did nothing. The election was over so far as I was interested in its result; but I was determined to have a parting word with the electors before leaving the town. I was mortified at the unblushing treachery and deception of my supporters.

I was next asked what I proposed to do. It was their object to get me out of the town as soon as possible, for if unsuccessful as a candidate, I might be troublesome in other ways. Such people are not without a sense of fear, if they have no feeling of shame.

I said I should do nothing but take a stroll by the river, the day being fine, and come back when the poll was declared and make them a little speech.

The little speech was exactly what they did not want, so in the most friendly manner they informed me that a fast train would leave Barnstaple at a certain time, and that probably I would like to catch that, as no doubt I wished to be in town as early as possible to attend to my numerous engagements. If they had chartered the train themselves they could not have shown greater consideration for my interests. But I informed them that I should stop and address the electors, and with this statement they turned sulkily away.

At the appointed hour for the declaration of the poll I was on the hustings-- well up there, although the lowest on the poll. Stukely and Cave were first and second, Howell Gwynne and myself third and *last*!

When my turn came to address the multitude, I spoke in no measured terms as to the conduct of the election, which I denounced as having been won by the most scandalous bribery and corruption.

All who were present as unbiassed spectators were sorry, and many of them expressed a wish that I would return on a future day.

"Not," said I, "until the place has been purged of the foul corruption with which it is tainted."

I had resolved to leave by the mail train, and was actually accompanied to the station by a crowd of some 2,000 people, including the Rector, or Vicar of the parish, who gave me godspeed on my journey home.

This kind and sincere expression of goodwill and sympathy was worth all the boisterous cheers with which I had been received.

On the platform at the railway station I had to make another little speech, and then I took my seat, not for Barnstaple, but London. As the train drew out of the station, the people clung to the carriage like bees, and although I had not even honeyed words to give them, they gave me a "send-off" with vociferous cheers and the most cordial good wishes.

Thus I bade good-bye to Barnstaple, never to return or be returned, and I can only say of that enlightened and independent constituency that, while seeking the interests of their country, they never neglected their own.

I need not add that I learnt a great deal in that election which was of the greatest importance in the conduct of the Parliamentary petitions which were showered upon me.

Before I accepted the candidature of Barnstaple, a friend of mine said he had been making inquiries as to how the little borough of Totnes could be won, and that the lowest figure required as an instalment to commence with was £7,000.

After this I had no more to do with electioneering in the sense of being a candidate, but a good deal to do with it in every other.

CHAPTER XXVIII.

THE TICHBORNE CASE.

[The greatest of all chapters in the life of Mr. Hawkins was the prosecution of the impostor Arthur Orton for perjury, and yet the story of the Tichborne case is one of the simplest and most romantic. The heir to the Tichborne baronetcy and estates was shipwrecked while on board the *Bella* and drowned in 1854. In 1865 a butcher at Wagga Wagga in Australia assumed the title and claimed the estates. But the story is not related in these reminiscences on account of its romantic incidents, but as an incident in the life of Lord Brampton. It is so great that there is nothing in the annals of our ordinary courts of justice comparable with it, either in its magnitude or its advocacy. I speak particularly of the trial for perjury, in which Mr. Hawkins led for the prosecution, and not of the preceding trial, in which he was junior to Sir John Coleridge.

It is impossible to give more than the *points* of this strange story as they were made, and the real *facts* as they were elicited in cross-examination and pieced together in his opening speech and his reply in the case for the Crown. What rendered the task the more difficult was that his predecessors had so bungled the cross-examination in many ways that they not only had not elicited what they might have done, but actually, by many questions, furnished information to the Claimant which enabled him to carry on his imposture.]

The Tichborne trials demand a few words by way of introduction, for although there were two trials, they were of a different character, the first being an ordinary action of ejectment in which the Claimant sought to dispossess the youthful heir, whose title he had already assumed, under circumstances of the most extraordinary nature.

The action of ejectment was tried before Chief Justice Bovill at the Common Pleas, Westminster. Ballantine and Giffard (now Lord Halsbury) led for the plaintiff, the butcher, while on behalf of the trustees of the estate (that is, the real heir) were the Solicitor-General Coleridge, myself, Bowen (afterwards Lord Bowen), and Chapman Barber, an *equity* counsel.

I must explain how it was that I, having been retained to lead Coleridge, was afterwards compelled to be led by him; and it is an interesting event in the history of the Bar as well as of the Judicial Bench.

The action was really a Western Circuit case, although the venue was laid in London. Coleridge led that circuit and was retained. I belonged to the Home Circuit, and had no idea of being engaged at all for that side. I had been retained for the Claimant, but the solicitor, with great kindness, withdrew his retainer at my request.

I was brought into the case for the purpose of leading, and no other; but by the appointment of Coleridge to the Solicitor-Generalship in 1868, I was displaced, and Coleridge ultimately led. His further elevation happened in this way: Sir Robert Collier was Attorney-General, and it was desired to give him a high appointment which at that moment was vacant, and could only be filled by a Judge of the High Court. Collier was not a Judge, and therefore was not eligible for the post. The question was how to make him eligible. The Prime Minister of the day was not to be baffled by a mere technicality, and he could soon make the Attorney-General a Judge of the High Court if that was a condition precedent.

There was immediately a vacancy on the Bench; Collier was appointed to the judgeship, and in three days had acquired all the experience that the Act of Parliament anticipated as necessary for the higher appointment in the Privy Council.

Instead of leading, therefore, in the case before Chief Justice Bovill, I had to perform whatever duties Coleridge assigned to me. My commanding position was gone, and it was no longer presumable that I should be entrusted with the cross-examination of the plaintiff. I was bound to obey orders and cross-examine whomsoever I was allowed to.

[The one thing Mr. Hawkins was retained for was the cross-examination of the plaintiff. Lord Chief Justice Cockburn said, "I would have given a thousand pounds to cross-examine him." It would have been an excellent investment of the Tichborne family to have given Hawkins ten thousand pounds to do so, for I am sure there would have been an end of the case as soon as he got to Wapping.

Coleridge acknowledged that the Claimant cross-examined him instead of his cross-examining the Claimant.

When that shrewd and cunning impostor was asked, "Would you be surprised to hear this or that?" "No," said he, "I should be surprised at nothing after this long time and the troubles I have been through; but, now that you call my attention to it, I remember it all perfectly well." Coleridge said: "I am leader by an accident." "Yes," said Hawkins, "a colliery accident."]

I had also been retained by the trustees of the Doughty estate. Lady Doughty was an aunt of Sir Roger Tichborne, and it was her daughter Kate whom the heir desired to marry. Had the Claimant succeeded in the first case, he would have brought an action against her also.

No copy of the proceedings had been supplied to me, and I was informed that at this preliminary cross-examination they would not require my assistance; that their learned Chancery barrister was merely going to cross-examine the Claimant on his affidavits--a matter of small consequence. So it was in one way, but of immeasurable importance in many other ways. But they said *I might like to hear the cross-examination as a matter of curiosity.*

I did.

The Claimant had it all his own way. I was powerless to lend any assistance; but had I been instructed, I am perfectly sure I could then and there have extinguished the case, for the Claimant at that time knew absolutely nothing of the life and history of Roger Tichborne.

So the case proceeded, with costs piled on costs; information picked up, especially by means of interminable preliminary proceedings, until the impostor was left master of the situation, to the gratification of fools and the hopes of fanatics.

I was, however, allowed in the trial to cross-examine some witnesses. Amongst them was a man of the name of Baigent, the historian of the family, who knew more of the Tichbornes than they knew of themselves. The cross-examination of Baigent, which did more than anything to destroy the Claimant's case, occupied ten days. He was the real Roger's old friend, and knew him up to the time of his leaving England never to return. I drew from him the confession that he did not believe he was alive, but that he had encouraged the Dowager Lady Tichborne to believe that the Claimant was her son; and that her garden was lighted night after night with Chinese lanterns in expectation of his coming.

Admissions were also obtained that when he saw the Claimant at Alresford Station neither knew the other, although Baigent had never altered in the least, as he alleged.

There was another witness allotted to me, and that was Carter, an old servant of Roger whilst he was in the Carabineers. This man supplied the plaintiff with information as to what occurred in the regiment while Roger belonged to it; but he only knew what was known to the whole regiment. He did *not* know private matters which took place at the officers' mess, and it was upon these that my cross-examination showed the Claimant to be an impostor. I "had him there."

As Parry and I were sitting one morning waiting for the Judges, I remarked on the subject of the counsel chosen for the prosecution: "Suppose, Parry, you and I had been Solicitor and Attorney-General, in the circumstances what should we have done?"

"Plunged the country into a bloody war before now, I dare say," said Parry, elevating his eyebrows and wig at the same time.

I confess when I undertook the responsibility of this great trial I was not aware of the immense labour and responsibility it would involve; nor do I believe any one had the smallest notion of the magnitude of the task.

Instead of the work diminishing as we proceeded, it increased day by day, and week by week; one set of witnesses entailed the calling of another set. The case grew in difficulty and extent. It seemed absolutely endless and hopeless.

Within a few weeks of the start, a necessity arose for procuring the testimony of a witness from Australia, a matter of months; and the trial being a criminal one, the defendant was entitled to have the case for the prosecution concluded within a reasonable time. If we had no evidence, it was to his advantage, and we had no right to detain him for a year while we were trying to obtain it.

However, the Australian evidence came in time. Numbers of witnesses had to be called who not only were not in our brief, but were never dreamed of. For instance, there was the Danish perjurer Louie, who swore he picked up the defendant at sea when the *Bella* went down.

Instead of this man going away after he had given his evidence, he remained until two gentlemen from the City, seeing his portrait in the Stereoscopic Company's window in Regent Street, identified him as a dishonest servant of theirs, who was undergoing a sentence of penal servitude at the time he swore he picked Roger up. He received five years' penal servitude for his evidence.

I had pledged myself to the task, which extended over many months more than I ever anticipated. At every sacrifice, however, I was bound to devote myself to the case, and did so, although I had to relinquish a very large portion of my professional income.

What made things worse, there was not only no effort made to curtail the business, but advantage was taken of every circumstance to prolong it. The longer it was dragged out the better chance there was of an acquittal. Had a juryman died after months of the trial had passed, the Government must have abandoned the prosecution. It would have been impossible to commence again. This was the last hope of the defence.

[The trial before Bovill ended at last, as it ought to have done months before, in a verdict for the defendants and the order for the prosecution of the Claimant for perjury. It was this prosecution that occupied the attention of the court and of the world for 188 days, extending over portions of two years.

There is no doubt that Coleridge would a second time have deprived the country of Mr. Hawkins's services, but higher influences than his prevailed, and the distinguished counsel was appointed to lead for the Crown, with Mr. Serjeant Parry as his leading junior. It is not too much to say that no one knew the case so well as Mr. Hawkins, and none could have done it so well. Bowen and Mathews were also his juniors.

The whole case, from the commencement of the Chancery proceedings down to the commencement of this trial, had been a comedy of blunders. The very claim was an absurdity, every step in the great fraud was an absurdity, and every proceeding had some ridiculous absurdity to accompany it. It was not until the cross-examination of Baigent by Mr. Hawkins that the undoubted truth began to appear.

"You are the first," said Baron Bramwell, "who has let daylight into the case." It will be seen presently what the simple story was which the learned counsel at last evolved from the lies and half-truths which had for so many years imposed upon a great number even of the intelligent and educated classes of the community. And I would observe that until nearly the end of the trial the case was never safe or quite free from doubt; it was only what was elicited by Mr. Hawkins that made it so. No Wonder the advocate said to Giffard, who was opposed to him on the first trial: "If you and I had been together in that case in the first instance, we should have won it for the Claimant." Being on the other side, this is how the case stood when he had completed it:--

The real heir to the family was a fairly well-formed, slender youth of medium height. The personator of this youth was a man an inch and a half or two inches taller, and weighing five-and-twenty stone. His hands were a great deal larger than those of Roger, and at least an inch longer; his feet were an inch and a half longer. He was broader, deeper, thicker, and altogether of a different build. The lobes of his ears, instead of being pendent like Roger's, adhered to his cheeks. But he was not more unlike in physical outline than in mental endowment, taste, character, pursuits, and sentiment, in manners and habits, in culture and education, connection and recollection.

Roger had been educated at Stonyhurst, with the education of a gentleman; this man had never had any education at all. Roger had moved in the best English society; this man amongst slaughtermen, bushrangers, thieves, and highwaymen. Roger had been engaged to a young lady, his cousin, Kate Doughty; this man had been engaged to a young woman of Wapping, of the name of Mary Ann Loader, a respectable girl in his own sphere of life.

Roger's engagement to this young lady, his cousin, was disapproved of by the Tichborne family, and was the cause of his leaving England. But before he went he gave her a writing, and deposited a copy of it with Mr. Gosford, the legal adviser of the family.

This document was one of the most important incidents in the history of the case, and upon it, if the cross-examination had been conducted by Mr. Hawkins in Chancery, the case would have been crushed at the outset. It is not my task to show how, but to state what it all came to when the learned counsel left it to the jury to say whether the claimant *was* the Roger Tichborne he had sworn himself to be, or whether he was Arthur Orton, the butcher of Wapping, whom he swore he was not.

This document forms the subject of the "sealed packet" left with Mr. Gosford, and contained in effect these words: "If God spares me to return and marry my beloved Kate within a year, I promise to build a church and dedicate it to my patron saint."

Till his cross-examination in Chancery he had never heard of this packet, and when he was informed of it his solicitor naturally demanded a copy. Gosford had destroyed the original, and of course there was no end of capital out of it; a concocted original was made, which was to the effect that this gentleman, "so like Roger," *had seduced his cousin*, and that if she proved to be *enceinte*, Gosford was to take care of her. Luckily "Kate Doughty" had her original preserved with sacred affection. But such was the memory of this man's early life, contrasted with what *would* have been the memory of Sir Roger Tichborne.

He did not recollect being "at Stonyhurst, but said positively he was at Winchester, where certainly Roger never was. He did not remember his mother's Christian names, and could not write his own.

He came to England to see his mother, and then would not go to her; she went to see him, and he got on to the bed and turned his face to the wall. She did not see his face, but recognized him by his ears, because they were like his uncle's, then ordered the servant to undo his braces for fear he should choke.

Such a piece as this on the stage would not have lasted one night; in real life it had a run for many years. But then there never was a rogue that some fool would not believe in. How else was it possible that millions believed in this man, who had forgotten the religion he had been brought up in, and was married by a Wesleyan minister at a Wesleyan church, he being, as his mother informed him, a strict Roman Catholic from his birth? However, he did his best to reform his error by getting married again by a Roman priest, although he made another blunder, and forgetting he was Sir Roger Tichborne, married as Arthur Orton, the son of the Wapping butcher. When his dear mother reminded him of his being a Catholic, he wrote and thanked her for the information, and hoped the Blessed Maria would take care of her for evermore, little dreaming that the "Black Maria" would one day take particularly good care of himself.

So that he forgot the place of his birth, the seat of his ancestors, the friends of his youth, the face, features, and form of his mother, his education and religion, his brother officers in the regiment, the regiment itself, and the position he occupied, thinking he had been a private for fifteen days instead of a painstaking, studious, diligent officer, who was beloved by his fellows. He had forgotten all his neighbours, servants, dependants, as well as the family solicitor who made his will and was appointed his executor. He forgot his life in Paris, the village church of his ancestral seat--nay, the ancestral seat itself--and the very road that led to it. He forgot his old friend and historian, who swore he had never altered the least in appearance since Roger left--historian and picture-cleaner to the family. In short, there was not one single thing in the life of Roger that he knew. He forgot what any but a born fool would remember while he was in poverty and bankruptcy for a couple of hundred pounds; the real Roger had written home on hearing of the death of his uncle, from whom he derived his title and estates, saying, "Pray go to Messrs. Glyn's and exchange my letter of credit for £2,000 for three years for one for £3,000."

Imagine a man forgetting he had £3,000 a year and an estate in England worth £30,000, and earning his bread in a slaughter-house and in the Bush, borrowing money from a poor woman and running away with it.

But now another singular thing stamps this fraudulent impostor who makes so many believe in him. He, alleged by his supporters to be Sir Roger Tichborne, recollected all about a place that he had never been to; people he had never heard of, far less seen; events that he could *not* know and which never happened to him, but did happen to Arthur Orton. He knew Wapping well--every inch of it; Old Charles Orton, the father of Arthur; Charles Orton the brother, the sisters, the people who kept this shop and that; so that when on his return to England he went to the Wapping seat of his ancestors instead of Ashford, he asked all about them, and reminded them so faithfully of the little events of Arthur's boyhood, and resembled that person so much in the face, that they said, "Why, you are Arthur Orton yourself!" True, he paid some of them to swear he was not, but the impression remained.

Mr. Hawkins told the jury how he picked up his second-hand knowledge of the things he spoke about concerning the Tichbornes, for it was necessary to be able to answer a good many questions wherever he went, especially when he went into the witness-box.

There was an old black servant, quite black, who had been a valet in the Tichborne family. His name was Bogle; and the Claimant was told by the poor old dowager that if he could meet with him, Bogle could tell him a good many things about himself.

Bogle was an excellent diplomatist, and no sooner heard from Lady Tichborne that her son Roger was in Australia than the two began to look for one another, the one as black inside as the other was out. Bogle announced that he was the man before he saw him, on the mother's recommendation, and became and was to the end one of his principal supporters--so much so that "Old Bogle" spread the Claimant's knowledge of the Tichbornes abroad, and, like everybody else, believed in him because he knew so much which he could not have known unless he had been the veritable Roger, all which Bogle had told him.

But in the interests of justice "Old Bogle" and Mr. Hawkins became acquainted, much to the advantage of the latter, as he happened to meet Bogle in the witness-box, a place where the counsel unravelled the trickster's most subtle of designs. The advocate liked "Old Bogle," as he called him, because, said he, Bogle, having white hair, was so like a Malacca cane with a silver knob, white at the top and black below.

Bogle had sworn that Roger had no tattoo marks when he left England. In point of fact he had, and Bogle had to fit them to the Claimant, who had had tattoo marks of a very different kind from Roger's. The Claimant had removed his, and therefore was presented to the court without any.

"How do you know Roger had no tattoo marks?" asked Mr. Hawkins.

"I saw his arms on three occasions." This was a serious answer for Bogle.

"When and where, and under what circumstances?" followed in quick succession, so that there was no escape. The witness said that Roger had on a pair of black trousers tied round the waist, and his shirt buttoned up.

"The sleeves, how were they?"

"Loose."

"How came you to see his naked arms?"

"He was rubbing one of them like this."

"What did he rub for?"

"I thought he'd got a flea."

"Did you see it?"

"No, of course."

"Where was it?"

"Just there."

"What time was this?"

"Ten minutes past eleven."

"That's the first occasion; come to the second."

"Just the same," says Bogle.

"Same time?"

"Yes."

"Did he always put his hand inside his sleeve to rub?"

"I don't know."

"But I want to know."

"If your shirt was unbuttoned, Mr. Hawkins, and you was rubbin' your arm, you would draw up your sleeve--"

"Never mind what I should do; I want to know what you saw."

"The same as before," answers Bogle angrily.

"A flea?"

"I suppose."

"But did you see him, Bogle?"

"I told you, Mr. Hawkins, I did not."

"Excuse me, that was on the first occasion."

"Well, this was the same."

"Same flea?"

"I suppose."

"Same time--ten minutes past eleven?"

"Yes."

"Then all I can say is, he must have been a very punctual old flea."

Exit Bogle, and with him his evidence.

After the trial had been proceeding for some time, Baigent was giving evidence of the family pedigree.

Honeyman whispered, "We might as well have the first chapter of Genesis and read that."

"Genesis!" said Hawkins; "I want to get to the last chapter of Revelation."

One day Mr. J.L. Toole came in, and was invited to sit next to Mr. Hawkins, which he did.

At the adjournment for luncheon the Claimant muttered as they passed along, "There's Toole come to learn actin' from 'Arry Orkins."

There was one witness who ought not to be forgotten. It was Mr. Biddulph, a relation of the Tichborne family, a good-natured, amiable man, willing to oblige any one, and a county magistrate--"one of the most amiable county magistrates I have ever met, a man of the strictest honour and unimpeachable integrity."

He had been asked by the dowager lady to recognize her son.

"I don't see how I can," said he. "I am willing to oblige, but not at the expense of truth. Better get some one else who knew him better than I did. This man bears no resemblance to the man I knew. I cannot do it." And so he resisted all entreaties with that firmness of purpose for which he was remarkable.

"He was then invited," said Mr. Hawkins, "to a little dinner at another supporter of the Claimant's, and one somewhat shrewder than the rest." The Claimant described this party as consisting of a county magistrate, a money-lender, a lawyer, and a humbug.

This is how the advocate dealt with this little party in his address to the jury:-

"Gentlemen, can't you imagine the scene? Perkins, the lawyer, says to Biddulph, 'Come, now, Mr. Biddulph, you know you have had great experience in cross-examining as a county magistrate at Petty Sessions; now, cross-examine this man *firmly*, and you'll soon find he knows more than you think. If he's not the man, he's nobody else, you may be quite sure of that. But first of all,' says Perkins, 'what did you know of Roger? That's the first thing; let's start with that.'

"'Oh, not very much,' says Biddulph. 'He stayed at Bath once for a fortnight, while his mother was there.'

"'Pass Mr. Biddulph the champagne,' says Perkins. (Laughter.)

"'Now,' he adds, 'how did you amuse yourselves, eh?'

"'Well,' says Biddulph, 'we used to smoke together at the hotel--the--the--White something it was called.'

"'Did you smoke pipes or cigars?'

"'Well, I remember we had some curious pipes.'

"'Another glass of champagne for Mr. Biddulph,' (More laughter.) 'What sort of pipes?' asks the Claimant; 'death's-head pipes?'

"The magistrate remembered, opened his eyes, and lifted his hands. Thus the amiable magistrate was convinced, although he said, candidly enough, 'I did not recognize him by his features, walk, voice, or twitch in his eye, but I was struck with his recollection of having met me at Bath.' The death's-head pipes settled him.

"As for Miss Brain the governess, she was of a different order from Mr. Biddulph. She told us she had listened to the defendant when he solemnly swore that he had seduced her former pupil, that he had stood in the dock for horse-stealing, and had been the associate of highwaymen and bushrangers, and had made a will for the purpose of fraud; and yet this woman took him by the hand, and was not ashamed of his companionship. His counsel described her as a ministering angel. Heaven defend me from ministering angels if Miss Brain is one!"

The Claimant, while in Australia, being asked what kind of lady his mother (the dowager Lady Tichborne) was, answered, "Oh, a very stout lady; and that is the reason I am so fond of Mrs. Butts of the Metropolitan Hotel, she being a tall, stout, and buxom woman; and like Mrs. Mina Jury (of Wapping), because she was like my mother."

A witness of the name of Coyne was called to give evidence of the recognition of the Claimant by the mother in Paris, and the solicitor said to Coyne, "You see how she recognizes him."

"Yes," said Coyne; "he's lucky."

There was no cross-examination, and Mr. Hawkins said to the jury, "They need not cross-examine unless they like; it's a free country. They may leave this man's account unquestioned if they like, but if it is a true account, what do you say to the recognition?"

Louie, the Dane, said that while the Claimant was on board his ship he amused himself by picking oakum and reading "The Garden of the Soul."

There were several *Ospreys* spoken to as having picked up the Claimant after the wreck of the *Bella*, and the defendant had not the least idea which one was the best to carry him safely into harbour. The defendant's counsel, notwithstanding, had told the jury that he, Hawkins, had not ventured to contradict one or other of the stories of the wreck, and had not called the captain of the *Osprey* which had picked him up.

Comment on such a proposition in advocacy would be ridiculous. Mr. Hawkins dealt with it by an example which the reader will remember as having occurred in his early days:--

"'We don't know which *Osprey* you mean.' 'Take any one,' says the defendant's counsel, reminding me of the defence of a man charged with stealing a duck, and having given seven different accounts as to how he became possessed of it, his counsel was at last asked which he relied on. 'Oh, never mind which,' he answered; 'I shall be much obliged if the jury will adopt any one of them.'

"You remember, gentlemen, the touching words in which the defendant's counsel spoke of Bogle: 'He is one of those negroes,' said he, 'described by the author of "Paul and Virginia," who are faithful to the death, true as gold itself. If ever a witness of truth came into the box, that witness was Bogle.'

"Well, you have seen him--Old Bogle! What do you think of him? Was there ever a better specimen of feigned simplicity than he? 'Bogle,' cries the defendant, after all those years of estrangement, 'is that *you*?' 'Yes, Sir Roger,' answered Bogle; how do you do?'

"'Do you remember giving me a pipe o' baccy?' asks a poor country greenhorn down at Alresford. 'Yes,' answers the Claimant. 'Then you're the man,' says the greenhorn. Such was the way evidence was manufactured.

"A poor lady--you remember Mrs. Stubbs--had a picture of her great-great-grandfather's great-grandfather. In goes the Claimant, and in his artful manner shows his childhood's memory. 'Ah, Mrs. Stubbs,' says he, looking at another picture, 'that is not the *old* picture, is it?' (Somebody had put him up to this.) No, sir,' cries Mrs. Stubbs, delighted with his recollection--'no, sir; but please to walk this way into my parlour,' And there, sure enough, was the picture he had been told to ask for.

"'Ah!' he exclaims, 'there it is; there's the old picture!'

"How could Mrs. Stubbs disbelieve her own senses?"

One, Sir Walter Strickland, declined to see the Claimant and be misled, and was roundly abused by the defendant's counsel. One of the jury asked if *he was still alive*. "Yes," said the Lord Chief Justice, although the defendant expressed a hope that they would all die who did not recognize him....

"In a letter to Rous, my lord, where he said, 'I see I have one enemy the less in Harris's death. Captain Strickland, who made himself so great on the other side, went to stay at Stonyhurst with his brother, and died there. He called on me a week before and abused me shamefully. So will all go some day'--this," said Mr. Hawkins, "was not exhibiting the same Christian spirit which he showed when he said, 'God help those poor *purgured* sailors!'"

"Why should the defendant," asked Mr. Hawkins at the close of one of the day's speeches, "if he were Sir Roger, avoid Arthur Orton's sisters? Why, would he not have said, 'They will be glad indeed to see me, and hear me tell them about the camp-fire under the canopy of heaven,' as his counsel put it, 'where their brother Arthur told me all about Fergusson, the old pilot of the Dundee boat, who kept the public-house at Wapping, and the Shetland ponies of Wapping, and the Shottles of the Nook at Wapping, and wished me to ask who kept Wright's public-house now, and about the Cronins, and Mrs. MacFarlane of the Globe--all of Wapping.'"

The Judges fell back with laughter, and the curtain came down, for these were the questions with many more the Claimant asked on the evening of his landing.

"I shall attack the noble army of Carabineers," said Mr. Hawkins on another occasion. He did so, and conquered the regiment in detail.

One old Carabineer was librarian at the Westminster Hospital. His name was Manton, and he was a sergeant. He told Baigent something that had happened while Roger was his officer, and Baigent told the Claimant. Manton afterwards saw the huge man, and failed to recognize him in any way. But when the Claimant repeated to him what he had told Baigent, Manton opened his eyes. This looked like proof of his being the man. He was struck with his marvellous recollection, and was at once pinned down to an affidavit:--

"The Claimant's voice is stronger, and has less foreign accent," he swore; "but I recognized his voice, and found his tone and pronunciation to be *the same as Roger Tichborne's*, whom I knew as an officer."

Truly an affidavit is a powerful auxiliary in fraud.

While Mr. Hawkins was replying one afternoon, Mr. Whalley, M.P., came in and sat next to the Claimant. He was from the first one of his most enthusiastic supporters.

"Well," he said, "and how are we getting on to-day? How are we getting on, eh?"

"Getting on!" growled the Claimant; "he's been going on at a pretty rate, and if he goes on much longer I shall begin to think I am Arthur Orton after all."

I will conclude this chapter with the following reminiscences by Lord Brampton himself.]

I had a great deal to put up with from day to day in many ways during this prolonged investigation. The Lord Chief Justice, Cockburn, although good, was a little impatient, and hard to please at times.

My opponent sought day by day some cause of quarrel with me. At times he was most insulting, and grew almost hourly worse, until I was compelled, in order to stop his insults, to declare openly that I would never speak to him again on this side the grave, and I never did. My life was made miserable, and what ought to have been a quiet and orderly performance was rendered a continual scene of bickering and conflict, too often about the most trifling matters.

With every one else I got on happily and agreeably, my juniors loyally doing their very utmost to render me every assistance and lighten my burden.

Even the Claimant himself not only gave me no offence from first to last, but was at times in his manner very amusing, and preserved his natural good temper admirably, considering what he had at stake on the issue of the trial, and remembering also that that issue devolved mainly upon my own personal exertions.

Nor was the Claimant devoid of humour. On the contrary, he was plentifully endowed with it.

One morning on his going into court an elderly lady dressed in deep mourning presented him with a religious tract. He thanked her, went to his seat, and perused the document. Then he wrote something on the tract, carefully revised what he had written, and threw it on the floor.

The usher was watching these proceedings, and, as soon as he could do so unobserved, secured the paper and handed it to me.

The tract was headed, "Sinner, Repent!"

The Claimant had written on it, "Surely this must have been meant for Orkins, not for me!"

Louie's story of picking him up in the boat must have amused him greatly. If he was amused at the ease with which fools can be humbugged, he must also have been astounded at the awful villainy of those who, perfect strangers to him, had perjured themselves for the sake of notoriety.

I did what I could to shorten the proceedings. My opening speech was confined to six days, as compared with twenty-eight on the other side; my reply to nine. But that reply was a labour fearful to look back upon. The mere classification of the evidence was a momentous and necessary task. It had to be gathered from the four quarters of the world. It had to be sifted, winnowed, and arranged in order as a perfect whole before the true story could be evolved from the complications and entanglements with which it was surrounded.

And when I rose to reply, to perform my last work and make my last effort for the success of my cause, I felt as one about to plunge into a boundless ocean with the certain knowledge that everything depended upon my own unaided efforts as to whether I should sink or swim. Happily, for the cause of justice, I succeeded; and at the end, although nattering words of approval and commendation poured upon me from all sides, from the highest to the humblest, I did Hot then realize their value to the extent that I did afterwards. The excitement and the exertion had been too great for anything to add to it.

But I afterwards remembered--ay, and can never forget--the words of the Lord Chief Justice himself, the first to appreciate and applaud, as I was passing near him in leaving the court: "Bravo! Bravo, Hawkins!" And then he added, "I have not heard a piece of oratory like that for many a long day!" And he patted me cordially on the back as he looked at me with, I believe, the sincerest appreciation.

Lord Chelmsford, too, who years before had given me my silk gown, was on the Bench on this last day, and I shall never forget the compliment he paid me on my speech. It was of itself worth all the trouble and anxiety I had undergone.

Beyond all this, and more gratifying even still, my speech was liked by the Bar, from the most eminent to the briefless.

But greatest of all events in that eventful day was one which went deeper to my feelings. My old father, who had taken so strong a view against my going to the Bar, and who told me so mournfully that after five years I must sink or swim; my old father, who had never once seen me in my wig and gown from that day to this, the almost closing scene in my forensic career, came into court and sat by my side when I made successfully the greatest effort of my life.

CHAPTER XXIX.

A VISIT TO SHEFFIELD--MRS. HAILSTONE'S DANISH BOARHOUND.

The remembrance of my Sessions days will never vanish from my mind, although at the period of which I am speaking they had long receded into the distant past. Even *Nisi Prius* was diminishing in importance, although increasing in its business and fees.

Solicitors no longer condescended to deliver their briefs, but competed for my services. I say this without the smallest vanity, and only because it was the fact, and a great fact in my life. I was wanted to win causes by advocacy or compromise; and the innumerable compensation cases which continually came in with so steady and so full a tide were a sufficient proof that, at all events, the solicitors and others thought my services worth having. So did my clerk!

Those were the days of the golden harvest, the very gleanings of which were valuable to those who came after.

Lloyd must have made £20,000 a year with the greatest ease. What my income was is of no consequence to any one; suffice it to say that no expectations of mine ever came up to its amount, and even now when I look back it seems absolutely fabulous. I will say no more, notwithstanding the curiosity it has excited amongst the members of the profession.

Of course it was a step for me from the humble "*one three six*;" but I have had a more lively satisfaction from that little sum than from many a larger fee.

In the midst of all this rush of London business I still found time to run down to country places in cases of election petitions or compensation.

One day I found myself on my way to Sheffield to support the member against an attempt to deprive him of his seat in Parliament. I went with the Hon. Sir Edward Chandos Leigh, my distinguished junior on that memorable occasion.

The journey was pleasant until we got near the end of it, and then the smoke rolled over and around in voluminous dense clouds, for a description of which you may search in vain through "Paradise Lost."

We were met at the station with great state, and even splendour, and treated with almost boundless hospitality.

To keep up our spirits, we were taken for a drive by the sitting member a few miles out, into what they call "the country" in those parts. The suburban residence was situated in a well-wooded park, if that can be called well-wooded where there are no woods, but only stunted undergrowths sickening with the baleful fumes that proceed from the city of darkness in the distance, and black with the soot of a thousand chimneys. The member apologized politely enough for bringing us to this almost uninhabitable and Heaven-forsaken region; but I begged him not to mind: it was only a more blasted scene than the heath in "Macbeth."

"Yes," said he, still apologetically; "it *is* very bad, I admit. You see, the fumes and fires from those manufactories make such havoc of our woods."

This was apparent, but the question was how to pass the time amidst this gloom and sickening atmosphere.

I found his residence, however, to my great joy, was farther than I expected from the appalling city of darkness, and hope began to revive both in my junior's heart and mine.

Our friend and host, seeing our spirits thus elated, began, to talk with more life-like animation.

"The fumes from the factories, Mr. Hawkins, have so played the devil with our trees that the general impoverishment of nature has earned for the locality of Sheffield the unpleasant title of the 'Suburbs of Hell.'"

"I don't wonder," I answered; "no name could be more appropriate or better deserved; but if it were my fate to choose my locality, I should prefer to live in *the city itself*."

A curious incident happened to us during this Yorkshire visit. An excursion was arranged to see Warburton's, situated some few miles off, and notable for many oddities.

We were driven over, and when we arrived were by no means disappointed by the singularities of the mansion. It was enclosed within a high wall, which had been built, not for the purpose, as you might suppose, of preventing the house from getting away, but for that of keeping out rats and foxes; for there were birds to be preserved from these destructive animals. Next, this portion of the estate was surrounded by water, which afforded an additional security to its isolation, access to the island being attainable only by means of a bridge.

The mansion was occupied by a Mrs. Hailstone, whose duty it was to show visitors over the house and explain everything as she went along, ghost stories as well; and being a remarkably affable lady, with a great gift of language, we had a very intelligent and edifying lecture in every room we passed through, now upon ornithology, now chronology, next on pisciculture and the habits of stuffed pike and other fish. But this was not all. Our guide was wonderfully well read in architecture, and displayed no end of knowledge in pointing out the different orders and sub-orders, periods of, and blendings of the same, so that we were quite ready for lunch as soon as that period should mercifully arrive.

But it was not exactly yet. There were many other curiosities to be shown. For instance, we had not done the Warburton Library, which was a most singular apartment, as we were informed, I don't know how many stories high, at the top of a very singular tower, with as many languages in it as the Tower of Babel itself, and very nearly as tall. One only wished the whole thing would topple down before we could come to it.

At last, however, we climbed to this lofty eminence and revelled as well as we could amongst the musty old books, which themselves revelled in the dust of ages.

Having seen all the shelves and the backs of the books, and heard all the accounts of them without receiving any information, we commenced our descent by means of the winding staircase towards the garden. On our way a curious circumstance took place. There was an enormously great Danish boarhound, which had, unperceived by us, followed Mrs. Hailstone from the library; it pushed by without ceremony, and proceeded until it reached the lady, who was some distance in advance. He then carefully took the skirt of her dress with his mouth and carried it like an accomplished train-bearer until she reached the bottom of the stairs and the garden, when he let go the dress and gazed as an interested spectator. We were now in the midst of a very beautiful and well-kept garden, with a lawn like velvet stretching far away to the lake, where ultimately we should have to wait for a boat to ferry us along its placid water. This was part of our entertainment, and a very beautiful part it was.

But before we parted from Mrs. Hailstone, and while I was talking to her, I felt my hand in the boarhound's mouth, and a pretty capacious mouth it was, for I seemed to touch nothing but its formidable fangs.

It was not a pleasant experience, but I preserved sufficient presence of mind to make no demonstration. Dogs know well enough when a man or woman loves their kind, and I am sure this one was no exception, or he would never have behaved with such gentlemanly politeness. So soft was the touch of his fangs that I was only just conscious my hand was in his mouth by now and then the gentlest reminder. I knew animals too well to attempt to withdraw it, and so preserved a calm more wonderful than I could have given myself credit for.

While I was wondering what the next proceeding might be, Mrs. Hailstone begged me to be quite easy, and on no account to show any opposition to the dog's proceedings, in which case she promised that he would lead me gently to the other side of the lawn, and there leave me without doing the least harm.

All this was said with such cool indifference that I wondered whether it was a part of the day's programme, and rather supposed it was; but it turned out that she said it to reassure me and prevent mischief. I also learned that it was not by any means the first occasion when this business had taken place. It was the first time in my life that I had been in custody, and if I had had my choice I should have preferred a pair of handcuffs without teeth.

As I was being led away Mrs. Hailstone said,--

"Do exactly as he wishes; he is jealous of your talking to me, and leads any one away who does so to the other side of the garden."

Having conducted me to the remotest spot he could find, he opened his huge jaws and released my hand, wagged his tail, and trotted off, much pleased with his performance. He returned to his mistress and put his large paws on her arms--a striking proof, I thought, of the dog's sagacity.

There will be in this history some stories of my famous "Jack," but as he belonged to me after I became a Judge, they are deferred until that period arrives. The reminiscences of Jack are amongst my dearest and most pleasant recollections.

The changeful nature of popular clamour was never more manifested than on this visit.

The Claimant had been convicted and sentenced to penal servitude, but to deprive a man of his title and estate because he was a butcher's son did not coincide with the wishes of a generous democracy, who lingered round the Sheffield court, where the fate of their sitting member was to be tried. They believed in their member, and, not knowing on which side I was retained, when I went along the corridor into the court they "yah! yah'd!" at me with lungs that would have been strong enough to set their furnaces going or blow them out.

After the petition was tried, and I had been successful, they changed their minds and their language. This same British public, which not long before had "yah! yah'd!" at me, now came forward with true British hoorays and bravos. "'Orkins for ever!" "Hooray for Orkins!" "Bravo, Orkins!" "Hooray! a ---- hooray! Hooray for Wagga Wagga!"

This last cry had reference to a village in Australia where the great Tichborne fraud had its origin; where the first advertisement of the dowager seeking her lost son was shown to the butcher in his own little shop, the son of the respectable butcher of Wapping.

The number of people who professed to believe in the Claimant long after he was sent to penal servitude was prodigious, although not one of them could have given a reason for his faith, or pointed to a particle of unimpeachable evidence to support his opinion. It had never been anything other than feeling in the dark for what never existed.

CHAPTER XXX.

AN EXPERT IN HANDWRITING--"DO YOU KNOW JOE BROWN?"

I always took great interest in the class of expert who professed to identify handwriting. Experts of all classes give evidence only as to opinion; nevertheless, those who decide upon handwriting believe in their infallibility. Cross-examination can never shake their confidence. Some will pin their faith even to the crossing of a T, "the perpendicularity, my lord," of a down-stroke, or the "obliquity" of an upstroke.

Mr. Nethercliffe, one of the greatest in his profession, and a thorough believer in all he said, had been often cross-examined by me, and we understood each other very well. I sometimes indulged in a little chaff at his expense; indeed, I generally had a little "fling" at him when he was in the box.

It is remarkable that, at the time I speak of, Judges, as a rule, had wonderful confidence in this class of expert, and never seemed to think of forming any opinion of their own. A witness swore to certain peculiarities; the Judge looked at them and at once saw them, too often without considering that peculiarities are exactly the things that forgers imitate.

"You find the same peculiarity here, my lord, and the same peculiarity there, my lord; consequently I say it is the same handwriting."

In days long gone by the eminent expert in this science had a great reputation. As I often met him, I knew *his* peculiarities, and how annoyed he was if the correctness of his opinion was in the least doubted.

He had a son of whom he was deservedly proud, and he and his son, in cases of importance, were often employed on opposite sides to support or deny the genuineness of a questioned handwriting. On one occasion, in the Queen's Bench, a libel was charged against a defendant which he positively denied ever to have written.

I appeared for the defendant, and Mr. Nethercliffe was called as a witness for the plaintiff.

When I rose to cross-examine I handed to the expert six slips of paper, each of which was written in a different kind of handwriting. Nethercliffe took out his large pair of spectacles--magnifiers--which he always carried, and began to polish them with a great deal of care, saying,--

"I see, Mr. Hawkins, what you are going to try to do--you want to put me in a hole."

"I do, Mr. Nethercliffe; and if you are ready for the hole, tell me--were those six pieces of paper written by one hand at about the same time?"

He examined them carefully, and after a considerable time answered: "No; they were written at different times and by different hands!"

"By different persons, do you say?"

"Yes, certainly!"

"Now, Mr. Nethercliffe, you are in the hole! I wrote them myself this morning at this desk."

He was a good deal disconcerted, not to say very angry, and I then began to ask him about his son.

"You educated your son to your own profession, I believe, Mr. Nethercliffe?"

"I did, sir; I hope there was no harm in that, Mr. Hawkins."

"Not in the least; it is a lucrative profession. Was he a diligent student?"

"He was."

"And became as good an expert as his father, I hope?"

"Even better, I should say, if possible."

"I think you profess to be infallible, do you not?"

"That is true, Mr. Hawkins, though I say it."

"And your son, who, as you say, is even better than yourself, is he as infallible as you?"

"Certainly, he ought to be. Why not?"

Then I put this question; "Have you and your son been sometimes employed on opposite sides in a case?"

"That is hardly a fair question, Mr. Hawkins."

"Let me give you an instance: In Lady D----'s case, which has recently been tried, did not your son swear one way and you another?"

He did not deny it, whereupon I added: "It seems strange that two infallibles should contradict one another?"

The case was at an end.

One evening, after a good hard day's work, I was sitting in my easy-chair after dinner, comfortably enjoying myself, when a man, who was quite a respectable working man, came in. I had known him for a considerable time.

"What's the matter, Jenkins?" I inquired, seeing he was somewhat troubled.

"Well, Mr. Hawkins, it's a terrible job, this 'ere. I wants you to appear for me."

"Where?" I inquired.

"At Bow Street, Mr. Hawkins."

"Bow Street! What have you been doing, Jenkins?"

"Why, nothing, sir; but it's a put-up job. You knows my James, I dessay. Well, sir, that there boy, my son James, have been brought up, I might say, on the Church Catechism."

"There's not much in that," I said, meaning nothing they could take him to Bow Street for. "Is that the charge against him?"

"No, sir; but from a babby, sir, his poor mother have brought that there boy up to speak the truth, the whole truth, and nothing but the truth. And it's a curious thing, Mr. Hawkins--a very curious thing, sir--that arter all his poor mother's care and James's desire to speak the truth, they've gone and charged that there boy with perjury! 'At all times,' says his mother, 'James, speak the truth, the whole truth, and nothing but the truth;' and this is what it's come to--

would anybody believe it, sir? *Could* anybody believe it? It's enough to make anybody disbelieve in Christianity. And what's more, sir, that there boy was so eager at all times to tell the whole truth that, to make quite sure he told it all, he'd go a little beyond on the other side, sir--he would, indeed."

When he heard my fee was a hundred guineas to appear at the police court, I heard no more of truthful James.

In dealing with a case where there is really no substantial defence, it is sometimes necessary to throw a little ridicule over the proceedings, taking care, first, to see what is the humour of the jury. I remember trying this with great success, and reducing a verdict which might have been considerable to a comparatively trifling amount.

[In illustration of this Mr. Cecil A. Coward has given an incident that occurred in an action for slander tried at the Guildhall many years ago, in which Mr. Hawkins, Q.C., was for the defendant, and Mr. Joseph Brown, Q.C., for the plaintiff. The slander consisted in the defendant pointing his thumb over his shoulder and asking another man, "Do you know him? That's Joe Smith."

Mr. Joseph Brown, Q.C., had to rely upon his innuendo--"meaning thereby Joe Smith was a rogue"--and was very eloquent as to slander unspoken but expressed by signs and tone. After an exhausting speech he sat down and buried his head in his bandana, as his habit was.

Hawkins got up, and turned Mr. Joseph Brown's speech to ridicule in two or three sentences.

"Gentlemen," he almost whispered, after a very small whistle which nobody could hear but those close around, at the same time pointing his thumb over his shoulder at his opponent, "do you know him--do you know Joe Brown?" There was a roar of laughter. Joe looked up, saw nothing, and retired again into his bandana.

Again the performance was gone through. "Do you know Joe Brown, the best fellow in the world?"

Brown looked up again, and was just in time to hear the jury say they had heard quite enough of the case. No slander--verdict for the defendant.

It was one of the best pieces of acting I ever saw him do.]

CHAPTER XXXI.

APPOINTED A JUDGE--MY FIRST TRIAL FOR MURDER,

No sooner was the Tichborne case finished than I was once more in the full run of work.

One brief was delivered with a fee marked twenty thousand guineas, which I declined. It would not in any way have answered my purpose to accept it. I was asked, however, to name my own fee, with the assurance that whatever I named it would be forthcoming. I promised to consider a fee of fifty thousand guineas, and did so, but resolved not to accept the brief on any terms, as it involved my going to Indie, and I felt it would be unwise to do so.

In 1874 I was offered by Lord Cairns the honour of a judgeship, which I respectfully declined. It was no hope of mine to step into a puisne judgeship, or, for the matter of that, any other judicial position. I was contented with my work and with my career. I did not wish to abandon my position at the Bar, and my friends at the Bar, and take up one on the Bench with no friends at all; for a Judge's position is one of almost isolation. This refusal gave great dissatisfaction to many, and a letter I have before me says, "I got into a great row with my editor by your refusal." Another said he lost a lot of money in consequence: "I thought it was any odds upon your taking it."

Sir Alexander Cockburn gave me a complimentary side-cut in a speech he made to some of his old constituents.

"The time comes," said he, "when men of the greatest eminence are called upon to give up their professional emoluments for the interests of their country. In my opinion they have no right to refuse their services; no man has this right when his country calls for them."

But these animadversions did not affect me. I held on to the course which I had deliberately chosen, and which I thought my labours and sacrifices in the Tichborne case on behalf of my country entitled me to enjoy. Let any one who has the least knowledge of advocacy consider what it was to carry that case to a successful issue, and then condemn me for not taking a judgeship if he will. I was entitled to freedom and rest. A judgeship is neither, as one finds out when once he puts on the ermine. But it requires no argument to justify the course I took. I was entitled to decline, and I did. There is nothing else to be said; all other considerations are idle and irrelevant.

A judgeship was, however, a second time offered by Lord Cairns in 1876. This, after due consideration, I accepted, and received my appointment as a Judge of the Exchequer Court on November 2 of that year.

The first and most sensational case that I was called upon to preside over was known as the Penge case. Sir Alexander Cockburn had appointed himself to try it, on account of its sensational character; but as it came for trial at a time when the Lord Chief Justice could not attend, it fell to the junior Judge on the Bench.

I am not going to relate the details of that extraordinary case,[A] which are best left in the obscurity of the newspaper files; but I refer to it because it cannot well be passed over in the reminiscences of my life. I shall, however, only touch upon one or two prominent points.

[Footnote A: The great sensation of the case was almost overpowered by the great sensation that "a new power had come upon the Bench." These are, as nearly as I can give them, the words of one of our most distinguished advocates, and one of the most brilliant who was in the Penge case:--

"We felt, and the Bar felt, that a great power had come upon the Bench; he summed up that case as no living man could have done. Every word told; every point was touched upon and made so clear that it was impossible not to see it."

Another distinguished advocate said there was no other Judge on the Bench who could have summed that case up as Sir Henry Hawkins did.--R.H.]

"Every person," I said in my summing up, "who is under a legal duty, whether such duty was imposed by law or contract, to take charge of another person must provide that person with the necessaries of life. Every person who had that legal duty imposed upon him was criminally responsible if he culpably neglected that duty, and the death of the person for whom he ought to provide ensued. If the death was the result of mere carelessness and without criminal intent, the offence would be manslaughter, provided the jury came to the conclusion that there had been culpable neglect of the duty cast upon the individual who had undertaken to perform it."

With regard to the evidence of one of the witnesses who was said to be an accomplice, so that it was necessary that she should be corroborated, I said a jury might convict without it, but recommended them strongly not to take for granted her evidence unless they found there was so much corroboration of her testimony as to induce them to believe she was telling the truth.

As to one of the accused, I said: "If she had no legal object to fulfil in providing the deceased with the necessaries of life, the mere omission to do so would not render her guilty; but if she did an act wrongfully which had a tendency to destroy life, but which was not done with that intention, she would be guilty of manslaughter."

The jury found a verdict of guilty against all, but with a strong recommendation in favour of one, in which I joined.

When a verdict of guilty of wilful murder is returned, a Judge, whatever may be his opinion of its propriety or justice, has no alternative but to deliver the sentence of death, and in the very words the law prescribes. It is not *his* judgment or decision, but it is so decreed that the sentence shall in no way depend upon the sympathy or opinion of the Judge. Whatever mitigating circumstances there may be must be considered by the Secretary of State for the Home Department as representing the Sovereign, and upon his advice alone the Sovereign acts.

But the Home Secretary never allows a sentence of death to be executed without the fullest possible inquiry as to mitigating circumstances, and it is at this stage that the opinion of the Judge is almost all-powerful.

My judgment in this case was the result of much anxious thought and consideration. The responsibility cast upon me was great. The case was as difficult as it was serious; but my line of duty was plain, and it was to leave the facts as clearly as I could possibly state them, with such explanation of the law applicable to each case as my ability would allow, and then leave the jury to find according to their honest belief. No duty more arduous has ever since been imposed upon me, and I performed it in my honest conscience, without swerving from what I believed, and believe still, to be my strict line of duty.

I have had many opportunities of reconsidering the whole circumstances, but I have never changed or varied my opinion after all these years, and am certain I never shall--namely, that I did my duty according to the best of my judgment and ability.

A Judge may go wrong in many ways, and often does in one way or other, especially if he does not know his own mind--the worst of all weaknesses, because it usually leads to an attempt to strike a medium line between innocence and guilt.

One great weakness, too, in a Judge is not having the faculty of setting out the facts in language which is intelligible to the jury, or in not setting them out at all, but repeating them so often and in so many forms that they are at last left in an absolutely hopeless muddle. A Judge once kept on so at the jury about "if you find burglarious intent, and if you don't find burglarious intent," that at last the jury found nothing except a verdict of not guilty, giving the "benefit of the doubt as to what the Judge meant."

As an illustration of the necessity of giving the jury a clear idea of the evidence in the simplest case, I will state what took place at Exeter. Juries are unused to evidence, and have very often to be told what is the bearing of it. In a case of fowl-stealing which I was trying, there was a curious defence raised, which seemed too ridiculous to notice. It was that the fowls had crept into the nose-bag in which they had been found, and which was in the prisoner's possession, in order to shelter themselves from the east wind.

Forgetting that possibly I had an unreasoning and ignorant jury to deal with, I thought they would at once see through so absurd a defence, and did not insult their common sense by summing up. I merely said,--

"Gentlemen, do you believe in the defence?"

They put their heads together, and kept in that position for some time, and at last, to my utter amazement, said,--

"We do, my lord; we find the prisoner *not guilty*."

It was a verdict for the prisoner and a lesson for me.

It was always my practice, founded on much calculation of the respective and relative merits and demerits of prisoners, to do what no other Judge that I am aware of ever did, which was to put convicted prisoners back until the whole calendar had been tried, then to bring them up and pass sentence after deliberate consideration of every case. I thus had the opportunity of reading over my notes and forming an opinion as to whether there were any circumstances which I could take into consideration by way of mitigation, or, in the same manner, as to whether there were matters of aggravation, such as cruelty or deliberate, wilful malice. The result of this plan on one occasion at Stafford Assizes, which I remember very well, was this. Two men were convicted of bigamy. The offence was the same in law as to both the prisoners. The one was altogether, physically and morally, a brute, cruel and merciless. The other man found guilty had been a bad husband to his wife before he went through the form of the second marriage; but as he had been already punished for his misconduct in that respect, I thought it fair that he should not be punished again for the same offence. Such is my idea of the law of England, although I fear it is sometimes forgotten. I therefore treated this man's crime as one of a very mitigated character, no harm having been done to the second woman, and released him on his own recognizances to come up for judgment if he should be called upon. I would not revisit upon him his past misdeeds. The other man I sent into penal servitude for five years.

CHAPTER XXXII.

ON THE MIDLAND CIRCUIT.

"That's Orkins hover there," said a burly-looking sportsman as I arrived one day at Newmarket Heath--"'im a-torkin' to Corlett. See 'im? Nice bernevolent old cove to look at, ain't 'e? Yus. That didn't stop 'is guvin' me *five of his wery best*, simply becorze by accident I mistook someb'dy else's 'ouse and plate-chest for my own. Sorter mistake which might 'appen a'most to henybody. There 'e is; see 'im? That's Orkins!"

I need not say I was frequently spoken of in this complimentary manner by persons who had been introduced to me at the Bar. I was once leading a little fox terrier with a string, because on several occasions he had given me the slip and caused me to be a little late in court. I led him, therefore, in the leash until he knew his duty.

On this day, however, as the crowd was waiting for me on the little platform of a country station, my fox terrier jumped out in front of me while I was holding him by the string.

"Good ----!" cried a voice from a gentleman to whom I had previously given a situation under Government, livery and all found; "why, blow me if the old bloke ain't blind! Lookee there, 'is dawg's a-leadin' 'im; wot d'ye think o' that?"

But persons in much higher station were no less at times fond of chaff, which I always took good-humouredly. A story of Lord Grimthorpe, who, many years after, had some fun with me at times over my little Jack, will appear in his reminiscences a little farther on. I used to lead Jack with a string in the same manner as I had done the other, for educational purposes, and Lord Grimthorpe jocularly called me Jack's prisoner. But I must let him tell his own story in his own way when his turn comes.

The Midland Circuit was always famous for its ill accommodation of her Majesty's Judges, and of late years even in the supply of prisoners to keep them from loitering away their days in idleness or lonely diversions.

I always loved work and comfortable lodgings, and may say from the first to the last of my judicial days set myself to the improvement of both the work and the accommodation.

Some Judges in their charges used to discourse with the grand jury of our foreign relations, turnips, or the state of trade; but I took a more humble theme at Aylesbury, when I informed that august body that the quarters assigned to her Majesty's Judges were such that an officer would hardly think them good enough to billet soldiers in.

"My rest, gentlemen, has been rudely disturbed," said I, "in the lodgings assigned to me. My bedroom was hardly accessible, on account of what appeared to be a dense fog which was difficult to struggle through. I sought refuge in the dressing-room. Being a bitterly cold night and a very draughty room, some one had lighted a fire in it; but, unfortunately, all the smoke came down the chimney after going up a little way, bringing down as much soot as it could manage to lay hold of. All this is the fault of the antiquated chimneys and ill-contrived building generally. My marshal was the subject of equal discomfort; and I think I may congratulate you, gentlemen, not only on there being very few prisoners, but also on the fact that you are not holding an inquest on our bodies."

The grand jury were good enough to say that there was "an institution called the Standing Joint Committee, who will, no doubt, inquire into your lordship's subject of complaint." The "Standing Joint Committee" sounded powerfully, but I believe no further notice was taken, and the question dropped.

"That's a nice un," said one of the javelin-men at the door when a friend of his came out. "Did yer 'ear that, Jimmy? Orkins is a nice un to talk about lodgings. Let him look to his own cirkit--the 'Orne Cirkit--where my brother told me as at a trial at Guildford the tenant of that there house wouldn't pay his rent. For why? Because they was so pestered wi' wermin. And what do you think Orkins told the jury?--He was counsel for the tenant.--'Why,' he says, 'gentlemen, you heard what one of the witnesses said, how that the fleas was so outrageous that they ackshally stood on the backs o' the 'all chairs and barked at 'em as they come in.' That's Orkins on his own circuit; and 'ere he is finding fault with our lodgings."

It was not long after my arrival at Lincoln, on the first occasion of my visiting that drowsy old ecclesiastical city, that I was waited upon, first by one benevolent body of gentlemen, and then another, all philanthropists seeking subscriptions for charitable objects.

One bitterly cold morning I was standing in my robes with my back to the fire at my lodgings, waiting to step into the carriage on my way to court, when a very polite gentleman, who headed quite a body of other polite gentlemen, asked "if his lordship would do them the honour of receiving a deputation from the L. and B. Skating Club." I assented--nothing would give me more pleasure; and in filed the deputation, arranging themselves, hats in hand, round me in a semicircle.

"We have the honour, my lord, to call upon your lordship in pursuance of a resolution passed last night at a special meeting of our club--"

"What is the name of your club?"

"The L. and B. Skating Club, my lord."

"What is its object?"

"*Our* object, my lord?"

"No, the object of your *society*. I can guess your object."

The leader answered with a smile of the greatest satisfaction,--

"Er--skating, my lord."

"Your own amusement?"

The head of the deputation bowed.

"Do you want *me* to skate?"

"No, my lord; but we take the liberty of asking your lordship to kindly support our club with a subscription."

"When I see," I replied, "so much poverty and misery around me which needs actual relief, and when I look at this inclement weather and think how these poor creatures must suffer from the cold, it seems to me that *they* are the people who should apply to those who have anything to bestow in charity; not those who are the only people, as it would appear, who can take pleasure in this excruciating weather. See if your club cannot do something for these poor sufferers instead of collecting merely for your own personal amusement; contribute to their necessities, and then come and see me again. I shall be here till Monday."

The head of the deputation stared, but it did not lose its presence of mind or forget its duty. The deputation made a little speech "thanking me heartily for the kind manner in which they had been received."

I never saw anything more of them from that day to this.

[In a case at Devizes Sir Henry showed in a striking manner the character he always bore as a humane Judge. He was not humane where cruelty was any part of the culprit's misdeeds, for he visited that with the punishment he thought it deserved, and his idea of that was on a somewhat considerable scale.]

I was down upon cruelty, and always lenient where there were any mitigating circumstances whatever, either of mental weakness, great temptation, provocation, or unhappy surroundings.

A woman was brought up before me who had been committed to take her trial on a charge of concealing the birth of a child. For prisoners in these circumstances I always felt great sympathy, and regarded the moral guilt as altogether unworthy of punishment. The law, however, was bound to be vindicated so far as the legal offence was concerned. She had already been in prison for three months, because she was too poor and too friendless to find bail. I am always pointing out that if magistrates would send more cases to the Judges than they do, they would get some precedents as to the appropriate measure of punishment, which they seem badly to need. This woman had already been punished, without being found guilty, with three times the punishment she ought to have received had she been found guilty. A month's imprisonment would have been excessive.

Prisoners should always be released on their own recognizances where there is a reasonable expectation that they will appear.

The result was that the unhappy woman, who had been punished severely while in the eye of the law she was innocent, was discharged when she was found to be guilty.

We have seen how Mr. Justice Maule examined a little boy as to his understanding the nature of an oath. I once examined a little girl upon a preliminary point of this kind, before she had arrived at that period of mental acuteness which enables one to understand exactly the meaning of the words uttered in the administration of the oath. The child was called, and after allowing the form of "the evidence you shall give," etc., and "kiss the book," to be gabbled over, I said, before the Testament could reach the child's lips,--

"Stop! Do you understand what that gentleman has been saying?"

"No, sir."

I think it is a great farce to let little children be sworn who cannot be expected to understand even the language in which the oath is administered, to say nothing of the oath itself. How can they comprehend the meaning of the phrases employed? And many grown-up uneducated people are in the same situation. Surely a simple form, such as, "*You swear to God to speak the truth*"--or, even better still, to make false evidence punishable without any oath at all--would be far better.

CHAPTER XXXIII.

JACK.

I was always fond of dogs, and never cease to admire their intelligence and sagacity.

My little Jack was given to me when quite a puppy by my old and very dear friend Lord Falmouth. He was brought to me by Lady Falmouth, and from that time his history was my history, for his companionship was constant and faithful; in my hours of labour and of pleasure he was always with me, and I believe, if I had had any sorrows, he would have shared them as he did my pleasures--nay, these he enhanced more than I can tell.

Of course he invariably came circuit, and sat with me in my lodgings and on the Bench, where he would patiently remain till the time came to close my notebook for the day. Whether he liked it or not I am unable to say, but he seemed to take an interest in the proceedings. About this, however, his reminiscences will speak for themselves. He always occupied the seat of honour in the Sheriff's carriage, and walked to it with a dignity worthy the occasion. I am glad to say the Judges all loved Jack, and treated him most kindly, not for my sake, but, I believe, for his own--although, I may add in passing, he sometimes gave them a pretty loud rebuke if they showed any approach to ill-humour on an occasional want of punctuality in coming into court. Some of them were exceedingly particular in being up to time to a *moment*; and I should have equal to the occasion at all times, but that I had to give Jack a run before we started for the duties of the day. It was necessary for his health and good behaviour. On circuit, of course, whenever there was little to do--I am speaking of the Midland particularly, although the Western was quite as pleasant--I gave him longer runs. For instance, in Warwick Park nothing could be more beautiful than to loiter there on a summer morning amongst the cedars on the beautiful lawn.

It may seem unreasonable to say so, but Jack almost seemed to be endowed with human instincts. He was as restless as I was over long, windy speeches and cross-examinations that were more adapted for the smoking-room of a club than a court of justice; and in order to repress any tendency to manifest his displeasure I gave him plenty of exercise in the open air, which made him sleep generally when counsel began to speak.

Having mentioned the commencement of my companionship with Jack, which in these reminiscences I would on no account omit, I shall let him hereafter tell his own experience in his own way.

JACK'S REMINISCENCES.

I was born into the family of my Lord Falmouth, and claim descent from the most well bred of my race in this kingdom, the smooth fox terrier. All my ancestors were noted for their love of sport, their keen sense of humour, and hatred of vermin.

At a very early period of my infancy I was presented to Sir Henry Hawkins, one of Her Majesty's Judges of the High Court, who took a great fancy to me, and, if I may say so without appearing to be vain, at once adopted me as his companion and a member of his family.

Sir Henry, or, as I prefer to call him, my lord, treated me with the sweetest kindness, and I went with him wherever it was possible for him to take me. At first my youthful waywardness and love of freedom--for that is inherent in our race--compelled him to restrain me by a string, which I sometimes pulled with such violence that my lord had to run; and on seeing us so amusing ourselves one morning, old Lord Grimthorpe, I think they called him, who was always full of good-natured chaff, cried out,--

"Halloa, Hawkins! What, has Jack made you his prisoner? Ha! ha! Hold him, Jack; don't let him get away!"

Well, this went on for several weeks, what I think you call chaff, and at last I was allowed to go without the string. It happened that on the very first morning when I was thus given my liberty, whom should we meet but this same old Lord Grimthorpe.

"Halloa!" he cries again--"halloa, Hawkins! Does your keeper let you go without being attached to a string?"

"No, no," says my lord--"no, no; Jack's attached to *me* now."

Thereupon dear old Grimthorpe, who loved a joke, laughed till his elbows rested on his knees as he stooped down.

"Well," said he, "that's good, Hawkins, very good indeed."

On one occasion one of those country yokels who always met us at Assize towns, and got as close up to our javelin-men as they could, so that we could not only see them but indulge our other senses at the same time, seeing us get out of our carriage, said to another yokel, "I say, Bill, blarmed if the old bloke ain't brought his dawg again--that there fox terrier--to go a-rattin'."

I did not know what "rattin'" meant at that time, and did not learn it till we got to Warwick. I thought it was rude to call my lord a "bloke," especially in his red robes; but did not quite know what "bloke" meant, for I had seen so little of mankind.

One morning before we opened the Commission at Warwick--I may as well come to it at once--my lord and I went for a walk along the road that leads over the bridge by Warwick Castle towards Leamington. There is a turning to a village which belonged to the old days, but does not seem now to belong to anything, and looks something like a rural watering-place, quiet and unexciting. We turned down this quiet road, and came alongside a beautiful little garden covered with flowers of all kinds.

I had occasion afterwards to learn whom they belonged to; but I will tell you before we go further, so as to make the situation intelligible. He was a countryman who used to make it his boast that he never had a day's schooling in his life (so that he ought to have been leader of the most ignorant classes), and this made him the independent man he was towards his betters. Then my Lady Warwick used to take notice of him, and this also gave him another lift in his own estimation. He learnt to read in the long run, for he really had a good deal of native talent for a man, and set himself up for a politician and a something they call a philosopher, which any man can be with a pint pot in front of him, I am told, especially at a village alehouse.

He was a great orator at the Gridiron beershop in the lane which runs round one part of my Lord Warwick's park, and it was said that old Gale--such was his name--had picked up most of his education from his own speeches. Gale was also the lawyer of the village--he could tell everybody what his rights were, if anybody had any besides Gale; but he declared he had been done out of *his* rights by a man who had lent his old father some money on the bit of land I am coming to.

As we went along, what should we see but a rat! I knew what he was in a moment, although I had never seen such a thing before, and knew I had to hunt him. My lord cries, "*Cis!--rat, Jack--rats!*"

Away I went after the rat--I did not care what his name was--and Sir Henry after me, with all the exuberance he used to show when he was following the "Quorn." Presently we heard the dreadful orator's voice using language only uttered, I am glad to say, amongst men.

"Where the h--l are you coming to like this?" he cried.

I forgot to say that our marshal was with us, and of course he took upon himself to explain how matters stood; indeed, it was one of his duties when Judges went out a-ratting to explain *who* they were. So when we arrived at the place where they were talking together, I heard the dreadful man say,--

"Judge o' th' land! He ain't much of a judge o' th' land to tear my flowers to pieces like that. Look at these 'ere toolips."

The marshal explained how that it was for the improvement of Sir Henry Hawkins's health that a little fresh air was taken every morning.

"Lookee 'ere," says Gale, "I didn't know it wur the Judge doin' me the honour to tear my flower-beds to pieces. I bin workin' at these 'ere beds for months, and here they are spilt in a minit; but I tell ee what, Orkins or no Orkins, he ain't gwine to play hell with my flower-beds like that 'ere. If he wants the ground for public improvement, as you call it, well, you can take it under the Act.

There's room enough for improvement, I dessay."

Now, instead of his lordship sending the man to prison, as I thought to be sure he must do, he speaks to him as mild as a lamb, and tells him he commends his spirit, and actually asks him what he valued the flowers at. A Judge condescending to do that! This mollified the old man's temper, and turned away his flowery wrath, so he said at once he wasn't the man to make a profit out o' the circum *starnce*; but right was right, and wrong worn't no man's right, with a great many other proverbs of a like nature, which are as hard to get rid of amongst men and women as precedents amongst Judges; and then the old man, much against his will and inclination, had a sovereign forced upon him by our marshal, which he put into his pocket, and then accompanied us to the gate.

Now came this remarkable circumstance. When we got back to our lodgings after being "churched," what should we find but a beautiful nosegay of cut flowers in our drawing-room from old Gale, and every morning came a similar token of his good-nature and admiration while we were there, and the same whenever we went on that circuit.

One of our servants was kind enough to make me a set of robes exactly like my lord's, which I used to wear in the Court of Crown Cases Reserved and at high functions, such as the Queen's Birthday or Chancellor's breakfast. In court I always appeared in mufti on ordinary occasions--that is to say, I did not appear at all ostentatiously, like some men, but sat quietly on my lord's robe close to his chair.

I well remember one occasion while we were at Hereford, a very pompous and extremely proper town, as all cathedral cities are; my lord and I were robed for the reception of the High Sheriff (as he is called) and his chaplain, who were presently coming with the great carriage to take us to be churched before we charged the grand jury.

Hereford is a very stately place, and enjoys a very high opinion of its own importance in the world. It is almost too respectable to admit of the least frivolity in any circumstances. You always seemed to be going to church at Hereford, or just coming out--the latter was nicest--so that there was, in my time, a sedateness only to be equalled by the hardness of a Brazil nut, which would ruin even my teeth to crack. I don't know if that is a proper way in which to describe a solid Herefordian; but if so, judge of the High Sheriff's surprise, as well as that of the chaplain, when I walked by the side of my lord into our drawing-room! I never saw a clergyman look so glum! We were both in robes, as I observed, and my lord was so pleased with my appearance that he held me up for the two dignitaries to admire. But Hereford does not admire other people; they confine their admirations within their own precincts.

On our way from the station to our lodgings, I ought to have said, both these gentlemen were full of praises. Who would not admire a Judge's companion?

Although Sheriff and chaplain were highly proper, the former could not restrain a hearty laugh, while the latter tightened his lips with a reproving smile. But then the chaplain, with a proper reverence for the State function, afterwards looked very straight down his nose, and, hemming a little, ventured to say,--

"My lord, are you *really* going to take the little dog to divine service in the cathedral?"

My lord looked quite astonished at the question, and then put his face down to me and pretended to whisper and then to listen. Afterwards he said,--

"No. Jack says not to-day; he doesn't like long sermons."

The chaplain would much rather I had gone to church than have heard such a reprimand.

But this is not quite the end of my reminiscence. I heard on the best authority that the sermon of the chaplain on that morning was the *shortest he had ever preached* as an Assize discourse, and my lord attributed it entirely to my supposed observation on that subject, so that my presence, at all events, was useful.

I have always observed that lesser dignitaries are more jealous of their dignity than greater ones. Here was an excellent example of it. The chaplain looked very severe, but when this little story reached the ears of the good Bishop Atlay he was delighted, and wished to see me. I was becoming famous. I made my call in due course, and let him see that a Judge's dog was not to be put down by a mere chaplain, and came away much gratified with his lordship's politeness. After this, during our stay in the city, the Bishop gave me the run of his beautiful new garden along the riverside. And there my lord and I used to gambol for an hour after our duties in court were over. This lovely garden was an additional pleasure to me, because I was relieved from a muzzle. There was only one thing wanting: the Bishop kept no rats.

After this his lordship never saw my lord without asking the question, "How's dear Jack?" which showed how much a Bishop could respect a little dog, and how much superior he was to a chaplain. I heard him say once we were all God's creatures, but that, of course, I was not able to understand at the time. I did not know if it included the chaplain.

I think I must now tell a little story of myself, if you will not think me conceited. It is about a small matter that happened at Cambridge. One day a very amiable but dreadfully noisy advocate was cross-examining a witness, as I thought, rather angrily, because the man would not say exactly what he wanted him to say. My lord did not take notice of this, and it went on until I thought I would call his attention to the counsel's manner, and, accordingly, gave a growl-- merely a growl of inquiry. Brown--which was the counsel's name--was a little startled at this unexpected remonstrance, and paused, looking up at the Judge.

"Go on," said my lord--"go on, pray," pretending not to know the cause of the interruption.

He went on accordingly for a considerable time, with a very noisy speech-- so noisy that one could not hear one's self bark, which I did two or three times without any effect. However, at last I made one of my best efforts.

But this was bad policy, inasmuch as it attracted too much attention to myself, who had been hitherto unseen.

My lord, however, thanks to his presence of mind, had the kindness to say,--

"Dear me! I wish people would not bring their dogs into court." Then turning to our marshal, he said, "Take Jack into Baron Pollock's room"--the Baron had just gone in to lunch, for he was always punctual to a minute--"and ask him to give him a mutton-chop."

And when, five minutes later, my lord came in, the Baron was enjoying his chop, and I was eating my lord's.

In another court the Judge administered a well-timed rebuke to a flippant and very egotistical counsel, and I could hardly restrain myself from administering another. During the progress of a dreadfully long address to the jury for the defence, he said,--

"Why, gentlemen, there is not sufficient evidence against the prisoner *on which to hang a dog*."

"And how much evidence, Mr. ----, would you consider sufficient to hang a dog?"

"That would depend, my lord, as to whom the dog belonged."

I thought how like human nature that young man was.

I used to have a very good view of all that took place in court, and could tell some very funny as well as interesting stories about persons I have seen.

One day I was amused *so* much that, had I not remembered where I was, I must, like my friends mentioned by Robert Burns in his "Twa Dogs," have "barked wi' joy," because I thought it so strange. Here was a Queen's Counsel, a man of so proper a countenance that I do not think it ever smiled in its life, and so very devoted to his profession that he would never think of leaving it to go to a racecourse. I should have as soon expected to meet him in our dogs' home looking for a greyhound to go coursing with on Primrose Hill,--and here he was standing up on his hind legs, and making an application to the court which my lord was never in his life known to grant.

It was the night before the Derby, and we always took care to have a full list of cases for that Wednesday, for *fear* the public should think we went to the Derby and left the work to look after itself. We generally had about a dozen in pretty early in the afternoon of Tuesday, so that the suitors and witnesses, solicitors and all others whom it concerned, might know where they were, and that *they* could not go to the Derby the following day.

What a scene it was as soon as this list was published! I used to sit and watch the various applicants sidle into their seats with the most sheepish faces for men I ever saw. In came the first gentleman, flustered with excitement.

"Would your lordship allow me to make an application?"

"Yes," said my lord--"yes; I see no objection. What is your application, Mr. ----?" I will not give his name.

"There is a case, my lord, in to-morrow's list--number ten. It is quite impossible, seeing the number of cases before it, that that case can be reached."

"If that is so," said my lord, "there is no necessity for making any application--if you know it is impossible to reach it, I mean to say--"

"It is *ex abundanti cautela*, my lord."

I think that was the expression, but, as it is not dog-Latin, I am not sure.

"It is a good horse to run, I dare say," said my lord, "but I don't think he'll win this time."

The counsel shook his head and would have smiled, I could see that, only he was disappointed. I felt sorry for him, because his clients had made arrangements to go to the Derby. As he was turning disconsolately away my lord spoke with a little more encouragement in his tone and a quiet smile.

"We will see later, Mr. ----. Is your client *unable* to appear to-morrow?"

"I'm afraid so, my lord, quite."

"Have you a doctor's certificate?"

"I am afraid not, my lord; he is not ill."

"Then you can renew the application later; but understand, I am *determined to get through the list*."

That was so like my lord; nothing would turn him from his resolution, if he sat till midnight, and I nearly barked with admiration.

Then came number six on the list, with the same complaint that it was not likely to be reached.

"I'm not so sure," said Sir Henry. "I have just refused number ten; yours is a long way before that. Some of the previous ones may go off very soon; there does not seem to be anything *very long* in front of you, Mr. ----. What's your difficulty about being here?"

"The real difficulty, my lord--" And as he hesitated the Judge said,--

"You want to be elsewhere?"

"Frankly, my lord, that is so."

"Very well; if both sides are agreed, I have no objection. If I am not trying your case I shall be trying some one else's, and it is a matter of perfect indifference to me whose case it is."

An hour after in came a brisk junior stating that his leader was unavoidably absent.

"What is the application, Mr. Wallsend?"

"There's a case on your lordship's list for to-morrow, my lord."

"Yes. What number?"

"Number seven, my lord. I am told number six is a long case, and sure to be fought. My application is that, as that case will last over Friday--"

"Friday? Why Friday?"

There was a little laughter, because it happened to be the Oaks day.

"I'm told it's a long case, my lord."

"Yes, but number six has gone, so that you will stand an excellent chance of coming on about two o'clock, perhaps a little before. What is the nature of your case?"

"Illegal imprisonment, my lord."

"Very well; if it is any convenience to you, Mr. Wallsend, I will take it last."

By the look of the young man it seemed of no great convenience.

"That will give your witnesses time to be here, I hope."

The counsel shook his head, and then began to say that the fact was that his client had an engagement, and his lordship would see it was the great race of the year.

"I do not like these applications made in this random manner. I am willing to oblige the parties in all cases if I can, but these constant motions to postpone interfere very much with the public convenience, and I mean to say that the public are to be considered."

Now came the gentleman who never attended races, and devoted himself to business. He could not have told you the name of a horse to save his life. But he also made his application to postpone a case until Thursday. Delightful day, Thursday; such a convenient day, too--between the Derby and the Oaks.

Said my lord, who was very friendly to the learned counsel, and liked him not only as a member of his old circuit, but as a brother Bencher and a clever advocate,--

"Oh, I see; I see where *you* want to be to-morrow."

"My lord!"

It was no use; in spite of the gentleman's remonstrance and protestations, he said,--

"You may go, Mr. ----, and I hope you will enjoy yourself."

I need hardly say nothing was left of the list by twelve o'clock the next day, and Sir Henry had the honour of going in the royal train and dining at Marlborough House in the evening.

I ought, perhaps, to mention that there was a case proceeding when all these interruptions took place. I don't know the name, but two counsel were in it, one of whom was remarkable for the soul of wit which is called *brevity*, and the other was not. One was Frank Lockwood, Q.C., a very amusing counsel, whom I always liked, because he often sketched me and my lord in pen and ink.

Mr. Jelf, Q.C., was the other learned counsel. Although I liked most of the barristers, I often wished I could teach them the invaluable lesson *when to leave off*. It would have saved many a verdict, and given me the opportunity of hearing my own voice.

Lockwood was cross-examining, and appeared to me dealing rather seriously with Jelf's witnesses, who were a pious body of gentlemen, and prided themselves, above all things, on speaking the truth, as though it was a great credit not to commit perjury.

At last Mr. Jelf, tired with being routed in so ruthless a manner, cried in a lamentable voice,--

"Pray, pray, Mr. Lockwood!"

"So I do," said Lockwood--"so I do, Mr. Jelf, at fitting and proper times."

CHAPTER XXXIV.
TWO TRAGEDIES.

[The *Daily Telegraph*, speaking of the necessity for Justice sometimes "to strip the bandage from her eyes and look into the real merits of a case, mentions the following case as showing Sir Henry's unequalled knowledge of human nature and the sound equity of his decrees:--

"A young, respectable woman had been led away by a villain, who was already married, and under a promise of marriage had betrayed her. He induced her to elope with him, and suggested that she should tear a cheque out of her father's cheque-book and forge his name. So completely was she under his influence that she did so. He sent her to different banks to try and cash it, but it was not till she got to a local bank, where she was known, that this was accomplished. The cheque was for £200. But the seducer never obtained the money; the girl was apprehended before she reached him.

"Sir Henry openly expressed his strong sympathy for the unhappy girl, and ordered her to be bound over in her own recognizance of £20, to come up for judgment when called upon."]

During the early years of my tenure of office as a criminal Judge I became, and still am, firmly impressed with the belief that to enable one filling that office to discharge the twofold duty attached to it--namely, that of trying the issue whether the crime imputed to the prisoner has been established by legal evidence, and if so, what punishment ought to be imposed upon the prisoner, assuming the presiding Judge to be the person to determine it--it is absolutely essential that he should keep the whole of the circumstances in his mind and carefully weigh every fact which either forms an element in the constitution of the offence itself or has a substantial bearing as affecting the aggravation or mitigation of the punishment; for it is not only essential that these matters should be known to and appreciated by the Judge who tried the case, but that they may be also presented for the information of the Home Secretary, who ought to be acquainted with them, so that he may form a satisfactory view of the whole of the circumstances surrounding the case.

A strange story that will ever stand out in my memory as one of the most dramatic of my life was that of a young lady who was a professional nurse at the General Hospital at Liverpool. She was young, clever, and, I believe, beautiful, as well as esteemed and loved by all who knew her.

She had become engaged to an engineer, and it had been arranged that she should pay a visit to her mother in Nottingham on a Friday, so as to acquaint her with their engagement, the intended husband having arranged to come on the following Monday.

The parents were poor, respectable people, and the girl herself was poor, so that she had no change of attire, but went in her professional nurse's dress. It was her intention, however, to buy an ordinary dress at Nottingham.

There was a dressmaker in that city whom her mother knew, and with whose children in their early days her daughter had played. Accordingly in the evening the nurse with a younger sister went to the cottage to make the necessary arrangements.

While she was there the son of the dressmaker came in, and was at once attracted by the beauty and the manner of the girl. As they had known one another in childhood, it was not surprising that they should talk with more familiarity than would have been the case had they been strangers.

When the nurse rose to go, the young man asked permission to accompany her to her mother's. She declined, but he persisted in his request.

This man was a clever mechanic, and had invented a machine for making chenille. Sad to say, this invention he used for the purpose of inveigling the girl into his workshop, which was situated on the second floor of an extensive range of warehouses in a yard at Nottingham. He asked her to come on the Monday morning, and when she informed him that her lover was to come by the 12.30 train at Nottingham Station, he said if she came at eleven she would have plenty of time to see his invention, and then meet him. She at last consented.

I now come to a series of facts of a sensational character. On the Monday morning she went, according to the appointment, and was seen to go with this man up a flight of steps which led from the yard to the first floor. The door opened on to the landing outwardly. In about a quarter of an hour after she was seen staggering down the steps, and crossing the yard in the direction of the street. In the street she fell, and was conveyed to a neighbouring house. She was afterwards taken to a hospital.

In the course of some minutes the man himself came down the steps, and was informed that a girl had been seen coming out of his premises bleeding, and had been taken to a cottage.

"Was there?" said he, and walked away.

In the afternoon he was apprehended. He said he was very sorry, but that he was showing the girl a little toy pistol, and that it had gone off: quite accidentally. He wished to be taken to the hospital where she was.

The magistrate in the meanwhile had been informed of the occurrence, and with his clerk attended at the hospital to take her dying deposition.

There was an amount of skill and ability about the prisoner which was somewhat surprising to me, who am seldom surprised at anything.

"Did you not think it was an accident?" he asked.

The dying girl answered, "Yes."

In re-examination by the magistrate's clerk at the end of the business, the following answer was elicited,--

"I thought it was an accident before the second shot was fired."

The extraordinary part of this story, to my mind, is that the able counsel-- and able he indeed was who defended him--treated the matter as the most frivolous prosecution that was ever instituted. I know that he almost laughed at the idea of murder, and, further, that the junior counsel for the prosecution treated the charge in the same manner, and said that, in his opinion, there was no case.

The man was indicted for wilful murder, and I am bound to say, after reading the depositions, I could come to no other conclusion than that he was guilty of the most cruel and deliberate murder, if the depositions were correct.

I went with the counsel on both sides to view the scene of the tragedy, and it was agreed that the counsel for the prosecution should indicate as well as he could the case for the Crown by merely stating undisputed facts in connection with the premises.

The flight of steps, as I have said, led from the courtyard to the first landing.

The door opened outwards, and the first visible piece of evidence was that some violence had been exercised in forcing open the door on the occasion of some one making his or her escape from the building, for the staple into which the bolt of the lock had been thrust showed that the door had been locked on the inside, and that the person coming from the premises must have used considerable force in breaking through.

The key was not in the lock, neither had it fallen out, or it would have been found somewhere near. It had evidently been taken out and secreted, because it was found at the bottom of a dustbin a long way off from the staircase and in the room occupied by the prisoner.

There was one additional fact at this part of the view which I must mention. A bullet was picked up near the door. It had struck the opposite wall, and then glanced off and hit the other wall close to the door.

The bullet had been fired from the landing above; this was indicated by the direction as it glanced along the wall, and, further, by the mark it had left of its line of flight from the landing above, for it had struck against the low ceiling of that spot as though the person firing had fired in a hurry and had not taken sufficient aim to avoid it. It might be taken, therefore, that the person firing was not used to firearms, or he would not have hit what might be called the ceiling.

The bullet was produced by the chief constable.

On reaching the second landing, the mark of the bullet in the lintel showed clearly that it had been fired in the direction of some object below--some one, probably, descending the stairs.

On turning into the factory on this floor, which was quite empty, I saw on the wall near the doorway the mark of another bullet which had rested near and was found by the police. It was a bad aim, and showed, therefore, that the person who fired it was unused to firearms.

We went to the next room, into which we ascended by six steps; it was clear that it was from the head of these stairs that the course of the bullet was directed; its elevated position and the angle of incidence showed this. But as neither of these bullets had struck the deceased, for there was no mark of any kind to prove it, there was another bullet to be accounted for, and as the prisoner said that the pistol went off by accident, two or three matters had to be considered. Where was the spot where the accident occurred? and was aim actually taken?

The bullet had entered the hinder part of the neck, had taken a downward direction, and lodged in the spine. It did not, therefore, go off while he was explaining the pistol to her, otherwise it would have struck her at any other place than where it did.

Moreover, she had run in a state of intense fright the moment she was wounded--had commenced to run before, in fact, having escaped from the clutches of her murderer, for the skirt of her dress was torn from the gathers. It was proved that the prisoner had bought the pistol on the Saturday night, that he was unused to firearms, for he had to ask the man who sold it to explain the mode of using it. He was heard practising with it on Sunday, and when the accident occurred it was proved that the interval between the first and second shots exactly accounted for the space which intervened between the respective spots where the firing must have taken place.

Much was made of the fact that the poor girl had said she thought it was an accident, but I had to call the learned counsel's attention to the statement at the end of her examination, which was this: "I thought at first it was an accident, for I could not believe he could be so cruel, but after the *second shot* I believed he meant to kill me."

A somewhat novel incident occurred during the examination for the prosecution.

A wire stand had been dressed with the girl's clothes to show where the lower part of the dress had been torn from the gathers. It was placed on the table, and no doubt exactly resembled the girl herself. The prisoner was so much affected that he shuddered, and had to be supported.

He was condemned to death.

In the House of Commons and out of it sympathy was, of course, aroused, not for the unhappy girl who had been sent suddenly to her account, but for the lustful brute who had murdered her. A question was asked of the Secretary of State for the Home Department as to the prisoner being insane, and whether there was not abundant evidence of insanity at the trial.

The counsel for the prosecution wrote to the Home Secretary and requested him to lay his letter before the prisoner's counsel to ascertain whether he agreed with it. The letter was to this effect: "Not only was there no evidence of insanity, but the prisoner's counsel based his defence entirely upon the fact that there was no suggestion that the man was or ever had been insane. He must have been insane, argued the counsel, if he had committed a brutal murder of that kind; there was no insanity, and therefore it was an accident."

The humane questioner of the Home Secretary left the prisoner after that statement to his well-deserved fate.

I recollect at one Gloucester Assize a man was tried before me for the murder of a woman near Bristol.

The prisoner had given his account of the tragedy, and said he had made up his mind to kill the first woman he met alone and unprotected; that is to say, he had made up his mind to kill somebody when there was no witness of the deed. Humanitarians for murderers might call this insanity.

He went forth on his mission, and saw a woman coming towards him with a baby.

He instantly resolved to kill both, and probably would have done so but for the fact that some one was seen coming towards him in the distance.

The woman and child therefore escaped, the person he had seen in the distance also passed by, and then he waited in the lane alone. In a little time a poor woman came along.

The ruffian instantly seized her, cut her throat, and killed her on the spot.

No sooner had he accomplished his purpose than a young farmer drove along in his cart, and seeing the dead body in the road, and the murderer a little way off, jumped out of his cart and arrested him.

A little farther on the road there was a labouring man, who had not been visible up to this moment, breaking stones.

"Look after this man," said the farmer; "he has committed murder. Keep him safe while I go to the village and get a constable."

"All right," said the labourer; "I'll keep un."

As soon as the farmer was gone the labourer and the murderer got into conversation, for they had to while away the time until the farmer had procured the constable.

"Why," asked the stone-breaker, "what have you been a-doin' of?"

"Killin' a woman," answered the murderer.

"Killin' a woman!" said the mason. "Why, what did you want to kill a woman for? She warn't your wife, was she?"

"Nay," answered the murderer, "or I should ha' killed her afore."

The want of motive is always a strong argument with humanitarians, who pity the murderer and not the victim. I heard no particle of sympathy expressed for the poor woman, but there was abundance of commiseration for the fiend who had perpetrated the terrible deed.

There never was any *adequate* motive for murder, but there was never a deed committed or any act performed without motive.

Insanity on the ground of absence of motive was set up as a matter of course, but insanity should be based on proof apart from the cruelty of the act itself. It was a premeditated crime, a bloodthirsty desire to wreak his malice on some one; but beyond the act, beyond the malignant disposition of the man, there was no evidence whatever of insanity.

I refused to recommend him to the Royal clemency on that ground, or on any ground, for there was not the smallest pretence for saying it was not a deliberate cold-blooded murder. And the man was rightly hanged.

Society should be protected from murderers. This may be hard dealing with the enemies of society, but it is just to society itself. I was never hard on a prisoner. The least circumstance in mitigation found in me a hearty reception, but cruelty in man or woman an unflinching Judge.

Take another case. In Gloucestershire a man was convicted of killing a girl by stabbing her in no less than thirty-eight places.

Again the humanitarians besieged the Home Secretary. "No man in his senses would have been so cruel; and there was his conduct in the dock: he was so wild, so incoherent. There was also his conduct in the field where he had committed the deed: he called the attention of the passers-by to his having killed her." And, last of all, "there was the doctor whom the Home Secretary had consulted after the trial."

I was appealed to, and stated my opinion honestly: that I had closely watched the man at the trial, and was satisfied that he was shamming insanity.

And he shammed it so awkwardly that there was no doubt whatever that he was sane.

Another Judge was asked about the case who saw only the evidence, and he came to the same conclusion; and I was compelled to report that the doctor who certified that he was insane did so *without having seen him* as the doctors for the prosecution had at the trial and before.

He was hanged.

CHAPTER XXXV.

THE ST. NEOTS CASE.

This is the last trial for murder that I presided over. The object is not to show the horrible details of the deed, but my mode of dealing with the facts, for it is in the elimination of the false from the true that the work of a Judge must consist, otherwise his office is a useless form. I shall give this case, therefore, more in detail than I otherwise should.

The case was that of Horsford, in the year 1898, at Huntingdon Assizes. I say now, long after the event, the murderer was not improperly described by the *Daily News* as the greatest monster of our criminal annals, and yet even in that case some kind-hearted people said I had gone quite *to the limits of a Judge's rights* in summing up the case. Let me say a word about circumstantial evidence. Some writers have spoken of it as a kind of "dangerous innovation in our criminal procedure." It is actually almost the only evidence that is obtainable in all great crimes, and it is the best and most reliable.

You may draw wrong impressions from it, I grant, but so you may from the evidence of witnesses where it is *doubtful*; but you cannot fail to draw the right ones where the facts are not doubtful. If it is capable of a wrong inference, a Judge should be absolutely positive in his direction to the jury not to draw it.

I have witnessed many great trials for murder, but do not remember one where there was an eye-witness to the deed. How is it possible, then, to bring home the charge to the culprit unless you rely on circumstantial evidence? Circumstantial evidence is the evidence of circumstances--facts that speak for themselves and that cannot be contradicted. Circumstances have no motive to deceive, while human testimony is too often the product of every kind of motive.

The history of this case is extremely simple. The accused, Walter Horsford, aged thirty-six, was a farmer of Spaldwick. The person murdered, Annie Holmes, was a widow whose age was thirty-eight years. She had resided for several months at St. Neots, where she died on the night of January 7. She had been married, and lost her husband thirteen years ago. On his death he left two children, Annie and Percy. The latter was sixteen years of age and the girl fourteen. The prisoner was a cousin of the deceased woman. While she lived at Stonely the man had been in the habit of visiting her, and had become an intimate member of the family.

In the month of October the prisoner was married to a young woman named Bessie ----. The widow with her two children, and a third, which it would be idle affectation to suggest was the offspring of her late husband, went to reside at St. Neots in a cottage rented at about £8 a year. The prisoner wrote to Annie Holmes on at least two occasions.

Towards the close of the year Annie Holmes suspected herself to be pregnant. She was anxious not to bring another child into the world, and had some communication with the prisoner on the subject.

On January 5 he wrote to her that he would come and make some arrangement. The woman was deceived as to her condition, but that made no difference with regard to the crime. The letter went on to state: "You must remember I paid you for what I done.... Don't write any more letters, for I don't want Bessie to know."

On December 28 he purchased from a chemist to whom he was a stranger, and who lived at Thrapston, a quantity of poison, alleging that he wanted to poison rats. Prisoner called in a gentleman as a reference to his respectability, as the chemist had refused to sell him the poison without. At last a small parcel was supplied. It was entered in a book with the prisoner's name, and he signed the book, as did also the gentleman who was his introducer. The poison was strychnine, arsenic, prussic acid, and carbolic acid. No less than 90 grains of strychnine were supplied. He had written to say he would come over on the Friday which followed January 5. There is no reason to suppose he did not fulfil his promise. On the Friday the woman was suffering from neuralgia. In the evening, however, she was in her usual health and spirits, and did her ironing up to eight o'clock. She went to bed between half-past nine and ten, and took with her a tumbler of water. In ten minutes the little girl and her brother went upstairs. They went to the mother, who was in bed with her child. The tumbler was nearly empty. The mother asked for a "sweet," which the little girl gave. After this Annie got into bed; the mother began to twitch her arms and legs, and seemed in great pain. Dr. Turner was sent for, as she got worse. His assistant, Dr. Anderson, came, and, watching the patient, noticed that the symptoms were those of strychnine poisoning. She was dying. Before he could get to the surgery and return with an antidote the woman was dead. She who had been well at half-past nine was dead before eleven!

The police were communicated with, and a constable searched the house. Turning up the valances of the bed, he found a piece of paper crumpled up; this was sent to an analyst on the following day. An inquest was held and a post-mortem directed.

Horsford at the inquest swore that he had never written to the deceased or visited her.

On the evening of Saturday the 8th, after the post-mortem, Mrs. Hensman and another woman found between the mattress and the bed a packet of papers. These were also submitted for analysis. One of them contained 35 grains of strychnine; another had crystals of strychnine upon it. There was writing on one of the packets, and it was the handwriting of the prisoner; it said, "Take in a little water; it is quite harmless. Will come over in a day or two." On another packet was written: "One dose; take as told," also in the prisoner's handwriting.

The body had been buried and was exhumed. Three grains of strychnine were found by the county analyst in such parts of the stomach as were submitted to him. Dr. Stevenson took other parts to London, and the conclusion he came to was that at least 10 grains must have been in the body at the time of death, while 1/2 grain has been known to be fatal.

There was a singular circumstance in the defence of this case, one which I have never heard before or since, and that was a complaint that the counsel for the prisoner was "twitted" by the Crown because he had not called *evidence for the defence.* The jury were solemnly asked to remember that if one jot or tittle of evidence had been put forward, or a single document put in by him, the prisoner's counsel, he would *lose the last word on behalf of the prisoner*! Of course, counsel's last word may be of more value than some evidence; but the smallest "jot or tittle" of evidence, or any document whatever that even *tends* to prove the innocence of the accused, is of more value than a thousand last words of the most powerful speaker I have ever listened to. And I would go further and say that evidence in favour of a prisoner should never be kept back for the sake of the last word. It is the bounden duty of counsel to produce it, especially where evidence is so strong that no speech could save the prisoner. Neither side should keep back evidence in a prisoner's favour. I said to the jury,--

"We are assembled in the presence of God to fulfil one of the most solemn obligations it is possible to fulfil, and I will to the best of my ability assist you to arrive at an honest and just conclusion.

"The law is that if a man deliberately or designedly administers, or causes to be administered, a fatal poison to procure abortion, whether the woman be pregnant or not, and she dies of it, the crime is wilful murder.

"You have been asked to form a bad opinion of this deceased woman, but she had brought up her children respectably on her slender means, and there was no evidence that she was a loose woman. It more than pained me when I heard the learned counsel--*instructed by the prisoner*--cross-examine that poor little girl, left an orphan by the death of the mother, with a view to creating an impression that the poor dead creature was a person of shameless character.

"Again, counsel has commented in unkind terms on the deceased woman, and said the prisoner *had no motive* in committing this crime on a woman whom he valued at half a crown.

"He might not, it is true, care half a crown for her. It is not a question as to what he valued the woman at; we are not trying that at all; but it showed there *was* a motive.

"I have not admitted a statement which the woman made while in her dying state, because she may not fully have realized her condition. Probably you will have no doubt that, by whomsoever this fatal dose was administered, there is only known to medical science one poison which will produce the symptoms of this woman's dying agonies. One thing is surprising at this stage--that immediately after death the door of the house was not locked, and while the body was upon the bed a paper of no importance was found, and that afterwards several relatives went in. The object of the cross-examination was to show that some evil-disposed person had entered the house and placed things there *without any motive.* But whoever may have gone into that house, there was one person who *did not go*--one who, above all others, owed deceased some respect--and that is the prisoner; and unless you can wipe out the half-crown letter from your mind, you would have expected a man on those intimate terms with the poor woman to have gone and made some inquiries concerning her death. He did not go; he was at the Falcon Hotel at Huntingdon, and a telegram was sent telling him to fail not to be at the inquest.

"At the inquest he told a deliberate lie, for he swore he had never written to the woman, or sent her anything, or been on familiar terms with her. He had written to her, and if his letter did not prove familiar terms, there was no meaning in language.

"With regard to the prisoner's alleged handwriting on the packets and papers found under the woman's bed and elsewhere, I must point out to you that here is one on which is written, 'Take in a little water; it is quite harmless. Will come over in a day or two.'

"This was written on a buff paper, which Dr. Stevenson said must have contained 35 grains of strychnine, sufficient to kill thirty-five persons, and the direction written was, 'One dose; take as told.'

"These inscriptions were sworn to by experts as being in the prisoner's handwriting."

Here I pointed out the alleged resemblances in the characters of the letters, so that the jury might judge if the prisoner wrote them.

"If the prisoner wrote the words 'take as told,' you must ask yourselves the meaning of it.

"Also, you will ask whether it was not a little strange that the death occurred on that very Friday night when he said he would go over and see her. Again, the word 'harmless' is of the gravest character, seeing that within the folds of that paper were 35 grains of a deadly powder, which even for rat-powder would be mixed with something else.

"Again, as to motive, upon which so much stress has been laid by the defendant's counsel. If the prisoner had no motive, who else had? Is there a human being on earth who had ill-will towards her, or anything to gain by her death? The learned counsel carefully avoided suggesting any one; nor could he suggest that any one in the neighbourhood wrote the same handwriting as the prisoner. I will dismiss the theory that some one had imitated the prisoner's writing in order to do him an injury, and ask if you can see any reason for any one else giving the woman the powder.

"There is one fact beyond all dispute: in December the prisoner bought a shilling's worth of strychnine. He said he bought it for rats, but no one on the farm had been called to prove it. What has been done with the rest of the powder?

"Where was he on that Friday? His counsel said he could not prove an *alibi*. But if he was at Spaldwick after saying he was going to St. Neots to see this poor woman, he *could* have proved it.

"The prisoner's counsel said that the accused did not speak of the woman's murder after the inquest, and said it was not necessary; he did not understand the 'familiar jargon' of the Law Courts.

"The familiar jargon of the Law Courts, gentlemen, is not quite the phrase to use with reference to our judicial proceedings. The Law Courts are the bulwark of our liberties, our life, and our property. Our welfare would be jeopardized, indeed, if you dismiss what takes place in them as 'familiar jargon.'

"The question is whether the charge has been so reasonably brought home to the prisoner as to lead you in your consciences to believe that he is guilty. If so, it is your duty to God, your duty to society, and your duty to yourselves, to say so."

Such was the summing up that was arraigned by the humanitarian partisans of the prisoner. If a Judge may not deal with the fallacies of a defence by placing before the jury the true trend of the evidence, what other business has he on the Bench? And it was for thus clearly defining the issue that some one suggested a petition for a reprieve, on the ground that the evidence was *purely circumstantial*, and that my "summing up was against *the weight of the evidence*." Truly a strange thing that circumstances by themselves shall have no weight.

But there was another strange incident in this remarkable trial: *the jury thanked me for the pains I had taken in the case.* I told them I looked for no thanks, but was grateful, nevertheless.

I have learnt that the jury, on retiring, deposited every one on a slip of paper the word "Guilty" without any previous consultation--a sufficient indication of their opinion of the *weight* of the evidence.

This was the last case of any importance which I tried on circuit, and if any trial could show the value of circumstantial evidence, it was this one. It left the identity of the prisoner and the conclusion of fact demonstrable almost to mathematical certainty.

A supposed eye-witness might have said: "I saw him write the paper, and I saw him administer the poison." It would not have added to the weight of the evidence. The witness might have lied.

CHAPTER XXXVI.

A NIGHT AT NOTTINGHAM.

Ever since the establishment of itinerant justices, now considerably over seven hundred years, going circuit has been an interesting and important ceremony, attended with great pomp and circumstance. I had intended to give a sketch of my own drawing of this great function, but an esteemed friend, who is a lover of the picturesque, has sent me an interesting description of one of my own itineraries, and I insert it with the more pleasure because I could not describe things from his point of view, and even if I could, might lay myself open to the charge of being egotistical.

"When Sir Henry Hawkins stepped into the train with his marshal, he felt all the exuberance which a Judge usually experiences on going circuit.

"Going circuit is a pleasant diversion, and may be a delightful holiday when the weather is fine and cases few. I am not speaking of those northern towns where hard labour is the portion of the judicial personage from the time he opens the Commission to the moment when he turns his back upon his prison-house, but of rural Assize towns like Warwick and Bedford or Oakham, where the Judge takes his white gloves, smiles at the grand jury, congratulates them on the state of the calendar, and goes away to some nobleman's seat until such time as he is due to open the Commission in some other circuit paradise where crime does not enter.

"At Lincoln station on this present occasion there is a goodly crowd outside and in, some well dressed and some slatternly, some bareheaded out of respect to the Judge, and others of necessity, but all with a look of profoundest awe.

"But as they wait the arrival of the train, all hearts are beating to see the Judge. Alas for some of them! they will see him too soon and too closely.

"Most conspicuous is the fat and dignified coachman in a powdered wig and tam-o'-shanter cap, and the footman with the important calves. Clustered along the platform, and pushing their noses between the palisade fencing, seem gathered together all the little boys of Lincoln--that is to say, those who do not live at the top of Steep Hill; for on that sacred eminence, the Mount Zion of Lincolnshire, are the *cloisters* and the closes, where are situated the residences of Canons, Archdeacons, and other ecclesiastical divinities. The top of this mountain holds no communion with the bottom.

"On the platform--for the signal has been given that the judicial train is entering the station--ranged in due order are the Sheriff of Lincoln, in full robes, his chaplain in full canonicals, and a great many other worthy dignities, which want of space prevents my mentioning in detail. All are bareheaded, all motionless save those bosoms which heave with the excitement of the occasion.

"Although the chaplain and the Sheriff hold their hats in their hands, it is understood in a well-bred town like Lincoln there will be no cheers, only a deep, respectful silence.

"And so, amid a hush of expectation and a wondering as to whether it's *Orkins*, some saying one thing and some another, the train draws slowly in; a respectful porter, selected for the occasion, opens the door, and out leaps--Jack.

"Then bursts from the crowd a general murmur. 'There 'e is! See 'im, Bill!' cries one. 'There's Orkins! See 'im? There 'e is; that's Orkins behind that there long black devil!'

"He was wrong about the black devil, for it was the Sheriff's Chaplain, who will preach the Assize Sermon next Sunday in the Cathedral."

[A somewhat humorous scene once took place at Nottingham. An indefatigable worker on circuit, Sir Henry seemed to have the constitution of the Wandering Jew and the energy of radium. No doubt he had much more patience than was necessary, for it kept him sitting till the small hours of the morning, and jurors-in-waiting and attendants were asleep in all directions. He was the only one wide awake in court.

Even javelin-men fell asleep with their spears in their hands; the marshal dozed in his chair, ushers leaned against the pillars which supported the gallery, while witnesses rubbed their eyes and yawned as they gave their evidence.

A case of trifling importance was proceeding with as steady a pace as though an empire's fate, instead of a butcher's honour, were involved. One butcher had slandered another butcher.

The art of advocacy was being exercised between an Irishman and a Scotchman, which made the English language quite a hotch-potch of equivocal words and a babel of sounds.

The slander was one that seemed to shake the very foundations of butcherdom throughout the world--namely, an insinuation that the plaintiff had sold Australian mutton for Scotch beef; on the face of it an extraordinary allegation, although it had to find its way for the interpretation of a jury as to its meaning. Amidst this costly international wrangle the Judge kept his temper, occasionally cheering the combatants by saying in an interrogative tone, "Yes?" and in the meanwhile writing the following on a slip of paper which he handed to a friend:--

"GREAT PRIZE COMPETITION FOR PATIENCE.

Hawkins   First prize.
Job   Honourable mention."

Much earlier in the evening an application had been made by way of finding out how far the Judge "would go," as the man tests the wheels of an express. Every wheel had a good ring. He was prepared for a long run. Every case was to be struck out if the parties were not there.

After a while a feeling of compunction seemed to come over him.

"One moment," said he, after the case in hand had proceeded for an hour or so. "This case seems as if it will occupy some time; it is the last but three of the common jury cases, and--I mean to say--if the gentlemen of the special jury like to go till--seven o'clock this evening, they may do so, or they may amuse themselves by sitting in court listening to this case."

There was a shuffling of feet and a murmur like that of bees.

"Gentlemen," he said, "do whatever will be most agreeable to yourselves. I only wish to consider your comfort and convenience."

"A damned pretty convenience," said a special juryman, "to be kept here all night!"

"Return punctually at seven, gentlemen, please; you are released till then."

Any person who knows Nottingham and has to spend in that city two weary hours, between 5 o'clock and 7 p.m., wandering up and down that vast marketplace, will understand the state of mind to which those special jurymen were reduced when they indulged in audible curses.

There was, however, an element in this condition of things which his lordship had not taken into consideration, and that was the *Bar*.

Several members were unnecessarily detained by this order of the court. Their mess was at the George Hotel; at seven they must be in court or within its precincts; at seven they dined. They chose the precincts, and sending for their butler, ordered the mess to be brought to the vacant Judge's room, the second Judge having gone away.

At seven the mess was provided, and those who were not engaged in court sat down with a good appetite and a feeling of delightful exultation.

Meanwhile his lordship proceeded with his work, while the temperature was 84°. Juries wiped their faces, and javelin-men leaned on their spears.

Now and then the sounds of revelry broke upon the ear as a door was opened.

At ten his lordship rose for a few moments, and on proceeding along the corridor towards his room for his cup of tea, several champagne bottles stood boldly in line before his eyes. He also saw two pairs of legs adorned with yellow stockings--legs of the Sheriff's footmen waiting to attend his lordship's carriage some hours hence.

The scene recalled the scenes of other days, and the old times of the Home Circuit came back. Should he adjourn and join the mess? No, no; he must not give way. He had his tea, and went back to court. He was not very well pleased with the cross-examination of the Irish advocate.

"Do you want the witness to contradict what he has said in your favour, Mr.----?"

"No, my lord."

"Why do you cross-examine, then?"

Now the catch of an old circuit song was heard.

"Call your next witness, Mr. Jones. Why was not this case tried in the County Court?"

(Sounds of revelry from the Bar mess-room.)

"Keep that door shut!"

"May the witnesses go in the third case after this, my lord?"

"I don't know how long this case will last. I am here to do the work of--"

("*Jolly good fellow!*" from the mess-room.)

"Keep that door shut!"

"What is your case, Mr.----?"

"It's slander, my lord--one butcher calling another a rogue; similar to the present case."

"Does he justify?"

"Oh no, my lord." It was now on the stroke of twelve.

"I don't know at what time your lordship proposes to rise."

"Renew your application by-and-by."

("*We won't go home till morning!*" from the mess-room.)

"Keep that door shut! How many more witnesses have you got, Mr. Williams?"

Mr. Williams, counting: "About--ten--eleven--"

"And you, Mr. Jones?"

"About the same number, my lord."

It was twenty minutes to one.

"I shall not sit any longer to oblige any one," said Sir Henry, closing his book with a bang.

The noise woke the usher, and soon after the blare of trumpets announced that the court had risen, as some wag said, until the day after yesterday.]

CHAPTER XXXVII.

HOW I MET AN INCORRIGIBLE PUNSTER.

As the Midland Circuit was perhaps my favourite, although I liked them all, there would necessarily be more to interest me there than on any other, and at our little quiet dinners, for which there was no special hour (it might be any time between eight o'clock in the evening or half-past one the next day), there were always pleasant conversations and amusing stories. With a large circle of acquaintances, I had learnt many things, sometimes to interest and sometimes to instruct. Although I never sat down to open a school of instruction, a man should not despise the humblest teaching, or he may be deficient in many things he should have a knowledge of.

There was once an old fox-hunting squire whose ambition was to be known as a punster. There never was a more good-natured man or a more genial host, and he would tell you of as many tremendous runs he had had as Herne the hunter. After-dinner runs are always fine.

The Squire loved to hunt foxes and make puns.

We were sitting on a five-barred gate one evening in his paddocks, and while I was admiring the yearlings, which were of great beauty, I suddenly saw looking over his left shoulder the most beautiful head of a thoroughbred I ever beheld, with her nose quite close to his ear.

"Halloa, my beauty!" said he. "What, *Saltfish*, let me see if I've a bit of sugar, eh, *Saltfish*?--sugar--is it?"

His hand dived into the capacious pocket of his shooting-coat and brought out a piece of sugar, which he gave to the mare, and then affectionately rubbed her nose.

"There, *Saltfish*--there you are; and now show us your heels."

I knew by his mentioning the mare's name so often that there was a pun in it, so I waited without putting any question. After a while he said (for he could contain his joke no longer),--

"Judge, do you know why I call her *Saltfish*?"

"Not the least idea," said I.

"Ha!" he explained, with a prodigious stare that almost shot his blue globular eyes out of his head: "because she is such a capital mare for a *fast day*! Ha, ha!"

Suddenly he stopped laughing from disappointment at my not seeing the joke. He repeated it--"fast day, fast day"--then *glared at me*, and his underlip fell. At last the old man tossed his head, and whipped his boot with his crop. I have no doubt I deprived that man of a great deal of happiness; for if anything is disappointing to a punster, it is not seeing his joke. He had not done with me yet, however, and before abandoning me as an incorrigible lunatic, asked if I would like to see Naples.

"Naples! By all means, but not at this time of year."

"Oh, I don't mean the town--no, no; but if you don't mind a little mud, I'll show you Naples. Come along this lane."

"Watercourse, you mean. I don't mind a little mud," said I; "it washes off, whoever throws it"--and I looked to see what he thought of that, knowing he would tell it at dinner.

"Good!" said he; "devilish good! Wash off, no matter who throws it--devilish good!"

Down we came off the gate, and through the mud we went, he leading with a fat chuckle.

"You don't see the joke, Hawkins--you don't see the joke about that fast day;" and he gave me another look with his great blue eyes.

I didn't know it was a joke; I thought it was the mare's name, and I heard him mutter "Damn!"

"This is the way," he said angrily. We seemed to travel through an interminable cesspool, but at last reached the open, and coming to another gate, he extended his arms on it, after the manner of a squire, and said,--

"There, there's *Naples*. Isn't she lovely?"

"Where?" I asked.

"There; and a prettier mare you never saw. Look at her!"

"She's a beauty--a real beauty!" I exclaimed.

He breathed rather short, and I felt easy. His manner, especially the distending of his cheeks, showed me that he was about to bring forth something--a pun of some sort.

"Do you know," he asked, with another turn of his eyes, "*why* I call her *Naples*?"

"No, I haven't the faintest idea. Naples? no."

"Well," he said, "I've puzzled a good many. I may say nobody has ever guessed it. I call that mare *Naples* because she's such a beautiful *bay*."

I was glad I was not sitting on the gate, for I might have fallen and broken my neck. As I felt his eyes staring at me I preserved a dignified composure, and had the satisfaction of hearing him mutter again, "Damn!"

"This is our way," said he.

I have no doubt he thought me the dullest fool he ever came near.

Our adventures were not ended. We went on over meadow and stile until we came to "The Park," a tract of land of great beauty and with trees of superb growth. He was sullen and moody, like one whose nerves had failed him when a covey rose.

I saw it coming--his last expiring effort. In the distance was a beautiful black mare, such as might have carried Dick Turpin from London to York. He was watching to see if I observed her, but I did not. "Look," he said, in his most coaxing manner, "don't you see that mare yonder--down there by the spinny?"

"What," I said, "on the left?"

"Down there! There--no, a little to the right. Look! There she is."

"Oh, to be sure, a pretty animal."

"Pretty! Why, there's no better bred animal in the kingdom. She's by ---- out of ----."

"She ought to win the Oaks."

"Come, now, *isn't* she superb?"

"A glory. A novelist would call her a *dream*."

"Ah, I thought you would say so. You know what a horse is."

"When I *see* one," I said. "I thought you said this was a mare."

This is what the Squire thought,--

"Well, of all the dull devils I ever met, you are the most utterly unappreciative!"

He was at his wits' end, although you must be clever if you can perceive the wits' end of a punster.

"That's *Morning Star*," said he. "Now do you know *why* I call her *Morning Star*?"

I answered truthfully I did not.

"Why," he said, with a merry laugh, "*because she's a roarer.*"

"What a pity!" I exclaimed. "But I don't wonder at it if she has to carry you and your jokes very far."

He took it in good part, and we had a pleasant evening at the Hall. He discharged a good many other puns, which I am glad to say I have forgotten. But there was a man present who was a good story-teller. Some I had heard before, but they were none the less welcome, while one or two I related were as good as new to my host and old Squire Fullerton, who had once been High Sheriff, and was supposed to know all about circuit business. He prefaced almost everything he said with, "When I was High Sheriff," so I asked him innocently enough how many times he had been High Sheriff, on which my host, being a quick-witted man, looked at him with a broad grin, while he balanced the nutcrackers on his forefinger.

"Well," said Fullerton, "it was in Parke's time."

"Yes; but which of them?" I asked. "Are you alluding to Sir Alan? They did not both come together, surely."

"Now, lookee, Fullerton," said my old friend, tapping the mahogany with the nutcrackers, as though he was about to say something remarkably clever; "one of 'em, Jemmy, had a kind of a cast in one of his eyes--didn't he, Judge?"

"Yes," said I; "but their names were not spelt alike."

"No, no!" cried the squire; "I'm coming to that. One eye was a little troublesome at times, I believe--at least they said so in my time when *I* was High Sheriff--and that made him a little ill-tempered at times. Now, that Judge's name was spelt P-a-r-k-e" (tapping every letter with his nutcrackers), "so the Bar used to call him '*Parke with an "e"*;' and what do you think they used to call the other, whose name was Park?--Come, now, Judge, you can guess that."

I suppose I shook my head, for he said, "Why, you told me the story yourself four years ago--ah! it must be five years ago--at this very table, when old Squire Hawley had laid two thousand on Jannette for the Leger. 'This is it,' said you; 'they call one of them Parke with an "e," and the other Park with an "i."'"

"Very well," I said, after they had done laughing at the way in which my host had caught me; "now I'll tell you what the Duke of Wellington said one morning. You recollect his Grace met with an accident and lost an eye, which was kept in spirits of wine. On asking him how he was, the Duke answered,--

"'Oh, Lord Cairns asked me yesterday the same question; and I said, "I am rather depressed, but I believe my eye is in pretty good spirits."'"

CHAPTER XXXVIII.

THE TILNEY STREET OUTRAGE--"ARE YOU NOT GOING TO PUT ON THE BLACK CAP,

MY LORD?"

One evening, while sitting with some friends in Tilney Street, there was one of the most tremendous explosions ever heard. It seemed as if the world was blown up. But as nothing happened, we did not leave the room, and went on with the conversation.

It was not until the next day it was ascertained that an attempt had been made to blow in Reginald Brett's front door, which was a few houses off, and that it had been perpetrated by some Fenians, whose friends had been awarded penal servitude for life for a similar outrage with dynamite. Why their anger was directed against Mr. Reginald Brett--a most peaceful and excellent man--it was difficult to say, for he was very kind-hearted, and, above all, the son of the Master of the Rolls, who never tried prisoners at all, only counsel.

Having made inquiries the next morning--I don't know of whom, there were such a number of people in Tilney Street--I was astonished to hear some one say, "They meant to pay *you that visit, Sir Henry.*"

"*Then they knocked at the wrong door,*" said I.

The stranger seemed to know me, and I had a little further conversation with him. It turned out he was a Chancery barrister, and a friend of Brett's.

"Why," I asked, "do you think they meant the visit for me?"

"Well," he answered, "it was."

"If it was intended for me," I replied, "I can only say they, were most ungrateful, for I gave their friends all I could."

"Yes--penal servitude for life."

"Very well," I added; "if they think they'll frighten me by blowing in Reginald Brett's front door, they are very much deceived."

Lord Esher, I believe, always considered that *he* was the object of this attack, and as I had no wish to disturb so comforting an idea, took no further notice, and the Fenians took no further notice of me. Years after, however, my name was mentioned in Parliament in connection with this case; nor was my severity called in question.

There were no more explosions in Tilney Street, but a singular circumstance occurred, which placed me in a position, if I had desired it, to deprive Lord Esher of the satisfaction of believing that he was the object of so much Fenian attention. But if it was a comfort to him or a source of pride, I did not see why I should take it away.

A reverend father of the Roman Church told me that a long while ago a man in confession made a statement which he wished the priest to communicate to me. It was under the seal of confession, and he refused, as he was bound to do, to mention a word. The man persisted in asking him, and he as persistently declined.

Some considerable time, however, having elapsed, the same man went to the priest, not to confess, but to repeat his request in ordinary conversation. This the father could have no objection to, and the culprit told him that he had undertaken to throw the bomb at the front door of Number 5, but that through having in the gas-light misread the figure, he had placed it against that of Number 2. He begged the priest as a great favour to assure me on his word that the bomb was certainly intended for me, and not for Brett.

On this subject the *Kent Leader* had some interesting remarks on the anarchists as well as their Judge.

"Speaking of dynamite," it said, "we have serious cause for alarm in our free land. The wretches concerned in the abominable outrage of Tuesday last cannot be too severely dealt with. It is evident that their intent was against Justice Hawkins, and the fact that Sir Henry was the presiding Judge at the recent anarchists' trial points the connection between the outrage and other anarchists....

"Justice Hawkins has been spoken of as a harsh Judge. Ever since the 'Penge mystery' trial many have termed him the hanging Judge. We have sat under him on many eventful occasions, and venture the opinion that no one who has had equal opportunity would come to any other conclusion than that he was painstaking and careful to a degree, and particularly in criminal cases formed one of the most conscientious Judges on the Bench. Hanging Judge! Why, we have seen the tears start to his eyes when sentencing a prisoner to death, and, owing to emotion, only by a masterful effort could his voice be heard. Above all, he is a just Judge."

[Many persons were not aware, and thousands are not at the present time, that when a verdict of "Wilful murder" is pronounced a Judge has no alternative but to read the prescribed sentence of death. If this were not so, the situation would be almost intolerable, for who would not avoid, if possible, deciding that the irrevocable doom of the prisoner should be delivered? In many cases the feelings of the Judges would interfere with the course of justice, and murderers would receive more sympathy than their victims, while fiends would escape to the danger of society.

And yet that Judges have sympathy, and that it can be, and is, in these days properly exercised, the following story will testify. I give the story as Lord Brampton told it.]

In a circuit town a poor woman was tried before me for murdering her baby. The facts were so simple that they can be told in a few words. Her baby was a week old, and the poor woman, unable to sustain the load of shame which oppressed her, ran one night into a river, holding the baby in her arms. She had got into the water deep enough to drown the baby, while her own life was saved by a boatman.

The scene was sad enough as she stood under a lamp and looked into the face of the policeman, clutching her dead child to her breast, and refusing to part with it.

At the trial there was no defence to the charge of wilful murder except *one*, and that I felt it my duty to discountenance. I think the depositions were handed to a young barrister by my order, and that being so, I exercised my discretion as to the mode of defence. In other words, I defended the prisoner myself.

In order to avoid the sentence that would have followed an acquittal *on the ground of insanity*, which would have entailed perhaps lifelong imprisonment, I took upon myself to depart from the usual course, and ask the jury whether, *without being insane in the ordinary sense, the woman might not have been at the time of committing the deed in so excited a state as not to know what she was doing.*

I thus avoided the technical form of question sane or insane, and obtained a verdict of guilty, but that the woman at the time was not answerable for her conduct, together with a strong recommendation to mercy. This verdict, if not according to the strictest legal quibbling, was according to justice.

I was about to pronounce sentence in accordance with the law, which it was not possible for me to avoid, however much my mind was inclined to do so, when the pompous old High Sheriff, all importance and dignity, said,--

"My lord, are you not going to put on the black cap?"

"No," I answered, "I am not. I do not intend the poor creature to be hanged, and I am not going to frighten her to death."

Addressing her by name, I said, "Don't pay any attention to what I am going to read. No harm will be done to you. I am sure you did not know in your great trouble and sorrow what you were doing, and I will take care to represent your case so that nothing will harm you in the way of punishment."

I then mumbled over the words of the sentence of death, taking care that the poor woman did not hear them--much, no doubt, to the chagrin of the High Sheriff and to the lowering of his high office and dignity. Nothing so enhances a Sheriff's dignity as the gallows.

[There was a great deal of unlooked-for appreciation of his merits, and from quarters where, had he been a hard Judge, one could never have expected it.

There was even the observation of the costermonger leaning over his barrow near the Assize Court when one morning Sir Henry was going in with little Jack.

"Gorblime, Jemmy! see 'im? The ole bloke's been poachin' agin. See what he's got?"

It was a brace of pheasants, and not going into court with his gun, but only his dog, it was taken for granted he had been out all night on an unlawful expedition.

Some one once asked Sir Henry what was the most wonderful verdict he ever obtained.

He answered: "It depends upon circumstances. Do you mean as to value?"

"And amount."

"Well, then," he said, "*half a farthing.*"

Some of the company were a little disconcerted.

"I'll tell you," said the Judge. "There was in our Gracious Majesty's reign a coinage of *half a farthing*. It was soon discountenanced as useless, but while it was current as coin of the realm I had the honour of obtaining a verdict for that amount, and need not say, had it been paid in *specie* and preserved, it would in value more than equal at the present time any verdict the jury might have given in that case."]

One of the most remarkable trials in which as a Judge I have presided was what was known as the Muswell Hill tragedy. It was a brutal, commonplace affair, and with its sordid details might make a respectable society novel. I should have liked Sherlock Holmes to have been in the case, because he would have saved me a great deal of sensational development, as well as much anxiety and observation.

Burglars are usually crafty and faithless to one another. They never act alone--that is, the real professionals--and invariably, while in danger of being convicted, betray one another. Such, at all events, is my experience. Each fears the treachery of his companion in guilt, and endeavours to be first in disclosing it. In the case I am now speaking of, this experience was never more verified than in the attempt on the part of these two murderers each to shift the guilt on to the other.

The ruffians, Milsome and Fowler, resolved to commit a burglary in the house of an old man who led a lonely life at the suburb known as Muswell Hill, near Hornsey.

The sole occupant of the cottage slept in a bedroom on the first floor. In his room was an iron safe, in which he kept a considerable sum of money, close by the side of his bed.

In the dead of night the two robbers found their way into the kitchen, which was below the bedroom. They made, however, so much noise as to arouse the sleeper in the room above. The old man rose, and went down into the kitchen, where he found the two prisoners preparing to search for whatever property they might carry away. Instantly they fell upon their victim, threw him on to the floor, and with a tablecloth, which they found in the room, and which they cut into strips for the purpose, bound the poor old man hand and foot, and struck him so violently about the head that he was killed on the spot, where he was found the following morning. The prisoners failed to obtain the booty they were in search of, and made off with some trifling plunder, the only reward for a most cruel murder. They escaped for a time, but were at last traced by a singular accident--one of the prisoners having taken a boy's toy lamp on the night of the burglary from his mother's cottage and left it in the kitchen of the murdered man. The boy identified one of the prisoners as the man who had been at his mother's and taken the lamp.

The men were jointly charged with the murder before me. Each tried to fix the guilt on the other, knowing--or, at all events, believing--that he himself would escape the consequences of wilful murder if he succeeded in hanging his friend. I knew well enough that, unless it could be proved that *both* were implicated in the murder, or if it should be left uncertain which was the man who actually committed it, or that they both went to the place with the joint intention of perpetrating it if necessary for their object, they might both avoid the gallows. I therefore directed my attention closely to every circumstance in the case, and after a considerable amount of evidence had been given without much result, so far as implicating both prisoners in the actual murder was concerned, an accidental discovery revealed the whole of the facts of the tragedy as plainly as if I had seen it committed.

I have said that the tablecover had been *cut* into strips to accomplish their purpose; and it was clear that a penknife had been used, for one was found on the floor. Suddenly my attention was called to the fact that *two* penknives, which no one had hitherto noticed, were produced. They belonged, not to the prisoners, but to the deceased man, and were usually placed on the shelf in the kitchen. But it came out in evidence, quite, as it seemed, accidentally, that they had been taken from that place, and were found on the floor where the cutting up of the tablecover had been performed, at some little distance from one another; but each knife *by the side of and not far from the deceased man*. They were at my wish handed to me; I also asked for some of the shreds which had bound the dead man. Upon examination it seemed that these were the knives that had been used to cut the tablecloth into shreds, and if so, the jury might well assume that *each* prisoner had used one of the knives for that purpose, for one man could not at the same time use two.

The tablecloth had jagged or hacked edges, which satisfied the jury that the knives had been used hurriedly, and that each man had been doing his share of the cutting. It was thus clearly established that both the men were engaged in the murder and equally guilty, and so the jury found by their verdict.

Whilst they were considering, the bigger of the two, a very powerful man, made a murderous attack upon the other, whom he evidently looked upon as his betrayer, and tried to kill him in the dock. The struggle was a fearful one, but the warders at last separated them.

They were both sentenced to death and hanged.

[The fact of these men making a noise in entering the house was strongly against them on a question of intent. Burglars work silently, and at the least noise decamp, as a rule. In the present case, there being only one old man to contend against, it was easy to silence him as they did, and as they doubtless intended, when they went to the house.]

CHAPTER XXXIX.

SEVERAL SCENES.

I think I have said that I had a favourite motto, which was, "Never fret." It has often stood me in good stead and helped me to obey it. I was once put to it, however, on my way to open the Commission at Bangor on the Welsh Circuit. The Assizes were to commence on the following day. It was a very glorious afternoon, and one to make you wish that no Assize might ever be held again.

I had engaged to dine with the High Sheriff, who lived three or four miles away from the town, in a very beautiful part of the country; so there was everything to make one glad, except the Assizes. Added to all this pleasurable excitement, the Chester Cup was to be run for in the meanwhile, and I had many old friends who I knew would be there, and whom I should have been glad to meet had it been possible.

The Sheriff had made most elaborate calculations from his Bradshaw and other sources as to the times of departure and arrival by train. I did not know what to do, so arranged with the stationmaster at Chester to shunt my carriage till the afternoon, having no doubt I should be able to fulfil my engagements easily.

It so happened, however, that the racing arrangements of the railway had been completely disturbed by the great crowds of visitors, and the result was that I did not reach Carnarvon at the proper time, and my arrival in that place was delayed for nearly an hour.

Nevertheless, I opened the Commission, and the High Sheriff asked me if I would allow him to go on to his house to receive his guests, whom he had invited to meet me, and permit the chaplain to escort me in the performance of my duties.

Having dressed in full uniform, I got into the carriage with the chaplain, who was quite a lively companion, of an enterprising turn of mind, and desirous of learning something of the world. I could have taught him a good deal, I have no doubt, had I allowed myself to be drawn. My friend had no great conversational powers, but was possessed of an inquiring mind. After we had ridden a little way, to my great amusement he asked me if I had any favourite *motto* that I could tell him, so that he might keep it in his memory.

"Yes," said I, "I have a very good one," and cheerfully said, "Never fret."

This, when I explained it to him, especially with reference to my business arrangements, seemed to please him very much. It was as good as saying, "Don't fret because you can't preach two sermons from two pulpits at the same time."

He asked if he might write it down in his pocket-book, and I told him by all means, and hoped he would.

"Excellent!" he murmured as he wrote it: "Never fret."

He then asked modestly if I could give him any other pithy saying which would be worthy of remembrance.

"Yes," said I, thinking a little, "I recollect one very good thing which you will do well to remember: Never say anything you think will be disagreeable to other persons."

He expressed great admiration for this, as it sounded so original, and was particularly adapted to the clergy.

"Oh," said he, "that's in the real spirit of Christianity."

"Is that so?" I asked, as he wrote it down in his book; and he seemed to admire it exceedingly after he had written it, even more than the other.

Then he said he really did not like to trouble me, but it was the first time he had had the honour of occupying the position of Sheriff's chaplain, etc.; but might he trouble me for another motto, or something that might go as a kind of companion to the others in his pocket-book?

This a little puzzled me, but I felt that he took me now for a sage, and that my reputation as such was at stake. I had nothing in stock, but wondered if it would be possible to make one for him while he waited.

"Yes," said I, "with the greatest displeasure: Never do anything which you feel will be disagreeable to yourself."

"My lord!" he cried in the greatest glee, "that is by far the best of all; that must go down in my book, it is so practical, and of everyday use."

I was, of course, equally delighted to afford so young a man so much instruction, and thought what a thing it is to be young. However, here was an opportunity not to be lost of showing him how to put to the practical test of experience two at least, if not all three, of the little aphorisms, and I said so.

"I should be delighted, my lord, to put your advice into practice at the earliest opportunity," he answered.

"That will be on Sunday," said I, "at twelve o'clock. Don't preach a long sermon!"

In due time we arrived at the Sheriff's house, and there found all the guests assembled and waiting to meet me. I was quite quick enough to perceive at a glance that they had been planning some scheme to entrap me--at all events, to cause me embarrassment. The ladies were in it, for they all smiled, and said as plainly by their looks as possible, "We shall have you nicely, Judge, depend upon it, by-and-by."

The Sheriff was the chief spokesman. No sooner had we sat down to table than he addressed me in a most unaffected manner, as if the question were quite in the ordinary course, and had not been planned. I answered it in the same spirit.

"My lord, could you kindly tell us which horse has won the Cup?" evidently thinking that I had been to the course.

There was a dead silence at this crucial question--a silence that you could feel was the result of a deep-laid conspiracy--and all the ladies smiled.

Fortunately I was not caught; nor was I even taken aback; my presence of mind did not desert me in this my hour of need; and I said, in the most natural tone I could assume,--

"Yes, I was sure that would be the first question you would ask me when I had the pleasure of meeting this brilliant company, as you knew I must pass through Chester Station; so I popped my head out of the window and asked the porter which horse had won. He told me the Judge had won by a length, Chaplain was a good second, and Sheriff a bad third."

The squire took his defeat like a man.

I was reminded during the evening of a singular case of bigamy--a double bigamy--that came before me at Derby, in which the simple story was that an unfortunate couple had got married twenty years before the time I speak of, and that they had the good luck to find out they did not care for one another the week after they were married. It would have been luckier if they had found it out a week before instead of a week after; but so it was, and in the circumstances they did the wisest thing, probably, that they could. They separated, and never met again until they met in the dock before me--a trysting-place not of their own choosing, and more strange than a novelist would dream of.

But there they were, and this was the story of their lives:--

The man, after the separation, lived for some time single, then formed a companionship, and, as he afterwards heard that his wife had got married to some one else, thought he would follow her example.

Now, if a Judge punished immorality, here was something to punish; but the law leaves that to the ecclesiastical or some other jurisdiction. The Judge has but to deal with the breach of the law, and to punish in accordance with the requirements of the injury to society--not even to the injury of the individual.

I made inquiries of the police and others, as the prisoners had pleaded guilty, and found that all the parties--the four persons--had been living respectable and hard-working lives. There was no fault whatever to be found with their conduct. They were respected by all who knew them.

I then asked how it was found out at last that these people, living quietly and happily, had been previously married.

"O my lord," said a policeman, "there was a hinquest on a babby, which was the female prisoner's babby and what had died. Then it come out afore Mr. Coroner, my lord, and he ordered the woman into custody, and then the man was took."

I thought they had had punishment enough for their offence, and gave them no imprisonment, but ordered them to be released on their own recognizances, and to come up for judgment if called upon.

Now came *my* sentence. The clergyman of the parish in which this terrible crime had been discovered evidently felt that he had been living in the utmost danger for years. Here these people came to his church, and for aught he knew prayed for forgiveness under the very roof where he himself worshipped.

He said I had done a fine thing to encourage sin and immorality, and what could come of humanity if Judges would not punish?

He denounced me, I afterwards learned, in his pulpit in the severest terms, although I did not hear that he used the same vituperative language towards the poor creatures I had so far absolved. Luckily I was not attending the reverend gentleman's ministration, but he seemed to think the greatest crime I had committed was disallowing the costs of the prosecution. That was a direct *incentive to bigamy*, although in what respect I never learned.

It sometimes suggested to my mind this question,--

What would this minister of the gospel have said to the Divine Master when the woman caught "in the very act" was before Him, and He said, in words never to be forgotten till men and women are no more, "Neither do I condemn thee"?

I thought those who loved a prosecution of this kind--whoever it may have been--*ought* to pay for the luxury, and so I condemned *them* in the costs.

CHAPTER XL.

DR. LAMSON[A]--A CASE OF MISTAKEN IDENTITY--A WILL CASE.

[Footnote A: In this and one or two other cases I am pleased to acknowledge my thanks to my esteemed friend Mr. Charles W. Mathews, the distinguished advocate, for refreshing my memory with the incidents.]

One of the most diabolical cases which came before me while a Judge was one which, although it occupied several days, can be told in the course of a few minutes. I mention it, moreover, not so much on account of its inhuman features as the fact that, in my opinion, Dr. Lamson led the prosecutors--that is, the Government solicitors--into a theory which was calculated by that cunning murderer to save him from a conviction, and it nearly did so.

The story is this:--There was in the year 1873 a family of five children, one of whom died that year and another in 1879, leaving two daughters and a poor cripple boy of eighteen. He was partially paralyzed, and had a malformation of the spine, so that he was an object of great commiseration. He was of a kind and cheerful disposition, and, excepting his spinal affliction, in good health. He seems to have been loved by everybody. His playmates wheeled him about in his chair so that he might enjoy their pastimes, and even carried him up and down stairs. One of this boy's sisters married a Mr. Chapman; the other married a man who was a doctor, or passed as one, of the name of Lamson. He was a man of idle habits, luxurious tastes, and a wicked heart. He was in debt, had fraudulently drawn cheques when he had nothing at the bank to meet them, and was so reduced to poverty that he had pawned his watch and his case of surgical instruments.

By the death of the brother in 1879, the two sisters received each a sum of £800. This boy, Percy, received the like amount, and if he should live to come of age would have a further sum of £3,000; but if he died before that period, one-half would go to Mrs. Chapman and the other half to Mrs. Lamson, the doctor's wife.

Lamson had bought a medical practice at Bournemouth in 1880, but very soon after writs and executions were issued against him.

For three years before Percy's death he had been at school at Blenheim House, Wimbledon.

It appeared from his statement while dying that he felt just "the same as I did once before, when I was at Shanklin with my brother-in-law," the doctor, "after he had given me a quinine pill." "My throat is burning, and my skin feels all drawn up." This pill, however, did not kill him, but it showed, as subsequent events proved, the murderous design of Dr. Lamson.

On December 3 the boy, being still at school and in good health, was amusing himself with his schoolfellows when his brother-in-law, the prisoner, called. Percy was taken into the room to see him. "Well, Percy, old boy," said the doctor, "how fat you are looking!" The doctor sat down, and Percy was seated near him. The visitor then took out of a little bag a Dundee cake and some sweets, and cut a small slice of the cake with his penknife. About fifteen minutes afterwards he said to Mr. Bedbury, the master, "I did not forget you and your boys: these capsules will be nice for them to take nauseous medicines in;" and he took several boxes of capsules from the bag and placed them on the table. One box he pushed towards Mr. Bedbury, asking him to try them.

No one had seen Lamson take a capsule out of the box, but he was seen to fill one with sugar and give it to the boy, saying, "Here, Percy, you are a swell pill-taker." Within five minutes after that the doctor excused himself for going so soon, saying if he did not he would lose his train.

Not long after his departure--that is, between eight and nine--the boy was taken ill and put into bed with all the violent symptoms which are invariably produced by that most deadly of vegetable poisons, aconitine, and he died at twenty minutes past eleven the same night.

Aconitine was found in the stomach; aconitine had been purchased by the doctor before the boy's death, and being well and having been well, the brother-in-law gave him the last thing he swallowed before the dreadful symptoms of the poison betrayed its presence. At that time no chemical test could be applied to aconitine, any more than it could to strychnine in the time of Palmer. But its symptoms were, in the one case as well as in the other, unmistakable, and such as no other cause of illness would produce.

Two pills were found in the boy's play-box, one of which was said to contain aconitine.

Such was the simple case which occupied six days to try. The jury were not long in coming to a conclusion, and returned into court with a verdict of "Guilty."

My awful duty was soon concluded. I told the prisoner the law compelled me to pass upon him the sentence of death; but gave him, both by voice and manner, to understand that in this world there could be no hope for such a criminal. I said, as I thought it right to say, that it was no part of my duty to admonish him as to how he was to meet the dread doom that awaited him, but nevertheless I entreated him to seek for pardon of his great sin from the Almighty. It was my opinion, and I believe that of the counsel for the defence, that, although so much stress was laid upon the *capsule* and the administration of the poison by that means, it was not so administered, but that the capsule was an artifice, designed to hoodwink the doctors and Treasury solicitors.

To have poisoned the boy in such a manner would have been a clumsy device for so keen and artful a criminal as Lamson; and I knew it was conveyed in another manner. It should be stated that in Lamson's pocket-book were found memoranda as to the symptoms and effect of aconitine, and as to there being no test for its discovery. Lamson therefore had made the poisoning of this boy a careful and particular study. He was not such a clumsy operator as to administer it in the way suggested. The openness of that proceeding was to blind the eyes of detectives and lawyers alike; the aconitine was conveyed to the lad's stomach *by means of a raisin in the piece of Dundee cake which Lamson cut with his penknife and handed to him.* He knew, of course, the part of the cake where it was.

My attention was directed to the artifice employed by Lamson, by the shallowness of the stratagem, and by the one circumstance that almost escaped notice--namely, the Dundee cake and the curious desire of the man to offer the boy a piece in so unusual a manner. So eager was he to give him a taste that he must needs cut it with his *penknife*. I was sure, and am sure now, although there is no evidence but that which common sense, acting on circumstances, suggested, that the aconitine was conveyed to the deceased by means of the piece of cake which Lamson gave him, and being carefully placed in the interior of the raisin, would not operate until the skin had had time to digest, and he the opportunity of getting on his journey to Paris, whither he was bound that night, to await, no doubt, the news of the boy's illness and death.

If the poison had been conveyed in the capsule, its operation would have been almost immediate, and so would the detection of the aconitine. As I have said, the contrivance would have been too clumsy for so crafty a mind. A detective would not expect to find the secret design so foolishly exposed any more than a spectator would expect to see the actual trick of a conjurer in the manner of its performance.

I was not able to bring the artifice before the jury; the Crown had not discovered it, and Lamson's deep-laid scheme was nearly successful. His plan, of course, was to lead the prosecution to maintain that he gave the poison in the capsule, and then to compel them to show that there was no evidence of it. The jury were satisfied that the boy was poisoned by Lamson, and little troubled themselves about the way in which it was done.

A singular case of mistaken identity came under my notice during the trial of a serious charge of wounding with intent to do grievous bodily harm. *Five* men were charged, and the evidence showed that a most brutal mutilation of a gamekeeper's hand had been inflicted. The men were notorious poachers, and were engaged in a poaching expedition when the crime was committed. One of the accused was a young man, scarcely more than a youth, but I had no doubt that he was the cleverest of the gang. The men were convicted, but this young man vehemently protested his innocence, and declared that he was not with the gang that night. His manner impressed me so much that I began to doubt whether some mistake had not been made. The injured keeper, however, whose honesty I had no reason to doubt, declared that this youth was really the man who knelt on his breast and inflicted the grievous injury to his hand by nearly severing the thumb. He swore that he had every opportunity of seeing him while he was committing the deed, as his face was close to his own, and *their eyes met.*

Moreover, the young man's cap was found *close by the spot where the assault took place.* About this there was no dispute and could be no mistake, for the prisoner confessed that the cap was his, adding, however, that he *had lent it on that night to one of the other prisoners.* The youth vehemently protested his innocence after the verdict was given.

So far as he was concerned I was *not* satisfied with the conviction. "Is it possible," I asked myself, "that there can have been a mistake?" I did not think that in the excitement of such a moment, and during so fearful a struggle with his antagonist, with their faces *so close together* that they stared into each other's eyes, there was such an opportunity of seeing the youth's face as to make it clear beyond any doubt that he was the man who committed the crime. The jury, I thought, had judged too hastily from appearances--a mistake always to be guarded against.

I invited the prosecuting counsel to come to my room, and asked him, "Are you satisfied with that verdict so far as the *youngest prisoner* is concerned?"

"Yes," he said; "the jury found him 'Guilty,' and I think the evidence was enough to justify the verdict."

"I *do not*," I said, "and shall try him again on another indictment." There was another involving the same evidence.

I considered the matter very carefully during the night, and weighed every particle of evidence with every probability, and the more I thought of it the more convinced I was that injustice had been done.

First of all, to prevent the men who I was convinced were rightly convicted from entertaining any doubt about the result of their conviction, I sentenced them to penal servitude.

I then undertook to watch the case on behalf of the young man myself, and did not, as I might have done, assign him counsel.

The prisoner was put up for trial, and the second inquiry commenced. It had struck me during the night that there was a point in the case which had been taken for granted by the *counsel on both sides*, and that that point was *the* one on which the verdict had gone wrong. As I have said, I did not doubt the honest belief of the keeper, but I doubted, and, in fact, disbelieved altogether in, the power of any man to identify the face of another when their eyes were close together, as he had no ordinary but a distorted view of the features. In order to test my theory on this matter, I took the real point in the case, as it afterwards turned out to be. It was this: *Five men* were taken *for granted* to have been in the gang and in the field on that occasion. The difficulty was to prove that there were only *four*, and then to show that the young man was not one of the four. These two difficulties lay before me, but I resolved to test them to the utmost of my ability. The Crown was against me and the Treasury counsel.

I knew pretty well where to begin--which is a great point, I think, in advocacy--and began in the right place. I must repeat that the prisoner boldly asserted, when the evidence was given as to the finding of his cap close to the spot where the outrage was committed, that it *was* his cap, but that he had not worn it on that night, having lent it to one of the other men, whom he then named. This was, to my mind, a very important point in this second trial, and I made a note of it to assist me at a later period of the case. If this was true, the strong corroboration of the keeper's evidence of identity was gone. Indeed, it went a good deal further in its value than that, for it may have been the finding of the prisoner's cap that induced the belief that the man whose face he saw was the prisoner's!

I asked the accused if he would like the other men called to prove his statements, warning him at the same time that it was upon his own evidence that they had been arrested, and pointing out the risk he ran from their ill-will.

"My lord," said he, "they will owe me no ill-will, and they will not deny what I say. It's true; I'm one of 'em, and I know they won't deny it."

Without discarding this evidence I let the case proceed. I asked the policeman when he came into the witness-box if he examined carefully the footprints at the gate where the men entered. He said he had, and was *quite positive* that there were the footprints of *four men only*, and further, that these prints corresponded with the shoes of the four men who had been sentenced, and *not* with those of the prisoner.

It shows how fatal it may be in Judge, counsel, or jury to take anything for granted in a criminal charge. It had been taken for granted at the former trial that *five* men had entered the field, and how the counsel for the defence could have done so I am at a loss to conceive. It was further ascertained that the same number and the *same footprints* marked the steps of those coming *out* of the field. It went even further, for it was proved that *no footprints of a fifth man were anywhere visible on any other part of the field*, although the most careful search had been made.

If this was established, as I think it was beyond all controversy, it clearly proved that only *four men* were in the field when the injuries were inflicted. But it might, nevertheless, be that the young man identified was one of the four. Whether he was or not was now the question at issue; it was reduced to that one point. To disprove this the prisoner said he would like the men to be called. I cautioned him again as to the danger of the course he proposed, feeling that he was pretty safe as it was in the hands of the jury. They could hardly convict under my ruling in the circumstances.

"No, my lord," he said; "I am *sure they will speak the truth about it*. They will not swear falsely against me to save themselves."

The man who was alleged to have borrowed the cap was then brought up, and I asked him if it was true that he wore the prisoner's cap on the night of the outrage. He said, "It is true, my lord; I borrowed it."

"Then are you the man who inflicted the injury on the keeper?"

His answer was, "Unhappily, my lord, I am, and I am heartily sorry for it."

When asked, "Was this young man with you that night?"

"No, my lord," was the answer.

The jury at once said they would not trouble me to sum up the case; they were perfectly satisfied that the prisoner was not guilty, and that what he said was true--that he was not in the field that night. They accordingly acquitted him, to my perfect satisfaction.

Of course, I instantly wrote to the Home Secretary, Mr. H. Matthews (now Viscount Llandaff), who at once procured a free pardon on the former conviction, and the prisoner was restored to liberty.

This case strikingly points to the imperative demand of justice that every case shall be investigated in its minutest detail. The broad features are not by any means sufficient to fix guilt on any one accused, and it is in such cases that circumstantial evidence is often brought in question, while, indeed, the *real* circumstances are too often not brought to light. Circumstantial evidence can seldom fail if the real circumstances are brought out. Nobody had thought of raising a doubt as to there being *five* persons in the field.

Upon such small points the great issue of a case often depends.

Another curious case came before me on the Western Circuit. A solicitor was charged with forging the will of a lady, which devised to him a considerable amount of her property; but as the case proceeded it became clear to me that the will was signed after the lady's death, and then with a dry pen held in the hand of the deceased, by the accused himself whilst he guided it over a signature which he had craftily forged. A woman was present when this was done, and as she had attested the execution of the will, she was a necessary witness for the prisoner, and in examination-in-chief she was very clear indeed that it was by the *hand of the deceased* that the will was signed, and that she herself had seen the deceased sign it. Suspicion only existed as to what the real facts were until this woman went into the box, and then a scene, highly dramatic, occurred in the course of her cross-examination by Mr. Charles Mathews, who held the brief for the prosecution.

The woman positively swore that she saw the testatrix sign the will *with her own hand*, and no amount of the rough-and-ready, inartistic, and disingenuous "Will you swear this?" and "Are you prepared to swear that?" would have been of any avail. She *had* sworn it, and was prepared to swear it, in her own way, any number of times that any counsel might desire.

The only mode of dealing with her was adopted. She was asked,--

"Where was the will signed?"

"On the bed."

"Was any one near?"

"Yes, the prisoner."

"How near?"

"Quite close."

"So that he could hand the ink if necessary?"

"Oh yes."

"And the pen?"

"Oh yes."

"*Did he hand the pen?*"

"*He did.*"

"*And the ink?*"

"Yes."

"There was no one else to do so except you?"

"No."

"Did he put the pen into her hand?"

"Yes."

"And assist her while she signed the will?"
"Yes."
"How did he assist her?"
"*By raising her in the bed and supporting her when he had raised her.*"
"Did he guide her hand?"
"No."
"Did he touch her hand at all?"
"*I think he did just touch her hand.*"
"When he did touch her hand *was she dead?*"

At this last question the woman turned terribly pale, was seen to falter, and fell in a swoon on the ground, and so *revealed the truth* which she had come to *deny*.

CHAPTER XLI.

MR. J.L. TOOLE ON THE BENCH.

Sir Henry Hawkins was sitting at Derby Assizes in the Criminal Court, which, as usual in country towns, was crowded so that you could scarcely breathe, while the air you had to breathe was like that of a pestilence. There was, however, a little space left behind the dock which admitted of the passage of one man at a time.

Windows and doors were all securely closed, so as to prevent draught, for nothing is so bad as draught when you are hot, and nothing makes you so hot as being stived by hundreds in a narrow space without draught.

He happened to look up into the faces of this shining but by no means brilliant assembly, when what should he observe peeping over the shoulders of two buxom factory women with blue kerchiefs but the *head of J.L. Toole*! At least, it looked like Mr. Toole's head; but how it came there it was impossible to say. It was a delight anywhere, but it seemed now out of place.

The marshal asked the Sheriff, "Isn't that Toole?"

The answer was, "It looks like him."

We knew he was in the town, and that there was to be a bespeak night, when her Majesty's Judges and the Midland Circuit would honour, etc. Derby is not behind other towns in this respect.

Presently the Judge's eyes went in the direction of the object which excited so much curiosity, and, like every one else, he was interested in the appearance of the great comedian, although at that moment he was not acting a part, but enduring a situation.

In the afternoon the actor was on the Bench sitting next to the marshal, and assuming an air of great gravity, which would have become a Judge of the greatest dignity. There was never the faintest suggestion of a smile. He looked, indeed, like Byron's description of the Corsair:--

"And where his frown of hatred darkly fell, Hope, withering, fled, and Mercy sighed farewell."

A turkey-cock in a pulpit could not have seemed more to dominate the proceedings.

One very annoying circumstance occurred at this Assize. It was the cracking, sometimes almost banging, of the *seats* and wainscoting, which had been remade of oak. Every now and again there was a loud squeak, and then a noise like the cracking of walnuts. To a sensitive mind it must have been a trying situation, as Toole afterwards said, when you are trying prisoners.

Meanwhile Sir Henry pursued the even tenor of his way, speaking little, as was his wont, and thinking much about the case before him, of a very trumpery character, unless you measured it by the game laws. But no one less liked to be disturbed by noises of any kind than Sir Henry when at work. Even the rustling of a newspaper would cause him to direct the reader to study in some other part of the building.

Suddenly there was a squeaking of another kind distinguishable from all others--it was the squeaking of *Sunday boots*. In the country no boots are considered Sunday boots unless they squeak. At all events, that was the case in Derbyshire at the time I write of.

The noise proceeded from a heavy farmer, a juror-in-waiting, who was allowed to cross from one side of the court to the other for change of air. His endeavour to suppress the noise of his boots only seemed to cause them the greater irritation. There was a universal titter as the crowd looked up to see what line the Judge would take.

Sir Henry reproved quietly, and just as the farmer, who was prancing like an elephant, had got well in front of the Bench, he said,--

"If that gentleman desires to perambulate this court, he had better take off his boots."

The gravity of the situation was disturbed, but that of the farmer remained, unhappily for him, for, with one foot planted firmly on the ground, and the other poised between heaven and earth, he was afraid to let it come down, and there he stood. "We will wait," said the Judge, "until that gentleman has got to the door which leads into the street." The juryman, Toole told us afterwards, was delighted, for he escaped for the whole Assize.

Although there was much laughter, Toole knew his position and dignity too well to join in it; but he did what any respectable citizen would be expected to do in the circumstances--tried to suppress it, yet made such faces in the attempt that the whole house came down in volleys. But now he was resolved to set matters right, and prevent any further repetition of unseemly conduct. The way he did so is worthy of note. He took a pen, dipped it in the ink, and then, spreading his elbows out as one in great authority, and duly impressed with the dignity of the situation, wrote these words on a sheet of paper, which had the royal arms in the centre, his tongue meanwhile seeming to imitate the motion of his pen: "I have had my eye on you for a long time past, and if I see you laugh again I will send you to prison. Be warned in time."

"Just hand that," said he, giving it to a javelin-man, "to the gentleman there in the *green blouse* and red hair."

The paper was stuck into the slit of the tapering fishing-rod-like instrument, and placed under the nose of the man who had been laughing. It was some time before he could believe his eyes, but a thrust or two of the stick acted like a pair of spectacles, and convinced him it was intended for his perusal. The effect was instantaneous, and he handed the document to his wife. It was interesting to watch the face of Toole, suffused with good-humour and yet preserving its elastic dignity, in contrast with that of the farmer, which was almost white with terror as they interchanged furtive glances for the next half-hour. However, it all ended happily, for the man never laughed again. Toole was invited to dine at the Judge's dinner, but being himself on circuit, and not at liberty till *eleven*, when he took supper, an invitation to "look in" was accepted instead, if it were not too late.

After supper he accordingly went for his "look in," and arriving at half-past eleven, was in time for dinner, which did not take place till half-past twelve, the court having adjourned at 12.15. However, we spent a very pleasant evening, Toole telling the story of his going to see Hawkins in the Tichborne trial related elsewhere, and Sir Henry that of the Queen refusing once upon a time to accept a box at Drury Lane Theatre while E.T. Smith was lessee, which made Smith so angry that he could hardly bring himself to propose her Majesty's health at a dinner that same evening at Drury Lane. Nothing but his loyalty prevented his resenting it in a suitable and dignified manner. When one sovereign is affronted by another, the only thing is to consider their respective *commercial* values, for that, as a rule, is the test of all things in a commercial world. But the sequel was that E.T. said, "*Although me and her Majesty have had a little difference, I think on the whole I may propose the Queen!*" Fool is he who neglects his Sovereign, and gets in exchange Sovereign contempt. Such was Toole's observation.

It was at this little entertainment that Sir Henry told the story of the banker's clerk and the bad boy--a true story, he said, although it may be without a moral. The best stories, said Toole, like the best people, have no morals--at least, none to make a song about--any more than the best dogs have the longest tails.

A gentleman who was a customer at a certain bank was asked by a bank clerk whether a particular cheque bore his signature.

The gentleman looked at it, and said, "That is all right."

"All right?" said the bank clerk. "Is that really your signature, sir?"

"Certainly," said the gentleman.

"Quite sure, sir?"

"As sure as I am of my own existence."

The clerk looked puzzled and somewhat disconcerted, so sure was he that the signature was false.

"How can I be deceived in my own handwriting?" asked the supposed drawer of the cheque.

"Well," said the clerk, "you will excuse me, I hope, but I have *refused to pay on that signature*, because I do not believe it is yours."

"*Pay!*" said the customer. "For Heaven's sake, do not dishonour my signature."

"I will never do that," was the answer; "but will you look through your papers, counterfoils, bank-book, and accounts, and see if you can trace this cheque?"

The customer looked through his accounts and found no trace of it or the amount for which it was given.

At last, on examining the *number* of the cheque, he was convinced that the signature could not be his, *because he had never had a cheque-book with that number in it*. At the same time, his astonishment was great that the clerk should know his handwriting better than he knew it himself.

"I will tell you," said the clerk, "how I discovered the forgery. A boy presented this cheque, purporting to have been signed by you. I cashed it. He came again with another. I cashed that. A little while afterwards he came again. My suspicions were then aroused, not by anything in the signature or the cheque, but by the circumstance of the *frequency of his coming*. When he came the third time, however, I suspended payment until I saw you, because the *line under your signature with which you always finish was not at the same angle*; it went a trifle nearer the letters, and I at once concluded it was a FORGERY." And so it turned out to be.

"That boy," said Toole, "deserves to be taken up by some one, for he has great talent."

"And in speaking of this matter," said Sir Henry, "I may tell you that bankers' clerks are the very best that ever could be invented as tests for handwriting. Their intelligence and accuracy are perfectly astonishing. They hardly ever make a mistake, and are seldom deceived. The experts in handwriting are clever enough, and mean to be true; but every *expert* in a case, be he doctor, caligrapher, or phrenologist, has some unknown quantity of bias, and must almost of necessity, if he is on the one side or the other, exercise it, however unintentional it may be. The banker speaks *without this influence*, and therefore, if not more likely to be correct, is more reasonably supposed to be so.

"Do you remember, Sir Henry," asked Toole, "what the clever rogue Orton wrote in his pocket-book? 'Some has money no brains; some has brains no money; them as has money no brains was made for them as has brains no money.'"

"Just like Roger," said Sir Henry. This was a catch-phrase in society at the time of the trial.

Some one recited from a number of *Hood's Comic Annual* the following poem by Tom Hood:--

A BIRD OF ANOTHER FEATHER.[A]

[Footnote A: These lines appeared about 1874, and I have to make acknowledgments to those whom I have been unable to ask for permission to reproduce, and trust they will accept both my apologies and thanks.]

"Yestreen, when I retired to bed,
I had a funny dream;
Imagination backward sped
Up History's ancient stream.
A falconer in fullest dress
Was teaching me his art;
Of tercel, eyas, hood, and jess,
The terms I learnt by heart.

"He flew his falcon to attack
The osprey, swan, and hern,
And showed me, when he wished it back,

The lure for its return.
I thought it was a noble sport;
I struggled to excel
My gentle teacher, and, in short,
I managed rather well.

"The dream is o'er, and I to-day
Return to modern time;

But yet I've something more to say,
If you will list my rhyme.
I've been a witness in a case
For seven long mortal hours,
And, cross-examined, had to face
The counsel's keenest powers.

"With courteous phrase and winning smiles
He led me gently on;
I fell a victim to his wiles--
But how he changed anon!
'Oh, you're prepared to swear to that!'
And, 'Now, sir, just take care!'
And, 'Come, be cautious what you're at!'
With questions hard to bear.

"And when he'd turned me inside out,
He turned me outside in;
I knew not what I was about--
My brain was all a-spin,
I'm shaking now with nervous fright,
And since I left the court
I've changed my dream-opinion quite--
I don't think Hawkins sport!"

Before concluding the evening, Toole said,--
"You remember your joke, Sir Henry,
about Miss Brain and her black kids?"
"Not for the world, not for the world, my dear Toole!"
"Not for the world, Sir Henry, not for the world;
only for us; not before the boys!
You said it was the best joke you ever made."
"And the worst. But I was not a Judge then."]

CHAPTER XLII.

A FULL MEMBER OF THE JOCKEY CLUB.

I knew a great many men connected with the Turf, from the highest to the humblest; but although I have spent the most agreeable hours amongst them, there is little which, if written, would afford amusement: everything in a story, a repartee, or a joke depends, like a jewel, on its setting. At Lord Falmouth's, my old and esteemed friend, I have spent many jovial and happy hours. He was one of the most amiable of hosts, and of a boundless hospitality; ran many distinguished horses, and won many big races. I used to drive with him to see his horses at exercise before breakfast, and in his company visited some of the most celebrated men of the day, who were also amongst the most distinguished of the Turf. Amongst these was Prince B----, whose fate was the saddest of all my reminiscences of the Turf. I almost witnessed his death, for it took place nearly at the moment of my taking leave of him at the Jockey Club. There was a flight of stairs from where I stood with him, leading down to the luncheon-room, and there he appears to have slipped and fallen.

I don't know that it was in consequence of this accident, or whether it had anything to do with it, but I seemed after this sad event to have practically broken my connection with the Turf, and yet perhaps I was more intimately attached to it than ever, for Lord Rosebery asked me (I being an honorary member of the Jockey Club) whether there was any reason, so far as my judicial position was concerned, why I should not be elected a *full member*. I said there was none. So his lordship proposed me, and I was elected.

The only privilege I acquired by "full membership" was that I had to pay ten guineas a year subscription instead of nothing. I almost regularly had the honour of being invited, with other members of the club, to the entertainment given by H.R.H. the Prince of Wales on the Derby night--a festivity continued since his Majesty's accession to the throne. Nor shall I forget the several occasions on which I have had the honour to be the guest of his gracious Majesty at Sandringham; and I mention them here to record my respectful gratitude for the kindness and hospitality of their Majesties the King and Queen whenever it has been my good fortune to be invited.

Speaking, however, of racing men, I have always thought that the passion for gambling is one of the strongest propensities of our nature, and once the mind is given to it there is no restraint possible, either from law or pulpit. Its fascination never slackens, and time never blunts the keen desire of self-gratification which it engenders, while the grip with which it fastens upon us is as fast in old age as in youth. It will absorb all other pleasures and pastimes. I will give an instance of what I mean. There was a well-known bookmaker of my acquaintance whose whole mind was devoted to this passion; his lifetime was a gamble; everything seemed to be created to make a bet upon. Do what he would, go where he would, his thoughts were upon horse-racing.

I was staying with Charley Carew, the owner and occupier of Beddington Park, with a small party of guests invited for shooting. One morning there was to be a rabbit-killing expedition, and after a pretty good morning's walk, I had a rest, and then leisurely went along towards the trysting-place for lunch. It was a large oak tree, and as I came up there was Hodgman, the bookie, who did not see me, walking round the rabbits, which lay in rows, counting them, and muttering, "*Two--four--twenty*," and so on up to a hundred. He then paused, and after a while soliloquized, "Ah! fancy a hundred! One hundred *dead uns*! What would I give for such a lot for the Chester Cup!"

His mind was not with the rabbits except in connection with his betting-book on the Chester Cup. He was by no means singular except in the manner of showing his propensity. The devotees of "Bridge" are all Hodgmans in their way.

At the Benchers' table I was speaking of Clarkson in reference to the Old Bailey. He had been with me in consultation in a very bad case. We had not the ghost of a chance of winning it, and indicated our opinion to that effect to the unhappy client.

He turned from us with a sad look, as if desperation had seized him, and then, with tears in his eyes, asked Clarkson if he thought it advisable for him to *surrender* and take his trial.

"My good man," said Clarkson, "it is my duty as a loyal subject to advise you to surrender and take your trial, *but, if I were in your shoes*, I'll be damned if I would!"

The man, however, for some reason or other, *did* surrender like a good citizen, and the man who did not appear was his own leading counsel Clarkson. He never even looked in, and the conduct of the case, therefore, devolved on me. I did my best for him, however, and succeeded. The man was acquitted.

Not content with this piece of good fortune, for such indeed it was, he was ill-advised enough to bring an action for *malicious prosecution*. Lord Denman tried it, and told him it was a most impudent action, and he was astonished that he was not convicted.

During this conversation another, of no little importance, took place, and Lord Westbury is reported to have said,--

"I did not assert that the House of Lords had abolished hell with costs, although I have no doubt that the large majority would gladly assent to any such decree--all, in fact, except the Bishops."

As I never listen to after-dinner theology, I forbear comment on this subject; but before this time there had been a curious action brought by a churchwarden against his vicar for refusing to administer the Sacrament to him, on the ground that he did not believe in the personality of the devil. After the decisions in the courts below, it was finally determined by the House of Lords that the vicar was wrong. Hence it was that Westbury was reported to have said that the House of Lords had abolished hell with costs. "What I did say," said Westbury, "was that the poor churchwarden who did not at one time believe in the personality of the devil returned to the true orthodox Christian faith when he received his attorney's bill."

Turning to me, his lordship said,--

"My dear Hawkins, you shall write your reminiscences, and, what is more, they shall be printed in good type, and, what is more, the first copy shall be directed to me."

And so it should be, if I only knew his address.

CHAPTER XLIII.

THE LITTLE MOUSE AND THE PRISONER.

I come now to a small event which occurred during my judgeship, and which I call my little mouse story.

I was presiding at the Old Bailey Sessions, and a case came before me of a prisoner who was undergoing a term of two years' imprisonment with hard labour for some offence against the Post Office.

The charge against him on the present occasion was attempting to murder or do grievous bodily harm to a prison warder. This officer was on duty in the prisoner's cell when the assault took place.

The facts relied on by the Crown were simple enough. The warder had gone into the cell to take the man's dinner, when suddenly the prisoner seized the knife brought for his use, and made a rush at the warder with it in his hand, at the same time uttering threats and imprecations.

Believing his life to be in danger, the warder ran to the door and got outside into the adjoining corridor, pulling the cell door to after him and closing it.

He had no sooner escaped than the prisoner struck a violent blow in the direction the warder had gone, but the door being closed, it fell harmlessly enough. It left such a mark, however, that no doubt could be entertained as to the violence with which it was delivered and the probable result had it reached the warder himself.

Thus presented, the case looked serious. Mr. Montagu Williams, who was counsel for the Crown, felt it to be, as it undoubtedly was, his duty in common fairness to present not only the bare facts necessary for his own case, but also those which might be relied upon by the prisoner as his defence, or at all events in mitigation of punishment. In performing this duty, he elicited from his witness a very touching little history of the origin and cause of the crime. It was this:--

A poor little mouse had, somehow or other, managed to get inside the prisoner's cell; and one day, while the unhappy man was eating his prison fare, he saw the mouse running timidly along the floor. At last it came to a few crumbs of bread which the prisoner had purposely spread, and ran away with one of them into its hiding-place. The next day it came again, and found more crumbs; and so on from day to day, the prisoner relieving the irksomeness and the weary solitude of his confinement by tempting it to trust him, and become his one companion and friend, till at last it became so tame that it formed a little nest, and made its home in the sleeve of the prisoner's jail clothes. During the long hours of the dreary day it was his companion and pet; played with him, fed with him, and mitigated his solitude. It even slept with him at night.

All this was, of course, against the prison rules. But the mouse had no reason to obey them.

One unhappy day a warder came into the cell, when the poor mouse peeped out from his tiny hiding-place, and the officer, I presume, as a matter of duty, seized the little intruder on the spot and captured it.

God help the world if every one did his strict duty in it! But--what to the prisoner seemed inexcusable barbarity--he killed the poor little mouse in the sight of the unhappy man whose friend and companion it had been.

This infuriated him to such an extent that, having the dinner-knife in his hand--the knife which would have assisted at the mouse's banquet as well as his own--he rushed at the warder, who fortunately escaped through the open door of the cell, the prisoner striking the knife into the door.

In the result the prisoner was indicted on the charge of attempting to murder the warder. The defence was that, as murder in the circumstances was impossible, the attempt could not be established, and on the authority of a case (which has, however, since been overruled) I felt bound to direct an acquittal; and I confess *I was not sorry* to come to that conclusion, for it would have been a sad thing had the prisoner been convicted of an offence committed in a moment of such great and not unnatural excitement, and one for which penal servitude must have been awarded.

The poor fellow had suffered enough without additional punishment. I can conceive nothing more keen than the torture of returning to his cell to grieve for the little friend which could never come to him again.

CHAPTER XLIV.

THE LAST OF LORD CAMPBELL--WINE AND WATER--SIR THOMAS WILDE.

Life, alas! must have its sad stories as well as its mirthful. I have told few of the former, not because they have not been present to my mind, but because I think it useless to perpetuate them by narration. But for its occasional gleams of humour, life would indeed be dull, and ever eclipsed by the shadow of sorrow.

One of the stories the Chief Baron told me is as indelibly fixed on my memory as it was on his. Lord Campbell had been so long and so prominently before the country that his death would be a theme of conversation in the world of literature, science, law, and fashion. But it was not his death that impressed me; it was the incidents that immediately attended it.

"His lordship"--thus was the event related--"had been entertaining a party at dinner, and amongst them was his brother-in-law, Colonel Scarlett. In its incidents the dinner had been as lively and agreeable as those events in social and refined life usually are. Scarlett had an important engagement with Campbell in the city on the following Monday, this being Saturday night. As he rose to go Scarlett wished his host good-night with a hearty shake-hands.

"'Good-night--good-night; we shall meet again on Monday.'"

Alas! Campbell died that night suddenly, and by a singular interposition of Providence, Scarlett died suddenly the next day, Sunday. They met no more in this world.

In the course of my life I have suffered, like many others, from nameless afflictions--nameless because they do not exist. No one can localize this strange infirmity or realize it. You only know you have a sensation of depression. In every other respect I was perfectly well, yet I thought it was necessary to see a doctor. So it was, if I wished to be ill.

Being in this unhappy condition, I consulted Sir James Paget, then in the zenith of his fame.

It did not take him very long to test me. I think he did it with a smile, for I felt a good deal better after it.

"Just tell me," said he, "do you ever drink any water?"

"Now it's coming," I thought; "he's going to knock me off my wine." I thought, however, I would be equal to the occasion, and said,--

"I know what you are driving at: you want to know if I ever mix a little water in my wine."

"No, no, I don't," said he; "you are quite wrong, for if your water is good and your wine bad, you spoil your water; and if your wine is good and your water bad, you spoil your wine."

I took his advice--which was certainly worth the fee--and never mixed my wine with water after that, although I have some doubt as to whether I had ever done so before.

I came away in good heart, because I was so delighted that there was not a vestige of anything the matter with me.

With a view to enable me to give each case due consideration before fixing the poor wretch's doom after conviction, I invariably ordered the prisoner to stand down until all were tried.

I then spent a night in going through my notes in each case, so that if there were any circumstances that I could lay hold of by way of mitigation of the sentence, I did so.

I do not mean to say that I did this in trifling cases, such as a magistrate could dispose of, but in all cases of magnitude possibly involving penal servitude.

Once, however, I had made up my mind as to what was, in accordance with my judgment, the sentence to be passed, I took care never to alter it upon any plea in mitigation whatever.

For this line of conduct I had the example of Sir Thomas Wilde, when, as Lord Chief Justice of the Court of Common Pleas, he travelled the Home Circuit. He was a marvellous and powerful judge in dealing with the facts of a case. He had tried a prisoner for larceny in stealing from a house a sack of peas. The prisoner's counsel had made for him a very poor and absurd defence, in which, over and over again, he had reiterated that one pea was very like another pea, and that he would be a bold man who would swear to the identity of two peas.

This miserable defence made the Lord Chief Justice angry, and he summed up the case tersely but crushingly to this effect: "Gentlemen, you have been told by the learned counsel very truly that one pea is very like another pea, and if the only evidence in this case had been that one pea had been taken from the house of the prosecutor, and a similar pea had been found in the prisoners house, I for one should have said it would have been insufficient evidence to justify the accusation that the prisoner had taken it.

"But such are *not* the facts of this case; and when you find, as was the fact here, that on March 30 a sack appears in a particular place, marked with the prosecutor's initials, safe in his house at night, where it ought to have been but was not, on the morning of the 31st; and when you find that on that morning a sack of peas of precisely similar character was in the house of the prisoner in a precisely similar sack behind the door, the question very naturally arises, *How came* those peas in that man's house? He says he found them; do you believe him? Did it ever occur to you, gentlemen, to find a similar sack of peas in the dead of the night on any road on which you chanced to be travelling?

"The prosecutor says the prisoner stole them, and that is the question I ask you to answer. Did he or not, in your opinion, steal them?"

I need not say what the verdict was. The man was *put back for sentence*. That is the point I am upon.

On the following morning the Lord Chief Justice, still a bit angry with the prisoner's counsel for the miserable imposture he had attempted upon the jury, said,--

"God forbid, prisoner at the bar, that the defence attempted by your counsel yesterday should aggravate the punishment which I am about to inflict upon you; and with a view to dispel from my mind all that was then urged on your behalf, I have taken the night to consider what sentence I ought to pronounce."

Having said thus much about the speech for the defence, he gave a very moderate sentence of two or three months' imprisonment. Every sentence that this Chief Justice passed had been well thought out and considered, and was the result of anxious deliberation--that is to say, in the serious cases that demanded it. Of course, I do not claim for my adopted system an infallibility which belongs to no human device, but only that during some years, by patiently following it, I was enabled the better to determine how I could combine justice with leniency.

CHAPTER XLV.

HOW I CROSS-EXAMINED PRINCE LOUIS NAPOLEON.

I have been often questioned in an indirect manner as to the amount of my income and the number of my briefs. I do not mean by the Income Tax Commissioners, but by private "authorities." I was often *told* how much I must be making. Sometimes it was said, "Oh, the Associates' Office verdict books show this and that." "Why, Hawkins, you must be making thirty thousand a year if you are making a penny. What a hard-working man you are! How *do* you manage to get through it?"

Well, I had no answer. It is a curious inquisitiveness which it would do no one any good to gratify. I did not think it necessary to the happiness of my friends that they should know, and if it would afford *me* any satisfaction, it was far better that they should name the amount than I. They could exaggerate it; I had no wish to do so. It is true enough in common language I worked hard, but working by system made it easy. Slovenly work is always hard work; you never get through it satisfactorily. It was by working easily that I got through so much. "Never fret" and "*toujours pret*" were my mottoes, as I told the chaplain; I hope he remembers them to this day. If they would not help him to a bishopric, nothing would. But I will say seriously that nothing is so great a help in our daily struggles as *good temper*, and with that observation I leave my friends still to wonder how I got through so much.

Judges often talk over their experiences at the Bar. Sometimes I talked of mine, and on one occasion told the following curious incident in my long career.

I mention this circumstance as a curiosity only so far as the incident is concerned, but as more than a curiosity so far as the legality of evading the substance of the law by a technicality is concerned.

All men are not privileged to cross-examine royalty, and especially future emperors.

On July 1, 1847, which was not very long after my call to the Bar, Prince Louis Napoleon, who afterwards became Emperor of the French, was residing in England.

Of course, in looking back upon a man who afterwards became an Emperor, the proportions seem to have altered, and he looks greater than his figure actually was. He is more important in one's eyes, and therefore from this point of view the event seems to be of greater magnitude than the mere police-court business that it was. When a man becomes great, the smallest details of his career increase in value and importance.

The Prince had given a man of the name of Charles Pollard into custody for stealing and obtaining by fraud two bills of exchange for £1,000 each.

I was instructed by one Saul (not of Tarsus) to defend, and old Saul thought it would be judicious to cross-examine the Prince into a cocked hat, little dreaming what kind of a cocked hat our opponent would one day wear.

But Saul, not content with this ordinary drum-beating kind of Old Bailey performance, in which there is much more alarm than harm, instructed me to make a few inquiries as to the Prince's private life, and so *show him up* in public. Saul loved that kind of persecution. To him the witness-box was a pillory, notwithstanding there was more mud attaching to the throwers than to the mere object of their attention.

Young as I was in my profession, I had sense enough to know that to dip into a prosecutor's private history, and the history of his father and grandfather, and a succession of grandmothers and aunts, was hardly the way to show that the prisoner had not stolen that gentleman's property, but was a good way to prevent the Prince from recommending him to mercy.

I therefore, in my simplicity, asked old Saul what the uncle of the Prince and his voyage in the *Bellerophon*, etc., had to do with this man's stealing these two bills of exchange.

"Never mind, Mr. Hawkins, you do it; it has a great deal to do with it."

However, I made up my own mind as to the course I should pursue, and having carefully read my "instructions," found that the man had been unjustly accused by this Napoleon--there never was a man so trampled on--and every word of the whole accusation was false. *So* did some solicitors instruct young counsel in those days.

I started my business of cross-examination, accordingly, with a few tentative questions, testing whether the ice would bear before I took the other foot off dry land. It did not seem to be very strong, I thought. Some of them were a little bewildering, perhaps, but that, doubtless, was their only fault, which the Prince was desirous of amending, and he graciously appealed to me in a very sensible manner by suggesting that if I would put a question that he *could* answer, he would do so.

I thought it a fair offer, even from a Prince, if I could only trust him. I kept my bargain, and definitely shaped my examination so that "Yes" and "No" should be all that would be necessary.

We got on very well indeed for some little time, his answers coming with great readiness and truth. He was perfectly straightforward, and so was I.

"Yes, sir," "No, sir;" that was all.

As I have said, at this time I had not had much experience in cross-examination, but I had some intuitive knowledge of the art waiting to be developed. Napoleon gave me my first lesson in that department.

"I am afraid, sir," said his Highness, "you have been sadly misinstructed in this case."

"I am afraid, sir, I have," said I. "One or the other of us must be wrong, and I am much inclined to think it's my solicitor."

It was a nice little bull, which the Prince liked apparently, for he laughed good-humouredly, and especially when I found, as I quickly did, that my strength was to sit still, which I also did.

I had learned by this exhibition of forces that there *was* a defence, if I could only keep it up my sleeve. To expose it before the magistrate would simply enable Clarkson, who was opposed to me, to bring up reinforcements, and knock me into a cocked hat instead of Napoleon. Old Saul knew nothing whatever about my intended manoeuvre, nor did Clarkson or his solicitor.

I knew the man would be committed for trial; the magistrate had intimated as much. I therefore said nothing, except that I would reserve my defence.

Had I said a word, Clarkson would have shaped his indictment to meet the objection which I intended to make; the man, however, was committed to the Old Bailey in total ignorance of what defence was to be made.

The case was tried before Baron Alderson, as shrewd a Judge, perhaps, as ever adorned the Bench.

When I took my point, he at once saw the difficulty Napoleon was in--a difficulty from which no Napoleon could escape even by a *coup d'état*.

It was, in fact, this--simple as A B C:--

When the bills of exchange were received by Pollard, although he intended to defraud, they were *neither drawn nor accepted*, and so were not bills of exchange at all; another process was necessary before they could become so even in appearance, and that was forgery.

Moreover, there was included in this point another objection--namely, that the *stamps* signed by the Prince having been handed to him with the intention that they *should be subsequently filled up*, they were not *valuable securities* (for stealing which the ill-used Pollard was indicted) at the time they were appropriated, and could not therefore be so treated.

In short, the legal truth was that Pollard neither stole nor obtained either *bill of exchange* (for such they were not at that time) or valuable security.

Such was the law. I believe Napoleon said the devil must have made it, or worked it into that "tam shape!"

There were many technicalities in the law of those days, and justice was often defeated by legal quibbles. But the law was so severe in its punishments that Justice herself often connived at its evasion. At the present day there is a gradual tendency to make punishment more lenient and more certain--to remove the entanglements of the pleader, and render progress towards substantial instead of technical justice more sure and speedy. Napoleon's defeat could not have occurred at the present day--not, at all events, in that "tam shape."

In a case in which the member of St. Ives was petitioned against on the ground of treating, before Lush, J., I was opposed by Russell (afterwards Lord Chief Justice and Lord Russell of Killowen). A.L. Smith was my junior, and I need not say he knew almost everything there was to be known about election law. There was, however, no law in the case. No specific act of treating was proved, but we felt that general treating had taken place in such a wholesale manner that our client was affected by it. So we consented to his losing his seat--that is to say, that the election should be declared *void*--merely void. As the other side did not seem to be aware that this void could be filled by the member who was unseated, they did not ask that our client should not be permitted to put up for the vacancy, although this was the real object of my opponent's petition. He wanted the seat for himself, but knew that he had not the remotest chance against his unseated opponent.

His surprise, therefore, must have been as great as his chagrin when, the very night of the decision which unseated him, he came forward once more as a candidate. The petition had increased his popularity, and he won the seat with the greatest ease, and without any subsequent disturbance by the former petitioner.

I have told you of a curious trial before a Recorder of Saffron Walden, and my memory of that event reminds me of another which took place in that same abode of learning and justice. Joseph Brown, Q.C., and Thomas Chambers, Q.C., were brother Benchers of mine, and when we met at the Parliament Chamber after dinner it was more than likely that many stories would be told, for we often fought our battles over again.

At the time I speak of Knox was the Recorder of that important borough, and was possessed of all the dignity which so enhances a great officer in the eyes of the public, whether he be the most modest of beadles in beadledom, or the highest Recorder in Christendom. To give himself a greater air of importance, Knox always carried a *blue umbrella* of a most blazing grandeur. He was looked up to, of course, at Saffron Walden, as their greatest man, especially as he occupied the best apartments at the chief brimstone shop in the town. When I say *brimstone*, I mean that it seemed to be its leading article; for there were a great many yellow placards all over and about the emporium, which, perhaps, ought to have been called a "general shop."

There were three men up before Knox for stealing malt; a very serious offence indeed in Saffron Walden, where malt was almost regarded as a sacred object--until it got into the beer.

"Tom" Chambers (afterwards Recorder of London) was defending these prisoners, and I have no doubt, from the conduct of Knox, acquired a great deal of that discrimination of character which afterwards so distinguished him in the City of London. The degrees of guilt in these persons ought to be noted by all persons who hold, or hope to hold, a judicial position. As to the first man, the actual thief, there could be no doubt about his crime, for he was actually wheeling the two or three shovelfuls of malt in a barrow; so there was not much use in defending him.

About the second man there was not the same degree of certainty, for he had never touched the malt or the barrow, and there was no evidence that he knew the first man had stolen it. The only suspicion--for it was nothing more--against him was that he was seen to be walking *along the highway* near the man who was wheeling the barrow, and as it was daytime, many others were equally guilty.

The third man was still less implicated, for all that appeared against him was that *at some time or other* he had been seen, either on the day of the theft or just before, to be in a public-house with the thief and asking him to have a drink.

If it had not been at Saffron Walden, where they are so jealous of their malt and such admirers of their maltsters, there would have been no case against any one but the actual thief; and if the Recorder had known the law as well as he knew Saffron Walden, or half as much as Saffron Walden admired him, he would have ruled to that effect.

However, he pointed out to the jury the cases one by one with great care and no stint of language.

"Against the first," said he, "the case is clear enough: he is caught with the stolen goods in his possession. In the second case, *perhaps*, it is not quite so strong, you will think; but it is for *you*, gentlemen, not for *me*, to judge. You will not forget, gentlemen, he was walking along by the side of the actual thief, and it is for you to say what that means." Then, after clearing his throat for a final effort, he said,--

"Now we come to the third man. Where was he? I must say there is a slight difference between his case and that of the other two men, who might be said to have been caught in the very act; but it's for *you*, gentlemen, not for *me*. It is difficult to point out item by item, as it were, the difference between the three cases; but you will say, gentlemen, whether they were not all mixed up in this robbery--it's for *you*, gentlemen, not for *me*."

The jury were not going to let off three such rogues as the Recorder plainly thought them, and instantly returned a verdict of guilty against all.

"I agree with the verdict," said the Recorder. "It is *a very bad case*, and a mercantile community like Saffron Walden must be protected against such depredators as you. No doubt there are degrees of guilt in your several cases, but I do not think I should be doing my duty to the public if I made any distinction in your sentences: you must all of you undergo a term of five years' penal servitude."

Whereupon Tom Chambers was furious. Up he jumped, and said,--

"Really, sir; really--"

"Yes," said Knox, "really."

"Well, then, sir, you can't do it," said the counsel; "you cannot give penal servitude for petty larceny. Here is the Act" (reading): "'Unless the prisoner has been guilty of any felony before.'"

"Very well," said the Recorder; "you, Brown, the actual thief, and you, Jones, his accessory in the very act, not having been convicted before, I am sorry to say, cannot be sentenced to more than two years' imprisonment with hard labour, and I reduce the sentence in your cases to that; but as to you, Robinson, yours is a very bad case. The jury have found that you were *mixed up* in this robbery, and I find that you have been convicted of stealing apples. True, it's a good many years ago, but it brings you within the purview of the statute, and therefore your sentence of five years will stand."

CHAPTER XLVI.

THE NEW LAW ALLOWING THE ACCUSED TO GIVE EVIDENCE--THE CASE OF DR.

WALLACE, THE LAST I TRIED ON CIRCUIT.

I should like to make an observation on the recent Act for enabling prisoners to go into the witness-box and subject themselves, after giving their evidence, to cross-examination.

It must be apparent to every one, learned and unlearned in its mysteries, that no evidence can be of its highest value, and often is of no value, until sifted by cross-examination. I was always opposed to this process as against an accused person, because I know how difficult it is under the most favourable circumstances to avoid the pitfalls which a clever and artistic cross-examiner may dig for the unwary.

It did not occur to me in that early stage of the discussion on the Bill that a really true story *cannot* be shaken in cross-examination, and that only the *false* must give way beneath its searching effect.

I had to learn something in advocacy; indeed, I was always learning, and the best of us may go on for ever learning, as long as this wonderful and mysterious human nature exists.

However, I am not writing philosophical essays, but relating the facts of my simple life, and I confess that the case that came before me on this occasion totally upset my quiet repose in all the comfortable traditions of the past. Human nature had something which I had not seen: it arose in this way. A doctor was accused of a terrible crime against a female patient. I need not give its details; it is sufficient to say that if the girl's statement was true penal servitude for life was not too much, for he was a villain of the very worst character. Taking the ordinary run of evidence, if I may use the word, and the ordinary mode of cross-examination, which, in the hands of unskilled practitioners, generally tends to corroborate the evidence-in-chief, the case was overwhelmingly proved, and how sad and painful it was to contemplate none can realize who do not understand anything below the surface of human existence.

I had watched the case with the anxious care that I am conscious should be exercised in all inquiries, and especially criminal inquiries, that come before one. I watched, and, let me say, *especially watched*, for any point in the evidence on which I could put a question in the prisoner's favour.

Upon that subject I never wavered throughout the whole of my career, and the testimony of the letters which I received from the most distinguished members of the criminal Bar--not to say that they are not equally distinguished in the civil--will, I am sure, bear out my little self-praise upon a small matter of infinite importance.

Everything in this case seemed to be overwhelmingly against the unhappy doctor. No one in court, except himself, *could* believe on the evidence but that he was guilty.

I, who through my whole life had been studying evidence and the mode in which it was delivered, believed in the man's guilt, and felt that no cross-examination, however subtle and skilfully conducted, could shake it.

I felt for the man--a scholar, a scientist--as one must feel for the victim of so great a temptation. But I felt also that he was entitled, on account of all those things which aroused my sympathy, to the severest sentence, which I had already considered it would be my duty to award him.

Then, under the New Act, which I had spoken against and written against, as one long associated with all the bearings of evidence given in the witness-box, the poor doctor stepped into that terrible trap for the untruthful.

Let me now observe that, even before he was sworn, his *manner* made a great impression on my mind. And on this subject I would like to say that few Judges or advocates sufficiently consider it.

The greatest actor has a manner. The man who is not an actor has a manner, and if you are only sufficiently read in the human character, it cannot deceive you, however disguised it may be. A witness's evidence may deceive, but his manner is the looking-glass of his mind, sometimes of his innocence. It was so in this case.

The man was not acting, and he was not an actor.

This made the first impression on my mind, and I knew there *must* be something beneath it which only *he* could explain. I waited patiently. It was much more than life and death to this man.

The next thing that impressed me was that there was not the least confusion in his evidence or in himself. His tone, his language, could only be the result of conscious innocence.

It was not very long before I gathered that he was the victim of a cruel and cowardly conspiracy. It was absolutely a case of *blackmailing, and nothing else.*

I believed every word the man said, and so did the jury. His evidence *acquitted him*. He was saved from an ignominious doom by the new Act, and from that moment I went heart and soul with it: however much it may be a danger to the guilty, it is of the utmost importance to the innocent.

This case was not finished without a little touch of humour. When half-past seven arrived--an hour on circuit at which I always considered it too early to adjourn--the jury thought it looked very like an "all-night sitting," although I had no such intention, and one of their body or of the Bar, I forget which, raised the question on a motion for the adjournment of the house.

I was asked, I know, by some impatient member of the Bar whether a case in which *he* was engaged could not go over till the morning.

This gave immense encouragement to an independent juryman, who evidently was determined to beard the lion in his den, and possibly shake off "the dewdrops of his British indignation."

I never believed in British lions, except on his Majesty's quarterings; and although they look very formidable in heraldry, I never found them so in fact. Indeed, if the British lion was ever a native of the British Isles, he must have become extinct, for I have never heard so much as an imitation growl from him except in Hyde Park on a Sunday.

The British lion, however, in this case seemed to assert himself in the jury-box, and rising on his hind legs, said in a husky voice, which appeared to come from some concealed cupboard in his bosom,--

"My lord!"

"Yes?" I said in my blandest manner.

"My lord, this 'ere ---- is a little bit stiff, my lord, with all respect for your lordship."

"What is that, sir?"

"Why, my lord, I've been cramped up in this 'ere narrer box for fourteen hours, and the seat's that hard and the back so straight up that now I gets out on it I ain't got a leg to stand on."

"I'm sorry for the chair," I said.

He was a very thick-set man, and the whole of the jury burst into a laugh. Then he went on, with tears in his eyes,--

"My lord, when I went home last night arter sittin' here so many hours I couldn't sleep a wink."

I could not help saying,--

"Then it is no use going to bed; we may as well finish the business."

That was all very well for him, but another juryman arose, amidst roars of laughter, and lifted up a hard, wooden-bottomed chair, and beat it with his heavy walking-stick.

The chair was perfectly indifferent to the treatment it was receiving after supporting the juryman for so many hours without the smallest hope of any reward, and I then asked,--

"Is that to keep order, sir?"

The excitement continued for a long time, but at last it subsided, and I suggested a compromise.

I said probably the gentlemen in the next case would not speak for more than one hour each, and if they would agree to this I would undertake to sum up in *five minutes*.

The husky lion sat down, and so did the musician. The jury acquitted and went home.

These are some of the caprices of a jury which a Judge has sometimes to put up with, and it has often been said that Judges are more tried than prisoners. Perhaps that is so, especially when, if they do not get the kind of rough music I have mentioned from the jury-box, they sometimes receive a by no means complimentary address from the prisoner. One occurs to my mind, with which I will close this chapter.

I had occasion to sentence to death a soldier for a cruel murder by taking the life of his sergeant. It was at Winchester, and after I had uttered the fatal words the culprit turned savagely towards me, and in a loud, gruff voice cried, "Curse you!"

I made no remark, and the man was removed to the cells. Very humanely the chaplain went to the prisoner and endeavoured to bring him to a proper state of mind with regard to his impending fate.

On the day appointed for the execution I received by post a long letter from the clergyman, enclosing another written on prison paper.

The letter was to tell me that for ten days he could make no impression on the condemned man; but on the tenth or twelfth day he expressed his sincere sorrow that he had cursed me for passing on him the sentence he had so well deserved, and his great desire was to make a humble apology to me in person. He was told that that was impossible, as I could not come to him, nor could he go to me. Whereupon he begged to be allowed to write this humble apology. This he was permitted to do, and the letter from the culprit, who was hanged that morning, I was reading at the very moment of his execution. It contained, I believe, sincere expressions of contrition for the cruel deed he had done, but was mostly taken up with apologies to me for having cursed me after advising him to prepare for the doom that awaited him. He begged my forgiveness, which, I need not say, I freely gave.

CHAPTER XLVII

A FAREWELL MEMORY OF JACK.

Poor little Jack is dead!

It is a real grief to me. A more intelligent, faithful, and affectionate creature never had existence, and to him I have been indebted for very many of the happiest hours of my life.

Poor dear little Jack! he lived with me for many years; and at last, I believe, some miscreant poisoned him, for he was taken very ill with symptoms of strychnine, and died in a few hours in the early morning of May 24, 1894. I was with him when he died.

I never replaced him, and to this hour have never ceased to be sad when I think of the merciless and cruel fate by which the ruffian put an end to his dear little life.

He was buried under some shrubs in Hyde Park, where I hope he sleeps the sleep of good affectionate dogs.

It is ten years ago, and yet there is no abatement of my love for him, hardly any of my sorrow. He always occupied the best seat in the Sheriff's carriage on circuit, and looked as though he felt it was his right. He slept by my side on a little bed of his own. At Norwich, I think, he made his first appearance in state. The moment he entered the house he appropriated to himself the chair of state, which had been provided by the local upholsterer for the express use of Queen Alexandra, then Princess of Wales, on her first visit to Norwich to confer honour and happiness on Queen Victoria's subjects in the eastern counties.

Nobody, however, molested Jack in his seat, and, I believe, had it been one of the seats for the county there would have been no petition to disturb him. He would have been as faithful a member as the immortal Toby, M.P. for Barkshire, of Mr. Punch, to whom ever my best regards. Jack considered himself entitled to precedence wherever he went, and maintained it. He was a famous judge of upholstery, and the softest chair or sofa, hearthrug or divan, was instantly appropriated. This sometimes made the local dignitaries sit up a little. They might be accustomed to the dignity of one of her Majesty's Judges, but the impudence of her Majesty's "Jack"--for so he deemed himself on circuit--was a little beyond their aldermanic natures.

I was much and agreeably surprised to find that the Press everywhere sympathized with my loss of Jack, and many an extract I made containing their very kind remarks. My room might have been one of Romeike's cutting-rooms. Here is one I will give as a sample. I am sorry I cannot positively state the name of the journal, but I am almost sure it is from the *Daily Telegraph.*

> "An item of judicial intelligence, which may not everywhere be duly appreciated, is the death of Mr. Justice Hawkins's fox terrier Jack. Jack has been his lordship's most constant friend for many years. With some

masters such a useful dog as he was would have found going on circuit a bore; but with Sir Henry Hawkins, who knows what kind of life suits a dog, and likes to see that he enjoys it, going on circuit was a career of adventure. The Judge was always out betimes to give Jack a long morning walk, and when his duties took him to small county towns he often rose with the farmers for no other purpose."

Here is another paragraph; and I should like to be able to give the writer's name, for it is very pleasant at all times to find expression of true love for animals, whose devotion and faithfulness to man endear them to us:--

"Sir Henry Hawkins has my sincere sympathy in his great bereavement. Jack, the famous fox terrier who accompanied his master everywhere, is dead. Innumerable are the things told of Jack's devotion to Sir Henry, and of Sir Henry's devotion to Jack. I first made their acquaintance at Worcester Railway Station some years ago, when I saw Jack marching solemnly in the procession of officials who had come with wands and staves and javelins to receive Sir Henry Hawkins at the opening of the Assizes. Jack was on one or two special occasions, I believe, accommodated with a seat on the Bench; and at Maidstone, when the lodgings caught fire, Sir Henry rushed back at the risk of his life to save his faithful little dog."

These are small memories, perhaps, but to me more dear than the praises too often unworthily bestowed on actions unworthy to be recorded.

But here I pause. Jack rests in his little grave in Hyde Park, and I sometimes go and look on the spot where he lies. Many and many an affectionate letter was written to me bewailing the loss of our little friend.

Only one of these I shall particularly mention, because it shows how immeasurably superior was Jack to the lady who wrote it, in that true and sincere feeling which we call friendship, and which, to my mind, is the bond of society and the only security for its well-being. She was a lady who belonged to what is called "Society," the characteristic of which is that it exists not only independently of friendship, but in spite of it.

After condoling with me on my loss and showing her sweet womanly sympathy, she concluded her letter by informing me that she had "one of the sweetest pets eyes ever beheld, a darling devoted to her with a faithfulness which would really be a lesson to 'our specie,'" and that, in the circumstances, she would let me have her little darling for *five pounds*. I was so astonished and angry at the meanness of this "lady of fashion" that I said--Well, perhaps my exact expression had better be buried in oblivion.

BALLAD OF THE UNSURPRISED JUDGE, 1895.[A]

[Footnote A: It was a well-known expression of Sir Henry Hawkins when on the Bench, "I should be surprised at nothing;" and after the long and strange experiences which these reminiscences indicate, the literal truth of the observation is not to be doubted. This clever ballad, which was written in 1895, seems sufficiently appropriate to find a place in these memoirs, and I wish I knew the name of the writer, that my thanks and apologies might be conveyed to him for this appropriation of them.]

("Mr. Justice Hawkins observed, 'I am surprised at nothing,'"--*Pitts v. Joseph*, *"Times"* Report, March 27.)

All hail to Sir Henry, whom nothing surprises!
Ye Judges and suitors, regard him with awe,
As he sits up aloft on the Bench and applies his
Swift mind to the shifts and the tricks of the law.
Many years has he lived, and has always seen clear things
That Nox seemed to hide from our average eyes;
But still, though encompassed with all sorts of queer things,
He never, no, never, gives way to surprise.

When a rogue, for example, a company-monger,
Grows fat on the gain of the shares he has sold,
While the public gets lean, winning nothing but hunger
And a few scraps of scrip for its masses of gold;
When the fat man goes further and takes to religion,
A rascal in hymn-books and Bibles disguised,
"It's a case," says Sir Henry, "of rook *versus* pigeon,
And the pigeon gets left--well, I'm hardly surprised."

There's a Heath at Newmarket, and horses that run there;
There are owners and jockeys, and sharpers and flats;
There are some who do nicely, and some who are done there;
There are loud men with pencils and satchels and hats.
But the stewards see nothing of betting or money,
As they stand in the blinkers for stewards devised;
Their blindness may strike Henry Hawkins as funny,
But he only smiles softly--he isn't surprised.

So here's to Sir Henry, the terror of tricksters,
Of law he's a master, and likewise a limb;
His mind never once, when its purpose is fixed, errs:
For cuteness there's none holds a candle to him.
Let them try to deceive him, why, bless you, he's *been* there,
And can track his way straight through a tangle of lies;
And though some might grow gray at the things he has seen there,
He never, no, never, gives way to surprise.

By the courtesy of Sir Francis Burnand, who most kindly obtained permission from Messrs. Bradbury and Agnew, I insert the following poem, which appeared in a February number of *Punch* in the year 1887:--

THE WOMAN AND THE LAW.

(A true story, told before Mr. Justice Hawkins at the recent Liverpool Assizes--*vide Daily Telegraph*, February 8.)

In the criminal dock stood a woman alone,
To be judged for her crime, her one fault to repair,
And the man who gave evidence sat like a stone,
With a look of contempt for the woman's despair!
For the man was a husband, who'd ruined a life,
And broken a heart he had found without flaw;
He demanded the punishment due to the wife,
Who was only a Woman, whilst his was the Law!

A terrible silence then reigned in the Court,
And the eyes of humanity turned to the dock;
Her head was bent down, and her sobbing came short,
And the jailer stood ready, with hand on the lock
Of the gate of despair, that would open no more
When this wreckage of beauty was hurried away!
"Let me speak," moaned the woman--"my lord, I implore!"
"Yes, speak," said the Judge. "I will hear what you say!"

"I was only a girl when he stole me away
From the home and the mother who loved me too well;
But the shame and the pain I have borne since that day
Not a pitying soul who now listens can tell!
There was never a promise he made but he broke;
The bruises he gave I have covered with shame;
Not a tear, not a prayer, but he scorned as a joke!
He cursed at my children, and sneered at my fame!

"The money I'd slaved for and hoarded he'd rob;
I have borne his reproaches when maddened with drink.
For a man there is pleasure, for woman a sob;
It is he who may slander, but she who must think!
But at last came the day when the Law gave release,
Just a moment of respite from merciless fate,
For they took him to prison, and purchased me peace,
Till I welcomed him home like a wife--at the gate!

"Was it wrong in repentance of Man to believe?
It is hard to forget, it is right to forgive!
But he struck me again, and he left me to grieve
For the love I had lost, for the life I must live!
So I silently stole from the depths of despair,

And slunk from dark destiny's chastening rod,
And I crept to the light, and the life, and the air,
From the town of the man to the country of God!

"'Twas in solitude, then, that there came to my soul
The halo of comfort that sympathy casts;
He was strong, he was brave, and, though centuries roll,
I shall love that one man whilst eternity lasts!
O my lord, I was weak, I was wrong, I was poor!
I had suffered so much through my journey of life,
Hear! the worst of the crime that is laid at my door:
I said I was widow when, really a wife!

"Here I stand to be judged, in the sight of the man
Who from purity took a frail woman away.
Let him look in my face, if he dare, if he can!
Let him stand up on oath to deny what I say!
'Tis a story that many a wife can repeat,
From the day that the old curse of Eden began;
In the dread name of Justice, look down from your seat!
Come, sentence the Woman, and shelter the Man!"

A silence more terrible reigned than before,
For the lip of the coward was cruelly curled;
But the hand of the jailer slipped down from the door
Made to shut this sad wanderer out from the world!
Said the Judge, "My poor woman, now listen to me:
Not one hour you shall stray from humanity's heart
When thirty swift minutes have sped, you are free
In the name of the Law, which is Mercy, depart!"

CHAPTER XLVIII.

OLD TURF FRIENDS.

An announcement in the morning papers of the death of Mr. Richard C. Naylor of Kelmarsh, Northamptonshire, at the age of eighty-six, carried me back to the far-off days when, tempted by the hospitality and kind friendship of Lord Falmouth, I became a regular visitor of Newmarket Heath--an *habitué* during the splendid dictatorship of Admiral Rous!

I would like to mention the names of some of the celebrities of the Turf of those days, many of them my frequent companions, and no less my real and sincere friends. Time, however, fails. But in looking through the piles of letters with which the kindness of my friends has favoured me from time to time, I come across many a relic of the past that recalls the pleasantest associations. Even a telegram, most prosaic of correspondence, which I meet with at this moment, is a little poem in its way, and brings back scenes and circumstances over which memory loves to linger.

It is nothing in itself, but let any one who has loved country life and enjoyed its sports and its many friendships consider what forgotten pleasures may be brought to mind by this telegram.

Telegram.
DORCHESTER, *November* 2, '97.
Handed in at QUORN at 9.10 a.m.
Received here at 11.1 a.m.
To SIR H. HAWKINS, The Judges' House, Dorchester.

Just returned from Badminton to find the most charming present from you, which I shall always regard with the greatest value, and think you are too kind, in giving me such a present. Am writing.--LONSDALE.

"At *Quorn*," I repeat, and then I find the letter which Lord Lonsdale was writing. This is it:--

CHURCHILL COTTAGE,
QUORN,
LOUGHBOROUGH,
Tuesday, November 2, '97.

MY DEAR SIR HENRY,--How can I thank you enough for your magnificent present? It is, indeed, kind of you thinking of me, and I can assure you that the spurs shall remain an "heirloom" to decorate the dinner-table (a novel ornament) and match the silver spur poor old White Melville gave me. Why you should have so honoured me I do not know, but that I fully value your kindly thought I do know.

Is there any chance of your being in these parts? If so, *do* pay me a visit. nd with many, many thanks for your extreme kindness, Believe me

Yours very truly,

(Signed) LONSDALE.

Alas! almost all of them have passed away, yet they will live while the memory of the generation lasts which called them friends. They have vanished from the scenes in which they played so prominent a part, and yet their influence remains.

There was the old Admiral himself, the king of sportsmen and good fellows. Horse or man-o'-war, it was all one to him; and although sport may not be regarded as of the same importance with politics, who knows which has the more beneficial influence on mankind? I would have backed Admiral Rous to save us from war, and if we drifted into it to save us from the enemy, against any man in the world. Then there was his bosom friend George Payne, and the old, old Squire George Osbaldeston, Lord Falmouth, W.S. Crawfurd, the Earl of Wilton, Lord Bradford, Lord Rosslyn, Lord Vivian, the Duke of Hamilton, George Brace, General Mark Wood, Alexander, Lord Westmorland, the Earl of Aylesbury, Clare Vyner, Dudley, Milner, Sir John Astley ("The Mate"), Lords Suffolk and Berkshire, Coventry and Clonmell, Manton, Ker Seymer--the names crowd upon my memory; then, alas! a long, long while after, Henry Calcraft, Lord Granville, Lord Portsmouth, and "Prince Eddy," Lord Gerard, the Earl of Hardwicke, Viscount Royston, Sam Batchelor, and Tyrwhitt Wilson.

These are some of those whom I remember, and, by the way, I ought to add the Duke of Westminster and Tom Jennings, names interesting and distinguished, and indicative of a phase of life ever full of enjoyment such as is not known out of the sporting world, where excitement lends to pleasure the effervescence and sparkle which make life something more than animal existence.

This is true in hunting, racing, cricket, and I should think intensified in the highest degree in a charge of cavalry. Take Balaclava, for instance: the very fact of staking life at such odds must have compressed into that moment a whole life of ordinary pleasure.

I will mention a few more names, and then close another chapter of my memory. There was Mr. J.A. Craven, the Duke of St. Albans, the Duke of Beaufort, Montagu Tharp, Major Egerton, General Pearson, Lord Calthorpe, Henry Saville, Douglas Gordon (Mr. Briggs), Oliver Montagu, Henry Leeson, the Earl of Milltown, Sir Henry Devereux, Johnny Shafto, Douglas Phillips, Randolph Churchill, Lord Exeter, Lord Stamford.

Of the famous jockeys and trainers there were John Scott, Mat Dawson, Fred Archer. There were also James Weatherby, Judge Clark, and Tattersall.

CHAPTER XLIX.

LEAVING THE BENCH--LORD BRAMPTON.

At length the time came when I was to bid good-bye to the Queen's Bench and the Court No. 5 in which I had so long presided, where I had met and made so many friends, all more or less learned in the law. I had been a Judge since the year 1876, and Time, in its never-ceasing progress, had whispered to me more than once, "Tarry not too long upon the scene of your old labours, where your presence has made you a familiar object to all the members of every branch of your great and responsible profession; and while health and vigour and intelligence still, by God's blessing, remain to you, apparently unimpaired by lapse of years, take some of that rest and repose which you have earned, ere it be too late."

Thereupon, without any needless ceremony of leave-taking, at the close of the year 1898 I took my leave of the Bench with a simple bow. Silently, but with real affection for all I was leaving behind me, I quitted my occupation on the Bench. I considered this to be a far more dignified way of making my exit than meeting face to face the whole of the court and its practitioners and officers, and leaving it to the eloquent and friendly speech of the Attorney-General to flatter me far beyond my deserts in the customary farewell address which he would have offered to me. I thought it better to rely upon the expressions and conduct of those who knew me well, and to feel that they appreciated the discharge of the many arduous duties which I had been called on to perform. As some evidence of this, I would point to the good wishes from all kinds and classes of people which have followed me into private life, and the numerous letters which every post brought me, and which would fill a volume in themselves.

But the crowning honour was graciously conferred upon me by her late Majesty Queen Victoria on January 1, 1899, through the then Marquis of Salisbury, who signified that her Majesty intended to raise me to the peerage. His lordship's letter announcing the gracious act I recall with feelings of pleasure and gratitude, and I need not say that it will, while life lasts, be my greatest pride. I was subsequently sworn of her Majesty's Privy Council, and for more than two years attended pretty regularly in the Final Court of Appeal.

It does not behove me to say more on this subject than that the acknowledgment of my long services by the Sovereign must ever be my greatest pride and satisfaction.

On February 7, 1899, I was introduced to the House of Peers, and took my seat.

I chose for my name and designation the title of Baron Brampton, which her Majesty was pleased to approve. My little property, therefore, which I mentioned earlier in my reminiscences, conferred on me what was more valuable than its income--the title by which I am now known.

Speaking with reference to those long years ago when I was dissuaded from my career by those who doubtless had the most affectionate interest in my welfare, and to whose advice I proved to be so undutiful, I cannot help, whether vanity be attributed to me or not, contrasting the position of the penniless articled clerk in the attorney's office and the situation which came to me as the result of unremitting labour.

Let me state it with pride as well as humility that my rewards have been beyond my dreams and far above my deserts.

On February 7, in a committee room of the House, I was met by my supporters and those whose duties made them a portion of the ceremony, and realized the ambition that came to me only in my later life.

Some members of my family would have preferred the family name to be associated with the title. I must confess I had some attachment for it, as it had rendered me such good service, and it was somewhat hard to give it up.

If, however, I had had any hesitation, it would have been removed when one afternoon Lord ---- called on me, and in his chaffing manner said,--

"Well, I hear you are to be Lord '*Awkins* of '*Itchin*, 'Erts."

"Be ---- if I will!" said I; "Brampton's the only landed estate I have inherited, and although the old ladies who are life-tenants kept me out of it as long as they could, I shall take my title from it as the only thing I am likely to get out of it."

"Bravo!" said he. "I don't like 'Awkins of 'Itchin, 'Erts. *Brampton* sounds like a title; and so my hearty congratulations, and may you and her ladyship live long to enjoy it!"

"Mr. Punch" was good enough to furnish me with a beautiful and humorous coat of arms, done by that very talented artist Mr. E.T. Reed.

Since the commencement of this volume many of the old friends mentioned in it with affectionate remembrance have gone to their rest, and I am steadily approaching my own end. Trusting to the mercy and goodness of God, I patiently await my summons. I can but humbly add that to the best of my poor ability I have ever conscientiously endeavoured in all things to do my duty.

And now, as I lay down my pen, dreamily thinking over old names, old friends, and old faces of bygone years, I live my life over again. Everything passes like a picturesque vision before my eyes. I can see the old coach which brought me from my home--a distance of thirty miles in eight hours--a rapid journey in those days. This was old Kirshaw's swift procedure. Then there was the "Bedford Times" I travelled with, which was Whitehead's fire-engine kind of motor; but generally in that district John Crowe was the celebrated whip.

Then passes before me the old Cock that crew over the doorway in Fleet Street, a Johnsonian tavern of mighty lineage and celebrity for chops and steaks. And I see the old waiter, with his huge pockets behind, in which he deposited the tons of copper tips from the numberless diners whom he attended to during his long career.

Then I observe the Rainbow, by no means such a celebrity, although more brilliant than the Mitre by its side; and in the Mitre I see (but only in imagination) Johnson and Goldsmith talking over the quaint philosophy of wine and letters till three o'clock in the morning, finishing their three or four bottles of port, and wondering why they were a little seedy the next day.

And there sits at my side, enjoying his chop, Tom Firr, described as the king of huntsmen--a true and honest sportsman, simple, respectful, and respected, whose name I will not omit from my list of celebrities, for he is as worthy of a place in my reminiscences as any M.F.H. you could meet.

CHAPTER L.

SENTENCES.

There is no part of a Judge's duty which is more important or more difficult than apportioning the punishment to the particular circumstances of a conviction. As an illustration of this statement I would take the offence of bigamy, where in the one case the convicted person would deserve a severe sentence of imprisonment, while in another case he or she might be set at liberty without any punishment at all. Such cases have occurred before me.

The sentence of another Judge upon another prisoner ought not to be followed, for each prisoner should be punished for nothing but the particular crime which he has committed. For this reason the case of each individual should be considered by itself.

I dislike, also, the practice of passing a severe sentence for a trifling offence merely because it has been a common habit in other places or of other persons. For instance I have known five years of penal servitude imposed for stealing from outside a shop on a second conviction, when one month would have been more than enough on a first conviction, and two or three months on a second conviction. For small offences like these the penalty should always be the same in character--I mean not excessive imprisonment, and never penal servitude. As often as a man steals let him be sent to prison, and it may be for each offence the time of imprisonment should be somewhat slightly increased, but not the character of the punishment.

Years ago, in my Session days, I remember a poor and, I am afraid, dishonest client of mine being *transported for life* (on a second conviction for larceny) for stealing *a donkey*; but I doubt if that could happen nowadays. It seems incredible.

Nobody who has carefully noted the innumerable phases of crime which our criminal courts have continually to deal with, and the infinite shades of guilt attached to each of those crimes, will fail to come to the conclusion that one might as well attempt to allocate to its fitting place each grain of sand, exposed to the currents of a desert and all other disturbing influences, as endeavour by any scheme or fixed rule to determine what is the fitting sentence to be endured for every crime which a person can be proved, under any circumstances, to have committed.

The course I adopted in practice was this. My first care was never to pass any sentence inconsistent with any other sentence passed under similar circumstances for another though similar offence. Then I proceeded to fix in my own mind what ought to be the outside sentence that should be awarded for that particular offence had it stood alone; and from that I deducted every circumstance of mitigation, provocation, etc., the balance representing the sentence I finally awarded, confining it purely to the actual guilt of the prisoner.

I have noticed that burglaries with violence are rarely committed by one man alone, and that when two or more men are concerned in a murder, one or more of them being afraid that some one, in the hope of saving himself from the treachery of others, is anxious to shift the whole guilt of the robbery, with its accompanying violence, on to the shoulders of his comrades. It is well that this should be so, and that such dangerous criminals should distrust with fear and hatred their equally guilty associates.

Except for special peremptory reasons, I never passed sentence until I had reconsidered the case and informed my own mind, to the best of my ability, as to what was the true magnitude and character of the offence I was called upon to punish.

The effect of such deliberation was that I often mitigated the punishment I had intended to inflict, and when I had proposed my sentence I do not remember ever feeling that I had acted excessively or done injustice. I am now quite certain that no sentence can be properly awarded unless after such consideration. I speak, of course, only of serious crimes.

It has more than once happened that even after all the evidence in the case was before the jury, as was supposed, I have discovered that an accused man, in *mitigation of sentence*, has pleaded that which would have been a *perfect defence to the charge made against him*! One of these instances was very remarkable. It happened at some country racecourse.

A man was charged with robbing another who was in custody in charge of the police for "welshing." The prisoner had undoubtedly, while the prosecutor, as I will call him, was in custody, and being led along the course, rushed up to him, after jumping the barriers, and put his hand in his coat-pocket, pulling out his pocket-book and other articles. He then made off, but was pursued by the police and arrested. He was indicted for the robbery, and the facts were undisputed.

There was no defence set up, and I was about to ask the jury for their opinion on the case, which certainly had a very extraordinary aspect.

Suddenly the prisoner blurted out, as excusing himself,--

"Well, sir, *he asked me to take the things*. I was a stranger to him, and the mob was turning his pockets inside out and ill-treating him for welshing."

I immediately asked the prosecutor, "Is that true?" and he answered, "Yes." The prisoner said, "I only did it to protect his things for him."

Of course I instantly stopped the case and directed an acquittal. I then gave both parties a little advice. To the prosecutor (the welsher) I said, "Don't go welshing any more;" and to the prisoner, "If you ever again see a welsher in distress, don't help him."

I should like to say one word more. It should not be supposed that a man, when sentenced, is altogether bad because he uses insulting language to the Judge. He may not be utterly bad and past all hope of redemption on that account.

The want of even an approach to uniformity in criminal sentences is no doubt a very serious matter, and is due, not to any defect in the criminal law (much as I think that might be improved in many respects), but is owing to the great diversity of opinion, and therefore of action, which not unnaturally exists among criminal Judges, from the highest to the humblest, numbering, as they do, at least 5,000 personages, including Judges of the High Courts, commissioners, recorders, police magistrates, and justices of the peace.

When one considers the conditions under which the criminal law is administered in England, and remembers that no fixed principles upon which punishments should be awarded have been authoritatively laid down, and that the law has stated only a maximum (but happily at the present time not a minimum), and each Judge is left practically at liberty to exercise his own unfettered discretion so long as he confines himself within the limit so prescribed, it is no matter for wonder that so great a diversity of punishment should follow so great a variety of opinion.

Even in the most accurate and useful books of practice to which all look for guidance and assistance during every stage of the criminal proceedings, down to the conviction of the offender, no serious attempt has been made to deal, even in the most general way, with the mode in which the appropriate sentence should be arrived at.

The result of this state of things is extremely unsatisfactory, and the most glaring irregularities, diversity, and variety of sentences are daily brought to our notice, the same offence committed under similar circumstances being visited by one Judge with a long term of penal servitude, by another with simple imprisonment, with nothing appreciable to account for the difference.

In one or the other of these sentences discretion must have been erroneously exercised. I have seen such diversity even between Judges of profound learning in the law who might not unreasonably, *primâ facie*, be pointed to as safe examples to be followed; and so they were, so far as regarded their legal utterances. Experience, however, has told us that the profoundest lawyers are not always the best administrators of the criminal law.

Practically there are now no criminal offences which can be visited with the penalty of death. Treason and murder still remain. For the latter offence the Judge is *bound to pronounce sentence of death*, which is imperatively fixed and ordained by Act of Parliament, and any other sentence would be illegal.

There are certain principles which I consider ought never to be lost sight of.

In the first place, it must be remembered that for mere immorality, not made criminal by the common or statute law of the land, no punishment can be legally inflicted, and, in my opinion, no crime ought to be visited with a heavier punishment merely because it is also against the laws of God.

Take, for example, the crime of unlawfully knowing a girl under the age of sixteen years, even with consent. Assume that with her invitation the man committed himself. Go further, and establish the sin of incest. The latter sin ought to be *totally ignored* in dealing with the *statutory* offence.

I must not, however, be understood as intending my observations to apply to cases where the immorality is in itself an *element* of the crime. My view is that the rule ought to apply only in cases where the immorality is only a sin against God, and is severable from the *crime* committed against the laws of the land.

The case I have suggested is an illustration of what I mean.

Secondly, a sentence ought never to be so severe as to create in the mind of reasonable persons, having knowledge of the circumstances, a sympathy with the criminal, for that tends to bring the administration of the law into discredit, and while giving a Judge credit for having acted with the strictest sense of justice, it might give rise to a suspicion of his fitness and qualifications for the administration of the criminal law--a state of things which ought to be avoided.

The same observations apply, but not with equal force, to sentences which may to reasonable persons acquainted with all the circumstances appear to be ridiculously light, for it is more consistent with our laws to err on the side of mercy than on the side of severity.

The object of criminal sentences is to compel the observance by all persons, high and low, rich and poor, of those public rights and privileges, both as regards the persons and property common to all their fellow-subjects, the infringement of which is made criminal.

For the infringement of other rights of a private character the law has provided civil remedies with which we are not at this moment concerned.

Punishments, then, should be administered only as a necessary sequence to the breach of a *criminal* law, with the object of deterring the offender from repeating his offence.

Of necessity it operates to some extent as a warning to others; but that is not its primary object, for no punishment ought to exceed in severity that which is due to the particular offence to which it is applied. To add to a sentence for a very venial offence for which a nominal punishment ought to suffice an extra fine or term of imprisonment by way of example or warning to others would be unreasonable and unjust. Vengeance, or the infliction of unnecessary pain, especially for the sake of others, should never form part of a criminal sentence.

Reformation of the criminal by and during his imprisonment should be one chief object of his punishment, but a just sentence for the offence is not to be prolonged either for education or reformation, unless expressly sanctioned by law, as in the case of reformatories.

With regard to crimes of violence, it sometimes happens that long periods of restraint and imprisonment are imperative--where, for instance, the criminal is persistent in his threats, or has made it evident by his actions or words that on his liberation from imprisonment for criminal violence he intends to resume his criminal course, and will do so unless restrained.

Take, for instance, the case of a persistent burglar, the great majority of whose robberies are committed under circumstances calculated to create terror and alarm, and upon whom imprisonment, however long, has no restraining effect after his liberation. Take the confirmed highway robber, who to secure his booty does not scruple to use deadly violence upon his victim. It is rare that one short term of imprisonment, or the fear of another, induces him to abandon his criminal course. In such cases it is essential for the protection of the public that he should no longer be at liberty to pursue his dangerous and alarming course of life. For him, therefore, a much longer term of restraint is necessary than in the case of mere pilferers, whose thefts, although causing loss and vexation, are not productive of personal injury.

Lastly, I am strongly averse from abolishing the sentence of death in cases of deliberate murder. Even when the crime is committed under the influence of jealousy, I should take little pains to save the life of one who had cruelly and deliberately murdered another for the gratification of revenge or the purpose of robbery.

In the case of poor creatures who make away with their illegitimate offspring in the agony of their trouble and shame, there were, in my experience, almost always to be found very strong reasons for commutation, even to very limited periods of imprisonment.

CHAPTER LI.

CARDINAL MANNING--"OUR CHAPEL."

Cardinal Manning was a real friend to me, and I often spent an hour with him on a Sunday morning or afternoon discussing general topics. At my request, when I had no thought of being converted to his Church, he marked in a book of prayers which he gave me several of his own selections, which I have carefully preserved; but I can truly say he never uttered one word, or made the least attempt, to proselytize me. He left me to my own free, uncontrolled, and uncontrollable action. My reception into the Church of Rome was purely of my own free choice and will, and according to the exercise of my own judgment. I thought for myself, and acted for myself, or I should not have acted at all.

I have always been, and *am*, satisfied that I was right.

As to Cardinal Manning, his extreme good sense and toleration were my admiration at all times, and I shall venerate his memory as long as I live. His kindness was unbounded.

It was after his death, which was a great shock to me, that I was received into the Church by the late Cardinal Vaughan.

When the latter was showing Lady Brampton and myself over that beautiful structure, the new Westminster Cathedral, I thought I should like to erect a memorial chapel, and made a proposal to that effect. We resolved to dedicate it to St. Gregory and St. Augustine. It was afterwards called "Our Chapel."

The stonework was accordingly proceeded with, and afterwards the plans for decoration were submitted to the Archbishop and myself. For these decorations I subscribed a portion. The rest of the work was our own, and we have the satisfaction of feeling that Our Chapel is erected to the honour and glory of God.

The style of decoration adopted is Byzantine. The walls are embellished with many and various beautiful marbles. The eastern side has a representation of Pope Gregory sending St. Augustine with his followers to preach the gospel in England. Another scene is St. Augustine's reception by King Ethelbert and Queen Bertha in the Isle of Thanet.

The panels of the reredos contain pictures of St. Gregory and St. Augustine, with their four contemporaries, St. Paulinus, St. Justus (Bishop of Rochester), St. Laurentius, and St. Mellitus (Bishop of London).

On the north are figures of St. Edmund, St. Osbald, and the Venerable Bede; while opposite are St. Wilfred, St. Cuthbert, and St. Benedict.

On the west are St. John the Baptist and St. Augustine, and below these, figures of women pouring water from pitchers, symbolical of the river Jordan.

Under the arch of this side are most artistically designed panels containing the names of the four rivers of Paradise.

The floor is inlaid, and the windows, which are of opalescent glass, throw over the structure a soft white light, admitting of the perfect harmony of colours which everywhere adorn this very beautiful chapel.

Almost all whose names I have mentioned in these reminiscences are gone. There are many others equally dear about whom I cannot for want of time and space write here; most of them have also passed away.

They can no longer sing the old songs, or tell the old tales, but their memory remains, and the pleasant melody of their lives. I enjoy their companionship now in the quietude of my home, and their memory brightens even the sweet twilight of the evening hours. But it all reminds me that the signal has been given to ring the curtain down.

I therefore make a last and momentary appearance in the closing drama, only to bid all and every one with whom I have been associated in times past and in times recent, as the curtain falls,

AN AFFECTIONATE FAREWELL.

APPENDIX.

THE CROWN CALENDAR FOR THE LINCOLNSHIRE LENT ASSIZES.

Holden at the Castle of Lincoln on Saturday the 7th of March 1818, before the Right Honorable Sir Vicary Gibbs and the Honorable Sir William Garrow.

JOHN CHARLES LUCAS CALCRAFT, ESQ., SHERIFF.

1. William Bewley, aged 49, late of Kingston upon Hull, pensioner from the 5th Regt. of foot, committed July 29, 1817, charged on suspicion of having feloniously broken into the dwelling house of James Crowder at Barton, no person being therein, and stealing 1 bottle green coat, 1 velveteen jacket, 3 waistcoats, &c. Guilty--Death.

2. John Giddy, aged 22, late of Horncastle, tailor, com. Aug. 5, 1817, charged with stealing a silver watch with a gold seal and key, from the shop of James Genistan of Horncastle. Six Months Imprisonment.

3. George Kirkhan, aged 25, }
4. John Colston Maynard, aged 19, } both late of Stickney,

laborers, com. Aug. 22, 1817, charged on suspicion of feloniously entering the dwelling house of W'm Bell of Stickney, between 9 and 10 o'ck in the morning, and stealing one £5 note and 8 £1 notes. Acquitted.

5. George Crow, aged 15, late of Frith Ville, com. Sept. 23, 1817, charged on suspicion of having entered the dwelling house of S. Holmes of Frith Ville, about 7 o'ck in the morning, breaking open a desk, and stealing three £1 notes, 3s. 6d. in silver, and a purse. Guilty--Death.

6. Thomas Young, aged 17, late of Firsby, laborer, com. Sept. 23, 1817, charged with having, about 11 o'ck at night, entered the dwelling house of John Ashlin of Firsby, with intent to commit a robbery. Guilty--Death.

7. Robert Husker, aged 28,}
8. John Robinson, aged 28,} both late of Glamford Briggs,

laborers, com. Oct. 13, 1817, charged with burglariously breaking into the dwelling house of Chas. Saunby, of South Kelsey, and stealing therefrom several goods and chattels. Guilty--Death.

9. John Marriott, aged 19, late of Osgodby, laborer, com. Oct. 18, 1817, charged with maliciously and feloniously setting fire to an oat stack, the property of Thomas Marshall of Osgodby. Guilty--Death.

10. Sarah Hudson, alias Heardson, aged 25, late of Newark, Nottinghamshire, com. Oct. 24, 1817, charged on suspicion of feloniously stealing from the cottage of James Barrell of Aisthorpe, in the day time, no person being therein, 6 silver tea-spoons and a pair of silver sugar tongs. Discharged by proclamation.

11. Elizabeth Firth, aged 14, late of Burgh cum Girsby, spinster, com. Nov. 22, 1817, charged with twice administering a quantity of vitrol or verdigrease powder, or other deadly poison, with intent to murder Susanna, the infant daughter of George Barnes of Burgh cum Girsby. No true Bill.

12. John Moody, aged 28, late of Stallingborough, laborer, com. Dec. 24, 1817, charged with having committed the odious and detestable crime and felony called sodomy. Indicted for misdemeanor. Two years imprisonment.

13. William Johnson, aged 28, late of Bardney, laborer, com. Dec. 29, 1817, charged with having burglariously entered the dwelling house of W'm Smith, of Bardney, and wilfully and malliciously beating and wounding, with intent to murder and rob Wm. Kirmond, a lodger therein. Seven Years Transportation.

14. Richard Randall, aged 27, }
15. John Tubbs, aged 29, } both late of Lutton,

laborers, com. Dec. 29, 1817, charged with feloniously assaulting Wm. Rowbottom of Holbeach Marsh, between 11 and 12 o'ck in the night, in a field near the king's highway, and stealing from his person 3 promissory £10 notes, 8 or 10 shillings in silver, one silver stop and seconds watch, and various other goods and chattels. Both guilty--Death.

16. William Hayes, aged 20, late of Braceby, weaver, com. Jan. 6, 1818, charged with feloniously stealing a mare, together with a saddle and bridle, the property of Ed. Briggs of Hanby. Guilty--Death.

17. Thomas Evison, aged 24, }
18. Thomas Norris, aged 28, } both late of Alnwick,

laborers, com. Jan. 21, 1818, charged with feloniously setting fire to a thrashing machine and a hovel, containing a quantity of oats in the straw, the property of Thos. Faulkner, jun. of Alnwick, which were all consumed. Guilty--Death.

19. William Walker, aged 20, laborer, }
20. Elizabeth Eno, aged 19, spinster, } both late of Boston,

com. Jan. 28, 1818, charged with burglariously entering the dwelling house of Wm. Trentham, and stealing a sum of money in gold and silver, several country bank notes, and a red morocco pocket-book. Guilty--Death.

21. William Bell, alias John Brown, aged 30, late of Alvingham, laborer, com. Feb. 19, 1818, charged with burglariously breaking into the shop of Wm. Goy of Alvingham, and stealing 1 pair of new shoes, 1 half boot, and 1 half boot top. Guilty--Death.

22. John Hoyes, aged 48, late of Heckington, com. Feb. 24, 1818, charged with feloniously stealing 2 pigs of the value of £3, the property of John Fairchild of Wellingore. Acquitted.

23. Christiana Robinson, aged 24, }
24. Mary Stewart, aged 26, } both late of Glamford

Briggs, com. March 7, 1818, charged with breaking into Chas. Saunby's shop, &c. (same as Nos. 7 and 8). Not prosecuted.

PRISONERS UNDER SENTENCE.

George Houdlass, convicted at Lammas Assizes, 1815, of mare stealing.--Ordered to be transported for the term of his natural life. (The Prince Regent, in the name of His Majesty, having graciously extended the Royal Mercy to the said convict, his said sentence is commuted to two years imprisonment, commencing July 1, 1817.)

Martin Dowdwell, convicted at the Lent Assizes, 1817, of perjury.--Ordered to be impillored once and imprisoned for two years.

Susanna Pepper, convicted at the Lammas Assizes, 1817, of secreting the birth of her bastard child.--Ordered to be imprisoned for one year.

William Whitehead (the younger); at the Summer Assizes, 1817, was found by a jury to be of unsound mind.--Ordered to be imprisoned until His Majesty's pleasure be known.

Edward Croft, convicted at the Louth quarter sessions, held Jan. 12, 1815, of a felony.--Ordered to be transported for seven years.

John Caminack, convicted at the Spilsby quarter sessions, Jan. 17, 1817, of a felony.--Ordered to be transported for seven years.

William Busbey, convicted at the same sessions of a felony.--Ordered to be transported for seven years.

William Nubert, convicted at the Lent Assizes, 1817, of burglary.--Ordered to be transported for seven years.

William Patchett, convicted at the same Assizes of burglary.--Ordered to be transported for seven years.

Richard Clarke, convicted at the Summer Assizes, 1817, of having forged bank notes in his possession.--Ordered to be transported for fourteen years.

Thomas Maddison, convicted at the same Assizes of burglary.--Ordered to be transported for seven years.

James Donnington, convicted at the same Assizes of stealing a lamb.--Ordered to be transported for seven years.

Samuel Brown, convicted at the same Assizes of stealing a mare.--Ordered to be transported for the term of his natural life.

Joseph Greenfield, convicted at the same Assizes of stealing a heifer.--Ordered to be transported for fourteen years.

William Johnson, convicted at the Spilsby quarter sessions, July 25, 1817, of a felony.--Ordered to be transported for seven years.

William Willson, convicted at the Kirton quarter sessions, Oct. 17, 1817, of a felony.--Ordered to be transported for seven years.

Henry Thorpe, convicted at the Bourn quarter sessions, Jan. 13, 1818, of a felony.--Ordered to be transported for seven years.

George Croft, convicted at the Boston quarter sessions, Jan. 13, 1818, of a felony.--Ordered to be transported for seven years.

William Betts, alias Bungs, convicted at the Spalding quarter sessions, Jan. 16, 1818, of a felony.--Ordered to be transported for seven years.

James Tidwell, convicted at the same sessions of a felony.--Ordered to be transported for seven years.

Samuel Chapman, convicted at the Spilsby quarter sessions, Jan. 16, 1818, of a felony.--Ordered to be transported for seven years.

David Jones, convicted at the Kirton quarter sessions, Jan. 20, 1818, of a felony.--Ordered to be transported for seven years.

IN HIS MAJESTY'S GAOL IN THE CITY OF LINCOLN.

1. Daniel Elston, aged 34, late of Waddington, cordwainer, com. Sep. 22, 1817, charged with feloniously stealing from the dwelling house of Rd. Blackbourn, of Waddington, one silver watch, and a pair of new quarter boots.--Guilty of stealing only--7 years transportation.

2. William Kehos, aged 22, a private soldier in the 95th Regt. of foot, com. Nov. 17, 1817, charged with feloniously slaughtering and stealing from the close of Matthew White of Lincoln one wether hog.--Guilty--Death.

Printed by DRURY & SONS, Lincoln.

THE END.

Printed in the United Kingdom
by Lightning Source UK Ltd.
115352UKS00001B/274